Surrender t

Summer TEMPTATION

Start your summer with three sinful romances from Natalie Anderson, Nikki Logan and Amy Andrews!

Summer TEMPTATION

Natalie **ANDERSON**
Nikki **LOGAN**
Amy **ANDREWS**

Published in Great Britain 2014
by Mills & Boon, an imprint of Harlequin (UK) Limited,
Eton House, 18-24 Paradise Road, Richmond, Surrey, TW9 1SR

ISBN: 978-0-263-24652-0

012-0614

Harlequin (UK) Limited's policy is to use papers that are natural, renewable and recyclable products and made from wood grown in sustainable forests The logging and manufacturing processes conform to the legalenvironmental regulations of the country of origin.

Printed and bound in Spain
by Blackprint CPI, Barcelona

Waking Up In The Wrong Bed

Natalie
ANDERSON

Possibly the only librarian who got told off herself for talking too much, **Natalie Anderson** decided writing books might be more fun than shelving them—and, boy, is it that! Especially writing romance—it's the realisation of a lifetime dream, kick-started by many an afternoon spent devouring Grandma's romances... She lives in New Zealand, with her husband and four gorgeous-but-exhausting children. Swing by her website, www.natalie-anderson.com, any time—she'd love to hear from you.

For June—thank you for giving us such a great port in our ground-shuddering storm.
We would have been lost if it weren't for you.

CHAPTER ONE

Some wicked time beyond midnight, Ellie darted along the hallways of the luxury lodge in an almost sheer slip. The plush carpet absorbed the rapid beat of her bare feet. The puff of air-conditioning didn't cool the mad heat blushing her skin. She was on an indulgence mission and, imprisoned by hedonistic—champagne-riddled—impulse, sanity didn't stand a chance.

She danced down the stairs to the next level, to where she knew he was sleeping. She counted the doors—one, two, three—and opened the next.

But his bedroom was empty. The dim light of an almost moonless night invaded through open curtains, revealing no body-sized lump in the bed. In fact it was so smooth it looked like a perfectly iced cake.

Disappointment dashed her spirits—because she wasn't hungry for cake. She was starving for something way more meaty than that. She'd gone fun-free for too long. So, inspired by the fabulosity of the location, she'd decided to hell with it and to take what he'd been offering for weeks. Until now she'd parried his flirtatious invites, unsure of his integrity. But here, in this most seductive location, what did anything matter but the moment? And this moment she wanted to enjoy some male, *physical*, attention. In a place as beautiful as this, surely fantasy could come true?

Yes. Having finally got the courage, she wasn't going to let fate confound her. Reckless joie de vivre bubbled again and she slipped back out to the hall. Maybe she'd counted wrong, or had the wrong side of the corridor? She pivoted one eighty and counted again. One, two three. Carefully she turned the handle of the fourth door.

Occupied.

Her over-wired senses instantly assimilated the signs—warmth, gentle, regular breathing, a light spiced scent. She quietly closed the door behind her. A couple of steps in she nearly stumbled over the shoe. The size said it all—a man's boot. This was the one, then.

The ten-inch gap in the curtains let in what light that waning moon threw. A gap that wide had to be deliberate—he must like to see the sun, moon and stars too. Smiling, she blinked to adjust her vision. Then, yes, in the wonderfully huge bed, she could just make out his laid-back shape, right in the centre. His dark hair contrasted against the white pillow, his face turned away from her. Then cloud crossed the moon, dulling the room to nothing but shades of black.

But she crept forward, heated inside and out.

'Hey,' she whispered. 'Are you asleep?'

Dumb question when she could hear the regularity of that breathing for herself.

'Hey,' she murmured again as she stretched across the bed, her hand out to touch…*skin*.

Oh, he was hot.

She snatched her fingers back, suddenly shy. Her heart bashed her ribs as adrenalin flooded, forcing a too-fast beat. She took a second to breathe, because never before had she slipped into the driver's seat like this. Her throat blocked, she could think of nothing else to say. But sensation—temptation—drove her closer. Despite the goosebumps popping over every inch of her skin, she burned.

She knelt on the bed, boldness returning the closer she got to his heat. Slowly, she slid her hand towards the point where the bed was depressed by the weight of one big, warm male. Her seeking fingers hit the boundary from cool cotton to hot body, but she pushed through her last nervousness, sliding her fingers up and over his hair-roughened skin.

Every cell inside her squeezed. The hit of pure pleasure from that smallest of touches surprised her. She'd not expected such excitement from so little. But perhaps this was about risk as well and she, who'd always been risk averse, was beyond excited already.

In daylight she found him perfectly resistible—they'd never even kissed. It had mainly been talk and suggestion—a way to help pass the boring bits at work. And there'd been more dull moments than anything recently—all paperwork, no perks. She'd hoped for job satisfaction this weekend, knew this was part of why she'd been offered the trip. But this place had her thoughts turning to the personal. Yes, now, up this close to his heat and that scent she'd never before noticed, she couldn't wait to discover him in this dark night.

His skin was warm, the breadth and obvious strength of his muscles another surprise. Who knew that beneath his customary too-trendy suits was a body of awesome size? Clutching one hand to her chest, she gently swept the other over his stomach, sliding the sheet down as she searched him out. He was completely naked and as a result only one word remained in her brain—*amazing*.

She was lost in her unrestrained exploration, so it was a few seconds before she sensed the change in him. Then she felt the ripple as, beneath skin, his muscles responded to her touch.

Stimulated.

She was emboldened by those signs, her reach went further, firmer. And her own excitement built as she realised the extent of his. It wasn't just with her hand that she touched him now. Bending, she pressed her mouth to his thigh. His hands lifted, his fingers thrusting through her hair, gently massaging. So her instinct had been right.

He was awake.

She knelt, lifting a knee across so she straddled him.

'Oh, yeah.' Sleep-rusted, hoarse, hungry, his voice sounded strange.

'Yeah,' she agreed with a breathy laugh, heart racing at her daring and his rising to the occasion so magnificently. 'You're okay with this?'

'Oh, yeah,' he repeated with a groan.

She felt his big release of air. Felt his hands firmly curve around her thighs. His fingers stroked over her skin, but with enough strength to keep her there.

He wanted her there.

She closed her eyes, letting her fingers feel him—that hot, stretched skin. Her sensuality exploded, extremely intense. The delight in discovering her recklessness would have such reward made her all the more liberated. In the past she'd been shy sexually—cautious, self-conscious, half afraid of doing something wrong or not being good enough. She'd never have dared this. But none of those feelings came into play now. Under the influence of lush surroundings, rich food and drink, this inky midnight and his rapid response, she simply didn't care. She felt too heavenly. Scent filled the warm darkness—a mix of the citrus of her shampoo and the spice of his soap. Not his usual aftershave. She guessed it was the guest soap. She made a mental note to find out the brand because it tantalised—encouraging her to taste.

Bending forward again, she brushed her hair over his skin as she kissed across his chest, finding one of his nipples to lick. She ran her hand down his abs. His muscles were rock solid. Hell, *all* of him was rock solid.

He pushed her shoulders so she sat up. His hands slid over her slip, over her belly to shape her breasts. He suddenly moved, lifting to pull the fabric from her. She raised her arms so he could take it over her head and toss it, she didn't care where. His hands slipped back to her butt, clutching her close—his touch possessive. She liked it. She also liked the thick part of him that she had one hand around. He stayed strained upwards, so his mouth teased her breasts as his fingers had for those too few delicious seconds before. She trembled—amazed that she could be so close so quick.

'If I'd known it was going to be like this,' she muttered hotly, 'I wouldn't have held back so long.'

She could have been having sex this good for the last two months—how had she been so blind to this chemistry?

He buried his face harder into her curves. Clutching her closer, kissing down her neck all the more passionately.

All this time her other hand had been curled into a tight fist, and tucked in the middle of that was something she knew they needed—*now.* She reluctantly let go of him to take the packet in both hands, tearing it open. Then she tried to get the thing to work.

'You have to help me with this,' she panted. Her fingers not getting the slippery rubber to roll down right.

He lay back, his hands pushed hers out of the way, but she bent, following the downward stroke of his fingers with her mouth. He hissed a curse—a whisper so stretched with desire it broke.

She laughed, delighted, and lost her last fragment of inhibition. The breathlessness, the haste, the heat, all turned her on to an extreme degree. He seemed to have the same reaction. His erection strained flat against his stomach. She straddled, shifting closer to him, letting her core rest just on the base of him, his tight balls just beneath her butt. She teased them both with tiny squeezes of her muscles, like little kisses from her intimate lips. The hard ridge of him was delicious torment on her sweet spot and grinding against him set her on an even faster track to ecstasy. Oh, yeah, now it was carnal, now it was *insane*. Never so raw and passionate and quick. He growled and firmly slid his big hand up her thigh, then forced his fingers between their bodies. She moaned, abandoned, as he used his thumb to tease her. He sat up to kiss her breasts again as he toyed with her, circling her rhythmically, occasionally slipping deep. She was dripping with desire, unashamedly writhing as he flicked his fingers, as he licked and kissed up to her neck, then down to her breasts again. Almost at the point of climax she pushed him back, her strength catching him by surprise. A loud smacking sound clapped in the room as she broke the seal of his mouth on her skin. He fell back on the mattress and she held him there with a hard hand on his shoulder.

'I want to do it,' she growled, grabbing his rigid length in a wide fist, hovering above him for one moment of ecstatic anticipation.

She gasped as she slid, instinctively clamping tight and twisting down on him. He roared and she felt his muscles flex. She smiled, thrilled he was as turned on as she. He arched uncontrollably again; whatever words he muttered were unintelligible.

She pressed her palms to his big, taut biceps for leverage, for control. Her fingers curled into the solid muscle as she began to ride him. Filled with limitless energy and endurance, she took him deeper and deeper, over and over. He was big and powerful and she loved having him beneath her. Oh, yeah, he was the most incredible ride. Perfect—big enough to fill her ravenous appetite—too big really. But that was exactly what she'd wanted—an extreme experience of pleasure.

His hands cupped her breasts, teasing her nipples between finger and thumb, until—mere seconds later—she lifted and sank on him too fast for him to keep grip, so he swept his palms over her curves, slipping down to her waist, smoothing the sudden slick of sweat over her body. And then his hands spread wide on her thighs, his fingers firmed, holding her soft flesh as tightly as she was gripping his biceps. Suddenly he thrust hard, meeting her in a massive movement. She roared with pleasure then, as the duel for dominance began. Her fingers curled deep into his, pressing down as he pushed up, ratcheting the friction. They drove hard, slamming together faster and faster, each forcing the other to ecstatic abandonment.

'So good, oh, so good,' she panted, almost inaudible. 'Oh, it's never been so good.'

So good it was only seconds before she came with a harsh, high cry. Only one more before he came hard after.

* * *

Rapid, jerky breathing filled her head—her own and his. Sensual joy surged through her in a final squeeze. If she had the energy she'd laugh. But she was sweaty and breathless and so zapped she was fast sinking into a lax, sleepy mass.

She heard footsteps—the clipping sound of high heels on concrete. A cough, then laughter rising up from the courtyard below the window. She froze. People were still up, still awake. Could have heard… The realization brought reality back with a crash.

The morning after hadn't been a very much thought-upon part of her plan. Now all the decisions came to her split-second: this would change nothing between them. They'd be colleagues who'd had a carefree kick together *one* night. That was all. She knew he flirted with every woman he met and that this would mean nothing to him. So it had to mean nothing to her too. She liked to think he'd keep his mouth shut. While in their industry hook-ups were common, this was her first. But she knew it would hardly become notorious news—there were people far more important than her for others to talk about. And she was not going to let this get ugly. It was over already.

She peeled her chest from his, preparing to slide off his body and get back to her own room. But he pulled her back against him. He was stronger than she'd thought he'd be. He was more everything than she'd thought he'd be.

'Stay.' A low, sleepy word—but a command none the less. His embrace tightened. Inescapable but so irresistible.

She hadn't expected this caring comfort either. He rolled them both in a smooth movement, settling them into a sleep position—still devastatingly intimate.

The moment of clarity she'd had before now melted in lax drowsiness as she physically melted back into his warm strength. He lifted a heavy leg over hers, his arms curled tighter—cradling her ultra-close. Consciousness slipped. Her muscles were spent, that yearning in her depths sated. The last thing she heard was another burst of laughter coming through the open window. A man's laugh. With the last fragment of conscious energy she frowned—she recognised that laugh.

Hours later she slowly woke to a low moan echoing in her ears. Her *own* moan as she released a breath that seemed to have been held for ever. Her heart was pumping, her skin—and other bits—damp and *so* hot. She was having the most vivid, gorgeous dream. She resisted opening her eyes, wanting to stay in the sizzling fantasy. And in that fantasy she was imprisoned in the arms of one very hot, hard body—part of that body was very, *very* hard. His fingertips gently brushed down her lower belly. The urge to flex her hips—to invite—was irresistible. As she rocked back against him she felt the rebellious ache in her muscles, but she didn't care. Not as the memories cleared—the wildness of that ride coming into focus. Not when his hips teased right back and his fingers went…

'Good morning.' His voice was less sleep-rusted than it had been last night, but it was still strange.

Ellie froze. Her heart stopped, totalling her oxygen supply. Then she spun, inadvertently trapping his hand between her legs. The molten-brown eyes intently focused on her weren't the pale green ones she'd expected.

'Oh, my God!' She jerked to a sitting position, trapping his hand all the more. Clutching the sheet to her chest with hands curled into claws, she squawked, utterly breathless, 'Who the hell are you?'

CHAPTER TWO

RUBEN THEROUX had never had a bedmate regret frolicking with him and he had no intention of breaking that record now. He didn't care that he hadn't a clue who his sexy intruder was. No, the question he'd spent the last twenty minutes musing over was what colour her eyes were. Now he knew. Cornflower blue and crazy big. And though shock had whitened her face, she was still the prettiest thing he'd woken to find in his bed. Then again, he hadn't woken to anyone in his bed in a while. Relationships and Ruben were like oil and water, and he'd been too busy in recent times for even a five hour fling. So maybe it wasn't surprising he'd spent so long studying the soft woman soundly sleeping—until he'd succumbed to the temptation to tease. And, oh, my, she was hot to tease.

'You're not Nathan.' Strangled sound emerged as she stated the obvious.

'No,' he answered calmly, not moving a muscle so as not to freak her out more. But who the hell was Nathan and how could she have made such a mistake?

'How can you not be Nathan?' she gasped.

Yeah, his thoughts exactly. 'Well.' He stated it quietly. 'This isn't Nathan's room. This is my room.' Literally. Every room in the place was his.

Her mouth opened and closed a couple of times. He waited—motionless—to see how this was going to go. She didn't seem to realise her thighs were sandwiching his hand in a hot, smooth vice and he wasn't going to make any sudden kind of movement. But the memory of those limbs straddling his hips wasn't helping him recover his equilibrium. All he could feel were those lush, strong curves. He wanted the rest of him to be in the midst of them again.

She flicked a wild glance around the room and then arrowed all her attention right back at him. 'But this has to be his room—I counted the doors. The other one was empty.'

He pressed his lips together to stop the chuckle sliding out because he didn't want to make the situation worse for her.

'Are you sure you're in the right room?' she asked, her eyes still shocked wide.

'Positive. I got in late last night.' He'd been so tired it had been all he'd been able to do to stumble from the shower straight to what was definitely *his* bed. 'I came to bed and then the best dream ever turned out to be real.'

Only his dream-turned-real lover was now turning fifty shades of red—embarrassment staining her skin in a swift sweep. Her murmurs of pleasure came back to him—her rough claim that she hadn't known it would be so good. Yeah. The sweetheart *had* made a mistake. She'd meant that passion for some other guy. A sharp claw of envy swiped his ribs, puncturing his enjoyment of his best ever wake-up. But it hadn't been some other guy who'd pleased her so much. It had been *him*.

'You're a guest here?' she asked in a low choked voice.

'Actually I—'

She didn't give him the chance to introduce himself; instead she launched into a monologue of mortification and panic. 'Oh, I can't believe this. I can't believe it. I'm so sorry. I am so, so sorry.'

Partly because he wanted to see her reaction, but mainly because he couldn't resist, he let his fingers stroke—just the once, so very gently—in the hot, damp prison she gripped them in.

The incessant apologies ended instantly on a breathless gasp. Her mouth reddened, her muscles tightened and her temperature sizzled. His eyes locked on hers, watching the blue go brilliant, then her black pupils absorbed that colour as they swelled super fast. Her flush deepened. He felt the spasms before she twisted, releasing him as she scuttled to the far edge of the bed.

'You don't need to apologise,' he said, wondering if he should be the one saying sorry now. But he couldn't quite regret it. She'd been waking up so wonderfully willing in his arms when she'd thought he was this Nathan, but just then? That had been a raw response to *him*. She was hot and hungry for *him*. As she'd been last night when *he'd* been the one to meet her demands.

A swift glance told him what he needed to know—there were no rings between those white knuckles. No guy had staked a permanent claim and the Nathan guy was a fool for not taking her to bed sooner. The woman was passionate and hungry, literally a dream lover.

He coughed to ease the constriction in his chest. 'I'm sorry I'm not Nathan.'

Only because he wanted what she'd meant for the other guy—that invitation and pleasure. Hell, he wanted it now. He was stiffer than a steel pipe and feeling her sensual response spike like that had worsened it. But he fought the impulse to drag her close again, wincing at his new-found Neanderthal leanings.

The poor woman was completely mortified and he was all rampaging lust, desperate to sleep with her again. What kind of human was he?

Definitely one who'd been without too long. Because try as hard as he could he couldn't seem to 'relax'.

'Don't be sorry.' She emphatically shook her head.

Her deepening discomfort bothered him more than his uncontrollable body. Somehow he had to limit the damage here and help her find a funny side. And nothing smoothed a situation more than some humour.

Ellie struggled to hide her breathlessness. Shock still had her lungs in a tight grip, but so did desire—she was seconds from orgasm and, frankly, that doubled her shock.

She stared at the complete stranger only a couple of feet from her. The stranger that she now knew so *intimately.* And just looking at him sent her heart rate through the ceiling.

'You're okay?' The soft query delivered between dangerously curved lips. That gorgeous smile was as natural to him as the stripes were to the tiger. Oh, yeah, he'd been blessed with beautiful lips, upturned at the ends so he looked as if he was always in good humour. Which, given all his other assets, he probably was.

She clutched the sheet closer. Only her action dragged the sheet completely off him and, yeah, this was definitely *not* Nathan. And his natural assets were…sizable.

'I'm so sorry this happened,' she said again, determined to ignore the savage desire rippling through her like some internal beast that refused to be tamed. What kind of depraved animal had she turned into?

'I'm not.'

She hardly heard him as she apologised another ten times, interspersing the phrase with a few more choice words beneath her breath. Clutching the sheet to her with one hand, she put her now freezing hand to her face.

He sat up, resting his weight on one hand behind him, and spoke more forcefully. 'You didn't do anything I didn't want you to.'

That silenced her for all of a second. 'You didn't have much choice.' She looked across the bed at him. 'I *seduced* you.' The guy had been sound asleep and she'd been stroking him all over. Like everywhere.

His smile burst forth again. 'Yeah, well, it wasn't like I said no.' He chuckled. 'And it wasn't like I was a virgin.'

Well, no, he hadn't been that. Ellie bit her lips to stop from smiling. He'd had all the moves. And he executed another now—a languorous stretch that drew her attention once more to his completely fit length.

Hell, she had to move away before she did something stupid again. So she stood, taking the sheet with her. She didn't care about leaving him exposed, he didn't seem to be bothered by it. Whereas all she wanted to do was *hide*. She tried to wind the sheet around herself, glanced up to see him watching close—with undisguised amusement—and arousal. Man, was he aroused.

'You're free to take advantage of me any time you like,' he said softly, lying back down again. 'Or, you can come back to bed and let me take advantage of you this time.'

Oh, she so nearly had already and they both knew it. She felt her blush deepen. 'I really am sorry.'

'Sweetheart,' he drawled, but with an underlying

hint of seriousness. 'I could have stopped you if I'd wanted to.'

And there was the question. She looked up from her twisted toga attempt—facing his gaze direct. 'Why didn't you want to?'

He roared with laughter, his whole body clenched into an expression of enjoyment. Her gaze skittered south all of its own accord. *Built* for enjoyment—his clearly defined muscles spelled strength and stamina and gloriously good reproductive genes. And his reaction proved he was *such* a man. An all-about-fun man. She'd been a sexual toy for the night—as of course he had been for her. A really *good* toy.

Ellie tried to get her thoughts back on track—berating herself with worst-case scenarios. Imagine if he'd been married. What if he hadn't been alone in the room? She didn't know which would be worse. All she knew was that his utterly relaxed acceptance of her mistake was astounding.

'What were you thinking going along with it? Do women leap on you all the time?' Actually, looking at him? They probably did.

'I was asleep. At first I thought it was just an amazing dream.'

'A 4D dream,' she said sceptically.

'Yeah, hot and wet,' he half groaned, movement rippling down his muscles. 'You're sure you don't want to come back to bed?'

'Quite sure.' She clipped out the lie, all of a sudden desperate to get out of there before she threw caution to the wind and went for a repeat of last night's decadence.

'Honey, relax. I'm single, you're…' He paused, his voice lifting in question, his eyes unwaveringly focused on hers.

'Single,' she confirmed.

He paused as his expression seemed to sharpen. 'So tell me about Nathan.'

'He's no one.' She so didn't want to go there.

'He's not your boyfriend or your benefits guy or whatever?'

'No.' She squeaked out an answer from her strangled-feeling throat. She supposed she did owe the guy some kind of explanation but it was just so mortifying. 'We're colleagues. He'd been flirting and I... For once I just felt like...' She trailed off, her toes curling into the plush carpet. Now she wanted to disappear into the sheet completely.

'Nothing wrong with feeling like it.' Her naked lover shrugged his shoulders. 'So it wasn't because you're secretly in love with the guy and want to have his babies?'

'No babies,' she answered faintly. 'Don't worry.' She inhaled a hit of oxygen for courage. 'What we did was... It was safe.'

He sat up slowly. 'I remember.' His gaze lingered on her mouth. 'So no babies but you're not in love with him either?'

She shook her head. 'I just thought I'd say yes for once. Take the bull by the horns, so to speak.'

'You like rodeo?' His irrepressible smile quirked.

'Actually I don't think it's really for me,' she muttered, all but dying.

'But you ride so beautifully. Great seat, great rhythm. You're a natural,' he teased, chuckling at her baleful look. 'So you don't often do random seductions?'

The idea of her being some vixen seductress was so far off the mark it was hysterical. But she wasn't going to get hysterical herself. No, she took a calming breath and reckoned she could manage to get into the tease zone too. That was the way to handle this. 'Only on full moons.'

'Oh, you're a were-woman?'

She flicked her brows and then dropped the pretence. 'Honestly, the location helped.' She fiddled with the sheet and couldn't look at him. She knew this guy of all guys wasn't going to get hung up on double standards, but she was still embarrassed.

'The *chateau*?'

'It's so luxurious.' She nodded, truly meaning it. 'All the fabric, the furnishings. It's beautiful.'

'Yeah,' he said slowly. 'But I've never thought of it as an *erotic* destination. It's not like there are mirrors on the ceiling, tie-me-down bed ends, or twenty types of massage oil in the bathroom cabinet.' He glanced around the utterly tasteful room with a perplexed look.

Ellie was smoking-hot over his list of essentials for an erotic destination. She'd never thought she'd be into anything more than vanilla but the man had said 'tie-me-down' and she was ready to hunt out the ropes. She banished the image but couldn't help smiling as she tried to explain it more. 'It has this kind of discreet decadence. And it was a warm night. I'd had the most amazing shower.' She put her hand to her head because this so wasn't enough. 'And they serve French champagne.'

'Ah-h-h.' He nodded as if that explained it all. 'French champagne.'

She shrugged and gave up at that. She truly hadn't been tipsy. She'd just been bewitched and decided to please herself.

'This place was once dubbed Frenchman's Folly, did you know that?' he asked softly.

'No.' She frowned. 'No one could call this place a folly. It's more a fantasy.'

And you had to have a fantastical bank balance to be able to stay here. A guy this fit was probably some elite athlete or something. She wondered if she ought to recognise him.

'Perhaps people thought his folly was his marriage.'

'Oh.' Ellie paused. 'Shame if he was heartbroken. This isn't a place for heartbreak.'

Her naked lover chuckled. 'Only for pleasure, huh? But you and your colleague were here for business?'

'I wasn't supposed to come here at all.' She flushed deeper at the unintended entendre. 'It's not one of my files but last minute our boss wanted me to be here for backup.'

'So what's the business?'

'I work as a location scout. You know—finding places to film movies and stuff.'

His brows lifted as he picked up her lack of enthusiasm. 'You don't think this would be a good location?'

'It would be an amazing location,' Ellie said fervently. 'And I know it sounds like an amazing job and all—it's actually really not that much fun.'

'How can having to spend time in places like this not be fun?' he challenged her.

'I don't get to come on the trips much.' She coloured again as she saw him smile. 'I'm usually stuck in the office working on the paperwork. I've not been there that long.' She shrugged. Trouble was she excelled at paperwork—every job she had she'd done too well in the admin department to be let out of it. Frustrating wasn't the word.

'And so to make sure you got the most out of this

trip, you went hunting for some pleasure as well?' He was laughing as he said it.

And what could she do? There was no hope in denying it or in explaining the mad moment of need for contact that she'd experienced. So she nodded. 'Massive mistake.'

'Yeah, but not a disaster.'

Not a disaster, no—she'd had the best sex of her life. But it had been with a total stranger. They hadn't even kissed. There was absolutely no emotional connection between them. It just wasn't supposed to work that way. And she couldn't want more—could she? She tried to claw back her common sense—because what kind of a guy happily screwed complete strangers? A playboy. With a smile that cheeky and attitude that cocky? Yeah, as he'd admitted, he was no innocent.

She closed her eyes and groaned. 'Why didn't I turn on the light?'

'Given the way you're clutching that sheet around you, I'm guessing you like it best in the dark.' He laughed. 'Typical.'

'Excuse me?' Indignance rose, she couldn't restrain her reaction to his tease.

'Hiding your body.' He shook his head. 'What a waste.'

There was some truth to his accusation. Lights on for sex wasn't something that did it for her—fast-train to self-conscious. And it was then that she became aware of what she must look like—no doubt her hair would be bigger and more bouffant than some eighties rock-star's. Oh, fabulous. At least she wouldn't have panda eyes from smudged mascara. But still, this didn't really make up for the fact that she'd slept with the wrong guy. The guy she couldn't tear her eyes from.

He was smiling as dangerously as ever. 'But then you clearly have a latent wild streak.'

It seemed so. But next time she felt in need of satisfaction she'd mail order a vibrator. She clamped her elbows to her ribs, holding the sheet in place while she tried to cool her cheeks with her hands. She was getting turned on all over again just by looking at the guy. 'Look, I really should go. Let's just forget this ever happened.'

She attempted a march to the door. Only her sheet was a liability and his nudity gave him a speed advantage.

'You don't get away just yet.' He leaned against the door blocking her exit, all six feet four inches of bared magnificence. 'We have some more to talk about.'

Now he was standing up and towering over her, she had the melting sensation so deep it was unbearable. Her fingers itched; she could hardly stand still against the hot pull inside. Secret muscles flexed in excitement. Her heart thundered.

'Will you put some clothes on?' she asked desperately. He was too damn *hot* and she couldn't think with him like that.

His amusement flared again. 'Why? I'm not going to hide how attracted I am to you.'

It wasn't *her* he was attracted to, it was sex. And his nudity was messing with her hormones too. She'd gone completely animal. She half laughed on a gasp. 'Just please put some clothes on. Please.'

He shrugged his refusal, his expression one of total tease. 'I'm comfortable. You're really not comfortable with baring all, are you?'

What she wasn't comfortable with was her body's insane reaction to the sight of his—tall, toned and so sex-ready her insides were curling in on themselves. Her nerves clamoured for the sensation of him sliding in and out of her. This complete stranger had her more insanely excited than she'd ever been in her life. 'Well, can you please turn around while I get decent?'

'Really?' His full lips pouted. 'I don't get the peep show?'

'You've had more than enough, okay?' she choked. 'Please be the gentleman I know you are and turn around.'

'What makes you so certain I'm a gentleman?'

She fearlessly held eye contact. 'You let the lady go first.'

'Oh, that wasn't gentlemanly. That was for my own pleasure.' His lips curved more deeply into that delicious smile and he answered mock primly, 'But, okay, if you insist, I shall avert my eyes.'

He presented her with his rear view. She just gawped for a second, before remembering her intention and dropping the sheet to hurriedly dash back across the room, around the bed to find her slip. Glancing down, she saw a couple of light bruises colouring her thigh. The faintest of finger marks. She remembered his firm clutch with vivid clarity. The squeezes as she'd slid down to take him to the hilt over and over. She turned her head away and screwed her eyes shut tight, as if she could block the blush as the involuntary excitement skittered through her.

'Okay, I'm decent.' Breathing in, she watched him turn back to face her. He was no more physically 'relaxed'.

'You were wearing *that*?' He half gasped, theatrically pressing his hand against his ribs. 'Damn, I wish you *had* turned on the lights.'

'Stop it.' She laughed. 'You don't need to try and flatter me.'

'Yeah, I do.' He walked towards her, totally serious now. 'How can I not?'

She could see the muscles twitching under his skin. She'd never considered herself any kind of seductress before and she knew she wasn't really now—it was that sexual toy thing. They shared an illicit fantasy for real. The guy was no doubt sex-mad. Insatiable. One track. Only problem with that was his condition had rubbed off on her. Hell, the thought of him finding her so attractive put a zing in her step. But to do this again—stone-cold sober and in the cold light of day? She wasn't that *crazy*. She backed up, snatched up the towel from the low table next to her and threw it at him in defence.

He caught it and held it so it unfolded like a flag. 'What am I supposed to do with this?'

Oh, hell, she'd not got the towel—only the facecloth that had sat on top of it. Pocket-hanky-sized—ridiculously small hanging from his hand.

'I'm insulted,' he teased. 'I think you need a refresher in what I have to offer.'

'Oh, don't.' She giggled, unable to hide her all-over-body blush in just the slip—she needed the sheet back. 'Just…don't.'

He chuckled. 'I'm glad you can see the funny side.'

Biting her lip, she shook her head. 'Oh, this is such a nightmare.'

'Crazy, yes, nightmare, no. Don't regret it.'

She steadfastly met the sincerity in his eyes. And the smile on his mouth. Yeah, she bet he'd experienced many a morning after. 'You know how to give a girl a good time.'

'I like to think it's one of my strengths.'

Oh, it was.

He turned, his attention grabbed by something out of the window. 'This Nathan guy,' he muttered. 'Wouldn't have dark hair and laugh like a hyena?'

She reluctantly moved to stand next to him. Not a hyena, but a distinctive laugh. She remembered hearing it late last night, right when she shouldn't have. Right when she'd breathlessly been falling towards sleep, when her lover had still been inside her and caressing the base of her spine with gentle fingers.

'Oh.' She swallowed the swearword when she saw Nathan kiss the pretty young woman they'd met at the bar in the late afternoon yesterday.

Naked Guy's eyebrows had shot upwards. 'It looks like he might have been sharing his flirt around.'

Just a little.

'It's like a French farce,' Ellie muttered. But it was real. 'In a chateau and everything.' She felt her mystery lover turn his gaze on her and refused to show any kind of disappointment.

'I can't believe you mistook me for him,' Naked Guy accused in a tone of utter outrage. 'He's at least five inches shorter than I am. And not as fit.' He flexed his muscles in a preening display.

Yeah, they were poles apart. This guy was way more outrageous than Nathan. Bold in flirtation. In his demands. Desire. He tempted with humour and cheerful abandon.

'You were lying down,' she said through gritted teeth.

'And you hadn't slept with him.' He sounded pleased about that.

She didn't reply. She knew she'd admitted that last

night in her amazed gasps of pleasure. They both watched the couple in the courtyard for another moment.

Her tall lover was the one to break the silence, turning to face her directly. 'Well, I'll be frank, I think you got the better deal.'

She gaped at him. Then giggled. 'Arrogant much?' She laughed again only for the sound to die quickly as she shook her head and gave it to him. 'But I'll admit in this case, I think you might be right.'

'You *think*?' he asked, mock-outraged. 'Come on, you know that was spectacular.'

She felt her blush rising again as memories twisted between them, trying to draw them together.

'Well.' She breathed out, brazening her way through the most mortifying experience of her life. 'Okay. Yes. Thanks so much, it was…' She couldn't think of an appropriate adjective.

'Fantastic and you can't wait to see me again,' he inserted for her.

She shook her head. 'No.' She tempered the bad news with a smile. 'This was what it was.' One almighty screw-up. 'But we're not going there again.'

'Oh, come on.' He walked forward. 'That hot, that quick?' He shook his head. 'We'd be crazy not to enjoy that again. You want to as much as I do.' His gaze flickered to her chest. She didn't need to look down to know her nipples were turned on like bright beacons, begging for his touch again.

Oh, yeah, she was tempted.

'It had been a while for you, hadn't it?'

'Last full moon,' she said breathlessly.

'Liar.' He called her on it. 'You're blushing more than a gaggle of schoolgirls. You can hardly look at me. You're no vixen. Although it has to be said you have potential.'

She rolled her eyes. 'And you're offering to give me a bit more practice?'

'Of course I am,' he said simply. 'It had been a while for me too.'

She snorted. That she simply didn't believe.

His grin flashed. 'Truth. I've been busy at work and I haven't had any midnight callers. But you've really whet my appetite.'

Had she? It wasn't only his appetite piqued.

'I know it was an unconventional way of meeting, but we're good together.'

For a moment Ellie let fantasy rule—imagined being with him again for another round or thirty of spectacular sex. Fantasy morphed—from this they'd develop some wonderful relationship that would rival the highest-grossing Hollywood chick flick's happiest of endings… And, yeah, there was the problem. In the past she'd given too much where it wasn't wanted. She'd been crushed before; she wouldn't be daft enough to set herself up for a similar sort of heartache. She knew herself, before long she'd want the full fantasy. But a guy like this wasn't the sort to do happy ever after. She'd seen his unveiled edge—unashamed, reckless—a complete playboy. Someone who could go along with an anonymous one-night stand with such relaxed, outrageous humour? Too, *too* casual. And while she could live with a casual—frankly marvellous—mistake in her life, it had to be one-off. Her non-plan with Nathan had been for just the once. This *definitely* had to be just the once. Naked Guy here was just too fit for her to keep up with.

'It can't happen.' Her final decision.

'Not because of Nathan.' Statement not question.

'No. Because of me.' She'd get burned by Mr Naked & Too Hot to Handle. He was too much more everything than any other man she'd met—more gorgeous, more good-humoured, not only blessed by nature but more talented in bed than any guy had the right to be. She'd fall so hard, in a heartbeat.

He hadn't taken his eyes from hers, as if trying to read her thoughts. Looking right back at him, into those molten-chocolate eyes, Ellie felt her thoughts begin to splinter dangerously. One thought became dominant. Not a thought—an *urge*. Steam rose, blinkering her vision—all she wanted was to plant a kiss on those perfectly curved lips.

She breathed, blinked, stepped back. Not going to happen. She moved quickly, opening the door and stepping out of the insanity.

'Wait.' He stepped after her, apparently not caring that she was in the middle of the hall in a sheer slip and he had only a facecloth failing to protect his modesty. 'I don't know your name. Mine's—'

'Don't.' She held up her hand. 'Let's just pretend the whole thing was a dream.'

'But—'

'Bye!' She clutched her breasts so she could sprint down the hallway to the stairs.

'You're going to leave me like this?'

She turned at his holler, saw him standing outrageously proud, bolder than anyone she'd met in her life. He had a fascinating lack of care, and an ability to find amusement in anything—that made him all the more intriguing. But she forced another step back from temptation. 'I'm sure you'll figure something out.'

Yeah, it'd be no time 'til he tempted another woman into his bed. And Ellie would be all envy.

CHAPTER THREE

'ELLIE, where have you been?' Nathan pointedly looked at his watch when Ellie finally made it down to the breakfast table an hour and a shower later. There was no sign of his girl guest—or any other guests either.

She squared her shoulders, refusing to feel even a hint of regret about last night. Maybe she should feel worse, but the gorgeous Naked Guy had completely diffused any threat of angst with his humour and relaxed attitude. And Nathan here had been scoring someone else. At least *he* never had to know about her crazy intention last night. She really had got the better end of the deal.

'I've been waiting ages for you.' Nathan's tone turned more to the 'smooth' one he used so often.

And she really didn't think so. 'I didn't know we were in such a rush to get going,' she answered ultra matter-of-factly.

'We're not leaving.' Nathan surprised her. 'He's here.'

'Who?'

'The owner. He's turned up unexpectedly.'

'The French guy?' Son of the folly man? Given the old dude hadn't lived to see the chateau finished, she guessed the son to be in his late forties or fifties.

Nathan nodded vehemently. 'We have to do whatever it takes to convince him this is the place.'

Ellie didn't want to stay here a moment longer than necessary, not when she had that other guest to avoid. Besides, securing permission to film onsite wasn't usually a problem. Business owners were thrilled to get the exposure. Plus they were well compensated. Although this place was in a class of its own. The elite of the elite retreated here where every luxury was on tap—and the key was its privacy. 'What's your plan?'

Nathan was frowning at her outfit. 'I thought you might toy with the man or something?'

'Pardon?' Ellie asked, certain she'd heard wrong.

'You know, charm him.' He was still frowning at her outfit. 'Flirt him round your finger.'

Ellie blinked as the real Nathan was revealed. Yeah, now the smooth had been removed—she realised that was what *he* did. Oozed charm to get what he wanted. All those compliments and the coy flirting he'd done with her? What had he really been after? Clearly not sex. She'd known the industry she worked in was all about the illusion—but this was killing the dream too much for her. 'We might work for film-makers, but the casting couch doesn't happen when it comes to *locations*.'

Lying back in bed—still recovering from his interrupted sleep—Ruben was glad for the open window and the way words spoken in the courtyard were carried up to his ears. The conversation going on down there was supremely interesting.

'He's French, isn't he? Frenchmen love an elegant woman. Not sure they like jeans.'

'Actually denim was originally created in France,'

Ellie—Ruben liked her name—snapped back at the Nathan prat.

'Well, don't you have anything sexier? What about a skirt or something?'

'I don't think skin is going to get us far. He's probably married.'

Ruben bit back a chuckle at that suggestion.

'Can't you make the effort? This is a major deal—you know that, don't you?'

'I'm not going to prostitute myself just to land a contract, Nathan. That's not the way I operate.'

'You know this industry is *all* about image,' Nathan lectured her. 'I wanted you here because you're so boringly together with paperwork, but you have to step up to the plate when the heat is on.' Nathan began with the clichéd metaphors. 'You need the killer instinct. You do whatever it takes to impress him.'

Ruben couldn't believe she'd wanted to get it on with this idiot. What had she been thinking?

'You might flirt your way into getting what you want, but that's not what I'm about,' Ellie answered back.

Go, the spitfire.

'Don't you want to win?' the doofus asked.

'Not at that price,' she answered smartly.

No, he'd known she wasn't ruthless or cynical. Ruben frowned at the hint of real hurt in her tone. Had she really had feelings for the jerk?

'Fingers crossed the guy is gay, Nathan, so you can be the one to flash the skin.'

Ruben got out of bed and walked into his bathroom. He couldn't wait to get down there. But by the time he did, she was alone, the only sign of any lingering annoyance the light flush on her cheeks. A flush that deepened when she saw him.

'Good morning,' he said to her for the second time that day.

'Oh.' She looked startled he'd spoken, as if she'd thought he was a mirage or something. 'Hello.'

Ms Cautious herself.

'You never mentioned your plans this morning.' He walked to the table that was laden with breakfast options. 'It's a beautiful place—are you going to explore it some more?'

She shook her head and looked everywhere but at him. 'I'm here to work.'

'But you don't much like your work. You're supposed to come here to relax and escape. Have you hunted out the spa facilities yet?'

Her flush deepened again. 'I don't have time for the spa. I really have to work and I really do need to get on with it so…'

'Maybe you ought to have some breakfast first. You must be hungry after last night.'

He sat down at the table, aware of the frustrated look she directed at him. No, he wasn't going to leave her alone. He bit into a croissant to hide his smile.

'I think I'll just have a coffee.'

He reached for the pot before she did, pouring a cup and handing it to her with deliberate care.

'Thanks,' she mumbled.

Ruben sent her a hot look. He didn't like her reserve; he preferred the tease he'd seen up in his room. And he knew there was a bomb going off behind that frozen exterior.

'Ruben Theroux!' a guy called loudly, striding out

from inside, a huge smile on his face. 'Wonderful to see you.'

Ruben knew the difference between sycophantic and genuine warmth. This was a no-brainer. He glanced at Ellie—a total 'what were you thinking?' look. Then he turned back to Nathan.

'I'm sorry, I'm not sure who you are,' Ruben answered coolly, not bothering to stand, just looking up from the table.

But clearly Nathan had done his homework—unlike his sidekick.

'I'm Nathan, I'm here with CineSpace. You know we're interested in your fabulous property. It would be just perfect for—'

'I'd like to finish my breakfast first,' Ruben interrupted, blatantly dismissive. 'Perhaps we can talk later?'

'Oh.' Nathan rallied in less than a second, his reply too collegial. 'Of course.'

'Why don't you go down to the stables? I'll be sure to find you there.'

Having sent the pain in the neck away, Ruben looked at the stop-sign-red face of his curvy midnight caller and felt that foreign tug in his chest again. To cover the awkward moment he went for the usual—tease. 'So, what are you going to do next to impress me?'

Ellie forced back the faint feeling. The guy she'd slept with was the owner Nathan reckoned she had to 'do anything to impress'—and he'd *listened in* to that conversation?

'How else?' Her temper flared. Did he think last night had been her attempt at the casting couch? 'Look, I didn't know who you were. It was a genuine—'

His laughter cut her off. 'I know that, sweetheart. I got in really late, no one knew until this morning that

I was here. I know you weren't trying to convince me to say yes in time-honoured fashion.'

She still didn't believe he was the owner. 'You're supposed to be French.'

'I'm half French but I've lived in New Zealand since I was six.'

'You're not old enough to own this place.' He looked late twenties. Dressed in jeans and a tee he looked more like the gardener than the owner. But that fitting-too-good tee shirt had 'Lucky' emblazoned across his chest and Ellie already knew the guy got lucky—every, single, time.

'My father was an old man when I was born.'

And he'd had a folly of a marriage? To a much younger woman? Ellie decided to skip that can of worms—she had a huge enough one open already. 'You told me you were a guest.'

'You assumed that. I did try to explain who I was but you were too busy apologising to listen.'

'I'm not going to apologise any more,' she said defiantly. 'You should have told me. You should have stopped me making a fool of myself twice over.'

He stood and walked around to her side of the table. 'You never made a fool of yourself with me.'

She stood, speaking through a clamped jaw. 'Mr Theroux.'

He stepped closer. 'You can't be serious.' His voice dropped to an intimate whisper.

'Actually I am,' she declared firmly, shoring up her quivering response. 'You know it's inappropriate for us to talk further. You need to talk to—'

'Nathan.'

'That's right.' She inhaled—bad idea because she caught that deliciously spicy soapy scent.

'I don't want to deal with Nathan. I want to deal with you.'

Now she knew what menopause was going to feel like: the hot flash stunned her. 'You can't.' She snuck a breath. 'It would be unprofessional. Nathan will work on it alone.'

'There's nothing to work on.' He shrugged.

'Are you saying that because I'm leaving, you're not interested in negotiating?' she asked even more breathlessly. 'Are you trying to blackmail me?'

He hesitated. 'I'm open to negotiations. But I would prefer to talk with you.'

'But if I'm not available will you still be open?'

He grinned. 'I'm a businessman, not an idiot. I know there are benefits to be had from this place being used as a location. Not for just any movie, of course.'

She gazed at him through narrowed eyes. Not sure she could believe him.

'I enjoyed every second with you in my bed, but I'm not slimeball enough to use our fling in my business decisions,' he said quietly but firmly. 'Just as you're not slutty enough to think sleeping with me could make me change my mind, right?'

'Right,' she said. 'But the fact is we don't know each other very well.'

'And as far as you're concerned we're not going to get to know each other any better.'

'I think that's best, don't you?'

'Not at all,' he answered bluntly. 'But unlike your colleague I'm gentleman enough to respect your wishes. I'm not into harassing people.'

Just how much of that conversation with Nathan had he overheard?

'I'm capable of keeping my business and my personal life separate,' he continued easily. 'It won't make any difference.'

Well, he was more capable of that than she was—she couldn't think straight with the guy around.

'Truth is I'm in the midst of a new deal to take on two new boutique hotels so a cash injection plus publicity could be useful. That's why I'm more open to film negotiations now than I was a couple of months ago.'

'Well, you'll need to talk to Nathan. I no longer work for the location company.'

Utterly silent, he stared—his brown eyes shifting to black and hard in a whisker of a second. 'You got the *sack*?'

Ellie shivered in the face of iced fury. The ultimate in easy-going humour had a frozen fiery depth she hadn't anticipated. Ruben Theroux wasn't someone to make angry. And now she knew he hadn't listened in to the whole conversation she'd had with Nathan.

'Nathan didn't have the authority to sack me. I resigned,' she said, lifting her chin. 'With immediate effect.'

His jaw dropped. 'Why?' Now he looked even more angry. 'You're just going to quit and run from some silly little mess?'

It wasn't a silly little mess. It wasn't anything to do with Ruben. She'd seen the light. She'd been taken on by that company to keep the paperwork tidy and to flooze where necessary. She might be a complete pleaser but that was taking it too far.

He glanced down at her clothes—and, no, her jeans weren't designer like his. Hers had frayed at the edges from use, not been bought that way.

'What are you going to do?'

Pride surged. 'I'm not so stupid to throw in a job

without having something else lined up. It's all sorted already. I start next week.'

'Doing what?'

She didn't want to tell him the finer details—not that she was embarrassed, more that she sensed it would be safer to keep him distanced. He was in her 'past' already. 'Same industry, different job.'

'You've got a part in a film, then?' He suddenly grinned. 'Lead role?'

'No.' She bit back an answering smile. 'I'm not a wannabe actress.'

'But you have leading-lady looks.'

She vehemently shook her head. 'Please not the flirting again.'

'It's impossible not to,' he murmured. 'Come on, tell me.'

She shook her head. 'Not acting.'

'That's really not a fantasy?' he scoffed. 'Any woman who works in the industry has that fantasy.'

'Well, I don't. I can't think of anything worse than being judged harshly on a giant screen.'

He gave her a sideways look. 'Well, you got your new job organised pretty quick.'

'She's been after me for some time.' It was true. She'd only had to send a text asking Bridie if she was still keen and the emphatic 'yes, start Monday' had been received less than a minute later. 'I've been mulling it a while.'

Fact was she was tired of trying to please everyone—and of not progressing.

Ruben Theroux still looked troubled. Ellie's pride bit deeper. 'Don't think that my decision has anything to do with what happened with you.'

'It doesn't?'

'I've been thinking of a change for months.'

'You're not letting that Nathan drive you out, are you?' he asked carefully. 'Because he's not worth it. Trust me, no relationship is worth killing your career for.'

'You know this from personal experience?' she asked, happy to get the focus on him for a change.

'Possibly.' He shrugged. 'Just don't let anyone get in the way of what you want to achieve.'

'Okay.' She laughed, not needing the 'best friend' advice from her random-stranger lover. 'Actually I feel liberated.'

She wanted the fun back—to be involved in the industry where she was among her own kind: the fans. And that was what Bridie was offering her. They'd met one day at a location—Bridie took fans on set tours, and she knew just how much of a movie buff Ellie was.

'How liberated are you feeling?' Ruben Theroux's expression had sharpened.

Already she knew what that gleam meant. 'Not that liberated.'

'There's absolutely no conflict of interest now.'

'That's definitely not why I resigned.'

'But you know that, despite everything, we never did kiss.'

'We did a whole lot more than kiss.'

He shook his head. 'But we never kissed mouth to mouth. I remember that clearly. I've spent the last hour remembering every second we had, very clearly.'

She mirrored his head-shake. 'We're not going to kiss now.'

'You can't tell me you're afraid.'

His whisper stirred right where she refused to be stirred. 'You can't try to tease me into it.'

It wasn't right that she have the best sexual experience of her life with a complete stranger. One who'd no doubt share himself with the rest of the female population given half the chance. She convinced herself it had been so amazing because she'd been without so long. She'd been celibate for so many months, it had been like a cork releasing from an all-shook-up bottle of champagne. But these things didn't last. Another sip and she'd discover how flat it had gone. It had to be that one-off pop of pleasure.

'I think we should try just the once, just to see.' A winning, teasing, tempting smile.

She laughed. It was very apparent that Ruben Theroux wasn't used to having his plans thwarted. He got what he wanted. And while part of her wanted what he was offering, she knew she'd want more than what he was prepared—or even able—to give in the long run.

'No.' She could say that to him and mean it. Sure she could.

'There's nothing so simple as a kiss.'

'And nothing so complicated.' And unfortunately, nothing else she could think about. His lips caused the problem. That natural curve upwards made them so inviting. Then there was that screamingly masculine line to his jaw. And those wretchedly captivating, laughing eyes.

'Well, if you're sure…' He extended the invitation another few seconds.

'Thanks anyway.' She stepped back from it, turned and fled.

Up in her room it took all of thirty seconds to fling her things into her overnight bag. She giggled at the thought of his temptation. Terribly gorgeous guy, bound to be terribly unreliable.

He was waiting round the front of the chateau. Her car had been brought up by one of those invisible service people who were brilliant.

'I'll make sure Nathan gets home somehow,' Ruben said with a faint grimace.

'Shouldn't you be off talking with him already?' She stowed her bag in the backseat.

'He's not my number one priority at the moment.'

'Oh, you're so good at the flattery, aren't you?'

'Given you're so determined to leave, I guess I'm not that good.' He tempered the words with that charming smile.

She paused by her open driver door and met the look in his delicious eyes. 'Right now I don't have any regrets. I stay and I might get them. I don't want to have any.'

'What about what I want? What about my regrets?'

'I can only apologise. Again.'

He walked closer, taking hold of the door. 'Never feel you have to apologise to me. Never ever.'

Unable to answer that, she got in the car. She'd not been honest about her lack of regrets. She regretted nothing of what had happened, but of what else could have happened had they been different people with desires that converged.

He closed the door for her but remained right by the car, expectantly. She fired the engine and hit the button to wind the window all the way down. He bent and leaned in so his face was right near hers.

'You don't get away that easy,' he murmured, sliding his hand to her jaw.

She couldn't accelerate away or she'd take his arm—

and head—with her. But there was no mistaking his intention.

The smile said it all and those gorgeously curved lips arrowed in on hers. The touch was firm—but not totally dominant as she'd expected. No, he held back for all of a second or two. But then his hand cupped her head, angling her slightly better to meet his as his lips plundered hers. And in another instant she plundered right back, seeking more of that strong touch, that deliciousness—the full impact of his utter masculinity. The shivers skittered down her spine, the knots coiled tighter and tighter in her belly already. His tongue swept—playful, insistent, driving. How could so much be said with a kiss?

She had no idea why she was gripping the steering wheel so tightly, or why she had her foot pushed so hard on the brake. The car engine wasn't even running. But she just knew she was in danger.

He stepped back. Her gaze was glued to him—to the fit, taut body and the smile that held as much rue as it did tease now. His big eyes burned right through hers.

'*My* regret…' he nodded slowly '…was not kissing you. Of course *now* I regret not kissing you sooner.'

Breathless, she put her hand on his wrist, seeking one last touch of skin. 'Thank you for being so nice to me.'

His gaze narrowed. 'I'm not as nice as all that, Ellie.' His voice dropped so she leaned forward in her seat, nearer to hear him. 'You need to know something about me.'

She waited, lungs not breathing, heart not beating.

'I'm man enough to take no for an answer,' he said. 'But I'm also man enough to fight for what I want.'

Eyes not blinking, she had to ask. 'What do you want?'

'You again. Every way. Any way.'

Oh.

He broke the drilling intensity with one of those shattering smiles that gave him such an unfair advantage. 'So if you want to go, you'd better go now.'

CHAPTER FOUR

'AND now, people, the moment you have been waiting for!' Despite the pelting rain, Ellie smiled, hugely enjoying the moment as she stepped aside to let them enter the cave—scene of the villain's final destruction.

The crowd cheered and walked in, a cacophony of excitement.

Four and a half unnaturally long weeks had passed. But the days were getting quicker—sure they were. Being super busy at work helped. She'd progressed from the day and overnight tours, to the longer three to seven nights. This was good, because being responsible for the well-being of up to a dozen people twenty-four hours a day meant she had little time to dwell on what might have happened had she not gunned the car and gone from zero to ninety in less than three seconds.

'OMG this is amazing!'

'I can't believe I'm actually here.'

'*Xaynethe*—at last!'

Ellie grinned as she took photos, photos and, oh, yes, more photos for the tourists as they posed outrageously in front of the mother of all rocks that had been used in the penultimate scene of the mock-Greek-myth movie franchise.

Yeah, she too was the kind of girl who'd want to

dance in the *Sound of Music* summerhouse if she ever got to Salzburg. She'd go to Tiffany's and eat breakfast with her nose pressed to the window pane…so she totally got where her attendees were coming from. And she wanted them to have that experience of their lifetimes, for it to be worth the massive journeys they'd taken. They were die-hard fans, and die-hard fans did not like to be disappointed.

'Okay, random dialogue time—spot prize to the person who answers this.' She broke into a speech, one of the less famous quotes that eventually led into one of the film's greatest scenes.

One guy stepped up immediately, answering her bit-part player's throwaway comment with the hero's 'impassioned plea'. She continued the scene—taking another character's part, wanting to see how far he'd go and whether he could achieve UFS—Ultimate Fan Status. She set the bar super high so not many did, but she had a good feeling about this guy.

As she'd suspected, her tour 'hero' kept the exchange up for the entire scene—and when it ended, the rest of the group clapped and whistled. Laughing, Ellie took his hand and guided him to take a bow. Yeah, it really was the best job ever.

She checked her watch to ensure they weren't getting behind schedule. The movie re-enactment had gone on longer than she'd expected when he'd made it to UFS. 'Okay, everyone, you've got another fifteen here. I'll be at the bus finding Kenny's prize.'

Back outside the rain had eased—slightly. She bent her head, getting ready for the dash across the car park.

'You can't tell me you don't want to be an actress.' A drawl, right in her ear. 'Diva.'

She jumped, dropping her clipboard as she clutched

her chest—stopping her heart from literally leaping out of it.

'Ruben,' she puffed as she turned. 'You're here because…?'

He handed her the clipboard he'd already retrieved. 'I was visiting the cave. Lucky coincidence, huh?'

Ellie wasn't convinced—not when his eyes twinkled like that.

'You're amazing,' he continued, ignoring her astounded snuffle. 'You have them eating out of your hand. They're loving it. Even in the sodding rain they're loving it.'

He'd been watching them in there? Oh, that wasn't embarrassing at all.

'It's not me.' She rushed to snuff that burn in his eyes—and douse the roaring inferno that had combusted in her belly at the mere sight of him. 'It's because they're such fans of the film. Doesn't matter what I do, they're still going to be blown away by being here.'

He shook his head. 'No, you do everything for them and more. No small hassle too much trouble. Your patience with the camera posing is phenomenal.'

He'd been watching a while, then? She giggled—and immediately cringed at her girlishness. 'I'm gritting my teeth over some of it. There are always one or two more difficult clients.'

'And one or two desperate to get into your pants.'

'Oh, that's not true.' But she blushed.

'That guy Kenny was all over you.'

'He was acting the part.' And she hadn't let him end that scene with the kiss that had happened in the movie.

'No, you're his leading lady now,' Ruben teased, stepping nearer. 'He's over his comic-book-heroine crush and fixed on someone real for the first time in his life.'

'He's just being friendly.'

'He's just being unsubtle.'

'And you're not?' She raised her brows at the way he'd moved in on her while speaking.

'Naturally I'm being as unsubtle as possible to let him and the rest of them know that you're not available.'

She glanced over his shoulder, panicking that some of her charges might come out of the cave and see her standing unprofessionally close to a random stranger. 'But I'm not available for you either.' A breathless rush of determined denial.

'I'm conveniently forgetting that for this moment.'

Hadn't she known he'd be difficult to handle? Totally the kind to tumble a girl to her back, and have her breathless and delighted before she'd so much as blinked. 'This isn't a good time,' she began.

'It's a perfect time. You have fifteen minutes before you have to round them back up on the bus.' He took her hand and led her across the car park, to the shelter of the trees on the far side. Out of anyone's view. 'Fifteen minutes…'

'Ruben…' Oh, this was not a good idea, but her heart was skipping and her limbs already sliding towards that warm, supple state. She inhaled deeply and valiantly strove for sanity. She was at *work*.

'Have you got any idea how gorgeous you look?' He sounded as if he wanted to eat her.

She needed to get a grip on both of them. 'I think you need to get to an optometrist—your vision appears to have gone soft-focus.'

He chuckled. 'Oh, no, I'm seeing very, very clearly.

In fact, I've got X-ray vision. I can see the lacy knickers even now.' He sighed. 'Lacy knickers under denim jeans.'

She couldn't help smile back at the sound of his laughter and the sight of his gorgeous—outrageous—face. So enticing. And exciting. Yeah, the rough denim was working its thing on her sensitive bits right about now.

'They are lacy, right?' he muttered in her ear as he swept her into his arms.

'What are you doing?'

'What do you think?' He laughed. 'I've wanted another kiss for weeks.'

She shook her head as she gazed up at him. She couldn't be so reckless again—certainly not now. 'You can't kiss me, you'll kill my lipstick.'

'It's alive?' One eyebrow up.

'It's neat and tidy and I don't want it all over my chin. I have to look good for them.'

His eyes narrowed. 'You look more than good. That Scottish sci-fi geek couldn't take his eyes off you.'

'It's the collectors' edition tee shirt—he wants it.'

'He wants what's in it. But he can't have it. I want it more.' His hands ran down her sides and it was all she could do not to melt into him.

Heaven help her, she was being turned on by macho possessive talk. 'I'm not an "it" and I'm at work.'

He nodded slowly and took a step back, his hands a feathering motion over her stomach as he stepped away. Too intimate and yet not enough. Damn. Her body screamed go-ahead-get-on-me. She didn't let that out; instead she strapped on a polite, *finite*, response. Because this guy would bring nothing but bad-boy trouble.

'I'd better get back to the bus, but thanks for stopping to say hi. It was nice to see you.'

His grin broadened, not seeming to take in her rebuff at all. 'Likewise.'

Ruben felt ridiculously pleased with himself for having tracked her down. It had taken less than five minutes in an online search. He'd hatched a cunning plan within another five. So now phase one was complete. Yes, having seen the bloom on her cheeks and the sparkle zing in her eye, he knew phases two and three were going to go so smoothly. He had the green light. An outsize amount of relief surged at her unguarded response because he was desperately—stupidly—hot for her. It wasn't as if he hadn't ever had a one-night stand before. He'd indulged in many a night of mutual thrills and minimal complexity. Just a 'hi' and a recognition of heat—that chemistry that guaranteed each would get their physical kicks. Enjoyable. Ultimately forgettable.

But Ellie Summers had not been forgettable. It wasn't even the sex that he remembered most—although he was getting off on some seriously good slow-mo mental replays. It was her priceless reaction the next day—the earnest apologies and then the gorgeous giggles. Yeah, that brave ability to see the funny side and parry his shameless flirt with a tart, bald humour. And dignity. He hadn't been sure if she was cut up by that Nathan guy or not. He suspected not, but he'd decided to give her space to lick her wounds anyway. And he'd expected his usual once-done, all-done attitude would kick in.

It hadn't. So that was why he was leaning against his car, not caring about the rain, watching her tour bus slowly move out of the cave's car park.

* * *

At 9:00 a.m. the next day Ellie was in the office, wearing more make-up than usual to cover the effects of her lack of sleep due to an embarrassing amount of Ruben obsessing. But two minutes later, natural effervescence had brought a smile to her face. 'I'm so pleased for you!' she squealed at her beaming boss.

'I'm pleased for me too! And I want to thank you so much.'

'It has nothing to do with me.' Ellie shook her head. The full-colour, double-page magazine spread featuring the popular movie-site tour company definitely had nothing to do with her given she'd only been on the payroll the last four weeks.

'Oh, yes, it has,' Bridie squealed back at her. 'You've already got a name as the best guide *evah*—did you know that group of German lads set up a Facebook page as a tribute to the tour? Although the page is mainly about you—they put your picture all over it.'

'They didn't.' Ellie gaped and embarrassment burned her skin from the inside out.

'Uh-huh. It's a brilliant piece of word-of-mouth marketing.' Bridie tapped on her computer, bringing up the website. 'Or pictures-of-tour-goddess marketing. Because as we know, a picture tells a thousand words. I put a link to it on our website as one of the testimonials, as well as liking it on our own Facebook page, of course.'

'You didn't.' Ellie winced at the picture of her mid-spiel in front of the remains of the futuristic epic that had been filmed a few kilometres up the road a few years ago—the one that had been a massive hit in Germany. They'd pinched the picture of her from the official company website too, but at least in that one she wasn't wearing a too-tight replica costume.

'Yes, and now we're fully booked for the next two

months and our Internet bookings are growing at a phenomenal rate and that's before this article came out.' Bridie's smile faded. 'Although I suspect some of our clients are going to be disappointed that it's not you taking this tour this weekend.'

'I'm not taking the tour?' Surprised, Ellie turned from the cringe-inducing page up on the computer. She was all geared up for it—more than happy to work weekends and extra shifts. It wasn't as if she had anything else to do. While she was the happiest she'd ever been career-wise in her life, her personal life was dead as a dodo—though she was happy about that too. She was in restorative mode, building her new career, working on her personal issues. That left no room for a man. And she refused, absolutely refused, to think about *him*. Of course last night she'd absolutely failed on that front. And the scenes her subconscious had chosen to replay in her dreams—well, they'd been equally impossible to control.

Now, for some reason, Bridie looked even more excited. 'No, because I'm sending you on a reconnaissance mission.'

'A what?'

Bridie looked about to burst. 'You know *Arche*?'

Of course she knew *Arche*. The multimillion-dollar dystopian fantasy duo had been filmed almost exclusively in New Zealand. It was one of her favourite film series; she'd listed it first in her tour-guide bio on the company website. There was one stop on her usual tour that had a twenty-second scene in the second film; she always stopped there and re-enacted it for the tourists. Inevitably there was at least one *Arche*-freak on the bus who loved it as much as she did.

'We might be granted access to it.' Bridie looked about to burst.

'What?' No one had been able to get into that set. The lower central South Island station where most of the action had been filmed was now one of those exclusive resort things for super-wealthy people. Some ancient South American rock star had opened it up for his equally famous and loaded buddies. Absolutely the kind of place she'd want to avoid—those kinds of exclusive retreat places made her think about not-so-distant mortifying events.

'They're thinking of allowing one tour operator in. And they want one of *our* reps to check it out.'

'And you want *me* to go?' Ellie gaped.

Bridie nodded furiously. 'By special request. They had a mystery shopper on all our tours and you're the guide who impressed them—so much so they want you to go check out the place and come up with some ideas for what you'd cover on a tour there.' Bridie jumped up from her seat and zipped around the office like a centipede on speed.

'But that's crazy,' Ellie screeched, collapsing into the nearest chair as her legs went woolly. 'I'm the newest recruit. You can't possibly trust me to do this.'

'It's not crazy. *You're* the one who knows those two films backwards—you can quote whole chunks of the dialogue, I heard you do it with one of those Brits the other day. You might be the newest recruit, but you're the best, most dedicated guide we've got.'

'But I can't represent you, I can't do the whole sales thing.' While she'd worked heaps on contracts at the location company, Ellie didn't have the experience to even think of it here.

'Don't worry about that. *I'll* be covering all access

and contract arrangements. All they're offering at the moment is the opportunity for you to tour the property and come up with the kind of spiel you'd do. They're concerned that as so much of the set was dismantled, there may not be enough there to build a tour around.'

Ellie rolled her eyes.

'I know.' Bridie chuckled near hysterically. 'Our film buffs would do anything just to see a blade of grass that might have been on screen. All you have to do is take a camera, think about the fans and we'll work on it when you get back.'

'You're not coming with me?' Ellie's hands went clammy with that mix of fear and excitement.

'It's the height of the season and our bookings have almost trebled. I'm taking your tour this weekend because you're the best asset to scope this new opportunity. And I'm trusting you with this because I don't want you head-hunted by another tour company and it's only a matter of time before they start calling you,' Bridie said, suddenly looking completely sober and intent. 'I know it's early days, but I know how much you love this and we both know how good you are. This is getting so big, so quick, I need someone like you heading it with me.'

Ellie had all but begged Bridie to give her this job when she'd hit the wall so hard at the location company. But it turned out it was the best thing she'd ever done because she loved it more than any other job—even the one where she'd got to fetch the twenty dollars a bottle water for that mega Hollywood star. It was hard work, but it was *fun*. And now? She couldn't believe she had this opportunity. 'Seriously?'

'Absolutely.' Bridie nodded, her smile returning.

'Okay, then, when am I going?'

Less than twenty-four hours later Ellie stepped off the plane at Queenstown airport dressed in her favourite-fitting jeans, white shirt, boots and her hair swished into a high ponytail. A man waited at the rail with her name scrawled on his board. He smiled and took her backpack.

'Ted Coulson, I'm driving you up there,' he introduced himself amiably. 'You'll need to save your questions for the boss, though. I only manage the deer farm business, not the lodge.'

'Okay.' She smiled, happy to feast her eyes on the amazing scenery for now anyway—the questions could come later. The snow-covered, spiky line of mountains was majestic and breathtaking. She could think of at least ten projects that had filmed in those Alps. She listed a few into her notebook and checked her watch to time the trip from airport to the station. But it wasn't too long before they left the main road and roared along a shingle one. Time disappeared as she breathed in the view—the mountains, the endless sky, the tussocky rolling land. Oh, yeah, no wonder the place was a popular choice for cinematographers—untouched beauty as far as the eye could see. Majestic.

But she blinked as the lodge came into view. 'Oh, wow.'

She knew there were several luxury properties around here, but this had to be one of the best. Man-made majesty this time.

'Something, isn't it?' Ted said dryly.

She breathed deep, trying to quell the nerves suddenly twanging just beneath her skin. 'It certainly is.' And she really, really didn't want to stuff this up.

Ted took the truck right up to the side of the house where there was a wide, covered porch, so passengers could alight unruffled by inclement weather. He was out of the car and opening her door before she'd managed to stop staring at the magnificence of the massive wooden door of the building. Yeah, just the door had her amazed.

She stepped out of the car, feeling like a pixie who'd mistakenly entered a giant's lair. She turned on the spot, checking out the view the house had of the surrounding mountains. This was out of her league. As Ted drove away—apparently in a hurry to get back to his deer—she heard that massive door swinging open and she turned, her biggest smile switched on. She wanted to make the best first impression ever.

Only her mouth gummed.

He had that 'Lucky' tee shirt on again. Those flattering blue jeans again. He had that smile again. The same chocolate ganache eyes—glossy, deep brown. And amused.

'Ellie Summers.' He held out his hand to shake hers, that smile full on his face.

'*You* were the mystery shopper?'

He just grinned more.

'You watched like five minutes.'

'I saw all I needed to. It's obvious you have a gift.'

'Don't try to flatter me.'

'Why would I when I already know that won't work with you? I'm merely stating a fact.'

She avoided looking him in the eye because she knew if she did she was going to laugh and she refused to let him away with it that easily. 'I'm not going to give you what you want.'

'How do you know what I want?'

'I can see it in your eyes.'

'You're not looking at my eyes.'

She closed her own, knowing her skin was sizzling—aliens in outer space would be able to see the glow from her cheeks. She was both disappointed and excited—a zillion thoughts ran through her head in a nanosecond. This couldn't be his place—and if it was, had he brought her here under false pretences?

'You don't own this lodge,' she asserted. 'It belongs to an Argentinian guitarist.'

'Andreas sold it to my company last year and I truly do want to open it up for tours,' he said calmly, apparently able to read her mind.

'But you asked for *me*.' Not her boss or the other more experienced employees.

'Because you're the best guide. Inventive, best when you're improvising rather than sticking to a script someone else has written. So I want *you* to write the script. You're good at creating the fun scenarios.'

The fun scenarios? 'And that's all you want from me?' Now she was blushing more because she'd made a massive fool of herself in assuming…

'Oh, no,' he said as calmly as ever. 'I also want to have wild animal sex with you for hours until neither of us can move. But perhaps it isn't very politically correct of me to admit that.' A flash of that wide, wicked smile.

She choked. 'Not really.'

'Better to be honest though, isn't it?' Complete charm now.

'Um.' Speechless, she just stared at him. It was kind of flattering to think that the beneficiary of her one attempt at seduction had enjoyed it so much he wanted another. Except he'd probably be disappointed in any replay—why mess with the memory? And more importantly, she had her job to think of. 'You don't think mixing business with…this…is a bad idea?'

'I'm capable of not letting my personal life interfere with my professional.' He lifted his shoulders and let them drop easily. 'Are you?'

'Oh, you're just Mr Perfect, aren't you?'

'I'm glad you think so,' he muttered. 'Because I can definitely be perfect for you. I know exactly how I'm going to make you come.'

She moved, because a mere glance at him had her heating in places no one ought to know about. 'Why are you staring at me like that?' she croaked.

'I'm concerned,' he answered expressionlessly. 'You're feeling hot? You've gone very red.' He brushed her cheek with the backs of his fingers—a light caress that didn't just tease, it singed through her skin to her most elemental cell.

She lifted her chin and stepped back out of reach. 'Actually, I am feeling hot,' she answered honestly. 'You should probably keep your distance. One of the passengers on last week's tour came down with the flu. Trust me, if I'm getting that fever, you don't want it.'

'No.' His smile came, slow and wicked. 'I want it no matter what.'

'Ruben—'

'Don't worry.' He held up both hands. 'I shan't touch until you ask me to. And if you insist we'll never discuss it again. I just thought I'd let you know my plans for the weekend. You can let me know if yours dovetail with mine.'

'I'm here for the tour company, for my career and for no other reason.' Absolutely.

'Sure.'

Oh, the guy was too confident—and pretty much

had every reason to be. 'I'm not messing around with you again,' she asserted vehemently.

'Sure.' Too casually, he turned away from her. 'So let's get started.'

CHAPTER FIVE

ELLIE followed Ruben inside—feeling like a pepper slow-burning over a bare flame. But while he might be all kinds of gorgeous, she was no longer Ms People-Pleaser Total Pushover. She'd drawn her line and she was holding it. She was here to work—and work was all that was important to her at the moment.

'You know the lodge wasn't used in the movies at all,' he said, leading her through the building, her overnight bag slung over his shoulder. 'So it won't be available for the tour. We're really just talking about those big hills and the remnants of the set buildings.'

'Okay, but they're going to need refreshments at some point. It's quite a hike to get here.' She was starving. The biscuit and coffee snack on the plane hadn't done much to fill her tummy's gap.

He nodded. 'There's a guest house further down the road. We can do morning tea or something. I have a cook.'

Of course he did.

'Actually, that cook has left something for us to eat tonight if you're hungry,' he said—still with that too-casual attitude.

She wished she had the reserves to say no but she knew it was in her best interests to get her blood sugar levels balanced or she'd be in danger of flying off yet another handle and doing something completely crazy. And merely watching his rear view fell into crazy category. Two minutes of following him had rendered her light-headed. The temptation to do *him* was lunatic.

'I'd love something to eat, thanks.' She'd think food, food, and nothing but food.

He turned, surprised at her easy acquiescence. 'Sooner rather than later?'

'Definitely.' She nodded enthusiastically. 'And I'd love a drink.'

He laughed, which really didn't help her battle to resist her attraction to him. 'No problem.' He led her to the massive, all-professional-equipped kitchen. 'There's a fantastic cellar here. Did you want red, white or bubbly?'

She rolled her eyes. 'Water straight from the tap will do me just fine, thanks.'

'You don't want any wine?' he asked in mock surprise. 'No French champagne tonight?'

'I'm not so stupid I'd make that mistake a second time,' she answered with spirit.

'You blame the bubbles?' He smiled.

She took the glass of chilled water he offered. 'No, but I don't think it helped. I'm grown-up enough to accept most of the madness was my own fault.'

He watched her from the other side of the granite-topped bench. 'What about the lodge—does the décor inspire you as much as the chateau's did?'

Ruefully she sipped, flushing her boiling system with the almost frozen water, and refused to answer. Instead she turned away from the gorgeously deluxe interior to look out of the window at the amazing skyline. 'How many of these places do you own?' She needed their addresses so she could avoid them at all costs. Just her luck that when she finally got to go somewhere gorgeous, her one most wicked encounter would have to be waiting.

'Last count it was five. I'm working on the sixth and seventh at the moment.'

'That's quite a stable.' Especially given each came with a multimillion-dollar price tag.

'They're not all as big as this one. But they keep me busy.'

She glanced back at him as he answered. Yes, there was the slightest hint of tiredness about his eyes. On the bench was the laptop, the tablet, the smart phones—all the paraphernalia of the businessman who worked 24/7.

'But the chateau was the first?' She pressed for more information. 'And it was your father who built it?' And who'd had the folly of the marriage?

'It had been his dream, but he got sick before he could finish it,' Ruben answered, no flicker of emotion crossing his face.

'Oh, I'm sorry.'

'Cancer.' He elaborated a fraction. 'He was older. It was only to be expected, I guess.'

'So you took it over?' She skimmed over his father's age reference for now. She was more interested in how on earth Ruben had managed to achieve all he had.

He nodded.

'How old were you?'

'Fourteen when he died, seventeen when I took on the chateau.'

'Seventeen?'

The roguish smile appeared at her amazed tone. 'My mother signed it over to me.'

'She did?'

He nodded as if it were completely everyday and then turned to the massive stainless-steel fridge. 'I wanted it, she didn't.'

Ellie was gobsmacked. Who on earth signed over a massive property to a teenager? 'Where's your mother now?'

'She went back to France a few months after he died. She didn't want to be hounded as a merry widow.'

'But you stayed?' All alone in New Zealand, barely old enough to leave school, let alone take on a massive business project?

'I wanted to finish the chateau.' He pulled a covered dish from the fridge and put it into the microwave, pressing the electronic controls, still speaking in that carefree way. 'I wanted to realise my father's dream. But Mama couldn't face it. I don't blame her for that.'

His mother had been that unhappy? And had their relationship been so fragmented she'd chosen to leave her only child behind? It seemed Ruben had some pain in common with Ellie's. 'Do you see her much?' Ellie couldn't resist asking and her curiosity didn't seem to bother him given the way he answered so easily.

'We use Skype and stuff but we're both busy. She has a small boutique she loves. I'm flat out,' he answered with that easy-going smile.

Okay, so maybe that relationship wasn't the greatest. But hadn't he had a better one with his dad? 'You must have been close to your father to want to finish his dream for him.'

Ruben's smile became fixed. 'He died a while back now.'

Yeah, but some wounds remained, never truly healing. While you got on with it, there was that permanent bruise beneath the skin. And though Ellie hadn't lost anyone close, she still understood heartbreak—in her case for what could have been, for what she'd missed out on from both parents. 'You don't have any other family?'

He shook his head. 'Nor do I want any.' He turned and caught her eye. His chocolate gaze held pointed meaning, despite the wicked seductiveness of his smile. 'I'm not a wedding-ring kind of guy.'

'Is that you trying to be subtle?' she asked, flipping to tart. 'You don't need to warn me. I'm not coming *anywhere* near you.'

'Oh, right.' He chuckled. 'My mistake.'

Arrogant sod. Of course, she couldn't help smiling and she couldn't help her curiosity. 'So, why no commitment? What's your marriage-avoidance excuse? You had a close shave with a stereotypically money-hungry woman or something?' She rolled her eyes at the cliché. Successful men always seemed to fear some big bad woman was going to come after half their assets in the divorce court or something.

'No.' He walked the few paces back to the business end of the kitchen, pulled a salad bowl from the fridge. 'It's a matter of priority. *Work* is my priority and has been for a while. It takes up every minute of every day and that's not about to change. I travel a lot between venues. I can't be at someone's beck and call.'

Beck and call? She frowned. 'We're talking marriage, not *servitude*.'

'There's a difference?' He smiled as if he was joking—kind of. 'I can't be anyone's husband. I can't be the guy who's going to be there for all those "important" things. It's not fair of me to promise that only to let someone down time after time. I don't want resentment to build and then be hurled against me.'

Was that what had happened? He'd been with someone who'd demanded too much of his time? But wouldn't a woman know what she was getting into in a relationship with a guy like him? That the career drive was an inseparable part of the man she'd fallen for? Just as a woman who married a military man would know that both she and he would have to sacrifice some things because of his duty? Didn't those relationships still work—*with* some work?

Yeah, maybe that was it. Maybe Ruben spent so much energy on his business, he couldn't be bothered working on sustaining a relationship. And why should he have to when he undoubtedly had billions of women throwing themselves at him?

'No, that's still just an excuse,' she said callously. 'You don't want to commit to a woman because you can get what you want from any number. Why would you limit yourself to just one?'

He filled a bowl from the rice cooker on the utility bench, grinning as he did so. And he didn't deny it. 'Let's eat.' He faced her with that smile. 'We'll feel better for it.'

'A microwave meal,' she gushed. 'I'm *so* excited.'

'Why don't you try it before casting judgment?'

Ellie met his challenge with a tilt of her chin and kept her chin high as he relentlessly watched her take first bite of the light curry.

'Okay, best microwave meal ever,' she mumbled, even though her mouth was still half full. There was no point trying to lie in the face of that piercing scrutiny.

He laughed softly and started in on it too.

Dinner passed too quickly because it was so damn delicious. She complimented his chef several times over—to his amusement. Conversation remained safe—

restaurants in Wellington, cafés on the wine trail. After, she helped him carry the dishes back to the bench, helped him rinse and stack them into the machine. And all that time she refused to let herself think on the fact that the guy was good company.

But he was. Really good company. And he was seducing her.

As that thought finally wriggled its way to the front of her brain she glanced at her watch. 'What time do we set out tomorrow?'

'After breakfast, which will be whenever you wake up. There's no real rush.'

'Well, I should probably—'

'Sit down on the sofa and look at the view,' he interrupted with that wolfish manner. 'It's nowhere near bedtime. We need to talk some more.'

'Don't you have work to do?' she asked, desperately aware she needed to get away from him. The longer she was in his presence, the more addled her brain became. It wasn't right that someone could exude such intoxicating heat. And now, as he walked her to the lounge with the amazing view and the sofas that were made for snuggling on, memories tormented, making her all the more susceptible.

'I always have work to do,' he answered carelessly. 'That's not the point.'

She took a seat, primly keeping her knees and ankles firmly together, avoiding looking at him. 'What did you want to talk about?'

'The movies,' he answered promptly, flopping onto the sofa opposite. 'Which of the two is your favourite?'

'Seriously?' She glanced at him. 'I wouldn't have thought you had much respect for movies. I'm guessing you don't have much *time* for them.'

'Not usually.' He blithely ignored her dig. 'But I made a point of watching them the other day and found they weren't bad. Talk me through the fandom.'

So she did. To her surprise, he really had watched them and remembered lots of detail. And had even enjoyed them. Then it turned out he'd watched a few classic films in his time. And a ton of French ones.

'Anything with Gérard Depardieu?' She giggled.

'Makes for a lot of movies.' He winked. 'My mother loves him and Dad used to try and impersonate him—badly.'

So there had been good times with his parents?

'How come you developed such a passion for the flicks?' he asked, switching the focus back on her.

'Oh, I just watched a lot as a kid. Habit.'

'Your parents liked them?'

No, she hadn't been curled up on a sofa between her parents watching a film as he probably had. She'd been in her own bedroom with her own telly—to her friends' envy—and watched them alone. She still had a massive DVD collection. 'They were just fun.'

A time-filler, a window into another, more friendly, world—where villains got their comeuppance, orphans found families and plain girls got the guys. Sure they might be fairy tales, but she enjoyed them.

'And you really like taking the tours?' he asked as if he couldn't understand why anybody would.

'Being with the fans is way more fun than working behind the scenes,' she explained. '*I'm* a fan—I understand that excitement. I mean, it's hard work, but I love it. And I love travelling. I love getting to meet these interesting people who've come from so far away. Who've been to other interesting places. Who love the movies I do. It's fantastic.'

The discussion was a timely reminder—she *wasn't* going to stuff up her perfect job by sleeping with one of the possible contacts. Again.

'I can see why you're popular. Your enthusiasm is infectious,' he said slowly, with a look in his eyes that she was sure wasn't good. 'You know there's a pool here,' he drawled.

Definitely not good. She had another melt moment and instantly rallied. 'I didn't bring my swimsuit. And don't even suggest skinny dipping.' Yeah, she'd caught the flicker of his smile.

'It's heated. There's a spa as well.'

She'd known staying to chat with him wouldn't be wise. She might be completely sober but she was suddenly as giddy as if she'd sucked a litre of champagne through a straw. 'I don't need to try all the things you have for your high-paying guests. I'll be with the scraggly film fans out in the muddy field.'

'I just thought it might help you relax.' He opened his hands in an oh-*so*-not innocent gesture.

'Let down my guard, you mean.' She wasn't here to relax.

'How about a ride, then?' He roared with laughter at her expression. Then clarified. 'We could just go along the fence-line, you could see the moon and the stars. Very much a movie scene.'

'I'm not really into horse-riding.' And she refused to blush. 'We have all day tomorrow to see the old set. I think it's best if I turn in for an early night.'

'You're afraid.'

'Of horses, yes.' She dared him to laugh at her. 'And I'm being sensible.'

He let out a theatrical sigh. 'Come on, then, Cinderella.' He scooped her bag from where they'd left it in the kitchen and then led her up the stairs—another wide, plush corridor that seemed to go for ever.

'Now.' He opened a door and put her bag just inside. 'This is your bedroom.'

'Thank you.' She walked into the room and quickly turned, her hand closing the door. But before she could slam it in his face he leaned in.

'Pay very close attention,' he drawled. 'My bedroom is a mere three doors along. Same floor and everything. You can't miss it. Even if there's a power cut and it's pitch black. Worst case just try them all, there's no one else staying here, only me to be found.'

'Dream on.'

'Oh, I do. Every night.' He shrugged, utterly unashamed. 'Just as you do.'

'There's a lock on this door, isn't there?' She looked down at it as if to ensure it.

'There's no full moon tonight,' he continued, ignoring her interruption. 'Just as there wasn't then. You don't need to pretend you're a horny were-woman, just do what you want to do.'

'*You're* not what I want to do,' she muttered, determined to believe it.

'I think I prefer it when you're agitated and honest rather than trying to be cool and lie.'

She choked—torn between laughter and outrage. 'You're so up yourself.'

'No, I'm just not so uptight I can't admit to something that feels good.'

She twitched. 'Look, what happened was a mistake. I'm all for learning from my mistakes.'

'Well, frankly, I'm glad you made the wrong room mistake and saved yourself from a mess-up with that other guy.'

'What happened with you was a mistake too.'

'How can you say that?' His voice dropped lower still. A whisper that slid over her like the faintest, warmest of breezes. 'You're as in thrall as I am.'

She had to end this somehow, before she went up in a puff of smoke. 'This is really flattering and all—' she sucked up some cool '—but I'm not available for anyone, or any kind of thing, right now. That night just showed what an idiot I was.'

'You weren't an idiot.' He looked concerned. 'That wasn't the act of a desperate woman.'

'Wasn't it?' Wasn't it exactly that?

It was one of the few moments in the evening where his expression was serious. 'There's nothing wrong with having needs and giving them free expression. You know what I think of you?' he asked.

She really didn't want to know.

'That you're a spontaneous, fiery, passionate woman who's as human as I am. Who makes mistakes, who has wants. It was refreshing. You were in total charge. You blew my—'

'Look, don't try to make out like I'm some kind of sex goddess just because you want back in my pants.' Ellie breathed in desperately. 'Truth is I don't want any kind of a relationship right now. I've got a new job that I really don't want to lose because I actually love it. I want to be in charge of both my career and my social life.'

'I don't want a relationship either.' His shoulders lifted. 'It's impossible for me. I'm in the middle of a new deal, I'm away every week to another hotel.' He half laughed. 'And that's not going to change any time soon. And not for anyone.'

'So there's really nothing to talk about, right?'

'There is just this one small thing.' He leaned closer.

'You said you wouldn't make a move.'

'I'm not.'

'You know you are.' She shook her head. 'Why don't you drive to the nearest bar or something? You could get sex any time you want it.'

'You're proving that statement wrong right this second.'

She swallowed.

'I have some fun when it feels right, but my field's been empty a while.' He maintained his intent, fiery gaze on her. 'I can admit to my needs, maybe you can't. But your actions that night showed you have them.'

'It can't happen.'

'Yes, it can. Just once more can absolutely happen.'

Just once more. Oh, so, so tempting.

'You promised you wouldn't touch me unless I invited it.' Her whisper was invitation enough and they both knew it.

She looked down to stop the mesmerising effect of his easy smile and dangerous eyes. But it merely made it worse because now she could *hear* the molten-chocolate quality in his words. She could feel his heat; her own instinct to draw nearer pulled.

'Look at me.' Now there was more than a thread of steely persuasion in that warm voice.

She fought the urge to obey—because he wasn't going to win her around. She wasn't going to roll over like so much of her *wanted* to.

He braced his hands in the door frame and leaned across the threshold.

And she felt it, she really did. His proximity was as good as a touch, spiking her adrenalin, sending shivers along her skin despite that inch of air between his body and hers.

'Ruben,' she barely breathed.

She could retreat into her room but she didn't want to back down in any kind of way. Besides, he'd simply follow her in and that would decimate her control.

'I'm not touching you,' he murmured, his sensual dominance merciless. 'Do you want me to?'

He didn't have to touch her to tempt her. But his incredible magnetism equally repelled her. More games with him would inevitably cause hurt for her—she always ended up the heartbroken, not the heartbreaker. She'd had only that one night of playing carefree seductress, whereas he'd had many as seducer. And worse, more games could cost her future with the best job she'd ever had. So despite the desire threatening to enslave her, she couldn't succumb to it.

'Good night.' She shoved him back through the doorway and quickly shut the door.

A split second of silence and then he called a teasing comment through the wood. 'Enjoy those dreams, darling.'

Oh, she would, but dreams were all they were going to be.

CHAPTER SIX

'It's supposed to be summer.' Stupidly forlorn, Ellie stared out of the window at the grey-blanketed land. The steady drizzle had drenched all her plans for the day. How were they going to get out and see the set remnants in this? How was she going to get through another hour under the same roof as Ruben and not jump him—even a roof as huge as this? She *had* to get out of there.

'It's not so bad.'

She turned. He was jeans-clad again. And it was worse than bad.

'Come and eat something.' He took her trembling for hunger of the food kind.

'We can still ride if you don't mind getting wet,' he commented, not quite idly, once she'd filled her cereal bowl.

Okay, maybe he knew exactly how much his mere presence tormented her. But she wasn't ever admitting how wet she already was.

'I'm not riding with you.' She glared at him, her spoon halfway to her mouth. She was a frustrated wreck who hadn't managed to get nearly enough sleep and infuriated with her inability to restrain her attraction to him.

'If you won't go on a horse, then it's the quad bike.

It's too far to walk and it's rough country, especially in this weather.' He shrugged. 'But lots of your tourists would like quad biking, right?'

Quad biking would mean her straddling the seat behind him, her arms around his waist. He was determined to breach her personal space again, wasn't he? And she was melting already. She shoved the loaded spoon into her mouth and chomped.

'I can ride one myself,' she declared once she'd swallowed. She was not cuddling him from behind.

'Of course.' He acted as if there'd been no other option anyway. 'Finish your breakfast. I'll go get the bikes ready.'

She was glad to see him go—truly glad: his back view didn't ever worsen any. Not with the casual jeans and clinging tee and, oh, so confident way he had of walking.

So he can walk—she winced at her fan-girly brainlessness—*many men can.* She returned her focus to the cereal and consumed the lot. If one type of hunger wasn't going to be sated, another would. At least her legs would lose the cotton-wool feeling.

But twenty minutes later she was astride a powerful machine, with her thighs vibrating. She'd never stand again at this rate. Oh, it was not good. She could *not* be getting turned on by a hulking great piece of metal. Of course she wasn't, she was *already* on.

'Which way?' she shouted breathlessly as he paused for her to come alongside his bike.

He just jerked his thumb in answer.

For almost an hour and a half they rode, stopping lots as he pointed out where filming had occurred. Then they powered out and let the machines roar. And she loved every damn second of it. Even in the drizzly, greyed-out day, the landscape was so majestic and ancient, it put all those pesky little things like unquenched lust into perspective—blowing away the sleepless bad temper and leaving exhilaration in its wake.

He, too, had the red-cheeked, bright-eyed excitement. 'Come on, we can go further up the valley.'

'The weather doesn't worry you?'

'No, are you okay?'

'I'm good.' Whether the scenery had been another character in a globally massive movie franchise or not, it was simply stunning. And she wanted more of this wild open air—with him. No matter that her jeans were mud splattered, that the drizzle had gone right through the light coat she was wearing over her jeans so her tee shirt was soaking. As the rain tumbled faster and heavier she was steaming up inside.

She followed his lead across the short tussocky track, down to the vast shingle riverbed. They were about two miles along that when the rain really began to fall. Their wheels churned up large globs of mud. She blinked rapidly to maintain clear vision but ahead of her Ruben's engine roared angrily as he pushed it. His bike jerked forward and Ellie winced, barely able to watch through half-screwed lids. Despite knowing what was about to happen, she was unable to do anything to help except shout. But even as she did Ruben jumped. His machine tipped, two wheels disappearing into a muddy bank. A half second later, Ruben rolled to his feet in total stuntman style.

'Hello, Mud-man,' she teased, hiding the relief that he wasn't injured. Thankfully they hadn't been going fast enough for a serious accident.

He was laughing, his eyes alight as he yanked off his

helmet and surveyed the damage. 'I'm going to need a truck to get the bike out of there.'

Ellie refused to notice how his hair had spiked in places, making him look more of a carefree rogue than ever. She hated to think what her own hair looked like now she'd removed her helmet too. More horrendous was the fact they were stuck miles from the lodge and had to share the one bike to get back.

'You did this deliberately, didn't you?' she accused, her adrenalin finding a vent in anger.

'I'm capable of many great things, but controlling the weather isn't one of them.' His laughter became more rueful. 'This part was more boggy than I expected. And if you must know, the rain bothers me more than it does you.'

'And why's that?' She didn't believe him.

'I had plans for today.'

Still astride her bike, she put her hands on her hips. 'Nefarious ones?'

'Utterly,' he admitted shamelessly. 'Now they're ruined.'

'So what are you going to do about it?'

'Oh, I always have a Plan B.' He chuckled.

Yeah, the guy was so confident in his ability to turn even the worst situation to something favourable. His plan involved charming the pants off her, no doubt. But while he was incredibly focused in his attention on her, somehow he made it impossible to get past *his* front. It wasn't that he wasn't genuine—unlike Nathan, she knew Ruben was honest in his desire to be with her. But while he answered her questions, he wouldn't let her past a certain point in his reserve. He closed conversation down or switched focus. But Ellie was both curious and determined not to let him have it all his own way.

'Don't think I'm handing over my bike to you,' she said, remaining firmly astride her vehicle. 'You're too reckless.'

He walked right in her path, leaning forward to put his hands over hers on the handlebars. 'You're going to make me walk back?'

'I'll drive, you give directions.'

'You do like to be in control of the situation, don't you?' he muttered.

In less than ten seconds she knew she'd made a mistake. He'd come round and climbed behind her and was now way too close with his hands too firm around her waist. If she'd been the one to take the rear position she could have made it less intimate.

'You don't have to hold so tight, you know,' she said firmly. 'I'm not going to drive that fast.'

All she felt then was the laughter vibrating in his chest. She wanted to lean back and absorb it some more. Instead, she put the engine on full throttle.

'Wow, you really know what you're doing,' he commented after she rode them out of the roughest part of the riverbed at high speed. 'You could go on one of those extreme environment survivor shows. Wild Mountain Woman or something.'

'Don't get too carried away.' She slowed down to hear him better. 'It's not like I'm going to rappel down a rock face using a rope I've plaited out of dental floss,' she scoffed. 'I know my own limitations.'

'Really? What's your limit?'

She ignored the innuendo and answered honestly. 'I still get a bit scared of heights.'

'Still?'

'I get a bit funny in the tummy but most of the time I can manage to control it.' She eased back more as she came to a badly bogged bit. 'My dad is really into rock-climbing and mountaineering and stuff. He'd be in his element here.'

'You go climbing with him?'

'When I was younger I did,' she said briefly. 'If I wanted to spend time with him, he was usually somewhere precarious so I had to suck it up.'

'And you wanted to spend time with him?'

'Sure.' He was her dad. All her life she'd wanted his attention and approval—until she'd grown up enough to accept it wasn't ever going to be forthcoming. 'I've never really understood his need to conquer nature, though. I mean, yes, appreciate the beauty, respect the elements, come and enjoy it. But why does he have to *beat* it? Where's the rush in risking life and limb? Man versus nature? Nature is always going to win.'

'Hmm.' Ruben grunted a kind of agreement. 'Where does he live?'

'He has an outdoor equipment store in one of those ski towns not too far up the road from here.'

'Oh.' A pause. 'Did you want to see him while you're down here?'

'No.'

Another slight pause. 'What about your mum? She's into the outdoors too?'

'No, she's the total opposite. While Dad's all mountain man, she's city-queen. She lives in Sydney.'

'They're divorced?'

'Have been for nearly twenty years.'

She heard his whistle. 'How'd they manage to meet and marry in the first place?'

'They were a fling, she got pregnant. They tried to make it work but, really, it was never going to. It would have been easier if they'd ended it sooner.'

'But they wanted you,' he said, as if that made it all okay.

Sometimes she thought it would have been better if they'd adopted her out to a couple who'd been desperate to have kids. Yes, she was grateful to them for making the decision to have her, but to raise her themselves? They were too selfish for that. Neither had wanted to give up the things important to them. Ellie had had to fit in—to tag along. But she'd never felt truly wanted, never once felt as if she could make them happy. Just once, just for once, she wanted to be the centre of the universe. Not to have to try to squeeze herself into some contortion to fit into the box of someone else's life. Every kid wanted her parents' undivided attention and love. No kid could ever have enough—especially if they'd been starved of it.

'They did the shared-custody thing, but that was because neither wanted me full time.'

His grip on her waist tightened as he pressed in even closer. 'What do you mean neither wanted you full time?'

'I mean exactly that.' Ellie hesitated—did she really want to go into this? Nothing put a guy off more than a woman who went on about her exes or unhappy home life. Men hated drama. And Ruben had already declared he wasn't into the whole 'being there' deal. Given that, it was probably *wise* to talk about it. Tell him all the crap to turn his interest off and shore up her own resistance. So she slowed more so he could hear her easily.

'You know, week about? One week with Mum, one week with Dad,' she explained. 'Everybody thinks it's great. You get double of everything. Different rules, different homes. Supposedly you can get away with stuff because you say the other parent "would let you".

But for me it wasn't like that. I wouldn't have minded a few more rules—at least then it might have felt like they cared.'

Some spats between them, some arguments over her welfare might have made things seem more normal. But the arguments had been because both her parents preferred their child-*free* week. The week they had scheduled with her was the one that hindered them. She'd heard the whispered fury when one had tried to get out of a weekend or a week of responsibility. The annoyance of having to have her—that her presence meant ruined plans. They'd each wanted their time *away* from her so badly. So instead of doing what *she* wanted, she'd tried so hard to do whatever it was that they wanted to do. To blend, to be good, to please. The only thing that had been easy was the actual move. Trying to fit into each destination was the exhausting bit. In the end she'd just kept quiet in her room, watching her favourite movies. And when old enough, hanging with some girlfriends, and then finding attention in the arms of guys who wanted what she had to offer, but didn't want to give what she needed.

'You're their only child?' he asked.

'Yeah, that's a good thing given the way they were. But it would have been nice for me to have had company.'

'So what, you have some Waltons family dream now?' he teased.

She laughed. 'I'm realistic enough to know that's a fantasy.'

'Hell, yes,' he said with feeling.

'How do you know it is a fantasy?' she couldn't resist challenging. 'You're an only child too.'

'But I grew up down the road from a number of

Waltons-esque families. And let me tell you, they were superficial images. I think it's better off staying small. *Very* small.' As in solitary. But even though he knew the answer, even though he knew this was a hopeless conversation, Ruben couldn't resist asking her, 'Are you into kids?'

'I'm not sure. Probably not.'

'Really?' Most girls didn't mean it when they went all definite denial. But Ellie hadn't been definite; she seemed more thoughtful.

'Not unless I meet the right guy, you know?' she finally expanded. 'He really has to be the *right* guy. I need him to be there and I need him to want the kid. It's not nice not to be wanted. I want any kids of mine to have two parents who want them, who love them, who are there for them. For everything.'

Ruben understood—she wanted her kids to have the kind of parents she *hadn't* had. He felt hurt for her, but impressed at the same time with her courage. Now she knew what she wanted and she wasn't going to settle for less. Not for some guy like *him*. Because he already knew he couldn't 'be' there. His one significant ex had wanted him to 'be' there—and that was just for her, not kids as well. If he couldn't be there enough for a grown woman, there was no way he could be there for children.

'I'm guessing you're a no-kids man?' Ellie sounded amused at his silence.

'I like kids but they wouldn't fit in my life. I'm not someone who can guarantee to "be there" for them. I've got things I want to do and I don't think it's fair to have a family when you can't give them everything they want.'

'That beck-and-call thing, huh?' she asked dryly.

She might be all sarcasm, but he meant it. He didn't

want a family holding him back from all he could achieve. He didn't have the ability or the desire to meet the demands of a long-term relationship. He'd tried it years ago with Sarah and failed miserably. And his father had succeeded in the relationship but failed on the business front. There was no such thing as managing it all. 'I'm years off being ready for it in terms of my career and I don't want to be old like my father was. I love him for having me, but I wish he'd done it sooner.'

'So your mum was quite a bit younger?'

'Try thirty years,' he admitted shortly. 'Hard to have everyone thinking he was your grandfather.' He chuckled to lighten it the way he always did. 'And the looks the two of them got when they were walking along the street, hand in hand and smooching like teen lovers. They just didn't give a damn.'

He felt her stiffen beneath his fingers and felt the old resentment burn in his gut. He hated intolerance.

'I thought they had an unhappy marriage?' Ellie had all but stopped the machine. 'Isn't that what you meant by his folly of a marriage?'

'Oh, no.' Ruben laughed, relieved her tension hadn't been in judgment of his parents. 'No, people couldn't cope with their age gap.'

'And gave you a rough time over it?'

'You can imagine the slurs at a small-town school back then.'

'What's wrong with two people making each other happy?' Ellie sounded as if she was frowning. 'Why can't people just be pleased for them? Doesn't everyone want to find a great love like that?'

He smiled at her naïveté—she'd watched too many Hollywood happy endings. 'People can be unkind when they don't understand or if it's something they've not been around much.' He hardly ever discussed it, he'd encountered too much intolerance—even in this supposedly modern world. There was just that inevitable smirk or comment—as if his dad were up there with Hugh Hefner or something. But Ellie's instant emo defence of them had him explaining more than he usually would. 'They really were a love match and really in love. Sickening really.' Sometimes even he'd felt excluded from it. This despite knowing he'd been the much-wanted, much-loved product of their relationship. And he'd been determined not to break their blissful ignorance and had never once told them of the taunts he'd suffered. He'd learned to handle the other kids his own way. When he'd first started school as an undersized six-year-old, with English as a second language, a weird accent in a small town with a father already almost at retirement age and a mother younger and more beautiful than everyone else's? It had been sink or swim—and Ruben had mastered the stroke. 'They just saw through each other's layers to the person within, and they loved what they saw.' He still felt that mix of happiness for them and frustration with them—because they'd been unable to achieve much else because of that total adoration of each other.

'Has your mum met anyone else since?' Ellie asked quietly.

'No. I kind of wish she would,' he found himself admitting aloud for the first time in his life. 'But she's adamant it isn't going to happen.'

'Because she buried her heart with him?'

'Yeah. I think she's scared of getting that hurt again.' He understood that too. The loss had been unbearable. 'She couldn't stay in New Zealand. Couldn't stay any place where she'd been with him.'

'But what about you? You were so young.' Ellie's body had gone taut beneath his fingertips again.

He laughed off her concern—the way he laughed off anything that touched too close to vulnerable aches. 'I wanted to finish what he'd started. I wanted to do that for him.'

'But it must have hurt her to leave you?'

Her sweet concern stabbed now and he didn't want it. 'Mama knew I was okay. And I was busy.' He'd made sure she'd thought he was okay. By then he was a master of hiding his hurt—those years of coping with childhood taunts had taught him well. You covered up—no one could grin and bear it like Ruben. He could turn any nightmare around with a comment and a smile, hiding how gutted he might be inside. He'd won them over with the ability to laugh and make others laugh—but he never let them close. Not when he knew too well how much it hurt to lose those you held close.

'It would have hurt her more to stay.' He dismissed the topic completely, switching to tell her something more about the mountain on their right, and then another anecdote from when Andreas had owned the lodge.

As the big building came into view he directed her to take the bike right up to the main entrance. He'd have it cleaned and put away later. For now it was the two of them who needed hosing down. Indeed, off the bike the first thing Ellie did was glower at his mud-covered clothes and then down at her own.

'I don't have any other jeans, you realise.'

Ruben couldn't contain his amusement. She looked like an earth goddess—a curvy sprite of a woman. Little curls had sprung around her temples, her face damp, her eyes shining. 'You can borrow some of mine.'

'Like they'd fit.'

'They'll be fine. Now come on, I'm freezing,' he lied. 'We don't want to get a chill.'

He'd taken the cover off the spa pool early this morning and he headed straight for it.

'I told you I didn't bring my swimsuit.' She followed him round the side of the lodge and stared at the pool with an unmistakably longing gleam in her eye.

Yeah, Ellie had a sensualist streak—he wanted her to embrace it.

'I'll give you a shirt that'll do.' She was going to have to peel off those blue jeans. He'd never appreciated denim as much before and he was a jeans-every-day guy. But hers were wet, hugging her curvy butt and thighs and he wanted to slide his hand down the tight front of them really badly.

He went into the pool house and grabbed a tee, tossing it at her and exiting before he turned into some kind of caveman and went for her mud and all.

He stripped poolside while she was in the change room, and forced himself to go under the outdoor shower—cold—sluicing away the streaks of dirt before quickly getting into the heated water. He badly needed to relax.

'You can't resist it, can you?' she teased as she came out of the pool house, ready to join him. She too had showered. Now his clean shirt was clinging to her wet body beneath.

Ruben pressed the spa bubbles on full to hide how horrifically extreme her effect on him was.

'Resist what?' he asked vaguely. Thinking about sex all the time? Hell, he wished he could get her out of his head, or at least get some other woman in. He'd never been unhealthily fixated on one lover like this.

He blamed it on the absolute excitement of waking to discover a hot, perfect lover straddling him. Pure fantasy come to life.

Of course he couldn't help thinking of it and nothing but. Of course he'd had to finagle a way of getting her back in his bed—even just for a weekend. Only it wasn't proving to be as simple as he'd planned.

'Seeking out pleasure.' She shook her head, shivering as she stepped carefully into the steaming water.

'I work hard so why shouldn't I enjoy playtime?' He sent her a sideways look and jeered lightly. 'Nothing wrong with relaxing and celebrating and enjoying pleasure. We should appreciate it when something feels good.'

'Don't think you can get me to yes by glamorising hedonism,' she answered equally flippantly.

'But you know how good it was. You *told* me how good it was.' And he'd loved hearing it. 'The best ever.' And he couldn't get past it now, not when she was doing the wet-tee-shirt thing in a hot tub.

'It's bad form to compare lovers,' Ellie said primly, sitting on the opposite side of the spa from him and determinedly not looking at his bare chest. She didn't believe for a second that he actually felt the same way—*she* hadn't been his best lover ever as well.

'I'm not doing that.' He laughed. 'I'm merely reminding you that that night with me was the best sex of your life. I can't understand why you don't want a repeat of that.'

'Because it wasn't real,' she said simply.

'It wasn't real?' Ruben's tease vaporised. 'Wasn't *real*?'

In a heartbeat the relaxed, teasing atmosphere

snapped to stormy. Ellie's suddenly feverish temperature couldn't be blamed on the bubbling water.

'No, it wasn't real,' she insisted.

He stared at her. 'It was the best sex of your life,' he declared again, almost defiantly daring her to deny it.

'Okay, I'll give you that.' She cleared her throat. 'But don't you think that's because it was such a fantasy? Like a dream?' Her half-dreaming state had made the memory even better. 'So good it *couldn't* have been real.'

His obsidian gaze narrowed in on her, compelling more explanation from her.

'I didn't know you. You didn't know me.' She faltered. 'We can't ever recreate that scenario.'

'So you think our being together again would be a disappointment?' he asked, incredulous.

'It would have to be,' she muttered. 'Don't you think?'

'No, I don't. You're not curious to know for sure?'

'I...' Of course she was curious. It was hard containing that curiosity. But she didn't want to taint that memory with disappointment, nor did she want to mess up her opportunity at work.

'You liked fantasy sex.'

'So did you,' she defended.

'Yeah,' he admitted with a wolfish grin. 'There are other kinds of fantasy sex.'

She swallowed. 'I'm not into kink.'

He chuckled. 'I can come up with many, many simple, sweet fantasies if you like.'

She licked her lips before realising what a revealing piece of body language she'd instinctively performed. She put her hand to her mouth and rubbed—as if she could deny the yearning there.

'Ellie.'

Oh, help, that had her toes curling, but the rest of her was paralysed. She couldn't walk, couldn't run. She just waited as he took the two paces through the water. So close she had to tilt her chin to maintain eye contact—which she was damn well determined to do. So close she could feel his breath, could feel her own muscles weakening as excitement erupted.

He inclined his head, lowering it almost enough. 'You want fantasy?' His lips barely moved as he challenged.

Ellie couldn't breathe at all now, couldn't hear a thing other than the echo of his words and the amplified thud of her heart. Blood shot to her extremities, her skin suddenly super sensitive. Every *cell* sensitive. And screaming out. Screaming so loud her reason was muted. So she was the one to tilt her chin that tiny bit further, bringing their lips into contact.

She was lost in that instant. She shut her eyes, only able to focus on the velvet warmth of his kiss. The insistence of his lips, his tongue. Oh, she opened, she let him in. She let him, let him, let him. Because what he demanded was exactly what she wanted—passion and need. So swiftly his touch swept her into that burning vortex where thought and caution were flung away because this ecstasy was all that mattered.

With every lush caress of his mouth, her resistance melted. *She* melted, her muscles sliding towards his strength, her mouth moving to welcome his demand. But there was a kernel of tension, slowly knotting, growing, sending the message that only his lips touching hers was not enough. Not nearly enough. She craved closer contact, craved for them to meld completely. Chest to breast, thigh to thigh, for their arms to curl and cling and for them to literally be locked in intimacy. Oh, she wanted that, she wanted that *now*.

She moaned—a song of need, a plea. The pressure of his mouth increased, his tongue flicking in an erotic tease that saw her tremble with it. For her body to move of its own accord—closer, closer, closer. They were inches apart in warm water, she wanted to feel his strong muscles, to press their wet skin together…

'That fantasy enough for you?' he asked, his voice rough as he stepped back. The water splashed as he sat down again on the opposite side of the tub.

Ellie couldn't believe he'd kissed her like that and then let her go. She couldn't believe the intensity in his expression—in his action—had suddenly vanished. 'You're the most awful tease.'

'Actually I think you're the one who can claim that crown,' he argued in that charming rogue way.

'I'm not teasing at all. You're the one who keeps crossing the boundaries.' She swept her sodden hair from her face.

'You keep tempting me to.' He shrugged.

'So it's all my fault?'

'Absolutely.'

Unable to help it, despite knowing it was what he wanted, she laughed.

'You think it's funny?'

She nodded. 'You're so good for a girl's ego.'

'Well, that is my raison d'être.' He inclined his head.

Ellie nodded. Yes, he'd gone back to form—a charming, carefree man made for good humour and good times. Yet she sensed that impenetrable wall only a millimetre beneath his surface.

Damn it, the whole complicated package fascinated her.

CHAPTER SEVEN

'PUT these on while we get your things cleaned and dried.'

'I didn't think I'd need more than one pair of jeans. I wasn't expecting a mudbath,' Ellie said with defiance born of embarrassment as she took the jeans and tee Ruben held out to her and then dived to her bedroom to get decent.

She figured that at least he was never going to get off on the 'she's wearing my clothes' thing—they totally swamped her. But suddenly she was feeling decidedly 'his' now wearing his jeans and tee. It was pathetically primeval but utterly seductive.

When she went out to the kitchen he was waiting with two giant mugs of coffee—perfect, as she'd been having some dangerous thoughts about heading to a nearby bed.

'What do you do when you're here alone and the weather's closed in like this?' she asked, desperate to make innocuous conversation.

'I read.'

'Let me guess, thrillers? Gory crime stories?'

'No.' He lifted his mug and led her down the hallway, pushing open the door to the large, plush study.

He walked to a bookshelf around a corner, further away from the others. 'Non-fiction.'

'Oh, wow.' Ellie gazed at the partially hidden display. Architecture books. Big, expensive, beautiful architecture and design books. Covering all kinds of buildings—not just hotels but homes and castles, inner-city apartments, outback homesteads and skyscrapers. The works.

'You've got a ton.' She moved in front of the shelf and pulled a couple out, then folded to sit cross-legged and opened the first book. It was the perfect safe time-killer.

He followed suit, leaning opposite her, soon burrowed in cushions and flicking through books. They talked, compared favourites, argued about the ugly. Almost two hours passed and Ellie couldn't help thinking that, despite his outrageous flirt moments, his life appeared to be all work.

'So where do you hang out most?' she asked, chuckling when she saw his startled expression. 'Don't worry, I'm not about to start stalking you.'

'At the hotels.'

'But where do you exercise? You play rugby or something?' Surely he was in a team. He totally had the fitness for it.

'I use the gyms in the hotels.'

Oh, of course he did. 'You don't actually have a *home* of your own?'

'There's no point.' He kept flicking pages and didn't look up to answer her. 'I visit the hotels on a constant rotation. I use a room in them. That way I can keep an eye on the quality of the service.'

Ellie glanced around the pristine interior of the place.

'Don't you have any personal stuff?' Aside from architecture books?

'Like what?' he asked absently, still looking at the book spread on his lap.

'Family photos?' *Anything?*

'I have some on my phone.' He shrugged. 'I guess I'm minimalist. I have an office at the chateau but most of the stuff I need is on my laptop.'

'And what do you do for fun?'

'Work is fun.' He looked up and smiled. 'I love what I do. Don't you love what you do?'

'Sure I do. I really do, actually.'

Ruben, now back in position leaning against cushions, had a sly look in his eye. 'You're meaning social fun, aren't you?' he asked.

She shrugged as if she weren't *that* interested. 'I'm guessing you enjoy your guests' company.'

'Some more than others,' he answered glibly. 'But not in the way you're thinking. You were an exception and you know it.'

Yes, but nothing could come of the flame between them—there was no future in terms of a *relationship.* She might bring tours here but she could avoid him completely if she wanted to.

Thing was, she *didn't* want to.

But she knew that if she agreed to a fling, when it was over there'd be no contact at all between them. It was how she worked and she was pretty sure it was how he'd work too.

The thought of not ever seeing him again squeezed her vulnerable heart hard. She wanted to see him. She wanted to know how his current deal worked out. She liked hanging out, she liked the aura of freedom he had, she liked how he made her laugh. Yeah, she wanted more of his company and she shouldn't. But if she worked out some boundaries—where she wouldn't give too much and thus not expect too much either—then maybe she could live with it.

'I think we should try to be friends,' she blurted decisively. 'We should put this on a friend level.'

Ruben choked on nothing but fresh air.

'I'm serious.' She smiled as she watched him gasp. 'We have a lot in common. We laugh together. We're similar in that work is important to us. We get on well.'

'And your point?'

She figured she could have him in her life as a friend, or not have him in her life at all. And though she knew she probably *should*, given how attractive she found him, she wasn't ready to cast him out of her life completely. She was still too curious. 'We can be civilised, can't we?'

'There's nothing civilised about the things I want to do with you.'

She closed her eyes for a second and waited for the blood to recede from her cheeks. 'But if we have a fling what do you think will happen in the end?'

He didn't answer.

'What usually happens?' she prompted.

He began to smile, that wry, rueful smile.

'Are you in contact with any of them?' she asked softly.

His shoulders lifted. 'If our paths cross we smile and wave and it's all lovely and amicable.'

'Because they have too much pride to show you how hurt they are inside,' Ellie said dryly.

His brows lifted. 'Honey, I'm not with any one woman long enough for her to get hurt.'

Ellie's laugh came out as a snort but his words made

her all the more resolved—she didn't want too few hot nights, she'd rather have long-term laughs.

'Well, okay, what about you?' he said firmly. 'Are you in contact with your exes?'

As if. 'I haven't had as many as you,' she said pointedly. 'But usually what happens is I have a relationship and, not too long later, the guy moves on. I *used* to try everything to please him, so he'd stick around longer, but I'm not going to bend myself into any more boxes in order to try to keep anyone.' She was never doing that again. 'I don't see any of them any more.'

'So you're not going to bend into any boxes for me?'

She shook her head with a laugh.

'I'm feeling a little insulted,' he said mildly.

'Don't be. Actually you should feel pleased. I want to stay in touch with you.' She really did.

'And that's a first? None of your other men?'

'How many do you think there've been?' She rolled her eyes when she saw the amused look on his face. 'No, I'm not in touch with any of the two hundred and eighty-four. They were jerks.'

He laughed. 'I don't want to be a jerk to you. I like you. I like talking to you.'

'Exactly!' Great, this was easier than she'd thought it would be.

'I still want to have sex with you, though.'

Okay, maybe not so easy. 'You'll get over that.'

'You're saying you're over it?' He moved towards her.

She darted sideways out of reach. 'Look—' she held him off firmly '—everybody says you have to feed passion, indulge it, have so much until you don't want it any more. But the only way to kill a fire is to starve it.'

'And you want to kill it?' He paused, clearly in disbelief.

'Well, that's best, right? Because I don't want us to lose all contact. I like hanging out with you.'

'I don't know whether to be pleased or insulted. You want me to be your buddy?' His unbelieving smile became positively evil. 'How about buddy with benefits?'

'No benefits. Too messy. It would never work.' She was adamant on that.

He stared at her. 'You really want to be friends more than you want to have sex again?' he asked, utterly incredulous.

She inhaled deeply. 'Yes.'

'I don't believe you. In fact I reckon I could get you to change your mind in about a minute or less.'

'If you put your mouth to that task, then I'd probably have to agree with you,' she admitted. 'But then I'd walk out of your life and that would be that. I don't want to have a fling with you. But I do want to be a friend.'

'You're giving me an ultimatum?' He sat an inch from her, clearly astounded.

'Think of it as a challenge.'

'Why would I put myself through that kind of a challenge?'

'How many friends do you have?' she asked, deadly serious.

'I have hundreds of friends.'

'I mean real, true, deep friends?' she asked.

'Friends are friends.' He shrugged off her scepticism. 'I like lots of them.'

'Then this should be easy, right?' she teased.

He sighed. 'You really don't want to be friends with benefits, or even just little perks?'

'That way lies mess and complication. This way lies companionship.'

'Companionship.' He all but spat the word.

'I know there's no such thing as commitment from a guy like you, Ruben.'

He turned into a statue before her eyes.

'To be honest, that's not what I want in my life at this stage either,' she reassured him with a smile. 'Things are exciting for me. I've got this great job with awesome opportunities…' She wanted to focus on succeeding with that.

'Do you really think we can get past the physical attraction?' Ruben really wasn't sure that was going to be possible.

'Sure we can. We're adults, not animals.'

'You like it animal,' he taunted softly, pleased that she still blushed for him.

'You'll forget that, eventually.'

He doubted that very much.

'Are you afraid you're going to fail at this, Ruben?'

Oh, she thought he would, didn't she?

'What do you get out of it?' he asked softly. 'Surely you have other friends already, right? So what is it you get from me that you get from no one else? If it isn't going to be stellar sex, what is it?'

Her flush deepened and she looked away.

He moved closer—not to touch her, but to really see her response. 'Answer me, or I say no to this and get you panting for it in less than a minute. Be honest. What do you get from me?'

'Just that, I guess.' She shrugged. 'I can be as rude as I like with you. I can be honest and you laugh at me and with me. I can completely be myself and it doesn't matter.'

That struck some long-buried nerve deep inside him. 'And you can't do that with anyone else?'

'Not quite the same, no.' She inhaled. 'I don't feel like I have to please you. I don't think I have to do anything but be me with you.'

Ruben looked into her blue eyes, trying to read her. He'd decided never to give a damn what anyone thought of him in life. Ellie's approach couldn't be more different. She cared too much about what people thought—she worked stupidly hard to please them. But it was both a weakness and a strength. It was part of what made her so good at her job, but clearly it had caused her some misery in terms of affairs. And she felt as if she could be free in his company?

Ruben narrowed in on the vulnerability in her blue eyes—and recognised blossoming fear. She was afraid he'd refuse her—that she'd asked for something he didn't want.

And what did he want? To have her in his life for a sex-filled night or two, or for longer as someone to hang with? He tried to think but looking into her eyes was a distraction. They were beautiful—wide and deep, like a vast ocean. Oddly he realised that her wanting just to hang out with him, feeling as if she *could*, made him feel good in a way he'd never felt before. A way that he didn't know how to analyse—couldn't—what with that weird ringing in his ears.

'Saved by the bell,' Ellie was muttering grimly.

Oh, there really was ringing—the doorbell. Ruben took her hand and marched her to the door with him. He didn't want her stropping off to her room because he'd taken too long to answer.

'Ruben?' An older woman stood in the entranceway,

impeccably groomed and dressed in summer country casual. 'I'm so glad you're home.'

'Oh, hi.' He drew a quick breath and put his photographic memory to good use. 'Margot, isn't it?' He'd placed her face—one of the society matriarchs in Queenstown. Lovely woman, very proper, probably wanted something for a good cause. He let go of Ellie and stepped forward to shake the older woman's hand.

'Yes.' She smiled.

'Margot, this is my friend Ellie.' He introduced them coolly, avoiding Ellie's eye as he labelled her the way *she* wanted. 'How can we help?'

'I'd heard you were in residence this weekend and stopped by to remind you of the gala in town tonight. Given you've donated so generously to the hospice, I thought you might like to attend.'

He donated to all the local hospices near his hotels. The care of people in the last stages of cancer in a homelike environment, with family able to be near, was something he felt very strongly about. He and his mother had cared for his father at home, alone. Had a hospice been nearby it might have made some moments almost bearable.

'My donations are supposed to remain anonymous.' He wanted no credit for it. No public recognition. Hell, his business was not built on personality but by private perfection. Quietly satisfied customers were his reward—return customers. He had no hunger for this kind of public approval; his assistance with hospices was intensely personal.

'Yes, and they will remain so.' Margot spoke with soft care. 'I only know about it because I'm the treasurer. But I thought you might like to see how your generosity has helped?' Margot smiled. 'There's a beautiful display at the restaurant and we have a wonderful speaker.'

He cleared his throat. 'Actually, Margot, we're really tired. We got bogged in the mud for a couple of hours this morning thanks to this.' He gestured to the damp fog—it had closed in even more while they'd been in the study.

'So you'll be spending the night here anyway as the airport is shut,' she noted brightly. 'Why not come just for the dinner? It doesn't have to be a late night. It starts at seven. It would be wonderful to see you there.'

He hesitated and glanced at Ellie. She was watching him closely. For a second he thought he saw sympathy in her eyes but she blinked and it was gone. She knew he didn't feel like socialising tonight. And she was right—he'd wanted to be utterly alone with her. He'd planned for them to be miles from anyone up in his mountain hut away from everything but temptation. The damn weather had thwarted those plans. And Ellie herself had thrown Plan B into complete disarray.

Nowadays he often had that nagging question as to whether a woman was interested in him mainly because of his business interests and accompanying bank balance. Ellie had been the one perfect exception to that. She'd had no idea who he was, she'd wanted his body, then she'd laughed with him. Apparently now she wanted to be some kind of buddy with him. He didn't get that at all—figured she'd partly done it because she didn't think he could. She thought she'd set him an impossible challenge and he understood there was a part of Ellie that liked to set a challenge. Just as there was a part of him that loved nothing more than a challenge. But she had no idea how determined he could be. He'd taken over a property aged seventeen, for heaven's sake.

He was totally capable of reining in his desires as an adult now. Of course he was…

But he was still looking at her and now a dozen other images flashed in his head.

Okay, the charity dinner wasn't his number one idea of fun but he could see himself failing on the friends thing if he stayed home alone with her tonight. She tempted too much. It would be safer to get out—and prove a point to her at the same time. After all, failure was never an option. And ultimately he had no intention of failing on getting what he really wanted from her. But he'd play it her way for now.

'Of course,' he said, turning to Margot, going for all-out charm. 'Ellie and I would love to be there. Thanks for stopping by.'

Somewhat stunned, Ellie watched Ruben's smile flash to mega-impact. Poor Margot actually reddened, her expression morphing from that of polite hostess to one suffused with genuine pleasure and surprise.

'Oh,' the older woman gasped. 'That's wonderful.' She flicked a glance to Ellie. 'It'll be lovely to have you both there. I'm looking forward to getting to know you better too, Ellie.'

Ellie merely smiled and saved her tongue for when the smartly dressed socialite had slipped back into her silver car and driven away.

'She seems very nice.' Ellie walked into the giant homestead. 'You'll have a great time.'

'You're coming with me,' he called after her, shutting the door behind them.

'No, I'm not.' She smiled sweetly as she shook her head and headed straight for the kitchen for some icy water. 'This is an opportunity for you to spend some time with your neighbours.'

'You're worried because you don't have anything to wear?' he asked. 'There are a bunch of expensive boutiques in Queenstown. We have time to hit them.'

He thought that was why she didn't want to go? 'Oh, please, don't make the mistake of thinking you're going to make me over.' She turned to face him tartly. 'Of course I have something to wear.'

'You only have an overnight bag with you.' He rested his hip against the kitchen counter, watching her fill her glass. 'And you said yourself you don't have a second pair of jeans, that's why you're wearing mine.'

His lascivious look told her he *was* all macho about her wearing his gear. She tried to ignore the hot clench of feminine satisfaction.

'I have a slip that doubles as an evening dress.' She faux demurely took a sip.

His jaw dropped. 'That blue thing?'

Ellie choked as she tried to swallow water while snorting with laughter. How could he sound both scandalised and horn-dog desperate? She shook her head and swallowed safely that time. 'No. Not a slip, it's a dress that doesn't need ironing so I can roll it up. I always have it in the bottom of my overnight bag.'

'What about shoes?'

'I have teeny, tiny strappy numbers. And I have make-up and glittery jewellery too. You never know when you might get that last-minute invite to a red-carpet event.' She was spouting complete rubbish of course—she'd never been to a red carpet event. But she had learnt a trick or two from hanging around on the set of a few ultra-budget short flicks. The make-up artists could work wonders with a tube of Vaseline and an eye pencil. And after the nightmare that had been Nathan and his insulting comments about her attire, she'd gone shopping for a kill-'em-at-any-occasion dress. And okay, it hadn't been Nathan she'd been thinking of. She'd been channelling her new-found inner seductress—basking in the conquest that had been Ruben and revelling in supreme sexual confidence for five seconds of madness in the shop's changing room.

'Impressive.' Ruben's expression went evil. 'So you have no reason to be able to refuse me, then.'

Too late she realised she'd been trapped. Oh, he was good. There was nothing for it but straight refusal. 'I'm not going as your date.'

'You have to. We've already told the immaculate Margot we'll be there and we can't disappoint her now.'

'Look.' She sighed. 'She's thrilled about *you* going. She won't mind my not being there. You don't need to do the host thing, I'm happy to have a nice quiet night here on my own. I'm really tired—it's been an exhausting day out facing the elements, you know.'

'And yet you're going to send me into the wolves' den, knowing I'm every bit as exhausted.'

'Hardly a den,' she mocked softly. 'They'll welcome you with open arms.'

'It's a dangerous place, the charity dinner. I'm not sure you understand the threat I'm facing.' Somehow he'd moved nearer.

'From all the women throwing themselves at you?'

He nodded soberly. 'It's frightening. I need you to protect me.'

'Oh, as if.' Arrogant sod. 'You need no protection. It's the other way round and you know it. You'll be waggling your eyebrows at all the waitresses and they'll fawn all over you.'

'I only waggle if they've got good racks. Of food.' He caught her eye and laughed. 'None of those women need fear me. Come with me. Please. It's what friends do.' He looked sly. 'And you're my *friend* now, right?'

Her eyes narrowed. 'I'd like to think that's possible. It remains to see whether you can manage it.'

'Well, friends support each other, don't they? Here's some truth for you. I'm shy.' He dropped his voice to a whisper. 'I admit it. I like my privacy and I find small talk…difficult sometimes.'

'Shy?' she scoffed. 'You're the guy who was happy to stand buck naked in a hotel corridor the morning we met. You're anything but shy. You're outrageous.'

'That was a special occasion.' He stared, all big brown puppy eyes.

'Oh, it was not. You don't care about what people think of you.'

'That's true.' He shrugged off the bashful routine.

Ellie nodded. 'You're stunning at schmooze. You just reduced society matriarch Margot to a blushing, tongue-tied wreck.'

'Doesn't mean I enjoy it. I have good managers at each of the lodges. I don't mix with the clients all that much. I'd rather wander round—'

'Looking like the gardener.'

'Exactly.' He'd edged closer still. 'Go on, come with me.'

She nibbled the inside of her lip, steadfastly ignoring the less than subtle undertone to his invitation. There was that irresistible desire to see what he was like at one of those events—to be out in public with him at her side. To indulge in that dangerous fantasy for a few hours would be far safer than to stay here another night alone with him.

'Okay.' She shrugged, feigning nonchalance. 'I'll go with you.'

'We have a couple of hours before—'

'Yeah, I'm going for a lie down.' She walked, quickly. *'Alone.'*

Two hours later she was running late, having spent too long messing around with all the luxury bathing products in the bathroom and thinking up movie-tour spiels. Wrapped in one of the luxurious robes supplied in the wardrobe, she raced to the kitchen to hunt out a snack. Munching a cracker, she caught him in the corridor on her way back to her bedroom.

She stopped, spilling crumbs as she unconsciously clenched her fist and crushed the cracker. How could any woman think 'friends only' when he looked as sex-in-a-suit as that?

He grinned as if he could read her thoughts. 'You like it?'

Oh, yeah, her *like* was all over her face. Way too late she pulled her jaw from the floor and got her tongue back behind her teeth. 'You're not playing fair.'

'I just thought it might be good to lift the challenge for you. Make you think about what you're giving up.'

As if she needed to think about that any more than she was already.

'You were wrong once—isn't there the possibility you might be wrong twice?' he asked slyly.

'What was I wrong about?'

'That it was fantasy sex that couldn't be repeated. But that kiss in the spa was way better than any fantasy. Just imagine what a whole night together would be like.'

'This is you meeting the friendship challenge, is it?' she asked.

He shrugged negligently. 'Oh, I can meet that challenge. But if you wanted to change your mind at any time, all you have to do is ask.'

And he'd do her? She merely smiled and went to set a challenge of her own. Twenty minutes later she walked into the lounge and waited for his response.

He stared—up and down, up and down, paused just north of her centre, and then up and down again. 'That was really in that tiny overnight bag?'

She twirled. 'It's a tiny dress.'

It was and all Ruben wanted to do was peel it off her. It was black and sleek—like cobwebbing over her breasts and an equally clinging skirt. Her legs were lightly tanned and framed with a pair of barely there sandals on her feet—only a strip of black sequins across her toes and a heel that gave her a slight chance of levelly meeting his gaze.

He managed to haul a couple of words together. 'We'd better go.'

There would have been a couple of hundred people there. The place glittered—diamonds adorned ears, necks, wrists and fingers everywhere. He glanced at Ellie's beautiful skin; diamonds would look good on her. Or sapphires to match her eyes. Although no gem, no matter how precious, could sparkle the way her eyes were now.

She was laughing at how he'd just waylaid a waitress and hoovered too many of her canapés before she'd been able to offer them to anyone else. But honestly, he'd not eaten for ages. The two hours Ellie had had her lie-down, he'd been working.

'You really don't give a damn about what these people think of you, do you?' Ellie teased.

'Why should I? It doesn't matter to me what anyone thinks.'

'But what about your business?'

'It speaks for itself. Each hotel or lodge is its own advertisement. I create them and then disappear into the background. It's not about me. Never about me. People don't go to a luxury retreat to hang out with the owner. They go for space, rest, privacy.' He shrugged.

He watched her talk with one woman about the scenery. Snowboarding. Turned out Ellie had never been snowboarding herself, but she got that other woman talking about it for the best part of twenty minutes. She really was interested in what the other was saying. Asked intelligent, thoughtful questions. She was so good at listening and paying attention to other people. At seeming to care. Watching her in action, he realised it was the skill set she'd learned as a lonely kid. By giving others attention, she got attention. It made her included.

He watched her show all through dinner. For the most part he just enjoyed her enthusiasm—as did those at their table. But she was interested in being friends with him because she *didn't* have to maintain that vivacious front the entire time with him. She could be ribald. She could be outrageous. She could be tired and grumpy. She could be selfish and take what she wanted. Hell, he wanted her to take what she wanted from him again. His body ached for her to.

Fortunately the band started up. While dancing was a very, *very* risky idea, it was also irresistible.

'Friends kiss each other, don't they?' he asked idly as they barely moved, swaying in the small, heated dance space.

'Oh, you're bad.' Glittering blue eyes sliced through him.

'We're also in a public place, so it's not like we can go overboard. Just a little, friendly kiss.'

'How friendly?'

'Well, given our history, I'd say we're *very* close friends.'

He stole a kiss and felt the fire both sharpen his need and melt his soul. This was what he wanted. Her giving in to him. Wanting him. Hot and sweet and soft. He pulled her closer, ached to have her lush body blanket his. Her warm lips welcomed. Oh, it was good. Blood fired—revitalised—around his body. He actually relaxed, the pressure in his head easing.

But she broke free. 'That was almost overboard,' she muttered, not looking at him.

He nodded but refused to let her out of his hold. Thank heavens for a crowded dance floor.

Ellie was almost out on her feet. No way could she handle more of this dancing and certainly not another 'friendly' kiss. She insisted on heading back to the bar where she stood alongside him and watched him attract people like the Pied Piper summoned every child in his town. He talked with men about farming, sport, politics, building developments. With the women it was more about the hotel business, the restaurants, the local events. Utterly sociable, he was the kind of person hosts loved at a party because he could carry conversation so well.

But it was all safe conversation. She noticed he never talked about himself—all topics were out in the public domain. While she made conversation by talking about the other person, he made conversation by talking about things or events or policies. He never broached the personal with any of them, but was utterly charming. And as the evening wore on it dawned on her that they were at a charity dinner for a hospice and he'd never once mentioned it in any of his conversations here. So that was too personal—she'd suspected so.

But his roguish smile and occasional outrageous joke had so many women giving him that look. And giving Ellie that look of envy.

She fell asleep on the drive home. Ruben pulled into the entranceway and quietly went round the car and opened her door. He scooped her up and carried her inside to the big sofa in the lounge. He didn't want the night to end just yet—not with them going to separate bedrooms.

So much for phases two and three being so easy. No matter the weather problems, the fact was she'd turned the tables on him and somehow he'd agreed to it. *Friends?* It was crazy.

With a soft murmur she stirred, looked at him, all big, blue drowsy eyes. Her heart right there in them—longing. His own heart did a weird flip-flop thing. It wasn't comfortable in the suddenly gaping cavern of his chest. Usually in this situation, when all the blood in his body had rushed south, he'd be on course for some highly satisfactory action. But today, despite the screaming tension from that most masculine part of himself, his brain wouldn't shut down. Amazingly the clarity of his thoughts was more acute than ever. And all he could think was how lovely she was.

'I'm really sleepy,' she said, scratchy-voiced.

'I'm not going to bed without you.' He didn't want to let her go.

'You're not going to bed with me.'

He smiled. A kiss and he'd have her mind changed. The glittering look she gave him beneath her lashes let him know she knew it too. But it had hit him hard—he didn't want to lose her from his life. Not yet. And knowing what he did—of her need for attention, her habit of running from rejection, of her refusal to ever communicate with an ex…not to mention his own dismal track record in maintaining any length of a relationship…

Yeah, now he knew he had to do what she'd asked. Reluctantly. 'Then I guess I'm not going to bed.'

He sat on the sofa, still holding her in his arms. She was soft and warm. He rested his head on hers.

'I had a nice night,' she murmured, settling closer.

So had he. And he was tired and too human to resist the temptation to kiss her again. Her sleepy, soft response deepened. She was deliciously lax in his arms, as if she'd let him do anything. Her breathy moan pretty much confirmed it. But they were friends and while friends kissed, that was all. And frankly? He'd never found kissing so rewarding. Long and luscious, kiss after kiss after way more than friendly kiss.

'Ruben.' She sighed.

He knew she was almost asleep, but she was also begging.

'You could kiss me all kinds of places.' A butterfly whisper.

Utter temptation. She had him so hard. And that was what she wanted, huh? To have her cake and eat it too. Or, more to the point, have him eat it. He smiled at his sleepy wanton woman and couldn't help trailing a finger up her thigh.

Just once. Just once he wanted to *see* her shudder in ecstasy thanks to him. Yeah, he was that selfish. He'd dreamed of it for too long and, breathing in her fresh scent now, there was no resisting. He was touching only a little. Delving into the soft heat. She clenched on him. He rubbed a couple more times and she was there—right there in his arms—vulnerable, beautiful, and, in that moment, completely his. He watched for a moment, but some emotion deep inside drove him to kiss her, to catch the last of her sighs, to inhale her energy.

The ache tearing him apart inside wasn't purely sexual. The craving ran too deep to be only that—but it was a yearning for something he couldn't ever admit wanting. So he clamped it—shutting it down, forcing his own need away.

Breathing hard, he looked at her peaceful expression. She was both vulnerable and strong. His sharp clarity returned. He didn't want her trying to bend into a box to keep any fling with him going. He had no illusions that a fling wouldn't end. Of course it would. In the past, a woman in a relationship with him soon grew tired—of his long absences due to constant travel, his mental and emotional absences. Ellie would soon get to the point where she'd had enough. She'd get mad and shout how selfish he was. How he didn't care.

Frankly he didn't want to care.

But he didn't want Ellie walking out on him in anger. She recognised his faults already. Knew what would happen. So she was removing that eventuality with immediate effect because she didn't want to lose touch with him altogether. She didn't want to disappear in the sunrise as another one-night stand. There was something in him she liked and wanted—other than sex.

And maybe all that was, was his acceptance of everything she was, without question or criticism. And he felt a simple honesty in return—he didn't want to screw her over. He didn't want to let her down. That was the last thing she deserved. And the only way he could ensure he wouldn't was to do as she'd asked.

CHAPTER EIGHT

ELLIE woke in a crumpled but cosy ball. Stretching out of it was the problem, given her muscles were stiffer than they'd been the day before. Half beneath her was Ruben, toppled sideways on the sofa, still in his tux and destined to have a hellish crick in his neck

They'd spent their first *almost* platonic night together. There'd been that sleepy kissing session and that moment just before she fell so deeply into sleep—the teasing luxury, the supposed relief he'd given her.

But it was no relief at all. It was like having the merest taste of some decadent gateaux that was now locked behind a glass cabinet and for ever out of bounds. All she could do was look at it with longing. Yeah, she wanted to devour the gateaux now—to indulge in every last bit. She could feel his hard length pressed against her thigh. Who was she kidding about the 'friends' thing? The desire to have him was too intense. 'Ruben?'

His eyes opened, his gaze warm and drowsy. Only as he woke he blinked a couple of times and a cool veil slipped down, masking that expression. She didn't like it.

She shifted her thigh so his thick erection pressed closer into her softness. 'You failed already.'

He shook his head. 'You're the one who got the "benefit" last night.'

'You teased me into it.' He was tempting her deliberately again now—wasn't he?

'You asked me to kiss you in the most inappropriate places,' he said softly. 'I was a complete gentleman.'

'With your hand in my pants?'

'You wanted my mouth there,' he countered. 'I went with the less intimate option.'

Oh, it was *all* intimate. Excitement skittered through her. Yes, the friends idea was a failure already…

'We'd better get going,' he said crisply, dropping his gaze from hers. He shifted slightly so he was no longer so intimately against her.

She slid off him—withdrawing too, chilling as she realised he wasn't out to tease her. He really was drawing the line she'd asked him to. 'You're so right. We had.'

Ruben drove them to the airport. It wasn't as foggy as the day before but it was still grey and wet. No doubt the flight would be bumpy. She sighed as they pulled up outside the terminal. The heartfelt sound gave away more than she meant it to.

'It'll be no problem,' he said, his hands tightly gripping the steering wheel.

'Of course,' she said, not believing it at that point in time. 'I'm off on a four-day tour next week.'

'I'm heading up to Taupo in the latter half of the week.'

'So there we go,' she said breezily, covering the ache of his absence that was already twisting her heart. 'Physical distance will take care of any last little itch.'

'Absolutely.'

'Don't come in, you can just drop me,' she said as he pulled into a park.

'Okay,' he answered readily. 'I'll be in touch.'

She wondered if that was a line. If the whole 'sure we can be friends' agreement had just been him being charming and polite to get through the weekend. Now she had some info for work, there was no reason for him to contact her directly again. He could do all the negotiations with Bridie and be absent if ever Ellie came on tour here. What a fool she'd been. She should have just taken his body for the weekend and been done with it, because she'd probably never hear from him again once she'd stepped from his car.

He seemed to read her doubts. 'I *want* to be friends.' He leaned across the car to brush a lock of her hair from her face. 'Truth is I like you. I had fun.'

'So did I.'

And not *that* kind of fun. Of course now the trouble was the yearning, for that was all she could feel right now. Especially after that sweet kissing session last night—those deep kisses had turned her heart completely inside out. It was one thing to have dynamite, animal sex. It was another to have tenderness and quietness and restraint. That had showed respect.

At the time she hadn't wanted it, but it had been *respect*, not rejection, that had stopped him from going down on her. From taking everything she'd been offering in her most vulnerable moment. She got out of the car quickly and didn't look back. She was in enough trouble without a longing parting glance.

Fortunately in the modern age there was that safe way to communicate—the text message. Where you could send just the smallest of sentences and wait to see what—if any—response you got. She was completely overthinking it already, mentally composing some silly thing she'd write the first time. Wondering again whether he'd even reply or whether he'd just been going along with her 'friends' idea merely for form's sake over the weekend…

Just as she was rolling her eyes at her own pathetic thoughts her phone chimed. She read the text right away.

Is it within friend boundaries to say I miss you already? Can't stop thinking about you.

She smiled and tapped out her reply.

No, I think that's ok. Friends do miss each other.

Yeah but you don't know what it is I'm thinking about doing with you.

That's possibly too close to the boundary.

I like to bend boundaries.

Ellie flexed her feet to rid even a fraction of the amount of tension from her overwrought body. He was hopeless. But even so, she was happier to have him as a hopeless charmer than not at all.

I'm turning my phone off, my flight's about to depart.

Ellie managed not to turn her phone back on after she'd landed—not 'til she was home and in her pyjamas and had one of her fave films loaded. It rang a mere five minutes later.

'Are you watching a movie?' He obviously heard it playing in the background.

She chuckled. 'Yes.'

'What is it?'

'*Casablanca.*'

'What happens?'

'You've never seen it?'

'No. Tell me about it.'

Somehow they ended up talking for over an hour.

* * *

A week and a half later Ruben lay back in bed and touched her name on his phone. He'd called her almost every night. He hadn't meant to, but it was so easy. Just a quick call for an update. It was always just before sleep time, in that most quiet of moments when he was alone in his room and she was all he could think of. She'd gone on tour again and had him in hysterics nightly with her descriptions of her clients and the way they were getting on with each other. He was looking forward to the latest anecdotes.

But part-way through the week, reluctant to break the connection too soon one night, he'd ended up talking to her about his own work. The deal was almost sealed—two more properties added to his collection and a million more hassles to work through. He confessed them to her—he, who'd worn all the worries alone for years, now found himself telling her the most stupid small details. She listened, she laughed and somehow helped him cut through the burden. She was a good listener. But it didn't make him want to see her any less.

'I'm flying back into Wellington on Monday. You want to do lunch next week?' he asked as soon as she answered his call. He wanted lunch on Monday but he was trying to keep it casual. Not desperate. They were friends now, so the driving need to see her could just ease off—yes?

'Oh, I can't, sorry, not going to be here.'

He sat bolt upright. 'Where are you going?'

'I'll be on the road again, back-to-back tours.'

'Damn it, Ellie, you've got to be kidding me.' Pissed off, he flung back the covers and got out of bed to pace. 'Why back to back? You'll be exhausted.'

'I'll be fine. It's fun. I'll call you.'

Yeah, but that wasn't quite enough. He found himself

thinking of her all the time. Wanting to tell her things, filing them away for when he called her. Wishing she could see his new place. Wanting to hear her ideas on what could be done with it.

'So how's your inspection going?' She filled the silence that had grown too long.

'Okay. A few staffing issues but then there always are. We can work through them. It's a stunning location. It's very different from the chateau and the lodge but just as beautiful. I think you'll love it.'

Now she took her time answering. 'I'm sure everyone will. You have a talent for spotting places that people will be drawn to.'

He wanted her to be drawn there—like the way she'd been drawn to both the chateau and the lodge. 'You must be tired from the last tour.' He knew just how much of herself she poured into those. There was no perfunctory checking names off a clipboard, she basically put on a show for the people. 'You should have a break.'

'I'm okay. It's nice to be busy,' she answered breezily. 'I'm really enjoying the work. Want to take up any opportunity Bridie gives me.'

'Don't let her take advantage of you.'

A low laugh. 'I won't.'

Eight days later Ellie's phone buzzed with yet another text message. He'd developed a skill for random comments during the day. Ellie was now in the habit of having her hand in her pocket, holding her phone, ready to answer instantly. But just as she was answering the text, he actually called. Unfortunately it was just as she was waiting for some stragglers to get to her bus.

'Aren't you flying to Auckland this afternoon?' She didn't bother saying hello.

'Yes, but I wanted to tell you about—'

'Nope, go pack or something,' she said.

'You're cutting me off?'

'Yes, I have a tour group waiting for me.'

'Oh, okay, I'll call you later.'

She put her phone back in her pocket and smiled at her waiting people—ignoring the fluttering buoyancy of her heart. But it was lifted high on that confidence that when she called back he'd be there to listen. And talk right back to her. She loved the way he talked to her about his work now, how familiar they were with what was going on in their lives. She was getting the hang of handling his friendship—sure she was.

'Ellie.'

She was properly awake in an instant. 'Is something wrong? It's the middle of the night.'

'I was thinking about you.'

She smiled but said nothing. She'd been thinking about him too. She clutched the phone closer and burrowed more into her warm bed.

'Ellie?'

'I'm here.' She giggled at the hint of belligerence in his tone. 'Have you been drinking?'

'No.' Defensive to the extreme. A sigh. 'I just can't get to sleep and I'm so tired.'

'Make yourself a mug of warm milk,' she said wryly.

'It's too hot here for milk.' He groaned, not appreciating her tone. 'It's really hot.'

'Turn on the air conditioner.'

'It's too noisy.'

'So you thought you'd ring me instead, at 3:00 a.m. Little bit spoilt of you, Ruben.'

'What can I say? I was an only child.'

She heard the smile then. Smiled back in response but was glad he wasn't there to see just how easily he brought her onside.

'You ever had phone sex?' he asked.

Boom. Lightning hit her heart, instantly sucking her into an intimate vortex. 'Are you sure you haven't been drinking?'

'Just answer the question.'

'No, I think I'd get the giggles.' Honesty prevailed.

'Yeah.' He chuckled. 'We could always have Skype sex. Then we'd get the visuals. I know you like a movie.' Oh, he was wicked.

And it had been weeks since her last orgasm. 'Except I don't have one of those fancy smart phones with the camera and all.'

'I could buy you a smart phone.'

She didn't want him to buy her anything. 'Ruben.'

'Yes?'

'We're supposed to be friends and not having any kind of sex.' She knew down to the hour how long it had been and, no, it wasn't getting easier. But it would. Sure it would.

'Oh, hell,' he muttered. 'I forgot about that.'

'Obviously.'

'I'll try harder.' He sounded contrite.

'Yeah, you need to try much, *much* harder.'

'Yeah,' he answered softly. 'You like it hard.'

'Ruben,' she warned him. Biting her lip because, hell, yes, she'd liked it hard from him.

'What'll you do to me if I slip up again?'

Slip up? Oh, yeah, she could think of the exact thing he'd slip up and into her.

'I'm sure I could come up with a suitable punishment.' Oh, this was ridiculous. She was getting turned on by the slightest smut talk? 'I'll find some way of restraining you.'

So many ideas of restraint just flooded her head. She heard the faintest strangled sound and smiled. She wasn't the only one sensing the innuendo.

'What if I fight back?' he asked softly. Ominously. 'You know I do like to tease. And I can keep that up for a long, long time.'

'You'd want to draw it out?' She slid lower into her bed. Her toes scrunching, trying not to let her hips flex the way they were begging to.

He sighed—oh, it was more of a groan. She could hear the sensual ache in it. Her hands yearned to touch, to relieve both of them.

'Draw out and then push back in. Deep. Over and over,' he muttered so soft. No double talk now. Direct, so close to dirty. And devastating. 'I keep seeing you…' His sentence drifted.

She bit her lip, her need to know overwhelming. Her hidden aches opening wide again. 'Seeing me what?' She hardly formed the words.

'You like my hand between your thighs.'

She sucked in a shocked breath.

'You do,' he insisted. 'It's one of your favourite things. It makes you come.'

She couldn't deny it.

'Do you wish my hand was there now?'

She rolled slightly, closing her eyes as she sank deeper into the bed—deeper into the half-dreamland he was conjuring with those low words.

'I know how hungry you are. How impatient you get,' he said, relentless now in his seduction. 'You have your hand between your thighs now, pretending it's mine.'

She gripped the telephone receiver harder. Her other hand curled exactly where he said, unable to resist the temptation.

'I know what you're going to do,' he said.

'What would that be?' She clenched her upper thighs together hard. The tension spiked her need higher. Every sense sharpened—her hearing acute, her skin a receptor of pleasure.

A soft pause, enough for her to sense this was no tease now. He was sharing an intimate truth—his private fantasy—and entwining it with hers. So intensely personal.

'You think of me. You can't help but touch.'

She'd been holding her breath so long, now a tiny gasp escaped.

'You have to touch. You touch where you want me to touch you. How you want me to touch you.'

She screwed her eyes tighter at the intimacy in his tone. The assurance of that direction. 'And what do you do?'

Another deep sigh. 'I want to watch, to listen, but I want to touch too. And then all I can think of is you riding me hard.' He swore. 'You rode me so good.'

Ellie trembled, holding back the release that was a single stroke away. They were having unintentional, accidental phone sex? How had that happened?

She turned her burning cheek, shifted her damp body onto a cool stretch of cotton sheet. Absorbing the chill, desperate to restore sanity. 'Ruben,' she whispered. 'I have to go now.'

'Ellie,' he whispered back.

'Yes?'

'Dream of me.'

She had been for weeks. Every damn night.

CHAPTER NINE

He didn't call for a couple of days, which was frankly a record. And the next time he did, she knew there was something they needed to get in the open if this was ever going to work out. She darted to the nearest bathroom for some privacy to talk to him, staring at her pale, sleep-lacking skin in the mirror.

'You know that if…if you meet up with someone else, you don't have to keep it secret from me. You can tell me. Okay?' She held her breath.

His answer was so long coming she'd nearly turned blue.

'Okay,' he said slowly. 'Same for you.'

'Of course.' She breathed out painfully. As if she could meet anyone as gorgeous as him.

'Have you met up with anyone else?' he asked.

'No. No.'

'Nor have I.'

She licked very dry lips. 'I know you have needs, Ruben. I'm not going to be…bothered. We're friends now.' As much as she'd hate it, maybe it would be better if he did hook up elsewhere. Then the agony of waiting for that nightmare would be over.

Again he took his time replying. 'And you'll tell me if you do?'

She laughed. 'I'm off the market for now. This job is taking up all my time. It's what I want to focus on for the next while.'

'What about your needs?'

She hesitated, hadn't meant for this conversation to be about *her* at all. 'I haven't got time to think about them.'

'Maybe you should think about them or they might sneak up on you again.'

She bit her lip, glad he couldn't see how she'd now gone red in the face—how her blood was zinging all round her damn willing body. 'That night in the chateau was a once only.'

'Yeah, and I don't think I'm ever going to forget it.'

It had been over three weeks since he'd last seen her and he'd thought he had it all under control. He'd been wrong on that.

'Hey,' he said as he got to her table—supposedly they were to have lunch. But it was crazy the way his pulse was pounding.

Her smile couldn't have been more rewarding. Her eyes glittering—deeper in colour than he remembered. She sparkled. And he had nothing under control. The less he saw of her, the more he thought of her. It wasn't supposed to be that way at all. Wasn't the maxim 'out of sight, out of mind'? But she was more than in his mind, she was in his body and in what little soul he had.

She was wearing jeans—heaven help him—with a white blouse and as she looked up at him he could see the lace edge of her bra. He'd become that much of a randy schoolboy he was reduced to sneaking glimpses down her shirt. It took only a second to decide to put the full plan into action. He'd suffered enough. And so too had she. He noted the flare in her eyes, the colour in her cheeks deepen, and, yes, he noticed the way her breasts responded to his less than subtle appreciation of them.

So he didn't sit down. Instead he extended his hand to pull her out of her seat. 'I've got a surprise for you.'

'What is it?' A flutter of caution cooled Ellie's pleasure at seeing him again because he didn't look that excited, if anything he looked more serious than she'd ever seen him. The edges of his beautiful mouth were held firm, not forming their natural curve up.

'There was a vital part of the station that you didn't get to see.'

'The station?' He was half dragging her out of the café and into his convertible. 'We're not going to the station.'

'Plane leaves in thirty, we've got just enough time to make it.'

'Ruben, we're only having *lunch*. I can't just go from work—'

'It's all arranged with Bridie. She's taking the tour this afternoon.'

'What?'

'You've worked too many days in a row anyway. You have to have a break some time.'

Ellie gazed at him. She was sure there was more to this, but he wasn't offering any deeper explanation this second.

It was less than an hour's flight from Wellington to Queenstown and he spent most of it typing into his phone. Not to be outdone Ellie read the inflight mag cover to cover. Once on the ground they didn't get into a car; instead he led her across the airfield to a helicopter.

'Ruben, I don't have any spare clothes with me.' She finally broke the silence.

He turned and looked at her—the old, utterly outrageous Ruben with that wicked smile and knowing expression. 'Sweetheart, you're not going to need any.'

With a stumble Ellie all but slithered into the helicopter. What had happened? There was no mistaking his intention now. Where on earth was he taking her?

The tragic thing was, she didn't much care. She was too excited to be back in his company and to know the spark was still as strong for him as it was for her. Hell, if anything it was worse. And this was him fighting for what he wanted.

Neither spoke while he flipped switches and made the rotor blades whirl. They still weren't loud enough to drown the din of her pulse in her ears.

She'd been in a helicopter before but not one as light as this or as plush inside. They zoomed, over the plains, heading further south, the mountains to their right. Then he pointed out the lodge so she got her bearings. He flew super low to follow the river in the valley, then up high, so close to the mountains, a breath away from the splash of a towering waterfall…

But she sat completely still in her seat. Her pulse slammed, her thoughts disordered—anticipation screwing with her head. They flew over one mountain, deeper into the range and there, hidden from possible view from anywhere other than the air, was an alpine lake. One of those that belonged in ancient myth and legend. Steely blue and still. He brought the helicopter down, landing on a small smooth edge.

'Come on,' he invited her.

He'd been here many times before, she could tell, and she totally got why. It was the most amazing colour, reflecting the cold clarity of the sky. It really was the scene from some ancient mystical, alternate world story—just like the movies. Only real. Fantastically real.

'It's beautiful.' It was so awe-inspiring she couldn't think of any words to fully describe the reaction within her. The reality of pure, unadulterated fantasy.

'It's also icy cold so don't dive in, because I don't want to have to jump in and rescue you.'

She laughed, glad he'd lightened the intensity. And yes, she did have the urge to dive in. It looked so inviting and, hey, maybe it would cool her burning senses.

She found a small flat stone and tried skimming it across the lake. He foraged in the short tussock for more and they had a contest for a while. And all that while—longer really—her ability to resist him curled into a smaller and smaller ball.

'We haven't talked about it,' he said, aiming another flat pebble across the lake.

'About what?'

'That phone call.'

She felt the flush ripple like a wave from her toes to the tip of her scalp. 'Oh.'

Oh was right—the guy had turned her on to nuclear with nothing but a few suggestions. Phone sex—a total first.

'It's not going to happen.'

'What?' she asked, confused.

'You being with anyone else.'

Oh, he meant *that* conversation?

'No one else, Ellie.' He turned to face her—all arrogance. 'You know you can't. Not until you've had enough of me.'

Oh, that wasn't fair—what if she'd *never* had enough of him? Because he'd have enough of her all too soon, she just knew it.

'So you have a choice to make.'

'I do?'

'Uh-huh.' He turned and skimmed another stone across the water. It bounced seven times. 'We could stay up here the night.'

'Where?'

'Just beyond that ridge there's a hut.'

This was why he'd brought her to an utterly isolated spot. Because he wanted…what *she* wanted.

'We could spend the night up here or we could go back to the station in the helicopter. I should warn you there's only one bed in the hut and it's not very big.'

Ellie's brain whirled—and then she stared up at the completely blue sky. 'It looks to me like there's a storm coming. It might be safer to stay up here.'

He walked towards her, holding her gaze imprisoned in his despite shaking his head. 'No storm, Ellie. No games. Just be honest. Do you want another night with me or not?'

Oh, his whole approach was outrageous. Excitement scudded in her belly, her innermost muscles stretching and flexing already. 'What kind of a question is that?'

'Just answer it.'

What did he want, her acquiescence written in blood? Or perhaps sweat? 'Okay, take me there.'

The chocolate-brown eyes were scorched. 'You're sure.'

'Yes.' She knew what she was doing. They were hardly lost in a snowstorm and forced to cling close to preserve life. This was a decision. *Her* decision. And she was tired of fighting the need.

He turned abruptly, climbed back into the helicopter. Ellie walked back towards the lake. It wasn't too late to change her mind but her mind and body were in sync already—she knew what she wanted.

Ruben got what he needed from the chopper and walked back to where she waited. It felt good to have her in place, ready to meet him. He drank in the signs—yeah, her blue eyes were deepening, just like the sky above them. She kept that intense eye contact, as if she was trying to see through him. His heart pounded—he briefly wondered if she could hear it, because he didn't like to be looked at that closely.

'Promise me something,' she said with that husky voice that gripped his attention completely. 'This one night. That's all. Nothing more afterwards. When we get back to civilisation, we're back to where we were. Just friends again. That's the only way this can happen. The fantasy, right?'

'Why do you keep trying to control this?'

'I'm not—'

'This isn't going to go away unless we deal with it. Your way isn't working.'

'One night.'

'The *whole* night.' He pressed his end of the bargain home. 'Not just once and then sleep. I want literally the whole, damn night.' Though he feared even that wasn't going to be enough.

'All night?' She paused, her tongue slipping over her lips.

She honestly thought they'd have just the once? Oh, she hadn't a clue. But she was on the edge. He stepped closer to her, acutely aware of the shifting signals—her shortened breathing, her flush, her almost invisible shiver. Oh, yes, it was going to be more than once. He'd get her over that line again and again. But he needed all night to do it. So they could leave tomorrow as ex-lovers, over this intensity, leaving no burning anxiety left. No more of this desire that had twisted him inside out the last few weeks.

Ellie was embarrassingly close to orgasm just from the suggestion of sex. And only a few steps into the walk to the hut she stumbled.

'Something's hurting?'

She shook her head. Nope, it was the unchecked wanton, wicked, desperate thoughts that had caused her loss of co-ordination. 'I'm fine.' She just wanted to be at the damn shack already.

He'd stopped and now stared stonily at her. Once more that uptilt of his mouth had flattened out to a thin line. Suddenly he lunged.

'What are you doing?' she shrieked.

In a blur and a thud he'd gone in low and hard and she was upside down. His grip was firm but apparently effortless given the pace he was striding up the mountain.

'What. Are. You. Doing?' She added some outrage to the question.

'Stopping you from doing yourself an injury.'

'Oh, please, this is just you unable to keep your hands off me.' Oh, yeah, and her excitement had just quadrupled.

'That too,' he confirmed, unapologetically running his hand up the back of her thigh and grabbing a handful of her butt.

'Well, put me down. You'll do *yourself* an injury.' She was no lightweight.

'We're nearly there anyway.'

'Ruben, seriously. I'm getting giddy.'

He squeezed her butt, then shifted, wrapping both arms around her as he slid her down his body to set her on her feet. For a moment she leaned against him, needing that closeness. All her personal space was his and, oh, it was good.

'Turn around.' He laughed.

'How do you expect me to when you're holding me so tight?' She was more breathless than he, which was embarrassing given he'd been the load bearer.

He turned her, holding her firm, pulling her body back close against his as soon as he could.

She drew an even deeper breath. '*That's* the hut?'

'Uh-huh.' As he laughed again she felt his chest rumbling against her back.

She smiled too, gazing at the small building, not hiding her amazement. 'So what are we doing here, glamping?' Glamour-camping. In by helicopter to a pristine lake and then a little trek to some deluxe boudoir?

'Hey, it's hardly five stars—look at the place. It's tiny and made out of tin,' he said in mock-defence. 'But we can get it really warm.'

Oh, she bet they could.

It *was* tiny, no more than a couple of metres squared. Two-storeyed and on stilts. A beautiful copper coloured tower. He strode ahead, pulling a set of keys from his pocket. He unlocked the padlocks on each side and pulled up the shades so they became awnings, revealing the massive windows beneath providing a view as far as the eye could see in each direction.

'Oh, my.' Ellie peered in the first window.

There was a log burner on the ground floor, with a pot on the top, a rug, a cupboard with a small amount of supplies—survival food, coffee. No sofa, just a wooden floor and a mountain of cushions. But that was what made it so damn glamorous. The wooden floor was polished, the rug hand woven, the cushions covered with the most expensive fabrics.

'You bring people here often?' Oh, she suspected him.

He shook his head. 'No. Honestly no.' His smile twisted. 'Let me get the fire going.'

It already was—a roaring inferno in her belly. 'You're not going to rub two sticks together?'

'Well, you only need one when it's a match.'

She kicked off her boots, as he did, and followed him inside.

'I'm guessing trampers and members of the public don't use this.' Every single item in the place was carefully selected, chosen for both use and quality, neat and tidy and perfect.

'No, it's not on any maps. It's my little getaway.'

'It's pretty amazing.' She turned around, taking it all in.

He waved a hand, encompassing that tiny space. 'You really like it?'

'Absolutely.' How could anyone not?

He looked boyishly, endearingly pleased. 'I designed it.' He coughed. 'And built it.'

'Really?'

'Is that so hard to believe?' He actually looked self-conscious.

Of course it wasn't. She suspected he was capable of many things, given all he'd achieved in the last ten or so years. 'You've designed other things?'

'Just this. It was all I wanted just for me.'

He owned several luxury lodges—massive ones—and he'd built himself a tiny annexe up in the wild heights.

'Have you brought any other women here?' She

shouldn't want to know this. Knowing this was irrelevant. But somehow it mattered.

He shook his head and too much satisfaction burned through Ellie's veins.

'Truth is I've never brought anyone here. I like being alone, appreciating the view. It's peaceful.'

Yes, this place offered serene simplicity. 'I'm not breaking that peace for you?'

'You're part of the fantasy.' He smiled. 'I think everybody needs an escape.' He bent to get the fire going.

'Especially those rich people who have it so hard,' she teased.

'Well, them no less than any other people. And they may want privacy and luxury furnishings. This is *my* escape.'

It was two square metres of heaven. An earthbound spot for angels to come down and enjoy the majesty of the Alps.

'But it really isn't glamping,' he muttered apologetically. 'The facilities are…uh…there.' He jerked his head to a spot out of the window where she could see a shovel. Beyond that, the privacy of tussock land.

'Great.' She grinned.

'There's a tap, the tank collects the rain water from the roof. There's some soap and stuff in the cupboard.' He stood. 'Come up and see the view before the light goes altogether.'

The flue of the log burner ran up the wall—radiating heat already—and further along from that was the ladder.

On that second floor there was a bed—not a giant bed, only slightly larger than a single and currently stripped of coverings. The walls were wooden, warm and cosy. There was only one window up here—a large rectangle cut out, facing the best view right up the spine of the Alps. While some might have wanted glass all round, like the lower level, the one window was like a painting. A frame for nature's greatest effort. It gave the eye a focal point, but the rest of the room offered a sense of safety, of security against that awesome, but ultimately uncaring environment. It really was a nest.

'It must be amazing here in the rain.' She'd love to lie in that bed and listen to a storm lash the tin.

'Yeah.' He pulled out an underbed storage box, opening it swiftly.

'There are sheets?' She laughed. She didn't know whether to be insulted that he hadn't jumped on her already, or touched that he was concerned for their comfort.

He looked a little sheepish. 'I get too hot in sleeping bags.'

She watched him flare the sheet out over the mattress.

'Told you it wasn't the world's biggest bed.' He grimaced.

She ran her hands down her thighs to stop the sudden damp nerves. 'Can I help?' She couldn't believe he was being so matter of fact and restrained about this, especially after the cave-man toss-her-over-his-shoulder approach of earlier.

'Pillows.' He nodded to the box in the corner.

She opened it and smiled. 'How many pillows do you need?'

He pulled a handful of pillowslips from the linen box and threw them at her. 'I *like* pillows.'

'So it's not just for the luxury look at the lodge?' She quickly covered a few and tossed them onto the now sheet-covered bed. 'How many do you have on your bed?'

He shrugged. 'Enough.'

'You cuddle a pillow,' she teased.

'At least it's not a soft toy,' he said, defensively snappy.

She giggled.

'I'm going to show you just how useful a couple of extra pillows can be,' he threatened.

Ellie swallowed, her toes curling in her socks.

'Except we should probably eat something first.'

Oh, he just *had* to be kidding. Was he deliberately torturing her? She shook her head and pushed her hands into her jeans pockets. 'I'm not very hungry.'

She wanted action. She wanted to be done with the ache that had haunted her so long. She wanted to burn the memory of that night. So she undid the first button of her blouse, then the second.

For a moment, he watched her. Then—to her relief—he moved. She smiled, hoping he was going to take over; she wasn't entirely comfortable with her attempted striptease. But to her surprise he moved only to switch on the battery-powered lantern that hung in one corner.

She paused. Completely self-conscious now.

'Oh, no,' he murmured. 'Don't stop. I didn't have the pleasure of seeing you last time.'

She couldn't.

He smiled. And that was when she saw the sheen of sweat on him—the film of heat that hadn't been there even after he'd lugged her up the mountain for five minutes. No, this sign of tension in him was new. And empowering. 'Only if you do the same for me.'

His wickedness flashed. 'You want me to strip for you?'

'Oh, yes.' She undid the last buttons and let her shirt fall. 'I go no further until you've matched me.'

She hadn't even blinked before that 'Lucky' tee shirt was whisked over his head and on the floor already. He unfastened his jeans. To her delight, he didn't take his briefs down with the denim. They were the close-fitting knit boxer type. They fitted him well.

'This is all for you, Ellie.' He knew exactly where she was looking.

'You and your size thing,' she mumbled.

'I'm not the one with body-conscious issues,' he taunted softly. 'But trust me,' he said. '*Look* at me. Look at what you do to me. I want you so much it hurts.'

And she wanted it all.

'So now it's your turn,' he said.

She slipped out of her jeans, taking her socks off—but, like him, leaving that last layer.

'Lace.' He nodded. 'Like your slip that night.' His gaze roved over her. 'You like the feel of it?'

'I like the feel of you.' She stepped towards him.

'Uh-uh.' He shook his head and backed a pace. 'It's not going to be quick this time.'

She needed it to be. She wanted that orgasm so badly. She licked her lower lip, so hot, so ready. So wanting. And given the pressure the front of his briefs was under, he was too. And so she went to the bed, removing her bra in the two paces it took to get there. She slipped off her knickers and stretched out on the mattress. Daring him to deny her now.

His grin disappeared for a moment as he watched her recline. Good, it was about time he felt as bothered as she was. Only then, to her surprise, his smile came back—more wicked than ever. He leaned over and took her hand, pulling her to sit up.

'Are you sure you don't want to star in a movie, Ellie?' he asked quietly.

'What?' Why wouldn't he just hurry up and lie down with her?

'Look at the window.' His voice a wicked tease, an invitation to decadence.

The night sky was now black—the moon had waned to the thinnest of crescents that threw little light. The stars not bright enough to fight back against the glow of the lantern in their room. So the window reflected the scene within—it had become a mirror.

'No one can see us. There isn't anyone for miles,' he said between teasing kisses everywhere on her face but her mouth. 'But we can see us. You can see us. You can watch.' He stepped in front of her, turned his back to the window and dropped to his knees.

She put her hand to her mouth when she saw what he meant. The clarity of their images. She was transfixed.

'Life-size screen,' he muttered, pressing a kiss to her throat.

He had to feel how her heart was racing. 'Ruben…'

'The lantern stays *on*,' he said firmly. 'The lantern stays on all night.' It was a decree. 'I want you to know it's me.'

That stabbed. 'I know that already.'

'*All* night,' he reiterated firmly. And then he kissed lower—down her neck, across her collarbones.

And she watched. Excitement liquefied her bones. Her body went as lax as a doll—his to toy with. Oh, yeah, she was starring in her own blue movie.

She licked her dried lips. 'I've never watched this kind of movie before.'

'Time you did.' He reached her breasts. 'But only with me.'

'Ellie Summers, porn star.'

'Ellie Summers, ultimate temptation.' He thumbed her taut nipple and looked up at her sceptical expression. 'You don't believe me?'

'I think you're quite good at saying nice things.'

'I'm quite good at doing nice things too. Things that feel nice.' He returned to task.

'Oh, my,' she breathed.

'You've never watched a woman be pleasured?'

'You're wicked.' Heat flushed through her.

'Watch while I do that for you,' he muttered.

'Oh.'

She'd never been very visual when it came to sex. She liked it in the dark, under the covers, the wobbly bits mostly out of the way. But the temperature in here was scorching—there was no way she wanted a sheet on her. And seeing a guy this built, on his knees in front of her. Yeah, that played to her hitherto unknown inner exhibitionist. She liked it. She liked what he was doing even more.

He cradled her breasts in his hands as if they were treasures he'd spent centuries searching for. His hands stroked down her sides, his palms flat, his reach broad and sure. He held her hips still as he bent forward to kiss her—from breast to breast, down her sternum. She lifted her hands, ran her fingers through his hair—so simple, but it was what she desired most. His kisses made her tummy tauten. His grip on her hips firmed as she unconsciously began to rock nearer him.

His smile was pleased. 'Getting warmer?'

She shook her head. 'Need more.'

She watched him tending to her, drank in the play

of muscles across his broad back. His body was beautiful—big in the right places, but lean so that definition could be seen. His butt taut, muscles clenching as he thrust his hips slightly in time to his nips and kisses on her breasts. Oh he was gorgeous. He reached to cup her other breast as his tongue lashed her nipple. She felt like a prized lover, in the care of masculine perfection. She lifted her gaze and looked at her own face. The flush in her cheeks, the heavy-lidded darkness of her eyes. The full-lipped smile, her skin grazed by his stubbled jaw. She looked the picture of hedonism. And he was her expert, demanding slave.

'You know I'll do anything you want.' He paused to look up at her.

Oh, yeah, captive lover. Her lungs were drawing in pure fire. 'Everything.' And now, because she was almost there already.

She put her hands on the top of her thighs, rubbing hard—applying pressure herself to try to ease the ache there. The desperate need for the pleasure of his weight, his invasion. His eyes glowed, tracking the slow, strong slide of her fingers. He put his hands over hers, spread her legs further, wider for him.

'Impatient, aren't you?' he murmured, his breath teasing her as he moved closer.

But to her infinite relief and exquisite torture, he bent his head and licked her there. A slow, lush taste.

She cried out, tightening her fingers on herself, hovering. 'Ruben.'

He lifted his head the merest fraction. 'Say—' a slide of his finger '—my name again.'

'Ruben,' she whispered.

He blew a shot of warm tormenting air above, while working his fingers inside. 'Say it again.'

'Ruben,' she pleaded, her body constricting.

His expression darkened. 'Scream it.' He bent forward and feasted.

She shrieked his name to the sky.

His hands remained hard on her thighs, mercilessly keeping her still for him, so he could continue applying his own brand of ecstatic torment. His tongue thrust deep, just as she wanted his erection to, or his fingers again, any part of him—just more. *All* of him. She threw her head back, her shriek not abating. Her hands clutched, trying to draw him closer. Wanting him to mount her, wanting him to ride her. Wanting it all harder than she ever had. Because she wanted as she never had. Oh, it was utter hedonism. She was spent, yet *starving*. She shook with the force of release, the savage orgasmic contractions going on and on. Until she begged over and over, 'I want you.'

He looked up, his fingers tracing back and forth softly across her slick, sensitive entrance. 'You want me to what?'

Panting, she swore at the amusement in his eyes. 'You know already.'

'How bad do you want it?'

She rocked harder into his hand. 'You know that already too.'

'I want you to tell me.'

He wanted it all? She reached, clenching his shoulders. 'Take me so hard I won't be able to walk.'

His cheeks flushed, his face went stern as determination gripped him. 'That hard?'

'Harder.' She wanted the furthest spectrum of pleasure. From him she'd settle for nothing less. This one night? This was all hers.

But he didn't rise and lie against her as she expected.

No, nothing was as she expected tonight. He stood and finally removed his boxers, got the protection.

She sat up, mouth watering. 'You want me to—'

'No.' A pained refusal. 'I won't last,' he growled.

He got onto the bed behind her, angling her slightly so they faced that reflection on the diagonal. He drew her to her knees, spreading them so his fitted between. His thighs were rock solid beneath hers. His erection strained against her soft flesh.

'Oh,' she gasped.

'Watch.'

She turned, gasped again at the erotic image in the window. She could see him behind her. His gaze met hers in that mirror. He held her waist firm in his hands and then encouraged her to rise up a little.

She did.

'Watch.' He leaned back, positioned her above him.

The instruction wasn't necessary—she couldn't tear her gaze from the sight of him thrusting upwards, from the sight of her swallowing him whole as he impaled her on him in one swift bite.

She screamed her joy. The excitement of watching their bodies fuse was too much. As was watching the play of his hand, now slipping down over her stomach to strum between her legs, the rippling of his thigh muscles as he flexed his hips, bumping her over and over, the sway of her own breasts—until he clutched them in his other palm. And then she watched the slide of his thumb over her nipples. She gasped for air, gasped to retain her sanity. And failed. Meeting his eyes in the reflection—she saw the glazed heat of lust that she felt mirrored within him too. The uncontrolled, animal lust. Until she couldn't watch any more. It was so overwhelming, she had to close her eyes to combat the intensity of the sensations. Because all this while, he was inside her, stroking deep, deep, deep inside her.

'Ellie,' he warned.

But she couldn't bear it any more. It was too hot, too intense—she just wanted another release *now*.

He moved. Lifting her, leaving her.

'Ruben.' She was furious, spun to face him, to pull him back.

But he pushed her down and, seeing the look on his face, she went, ecstatic. Lying back, panting, grateful for the cool cotton sheet beneath her. He loomed above, looking right into her eyes. There was no mistaking she was getting it all now.

All inhibition gone, all sense of reality gone, she smiled.

He held her apart, bent his head and kissed her. Then let her feel the immense power of him. She shook. This was what she'd wanted—his weight. *All* his weight pressing on her. Filling her. Almost smothering her with his strength. Her fingers spread, clutching his biceps, sliding round to his back to simply try to hang on. She arched her hips, trying to widen her legs more to cope with him. He owned her then. Thrusting again and again, filling her until her pleasure overflowed, releasing in harsh flashes, her nails digging, her screams raw as she revelled in his assault. She still couldn't get enough.

'Hell, you're demanding,' he choked. He gripped her hair and tilted her head back so he could see into her eyes. 'How much more do you want?'

'Every last damn bit,' she answered, throaty, unashamed, ravenous.

He threw back his head and thrust harder than ever. Slow and violent and so deep her groan was ripped from the core of her. It wasn't about fantasy any more; there was no game, no tease in his action. He was as unleashed, as uninhibited and as out of control as she. And she adored it.

Sweat slicked between their hot bodies. Skin sizzled where it touched, the burn such a pleasure she pushed closer still. Their movements deepened again, relentless, the pace now insane. She didn't want it to stop, never ever to stop. Yet she couldn't bear it a second longer.

He swore. 'I feel you, I can feel you—'

He broke off as her scream rose high, echoing round the unforgiving peaks of the mountains.

A long time later all she heard was his rough, rapid panting. His groan as he tried to control the frantic beat of his heart. Their sweat mingled. He was too heavy for her to push against. She didn't care. It was a heavenly way to suffocate.

With a pained moan he shifted slightly to the side. 'Can you breathe?'

'Just about.' Her throat was sore, she'd screamed so loud. Heat flooded her cheeks—not the lust kind. She'd been so *abandoned.*

He turned his head sharply. 'Don't regret a thing about it,' he said. 'Most awesome experience of my life.'

She nodded.

'It was even better than before,' he whispered. He shook his head hopelessly. 'All I want now is to do it all again. Again. Again.' He rolled right onto his back and growled up at the ceiling. 'But I have to catch my breath.'

And scratchy-voiced she reminded them both. 'Only tonight.'

CHAPTER TEN

HE WAS fitter than she, because he recovered far more quickly than she'd thought possible. But he was oh-*so*-kind, and let her just lie back while he explored. Deeply.

And then he leaned over her. 'Are you hungry?'

'You *can't* be serious.' She was aghast.

He roared with laughter. 'No, I mean your stomach.'

'Oh, that. Yes.'

He disappeared down the ladder and came back with long-life food. Yeah, muesli bars had never tasted so good.

'High energy.' He handed her a can. 'Drink that and have some chocolate. Not exactly gourmet but perfect given all that's required of you in the next ten hours.'

All that was required of her? Oh, she liked these demands. 'Aren't you planning to sleep at all?' She'd thought he'd been teasing about that, but now she wasn't so sure.

'Not a wink.'

Two hours later Ellie was *convinced* he'd want to sleep now. But the crazy thing was, although she was physically exhausted, the last thing she felt like was sleeping. 'Can we turn the lantern out?' she asked.

'No.' Ruben refused to let that happen. He didn't want to lose an hour of this to sleep.

'What if I promise to say your name, repeatedly, so you know I know who I'm with.'

He chuckled. 'Why do you want it out? You know we're not actually going to sleep any tonight.'

'I want to see the stars.'

He glanced at the big window. Okay, he could see how that would be good.

'I'll say your name lots.' She batted her eyelashes at him.

He knelt up and flicked the switch off. The moon wasn't big or terribly bright, but the white mass of stars was incredible.

She commando crawled to the end of the bed and leaned closer to the window. 'Ruben, this place is amazing.'

'I'm glad you like it.' He liked how she made him feel.

'Ruben, I don't just *like* it, up here we're practically in heaven. Ruben, this *is* heaven.'

Yeah, it was as close as he'd come to that.

'Ruben.' She said his name again in an exaggerated tease. 'Can you see *Lepus*?'

Given the way her eyes were reflecting the stars, he figured she meant a constellation. 'I can see the Southern Cross but that's about it.'

'Well, Ruben, if you look up there to the left, you'll see a bigger one, then three more in an almost circle around it,' she directed him. 'Do you see?'

'I think so,' he lied and heard her snort of disbelief. No fooling her, then.

But lying side by side staring up at the massive expanse of sky was nice. So was the way she played up the over-use of his name.

'Ruben, to the left.'

'Did your father teach you these?' he asked.

'Honestly, Ruben, he was more into the conquer-the-mountain thing. I learnt them myself. It was my personal reward for getting through the day's climb. Ruben, I'd lie there and look up at them and give thanks I made it through another day.'

'It really doesn't sound like fun.'

'It wasn't so bad, Ruben. At least I had him to myself for a bit, whereas Mum was always on the phone or something.'

Poor Ellie. Well, the least he could give her was his undivided, utterly focused attention—tonight.

He bit back the laughter at her repeat, repeat, repeat of his name. In the dark, lying sideways across the bed together, they looked at the stars. Somehow the conversation drifted. She joked her way through her assortment of odd jobs in the movie industry, then the focus turned to him—with her prompting he talked through the long, slow battle that had been the chateau. Ironic to think it had started with him begging any kind of work he could to get funds to develop it. He'd worked like a dog. Then all of a sudden success had snowballed. The acquisitions in recent years had him running faster than a hamster on speed—more hours than ever before. A week or so from one business to the next—he was driven to personally ensure each was on track. She listened in the dark, asked questions about the early years and commented, constantly beginning each utterance with his name.

And then she turned the clock back a year or so more and asked about his father—about the cancer. That dark period in his life when he'd lost his father and a few months later his mother had left.

Ruben rolled away but she wrapped her soft body around his and didn't let go.

'It's not something I can talk about,' he muttered beneath his breath.

She heard him. Softly whispered his name as she embraced him, refusing to let him shut off from her completely.

But he never ever discussed those days—had never admitted to anyone the heartbreak of nursing his terminally ill parent when his mother had been too tired and distraught to cope any more. He'd never unloaded the desolate loss, the helplessness, the hopelessness.

The kind of pain he never wanted to endure again. That unbearable loneliness.

'Ruben.' She whispered his name softly. Her voice, like her body, a caress—soothing and so very, very sweet. Somehow it was as if she understood and absorbed that deep, private hurt. And for the first time in his adult life Ruben relaxed into a loving embrace. She held him and he let her—until the melancholy moment suddenly passed and he could stand her quiet comfort no longer. It was something else he wanted from her, only that one thing—right?

'What are—? *Oh!*' Breathless, she forgot to say his name at the beginning of a sentence.

'Yeah.' He chuckled as she squealed again.

'What are you doing?' She managed to finish the sentence that time. Still sans his name.

'Turning the lantern back on.' He moved away quickly to do it.

'Why?'

He grabbed her by the legs and hauled her towards him. 'Because by the time I've done with you, you won't remember your *own* name, let alone mine.' It was that mindless pleasure he wanted. That beautiful, intense ecstasy.

Her star-filled eyes gleamed. 'Sounds fantastic.'

CHAPTER ELEVEN

Too few hours later Ellie woke. Blinking to banish the sleepy feeling, she frowned at the dull grey light. 'We've really fogged up the window.'

Ruben leaned across her to examine the glass. 'No, the fog is outside.'

'Really?' She sat up and swiped a finger across it. The grey remained. Clouds had descended, encompassing their tower. They couldn't see a thing.

'We can't fly out in this.' He sighed sleepily.

'But we can't stay here another night.' Panic threatened to drown her relaxed state as consciousness brought thought with it. One night she could manage. More was a definite no.

'We don't have a choice,' he replied. 'It's not safe to leave here until the fog lifts.'

Not safe physically perhaps, but this was her heart on the line. She'd let him in and more intimate time together would have her in trouble. She'd always known that. 'But—'

'Stop looking so worried.' He laughed roughly. 'We can't anyway. We're all out of condoms.'

'You're kidding.' Her jaw dropped.

He shook his head. 'It was only a three pack.'

How stupid had she been not to have any on her?

How stupid had he been not to buy in bulk? And had they really only had sex the three times? It felt like so much more. Mind you, there'd been other kinds of orgasms too.

'It's probably a good thing.' She closed her eyes and shook her head. 'This was enough.' Both her body and her heart were worn out. Now that fog just had to burn off super quick so she could keep as whole as possible and not leave that vital beating part of herself behind with him.

She felt him fall back on the pillows beside her. 'You're right.'

'I'm sorry?' She laughed, working up some humour to cover the sudden sense of devastation. She was learning tricks off him. 'Can you repeat that, please?'

'You're *right*,' he mumble grumbled.

'A little louder.'

He pulled the pillow out from under his head and threw it at her.

'Wow, a man who can admit when someone else—a woman—is right,' she teased, determined to jolly away the disappointment when she'd realised he couldn't come inside her again. And that for him this one night had truly been enough. 'Why haven't you been snapped up already?'

'Because I turn into a werewolf at full moon,' he teased back, reminding her of her old joke back that first morning after.

'Even more reason for you to have the ball and chain already. Women love a man in touch with his animal side,' she purred.

His brows lifted. 'You do like some animal in your man, don't you?'

She licked her lips and tipped her head back to utter a little howl.

He reached a long arm out and twisted his fingers into her hair. 'I like your hair like this. Neither straight or curly, but it definitely has this little kink.'

There was a time when Ellie would have ensured that every time she saw him next, her hair would be just so. She'd straightened it to a crisp for one boyfriend, curled it tight for another—always aiming to please. To do whatever to make a guy like her and keep liking her. Old habits died hard. But she wasn't going to do that for Ruben—it had never been that way between them and she wasn't going to slide backwards now. No, after last night she needed to make more than sure she stayed on top of her vulnerable trying-too-hard tendencies.

Despite only having a couple of hours' sleep in the early hours of the morning, she couldn't seem to get back to sleep now. Nor could Ruben. By unvoiced agreement they dressed and went downstairs, sat on the rug in front of the little log burner.

'We only have muesli bars left.' Ruben rummaged in the tin, pulling out packs of bars and bottled water. 'Sorry I don't have anything else.'

'I like muesli bars.'

'I don't even have a deck of cards,' he added ruefully.

'That's probably a good thing, I only know how to play poker.' Ellie glanced up and caught the look in his eye. Yeah, time to move the conversation along. 'I've got some news actually.'

Ruben took a bite out of his bar and chewed thoughtfully, taking satisfaction in the way her smile was bubbling out of her. That was his doing and it made him feel good.

'I'm up for a tourism award. Only a very minor one

of course. Rookie Guide of the Year—can you believe that?' She bounced on her knees. 'I've only been there a couple of months but I've been nominated! I'm so thrilled.'

So *that* was why she was glowing? It wasn't because she was still bathed in post-sex bliss? He felt stupidly deflated. 'That's awesome.' He nodded. 'When did you find out?'

'A few days ago,' she said.

A few days? But they talked on the phone every night. 'How come you didn't tell me already?' It niggled that she'd kept something so special a secret.

'I wanted to tell you in person.' She smiled, her pleasure iridescent. 'I wanted to see your reaction.'

'Oh.' He felt a bit better. 'Well, that's really cool. Good for you.'

'I've finally found what I'm meant to do.' She grinned and bit into her bar. 'It's the best job in the world.'

Impulse hit Ruben hard—he wanted to see if she won that award. He wanted to be there to give her a hug if she didn't. Okay, maybe he wanted to give her more than a hug. 'When do you find out if you've won?'

'There's a function—dinner and the awards and stuff—at the end of the week.'

'Do you get to take a date?'

She paused. 'I'm not sure.'

'If you do, will you take me?'

'You want to go?' She looked surprised and suddenly elated. The sun pierced through the clouds the same moment her smile exploded.

'Of course, that's what friends do.' He tried to get a grip. That was what this was about. Being a friend and supporter, right?

'Friends,' she echoed.

'We are still friends, right?' He blinked as the bright sunshine hurt his sleep-deprived eyes.

'Of course.' Her smile didn't dim.

Ruben was relieved the sun soon burned off the fog because he needed a little thinking space to assess quite where he was at. Satisfied, yes—but for how long? It was what she'd insisted on—one night—and then back to normal. But he really didn't feel quite right.

He flew them down to the airport—had booked her flight back to Wellington. He planned to stay at the lodge a couple of days and catch his breath. But when he said goodbye to her at the departures gate it was with a way-too-friendly, utterly breathless kiss. She melted into his arms and he unashamedly hauled her closer, revelling in her surrender. Maybe they'd take this one hook-up at a time. They could stay friends on the phone and lovers on the nights their schedules melded. No problem at all. And maybe their clashing out of town calendars could be just the thing to stop this affair from ending too soon.

Three days later Ellie was all but skipping around the office. She was supposed to be working on the plan for her next tour, but distraction in the form of random Ruben thoughts kept hitting her.

'You really can't concentrate, can you?' Bridie teased.

Fortunately her boss thought her dithering was about the awards tomorrow night, not the excitement of seeing Ruben again.

It was silly—he was coming tomorrow just as a friend. But she knew what might happen—he'd said it was enough, but that kiss goodbye at the airport?

Oh, she wanted more of that. She could control this added dimension to their friendship. Of course she could. Friends with benefits wasn't just a Hollywood set-up, maybe it could really work. Okay, so the realist in her sensed impending heartache, but there was that irrepressible flicker of hope—surely he wouldn't have offered to come with her if he didn't care even just a little, right?

Maybe, just maybe that wall of his was coming down—one brick at a time. They'd grown closer over the last few weeks—not physically but in all those phone calls. And then the physical had happened—and transported her to a whole other level. She'd never felt closer to anyone than she had with him in that hut. She'd never felt closer to heaven.

Ruben was staring at his calendar and planning future trips to Wellington for more nights with Ellie when his phone rang. It was a blocked number—and the call played to his innate ambition.

Anthony Mackenzie—of the Australian department store dynasty—was in the country with his sister. 'We'd love to have a meeting with you. We've heard you excel at discreet luxury.'

'Are you looking to stay at one of my venues?'

'We want you to come to Australia and build us some.'

Ruben paused for a 'wow' moment. Overseas expansion wasn't in his current plan but he'd be a fool not to make the connection. 'When did you want to meet?'

Ruben—still looking at his schedule—frowned as Anthony named the next day. It shouldn't matter—the meeting was in the afternoon, Ellie's gig was in the evening. So long as he made the flight he'd be there.

And if he missed the plane, he could charter his own. It wasn't going to be one of those clash of timing things at all. Fate wouldn't be so inconvenient. It was completely manageable.

The instant he hung up from Anthony, Ruben phoned Ellie. The opportunity made excitement burn all over and he wanted to share the buzz.

'Are you getting excited?' he teased her first when he heard an ultra-chirpy hello.

'No. I'm just going to relax and enjoy it. It's not about winning.'

Ruben smirked. It was *always* about winning. 'I've got a meeting in the afternoon.' Yeah, he was looking forward to the whole damn day.

'So you're not coming.' Not missing a beat, she leapt to the wrong conclusion. 'That's fine. I don't expect you to be there, I know you're really busy. If you can't make it that's cool.'

Something else burned in Ruben now. He paused, registering how effortless her shift to 'I don't mind' was. Had she *expected* him not to show? It had happened to her before, hadn't it? Her determined cheeriness to cover up any wound was too practised. Her parents probably. But Ruben didn't like that she trusted him so little.

'Of course I'm coming,' he said more sharply than he intended. 'I'll be flying in after. It's a short flight, you know. I'll be there.'

'You don't have to—'

'I want to, Ellie.' He sighed. 'Trust me.'

There was a moment of silence. 'Okay.' And then she finally asked, 'What's the meeting about?'

But the excitement of telling her about the connection

faded in the insecurity that whispered along the cellular network. 'Possibility of taking on a deal in Australia. New boutique hotels. Right from design stage.'

'Wow, that's big,' she said. 'That's really big.'

'It could be amazing.'

'Sure,' she agreed. 'But once you've nailed that, will it be enough?'

'What do you mean?'

'Once you've conquered Australia, what's next?'

'Indonesia maybe?' He ignored her underlying criticism and played up. 'Or Fiji?'

'Of course.' She sighed. 'You're going to end up with a massive chain.'

'No need to sound critical, you know I love a challenge.' And what would be so wrong with a massive challenge?

A small silence. 'Well, I hope the meeting goes really well. It sounds like it could be a great opportunity. And you're incredible at making the most of every opportunity that comes your way.'

He swallowed back the defence gagging in his throat. There was no point in fighting with her over the phone. Was she distancing—shoring up her defences in case he let her down?

Her determination not to care worried him. He didn't want to worry. He didn't want to have to mind how she might be feeling.

'So what are you planning to wear tomorrow?' He tried to tease them both out of it. 'The black slip dress would be good, with the sequined sandals.' He dreamed about that outfit all the time.

'You sound like my gay best friend, you know that?' she teased back.

He forced a chuckle but couldn't quite mask the bitter kernel burrowing deeper inside his chest. 'Isn't that what you wanted?'

Less than twenty-four hours later he shook hands with Anthony and Annabel Mackenzie—twin offspring of one of the wealthiest families in Australia. He was the playboy head of the department store conglomerate. She the former solo-sailing superstar. She was petite, beautiful and strong. He was tall and even stronger. Formidable competition, fantastic allies. Practically royalty. Ruben liked being his own boss, but he wasn't stupid. He'd forge a business alliance with the best of them. But only the best.

'Thanks for taking time out to meet us.' Anthony smiled.

'Pleasure,' Ruben replied. 'Thanks for the invitation.'

'We've been watching what you've been doing for a while,' Anthony said. 'We have some clients in common.'

Conversation quickly turned serious. They wanted him in on a consortium they were putting together to construct a couple of elite boutique lodges in Australia. Ruben would oversee it. But he wanted to know why they wanted him.

Annabel answered briskly. 'You're as driven as I am.'

'For different reasons.' They couldn't have more different backgrounds.

A smile showed her acknowledgement of that. 'You have the kind of focus that ensures success.'

He nodded slowly. Focus was everything. 'And you insist on success.'

'Absolutely.'

Yeah, this woman was driven. So was her steely-eyed brother. Ruben understood, he had that insatiable pit in his belly—the fire that needed constant fuel. They might have wildly different histories, but that commonality was there. And this would be some job. It wouldn't be days away, it would be *months*. It would be hours and hours of work. The kind of challenge Ruben relished.

'I'd need total control,' he said.

Anthony sat back and smiled. 'Naturally you would.'

As they talked Ruben glanced at Annabel. She was a woman well used to getting what she wanted, a beautiful, fit woman. A woman who had a lot in common with him. She had that ruthless, business-first ambition. Was the kind of person who'd made sacrifices—because no one could have it all. Especially those who dreamed big.

'I have the connections,' Anthony was saying. 'You design it.'

'We want your vision.'

But Ruben was struggling to concentrate and he'd *never* had trouble concentrating before. His work was everything to him. It had to be—for so long it had been all he'd had. No family, no friends, only wood and nails and garden had been the constants for him. He'd put his all into it and he'd reaped the benefits. As a kid it had been hard cultivating the 'I don't give a damn what you think' mentality, but now that attitude was second nature. It had seen him take massive risks that had paid off.

But Ellie's question circled—when would it be enough? Would it ever be enough? Or would the edge of dissatisfaction always be there?

He couldn't afford to care what Ellie thought. It limited him. He'd start to need approval and he'd needed approval from no one for decades. But he wanted to know what she thought of this. Her doubts made *him* doubt himself.

He agreed to research the idea and get back to them. Engrossed in thought, he took a taxi from their hotel for the airport. The Mackenzie siblings waved him off and for the first time Ruben felt his isolation keenly.

How could he feel lonely now?

He knew why and, damn it, he couldn't afford to be thinking about Ellie all the time. Couldn't afford to miss her. Couldn't afford to need to talk to her. She took up all his spare brain space. Plus the space he *didn't* have spare.

He didn't do relationships—not beyond superficial friendly or useful for business. None that required emotional investment. His business was his life. That was how he liked it and that was what made him happy. Thinking of her all the time was *not* making him happy.

He faced facts—it had to be over. He needed to cut her from his life so he could concentrate on what was most important to him. He'd tell her tonight, after the awards.

On a quiet Sunday morning, it could be only a twenty-minute drive to get to the airport, but in traffic like this it might be a good fifty minutes or more. His muscles clenched at the thought of seeing her again and having to say goodbye. He thought back on that conversation so late those few nights ago. The one that had turned him incandescent with rage and forced him into breaking the friendship boundary. His jaw clamped tighter but it was no use. He was powerless to resist, unable to block the constant dreams of her.

Starvation hadn't killed the sexual attraction. Nor had that night of indulgence. He thought of her more and more. Every phone call he heard the sultry in her voice.

Seeing her would only worsen it. So what was the point of tormenting himself even more? The sooner she was expunged, the better. And wouldn't seeing her once more only tempt him back into trouble?

The best idea would be for him to go to Australia as soon as possible and focus on that. Because what did she get from him really? He couldn't believe she really needed his friendship. She had plenty of other friends and she was already expecting him to let her down. Her reaction when he told her about the meeting had shown that. And even if, for just a second, he let himself dream of being with her, he knew he couldn't ask it of her. She loved her job. She was damn good at it. And it was completely incompatible with his. She didn't need him distracting her or holding her back. She'd been in it only a few months and she was up for an award already. It was her calling. What she was best at, and what she adored. She was becoming as bad a workaholic as he was.

He frowned at that. She was tired with all these back to back tours. She needed a rest. In his most private dream he'd take her back to the hut and pin her there until she'd caught up on all the sleep she needed. He groaned at the agony. Because it wasn't really sleep he was dreaming of.

And then he thought back to that call—the 'it's okay to meet someone else' call. Wasn't her staying 'friends' with him limiting her chances of meeting other people? Couldn't there be some guy she'd meet who'd be so much better for her? Some other tour guide or someone who had more to offer her. It would happen soon enough. There'd be some charmer on her tour who'd tempt her. Who'd treat her the way she ought to be treated.

He didn't want to be on the end of the phone when she told him about her new lover. Never.

He'd hurt Sarah with his unavailability. His 'lack of support' as she'd put it. Emotional—not financial, of course. He didn't want to hurt Ellie. Not any more than he had to. There was no future for their friendship. It couldn't ever work. It wasn't working *now.* And he couldn't bear the thought of feeling hurt himself. The sooner it was over, the better for the both of them.

He leaned forward in the seat and called to the driver. 'Actually, I've changed my mind. Turn back to the city, please.' He'd check into a hotel and get to work researching the Australians' proposal. That was his future.

He fished out his phone. He didn't want to speak to her. Not with this ache in his upper chest as if he were coming down with some infection—he didn't want her to hear him sounding husky. He'd text her. He stared sightlessly at the screen, deciding how to word it. Best to end it in a way that would be complete for her. To do what she expected in her heart. He paused, motionless.

He wasn't looking out of the window. He never saw the car at the intersection—the one not slowing down for the light as it should. He never heard the noise. Because at that moment, the only thing he could see was her sparkling eyes.

Ellie didn't wear the black slip dress. She went all out and bought a new one—that she couldn't really afford and that she'd probably wear only the once because it was too *luxe* for everyday life. French navy in colour, clingy—she felt a million dollars wearing it. Not to mention sensual, with cool silk skimming over her skin. Not that she was thinking sex either.

She did her make-up, blow-dried her hair, slipped her feet into the kind of shoes she could only bear to wear for minutes rather than hours—the sparkly, insane stiletto sort, with heels so high she'd be practically *en pointe*. But it would be fine—dinner was a sit-down affair, she'd taxi there. And Ruben would still be taller than her but she might be able to brush her lips over his with a mere tilt of her chin.

Of course, she took her imagination in a firm grip, she'd be brushing her lips across his cheek, not his mouth. They were *friends*. And she was not, not, *not* counting the hours until she saw him again. Absolutely did *not* know exactly how many seconds it had been since she last saw him.

'Oh, wow, you look amazing.' Bridie smiled at her when Ellie made it to the bar.

The venue for the awards was a couple of doors along. Ruben was coming straight from the airport. A hot flare of desire burst inside her at the mere thought of seeing him. She shivered, telling her skipping heart to calm down.

'You need another drink?' she asked Bridie, needing to move to work off some of her nervous energy.

She went to the bar, checked her phone while waiting to be served. No message. She was still giving herself a mental lecture even after the bartender had poured the drinks and she was carrying them back to the group. There could be traffic delays, flight delays, all kinds of reasons why he wasn't there yet. Twenty minutes later she bit the bullet and sent him a text.

Just 2 let u know we've gone into the convention centre for the awards. Yr name is on the door so u can get in, but let me know when u get here & I'll meet u.

She sat at the table. Silly to be nervous. Her hands

cold and clammy, her heart skipping beats uncomfortably. Restless. Time played with her mind—two minutes felt like twenty. A permanent state of waiting was a horrible way to live.

And then time sped up. The awards were all on and she wanted the clock hands to slow again. It wasn't as if she could ask them to delay the announcements. It was okay. She had Bridie on one side of her. An empty seat on the other but, hey, that didn't really matter—not when there were canapés to die for and an endless amount of wine. And a bunch of flirty tourism types who truly knew how to party.

'Do you think he's going to make it?' Bridie asked.

Ellie smiled with a careless shrug and was so glad she'd played down her relationship with Ruben. A friend, she'd defined him herself, right? She checked her phone again. Still no message. He didn't even have the decency to reply to her text?

'I don't know that he is.' She turned away so Bridie couldn't see her screen and lied to cover the fact she'd been stood up. 'Oh, no, his flight's been delayed.'

But she'd used her phone to check the airport website only ten minutes before—all flights were on schedule and operating normally. If he'd got the flight he'd be here already. And if he hadn't got the flight, why hadn't he contacted her to let her know?

Goosebumps feathered over her skin.

She knew why he hadn't contacted her. Because he didn't want to be there. If he'd really wanted to be there, he'd be there. It was like all those unfulfilled promises of her parents. One or other would promise to be there—a sports day, a special assembly—but more often than not they'd forget, too swept up in their own affairs, careers or better offers. Once or twice one or other had arrived just at the end—having missed her event. Never on time. Never truly there just for her. Something or someone else always came first.

And so it was with Ruben. For him work came first. It always would. And that was okay if she could put up with it. But she didn't want to put up with it. She didn't want to be second best. Just for once she wanted to be put first in someone's life. But that someone wasn't going to be Ruben.

That secret, hidden dream shattered.

What an absolute fool she'd been. He'd utterly played her with his acquiescence to her friendship request, with his phone calls and supposed sharing. He'd only been after the one thing—and he'd got it that night up in the mountain. There hadn't been any kind of amazing more-than-physical connection for him, there'd just been sex.

How naïve to think he'd show up tonight. How naïve to think a friendship could work. How point-blank stupid of her to have said yes to any damn benefits.

And how it hurt. It hurt worse than any of those damn sports days or disappointments from her parents. She'd given her heart and got nothing back. But she was determined to hide it—even from herself. She was damn well determined to have a good night out.

When it came to announcing the winner of the category she was nominated in, someone else's name was called. Someone else went up and collected their award. Ellie smiled lots and clapped loudly. Then she sipped some of that wine, ate another canapé and conversed enthusiastically with all those around her.

She *should* have been an actress—she could mask misery so easily.

But she went out with her colleagues, determined to find comfort in company. She'd hang with her true friends. And Ruben wasn't one of them.

CHAPTER TWELVE

RUBEN's head ached really badly. So did the rest of him. He was alone—just as he'd always believed he wanted. And, hell, he'd been wrong.

Sure there were people he could call. All those names in his contacts file—he could get any one of his 'friends' and they'd be there in a flash. But what would they do? Sit and talk sport or weather or politics? Not one of them really *knew* him—and he didn't really know them. He'd kept a certain distance so well it was second nature. And now he realised how alone it had made him.

Because there was one person who'd slipped through those barriers. One person he ached to see. One person whose comfort he wanted. Someone whose arms he wanted around him—someone he wanted to confide every last little thing to. Someone he'd been trying to contact for the last three days.

She didn't answer her phone. He rang five, ten, fifty times and every call went to the answer service. He tried ringing from a land-line so she wouldn't recognise the number. Still she didn't take the call.

So now he knew the reality of this new life. Accident or not, this would have happened anyway. He'd have finished that text and sent it, so the result would have been the same. She'd have been avoiding him. There'd be no contact.

And accident or not, he'd still be this bruised. Yeah, it wasn't those real cuts and bruises bleeding him, but that damn muscle in his chest. The injury that he had sole responsibility for and that radiated agony throughout the rest of him.

He was an idiot. A powerless idiot. Stuck in a hospital bed with an IV needle deep in his arm and cracked ribs that meant an airline wouldn't take him onboard. Not as far as Australia, so he couldn't escape as he'd planned to. But he couldn't escape anyway, aeroplane policy or not. He wanted to take it all back and start again. And while he might not be able to get on a plane, he could get into a campervan with a driver. He'd lie down most of the way, but he wasn't living through another day without trying to make things right. He'd been acting the coward too long as it was.

Ellie had a new phone—a very cute new smart phone that she could download a zillion apps on. She was just deciding which music to set as her ringtone when it rang with a real call. She didn't recognise the number. 'Hello?'

'Are you through punishing me?' he asked bluntly. 'Are you ready to talk to me yet?'

All kinds of emotions tumbled through Ellie. For a moment she couldn't cope with the spike in adrenalin that boosted the performance of every vital organ. 'I've been busy,' she finally breathed.

'This is how you treat your friends? Why have you been ignoring my calls?'

'I haven't been. I lost my phone.' Okay, so she'd thrown it in Wellington harbour. Not the most adult thing to have done but, hey, she'd got glum in the wee small hours after the chaotic clubbing scene of the awards after party.

'Good of you to give me your new number.'

How he'd managed to get it she didn't know.

He sighed. 'Can you just be mad with me, please? Just yell or something.'

She sat in a ball on the floor because her legs wouldn't work any more. 'There's nothing to yell about, Ruben. I'm fine.'

'Really?'

'Sure,' she said, pride surging. 'I'm not in some kind of decline just because you didn't turn up when you said you would. I had a really good night actually—it was quite a party.'

'I saw the photos on the company's Facebook page. I saw some others from the last tour too.'

'Yeah,' she reminisced with a fake smile that she hoped would sound real down the phone. 'They were a bit of a wild bunch.'

'And you had a good time with them.'

'It's my job to help them have a good time.'

'More Scotsmen.'

'What can I say? I seem to attract them.'

In one of those pictures she'd been wearing a Scottish flag and very little else. They'd had a toga party. It had been fun. There'd been bare-chested men in kilts. Nothing had happened with any of them, of course, but just the flirtation had made her feel better, right? She'd been popular. No matter that it was only temporary—for the two-day tour duration. She knew how to please people. But she'd once told Ruben that she didn't feel as if she had to please him. She wasn't going to please him now. She drew in a breath, dug up that deep resolve. 'You know this "let's be friends" deal?'

'Uh-huh.'

'It's not working for me.'

'Why not?'

'Well.' She screwed her eyes closed as she went for brutal honesty. 'I'm not going to meet anyone else when I'm still being "friends" with you.' She held her breath, heard his whistle in.

'You really want to meet someone else?'

'I think that would be the best thing for me, yeah.' Her toes curled and her skin goosebumped in revulsion at the thought of it. But it *was* the best thing. Ruben didn't want her beyond an occasional bed buddy and she didn't want to be mooning over him for the next millennia. She had to be kind to herself and cruel at the same time, because sending him away was hard.

'You're not even going to say this to my face?'

'Nope. I'm doing it over the phone. You're lucky it wasn't a text. It nearly was.' His mere presence was enough to tempt her. One smile enough to keep her hope afloat for weeks. She wanted to fall *out* of love with him. The cold turkey approach was the only way that could possibly work.

'Is this because I missed the show?'

'Oh, wow, you think?' Yeah, she'd just lost her grip on cool and capable.

'Ellie—'

'You don't have to explain it. I understand. You don't care for me.'

Silence. Then he got snappy right back at her. 'Our "friendship" isn't a one-way street, Ellie. You haven't been the best of friends to me either, you know.'

Well, that wasn't fair. But she was too hurt to argue.

The last thing she wanted to face was the fact that she loved his calls, loved hearing his tales. She got more than he did from this and she wanted more still. 'I don't think we were ever truly friends, Ruben. I think all those movies are right—men and women can't do platonic friendship. Let's call it a day, okay?'

She jabbed the end-call button, furiously blinking back the sting of rejection.

Someone instantly started hammering down her front door. She swiped the trickles from her cheeks and stormed the stairs. The door was rattling in the frame. She yanked it open. 'You were outside all this time?'

'I've had enough of the phone call rubbish.' He barged in, plucking her phone from her hand as he pushed past and flinging it across the room. His went with it.

Stunned, she watched them smash on the floor. 'You've probably broken both of them!'

'Good. So we're forced to speak face to face.'

She turned back and stared at him. For the second time that night her knees went completely weak. 'What the hell happened?'

'Car crash.'

Her lungs then failed too. 'You're kidding,' she wheezed.

'No. On the way to the airport the night of your awards.'

That was why he hadn't turned up? That was four days ago. 'And you're still this bruised?' He looked *awful*. Not even the jeans and the favourite 'Lucky' shirt could lift his near death-mask look. 'Why didn't you try to get in touch with me?' She was so shocked she shouted.

'When I regained consciousness the next day I did try. Just went to your answerphone.'

Oh, now she felt terrible. He'd had an accident—a horrible accident that could have been so much worse. And she hadn't been there for him. He'd been alone and abandoned again. That just broke her heart. But how was she to have known if he didn't tell her?

Ruben had decided on the trip down that he was going to fight hard—and dirty. No matter how, he was winning this woman.

'Friends are supposed to look out for each other,' he snapped, belligerent. Mad with himself as much as he was with her. 'Why didn't you call me to see where I was?'

'I sent you a text,' she snapped, equally defensive.

'One.' His hurt spilled. 'You never followed up. You never called that night or the next day. If we were such great friends how could you walk away so easily?' He breathed in and it hurt. Every breath hurt.

'So this is my fault?'

It was *all* her fault. 'You didn't care about me enough to wonder where I was or whether I was okay.'

She paled; her blue eyes weren't sparkling, but glistening. 'It never occurred to me you might not be okay.'

'No, you just thought the worst of me. That I'd let you down.' He breathed in hard and honesty—responsibility—slammed into him. Because he knew exactly why she'd not followed up with her call—she'd been afraid, yet certain, of his rejection. 'And you were right, that's exactly what I'd decided to do.'

Yeah, his chest burned. He saw the horror in her eyes at the sight of his bruises. But he couldn't win this that dirty after all. He didn't want to win her through sympathy. Her guilt was a hollow, bitter victory. He didn't want pity. He didn't want her to feel bad or obligated. He just wanted her to love him the way he loved her. But she deserved the truth. Even if it meant he might lose her.

'The accident doesn't matter,' he said huskily. 'I wasn't going to be there anyway.'

'What do you mean you weren't going to be there?' She'd backed up to the wall, as far from him as she could get.

'I'd decided to end it. I was texting you to say I wasn't coming when the accident happened.'

'You were texting while driving?' she screeched, anger flooding back.

'Actually I was in the back of a taxi.'

She stared at him and as the seconds ticked he didn't just see the pain he'd inflicted on her, he felt it himself. Her hurt was his—because his heart was hers.

'Why are you telling me this?' Ellie had suffered too many shocks already. She didn't get what the guy wanted or why he was here.

'I want to be honest with you. I want to clear this up.'

Clear it up? As in *over*? Hadn't she just tried to do that? What was with the torment?

'I don't want to be friends with you, Ellie. I want a relationship with you.' He looked less than impressed about it. 'I can't get you out of my head,' he growled.

She had no sympathy—nothing left to give in the face of this. 'Maybe you need to try harder.'

'Ellie.' He shook his head, his voice low. 'I can't stay away from you.'

'You can't stay away from *sex*. That's all it is.'

'No, that is not all it is,' he shouted back. 'We hadn't had sex in *weeks*.' He drew breath—the damn cracked rib kept poking him, forcing the honesty. 'Yes, that was a big part of it at first. But then it was you. *All* of you.'

She wasn't buying it. 'You only did the calls because you were frustrated that I hadn't put out. I was the challenge—and once you'd conquered me up on that mountain you weren't interested any more.'

'That's not true.'

'Well, what is it you want from me, then?' Oh, she hurt. So hurt. But she couldn't be second best. Not when he'd become her everything.

'Ellie.' His voice broke. He leaned back against her door, his body completely rigid, every muscle straining as he pressed his fists to his chest. 'I can't sleep. I'm barely eating. I can't concentrate on anything at work. I haven't for weeks. I don't want to be this *obsessed*. I've always been totally one track, but, now, *you're* the track. And I can't fight it any more. I don't care about anything else. All I care about is being with you.' He scrubbed his hands through his hair. 'But I've never had a relationship actually work for more than five minutes. And I can't...' He sighed. 'You deserve more than I can give you.'

Ellie stared at him—stunned and uncomprehending. 'Why do you think you can't give me what I need?'

'I've never been able to before,' he said harshly. 'And I've never wanted to. I hate feeling so out of control.' He straightened away from the door, and awkwardly walked to her lounge. 'My parents' relationship limited them. Neither achieved their ambitions. Dad had his dreams but they hardly got off the ground. They were too tied up with each other.'

'Is that so bad?'

'I know they were happy,' he admitted. 'And maybe because of the way the world viewed them they were an even tighter unit. But it was frustrating.' He hobbled about her lounge, not looking at her. 'We came out here when I was six. I had this French accent, an ancient dad and I loved him. But he bought this wreck of a property and said he was going to turn it into a *chateau*.' Ruben laughed painfully. 'He drew up these awesome plans. But that was about as far as he got.'

'So you did it for him.' Ellie knew this but she thought she had it all now. 'But you really think their relationship held your father back from achieving anything else?'

He winced. 'Not just him, they were both hopeless that way. No one can have it all. And if you want to do something you're better to be free to get on with it.'

'But maybe neither of them *wanted* to achieve those dreams that much. Maybe your father was just enjoying being a husband and a dad—you said yourself he never thought it was going to happen. Maybe he wanted to spend that time *imagining* his dreams with you—rather than *not* spending that time with you as he made them a reality. I'm sure he'd be thrilled with what you've done, but I don't know that he'd be so pleased with how you've isolated yourself to do it.'

He was silent a long moment. She could see the shifting emotions in him—saw the hopelessness lift.

But then he turned away. 'My ex resented the time I put into work. It came to a head—I had to pick her or the deal for the Taupo lodge. I chose the deal and she walked. At the time I was glad. But this time?' He shook his head. 'I don't want to hurt you like that. I don't want to lose you but how can I be fair to you?'

'But I'm not her. I want to *support* you, not hold you back.' She'd love to help him however she could. 'And

I want you to support me. Why can't we achieve our dreams together?'

He jerked his head, turning back to face her. 'You're the first woman I've ever put before work, the only woman who's made work seem utterly meaningless.' He walked towards her. 'You're the only woman I've chased. And I'm going to keep chasing as long as I have to.'

It wasn't going to have to be for much longer. Her eyes filled with tears.

'Ellie, you're everything and more to me.' He stopped in front of her. 'You don't need to be anything other than yourself. You're the perfect woman for me.' He stepped close enough to touch—so he only had to whisper. 'Just you. Just as you are. I need you in my life. I never knew how much I needed you until I tried to live without you.'

'This is you chasing, huh?' She swiped the streaming rivers from her cheeks.

'This is me being honest,' he said softly. 'I didn't want to hurt you but I did and I'm so sorry. But I didn't want to hurt myself either and I thought walking away would save me from that. I was so wrong.' His voice softened. 'Because the thing is, I *am* like my parents. I love as deeply. You. I *hate* being apart from you. I want to be with you all of the time. I don't want to go away. I don't want you going away from me.' He shook his head. 'It's crazy. I think about you all the time. I miss you like you wouldn't believe. It *hurts*. It's a physical ache. I never wanted to hurt like this.'

Oh, she knew that ache. The constant, incurable gnawing deep inside. The coldness in bed—despite summer heat or electric blankets. The sadness at the stretch of bed beside her. The inadequacy of a quick phone call. The inability to catch his eye, to smile at a joke she knew he'd get. She missed that magic language, that connection that she'd never had with another person. Only him. It was real heartache, that heaviness of his absence. He wasn't hers and she'd thought he couldn't ever be. Oh, that had hurt.

'I feel for you like I've never felt for anyone. I've fought it. I thought I could control it, but I can't. I just want to be with you.' He took her hand in his. 'I don't want to go anywhere else. Home is where you are.' He looked intently into her eyes. 'You're the most important thing in my life.'

She nodded. Swallowed. Trying to clear the blurring in her eyes, the building of emotion in her throat.

'That's the nicest thing anyone's ever said to me.' Her throat was so constricted from holding back her emotion that it was hardly a whisper that sounded. She put her fingers to her lips to stop the sobs from ripping free.

'Please let me love you,' he whispered back. 'I'll do whatever I have to.'

'You don't have to do anything *but* love me,' she whispered. 'I don't want you giving up things that are important to you.'

'I'm not.'

'What about those Australians?'

'The terrible twins?' He laughed. 'They'll find someone else. I'm not in the market for global domination. Just national.'

'Really?'

'I have lots of things to do round here—at work and with you.'

She smiled. 'So do I. Planning to be the best tour guide in the country, you know.'

'Of course.' He nodded. 'So maybe I could come on

tour sometimes?' That one eyebrow went even higher. 'I could learn all those lines and achieve Ultra Fan Status.'

She chuckled—well, it was more a hiccup. Because she didn't know if she could handle his presence when she was leading a tour. 'You might be too much of a handful on my bus.'

He winked. 'I do solemnly declare that I will never manhandle you on tour time. Only in the hotel every night.'

'It's not you I'm worried about.' She smiled. It was her own urges. 'But maybe I could travel with *you* sometimes?'

'Any time you want. I won't visit the lodges as much. I need to consolidate and I could stay in town more. Here.'

'You're going to move in with me?' Her eyebrow took the upwards escalator that time.

'If you'll have me.' He paused.

'Is it going to be enough for you?' What if he got bored and felt she was holding him back?

'I'm talking long-term commitment, Ellie. I'm talking life. Literally. I want a family,' he said softly.

'You're talking kids?' Her voice lifted a dozen octaves. *And* he'd used the C-word?

'And I want to be involved.' He nodded, seeming to miss her total astonishment. 'I don't want them turning themselves inside out to get my attention. I don't want to do that to our children. I want them to know how important they are.'

The security she *hadn't* been given by her parents. Knowing he understood that made her melt completely. She leaned against his chest. 'I think if you tell them…'

He shook his head. 'Words aren't enough,' he whispered. 'It's all in the actions. Words mean nothing if they're not backed up with action. I want to *show* them. Just as I want to show you.'

'You already have.'

'No, I've only just begun. I love you, Ellie. Let me show you how for the rest of our days.'

Not often did an actual climax live up to the fantasy of Ellie's unlimited—heavily Hollywood influenced—imagination. This moment wasn't like that. There was no cinematic tweaking, no flash mob dancing, no proposals in neon lights… But nothing could beat the sincerity shining in the light in his eyes. Nothing could beat the liquid joy racing in her veins. Nothing could stop her from smiling, from crying. She squeezed her eyes shut as her tears flowed faster. Warmth seeped into her skin—the feel of his skin, his strong body, his tight embrace. Yes, the blaze of passion was there, but it was based on an eternal flame, a lick of heat that was all security. All his love.

She'd never felt so treasured. So wanted. In every way that mattered. In that most special of ways. She was his partner in everything. His equal. And they were going to work it *together*.

'I love you.' She'd give him everything she had to give. It could never be too much, now she understood that. He wanted it all—wanted to give her the same.

He groaned. 'I need you.'

She couldn't believe he was so blown away to have her in his arms. That he too was so ecstatic and so relieved that she'd opened up to him. As if he'd really believed she might not.

He moved, lifting her.

'This is a bad idea,' she yelped. 'You're injured.'

'I'm fine,' he argued.

'You're not.'

'Hold me back any longer and I won't be. Please let me do this.'

She cupped his cheek with her hand. 'Only if you let me take care of you too.'

He smiled at her—that lucky, lovely smile—and carried her to the place they both needed to be. She muffled her gasps when she saw the extent of his bruising, but he'd already seen her distress.

'It looks worse than it is.'

'Liar.' She brushed a kiss over the purplish skin near his ribs.

'I love you.'

'We haven't had sex this simple,' she said softly as he carefully moved over her.

'This isn't simple,' he answered. 'And this isn't sex.'

She arched instinctively, her neck, her spine, her feet. Every muscle clenched on the pleasure of him, breathing hard already. Abandoned moans were a mere thrust away.

'This is love.' His biceps rippled as he braced over her, pausing before driving his point home. 'This is making love.'

She cried, 'Oh, yes.'

He groaned and pulled back, trying to slow down. 'It's not going to be a marathon.'

'Not a problem.' She arched again, the ripples starting already.

His grin was lopsided and strained. And so lucky. Their eyes met—vulnerable, revealing. Trusting.

In the aftermath he nuzzled closer, his weight so wonderfully heavy on her. She blew cool, teasing air over his face and neck.

'I think I'm the luckiest guy ever,' he whispered gruffly.

She looked at the lamp where his tee shirt had landed and saw the old slogan and smiled, the most secure and certain of anything in her life. 'Yeah,' she whispered. 'There's no one luckier than you. Except me.'

She felt his smile against her skin.

'We're going to spend the rest of our lives arguing that,' he teased.

Pure happiness radiated through her. She softened. His completely. Happy completely.

'I know.'

EPILOGUE

One Year Later.

'I'M NOT going to win, you know. Just to be nominated is amazing. I never expected it, not two years in a row.'

Scepticism was painted all over Ruben's face. 'Just to be nominated? No one actually believes that, you know. Everyone wants to win. You included.'

Ellie determinedly shook her head. 'It would be nice to win, but I'm not going to be devastated if I don't. I'm going to enjoy the night anyway.' She'd partied like a wild woman last year when she hadn't won. This year was going to be so much better than that because he was with her and they'd just had the best year ever.

'You are?'

She nodded. 'You by my side, a job I adore. Life can't get better.'

Those gorgeous lips of his curved a little deeper. 'I got you a little something.'

'A consolation prize?' She giggled. 'To make me feel better if I don't win?'

'I wouldn't say it's a consolation prize. But it's for later.'

'Can I have it now?' She sent him a flirt look.

'Your category hasn't even been announced yet.'

'I don't care.' She leaned close, brushing against him. 'I'm far more interested in what you've got for me.'

'It really is for later.'

'Please?'

He sighed. 'I can't say no to you.' He put his hand in his pocket. 'But hopefully you can't say no to me either.'

He opened his hand in front of her.

Ellie looked at the box. The noise of the crowded room was suddenly muted. The crowd had vanished too—she was conscious of only him and her. 'Oh, Ruben.'

'Bit of an odd place to do this, but…'

She looked up. She could see only him—his gorgeous brown eyes, that charming, lucky smile and the love that shone through.

'You'll say yes? You'll marry me?'

'Of course I will,' she said. Only she was so choked up with emotion it was little more than a whisper.

She didn't hear her name over the sound system, she was so busy kissing him.

It was Bridie who poked her in the back and informed her she'd just won Tour Guide of the Year.

She hit the stage, collected her award and was heading back to her seat with no recollection whatsoever of what she'd said or done. But the entire audience had laughed and cheered so it must have been okay. And he was waiting with eyes only for her and with all the love she could ever want.

She ran the last few steps into his embrace. Real life was so much better than anything Hollywood could conjure. And Ellie Summers had won her world.

* * * * *

Once a Rebel...

Nikki
LOGAN

Nikki Logan lives next to a string of protected wetlands in Western Australia, with her long-suffering partner and a menagerie of furred, feathered and scaly mates. She studied film and theatre at university and worked for years in advertising and film distribution before finally settling down in the wildlife industry. Her romance with nature goes way back and she considers her life charmed, given she works with wildlife by day and writes fiction by night—the perfect way to combine her two loves. Nikki believes that the passion and risk of falling in love are perfectly mirrored in the danger and beauty of wild places. Every romance she writes contains an element of nature and, if readers catch a waft of rich earth or the spray of wild ocean between the pages, she knows her job is done.

For Tracy Scarparolo.
And to Dan, the best office-mate and
friend a girl could have.

PROLOGUE

www.remembermrsmarr.com
Front row seats for a Beethoven symphony
Bungee jump in New Zealand
Run a marathon
Ride like The Man from Snowy River
Hunt for a dinosaur fossil
Commune with the penguins in Antarctica
Float in a Hot Air Balloon
Climb the Sydney Harbour Bridge
Take a gondola ride in Venice
Climb Everest
Abseil down a cliff face
Be transported by a touch
Get up close and personal with dolphins
Take a cruise
Hold my grandchild

www.rem—

SHIRLEY keyed the first letters of the web address into her browser before it auto-completed the rest. She visited enough that it knew exactly where she wanted to go.

www.remembermrsmarr.com

The simple site opened and she spent the first moments—as she always did—staring at the face of her mother, captured forever in time in a delighted, head-thrown-back kind of joy. Exactly as she would have wanted people to see her. Exactly as her students did see her. And exactly how Shirley chose to remember her now, with the benefit of distance.

Clicking through to the list she knew was on the next page only disappointed.

Still nothing in the first column—the one headed 'HT.'

After all this time.

Hayden Tennant had been her mother's all-time favourite student. He'd been the one—hurt and grieving—to suggest the tribute website in the first place. So that they could each do the items on her mother's bucket list. All the life experiences an unlicensed drunk-driver had robbed her of.

Hayden had pledged.

He'd *vowed* in that gorgeous, thick, grief-filled voice.

Yet every single square next to every single item on *www.remembermrsmarr.com* was empty where Hayden's initials should have been.

Today was an extra sucky day to be staring at the list and finding it empty. Because today was ten years since Carol-Anne Marr had taken her last breath. How many weeks had passed before he'd forgotten all about it? Or was it days? Hours? Did he think no one would notice? Did he think his teacher's only daughter wouldn't be watching? Shirley tapped her purple fingernails on the keyboard and enjoyed the sound of the slick keys under them.

Come on, Hayden. You've had a decade.

Something.

Anything.

Swimming with dolphins. Climbing the Harbour Bridge. Running a marathon. Even *she'd* done that one, back before she'd got boobs. Back when her schedule had been able to tolerate training for eight straight hours. It had taken her eighteen months to train up and get old enough to qualify, but then she'd placed in the middle of the under-sixteens category and held her medal to the heavens as she lurched across the finish line.

And then she'd never run again.

If I can tick that one off, surely you can, Tennant.

Hayden, with his long, fast legs. His intense focus. His rigid determination. He wouldn't even need to train, he'd just *will* himself to last the entire forty-two kilometres.

She'd hoped for a while that he was honouring her mother privately, keeping his own list the way she herself was.

But the truth had finally dawned.

All that angst, all that sorrow and despair at her funeral; all of that was simply the emotion of the moment. Like a performance piece. Terribly dramatic and intense. Terribly Hayden. None of it had been genuine. Amazing, really, that he was still forking out the cash annually to maintain the domain name.

She cocked her head.

The domain...

It took her just a few minutes to track down the site registration details and a few more for a contact number for the company it was registered to. Molon Labe Enterprises. That had to be him. He'd had a thing for Spartans the entire time she'd known him.

Known *of* him.

Watched him.

She chased down the contact details for the company right here in Sydney and its executive structure. He wasn't on it. Disappointed by that dead end, she called the company direct and asked for him outright.

'Mr Tennant does not take calls,' the receptionist told her.

Really? Too busy and important? 'Could you give me his email address, please?'

It took the officious woman nearly a minute to outline all the reasons why she couldn't. Shirley rang off, far from defeated. Chasing down story leads was what she did for a living. It wasn't stalking if you were a professional. A bit of reconnaissance, finding out where he was and what was so important it had made him forget the promises of a decade ago…

That was doable. He'd never even know.

Thank goodness for search engines.

Two hours went by before she surfaced, frowning deeply at the screen. Hayden Tennant was a time bomb. Her online search was littered with images of him stumbling out of one seedy venue or another on the arm of some blonde—always a blonde—going back six years. In most of them, it was hard to tell who was holding up whom, but the club security was always on hand to facilitate their departure.

She stared at one image. He looked nothing like the Hayden she remembered. He used to get around in a shabby kind of hip style—*the garret look,* her mother had used to joke and make Shirley promise never to go out in public like that. So of course she had instantly wanted to. The designer lank hair, holed jumper and frequently bare feet. Bohemian plus. She'd coveted everything about his personal style back then, as only a love-sick fourteen-year-old could.

But the Internet had him in some pretty fancy threads now, as carefully fitted as the women accessorising the sharp suit and cars.

Guess everyone grows up.

She searched up Molon Labe's website, flicked through to their corporate contacts and scribbled down the address. Maybe his reception staff would find it harder to say no to her face? Not that she had the vaguest idea of what she'd say if she saw him.

Or why she wanted to.

Maybe so she could ask him, personally, why he hadn't bothered to tick a single box. Maybe because she owed it to her mother.

Or maybe just so she could finally nail a lid on the last remnants of her childhood.

CHAPTER ONE

'PLEASE be a stripper.'

His voice was thick and groggy, as though she'd just roused him from sleep. Maybe she had. It was a gently warm and breezeless day and Hayden Tennant looked as if he'd been lying in that longish grass at the base of the slope behind his cottage for quite some time.

Shirley found some air and forced it past a larynx choked with nerves. This suddenly seemed like a spectacularly bad idea.

'Were you expecting one?' she breathed.

He scrutinised her from behind expensive sunglasses. 'No. But I've learned never to question the benevolence of the universe.'

Still so fast with a comeback. The man in front of her might have matured in ways she hadn't anticipated but he was still *Hayden* inside.

Somewhere.

She straightened and worked hard not to pluck at her black dress. It was the tamest thing in her wardrobe. 'I'm not a stripper.'

His head flopped back down onto the earth and his eyes closed again. 'That's disappointing.'

Discharged.

She stood her ground and channelled her inner Shiloh. She wouldn't let his obvious dismissal rile her. Silent minutes ticked by. His long body sprawled comfortably where he lay. She took the opportunity to look him over. Still lean, still all legs. A tiny, tidy strip of facial hair above his lip and on his chin. Barely there but properly manicured. It only half-covered the scar she knew marred his upper lip.

The biggest difference was his hair. Shorter now than when he'd been at uni and a darker blond. It looked as if someone who knew what they were doing had cut it originally, but she guessed they hadn't had a chance to provide any maintenance recently.

She pressed her lips together and glared pointlessly at him as the silence continued. Had he gone back to sleep?

'I can do this all day,' he murmured, eyes still closed. 'I have nowhere to be.'

She spread her weight more evenly on her knee-high boots and appreciated every extra inch they gave her. 'Me, too.'

He lifted his head again and opened his eyes a crack.

'If you're not here to give me a lap dance, what do you want?'

Charming. 'To ask you some questions.'

He went dangerously still. Even the grass seemed to stop its swaying. 'Are you a journalist?'

'Not really.'

'It's a yes/no question.'

'I write for an online blog.' *Understatement.* 'But I'm not here in that capacity.'

He pulled himself up and braced against one strong arm in the turf. Did that mean she had his attention?

'How did you find me?'

'*Molon Labe.*'

He frowned and lifted his sunglasses to get a better look at her. His eyes were exactly as blue and exactly as intense as she remembered. She sneaked in a quick extra breath.

'My office wouldn't have given you this address.'

No. Not even face to face.

'I researched it.' Code for *I stalked your offices.*

It had taken a few visits to the coffee shop over the road to spot what messenger company they used most regularly. A man at the head of a corporation he didn't visit had to get documents delivered to wherever he was, right? For signatures at least. Sadly for them, if Hayden ever found out, the courier company had been only too obliging when a woman purporting to be from Molon Labe had called to verify the most recent details of one of their most common delivery addresses.

His eyes narrowed. 'But you're not here in a journalistic capacity?'

'I'm not a journalist.'

'Or a stripper, apparently.' He glanced over her from foot to head. 'Though that seems wasted.'

She forced herself not to react. She'd chosen this particular outfit carefully—knee-high boots, black scoop-neck dress cinched at the waist and falling to her knees—but she'd been going more for *I am woman* and less for *I am pole dancer.*

'You used to say sarcasm was the lowest form of wit,' she murmured.

One eye narrowed, but he gave no other sign of being surprised that she already knew him. 'Actually, someone else did. I just borrowed it. I've come to be quite fond of sarcasm in the years since…?' He left it open for her to finish the sentence.

He didn't recognise her.

Not entirely surprising, given how different she must have looked when he last saw her. Fourteen, stick-insect-thin, mousy, uninspired hair. A kid. She hadn't discovered fashion—and her particular brand of fashion—until she was sixteen and her curves had busted out.

'You knew my mother,' she offered carefully.

The eyes narrowed again and he pushed himself to his feet. Now it was his turn to tower over her. It gave him a great view down her scoop neck and he took full advantage. His eyes eventually came back to hers.

'I may have been an early starter but I think it's a stretch to suggest I could be your father, don't you?'

Hilarious.

'Carol-Anne Marr,' she persisted, the name itself an accusation.

Was it wrong that she took pleasure from the flash of pain he wasn't quite fast enough to disguise? That she grasped so gratefully at any hint of a sign that he hadn't forgotten her mother the moment she was in the ground. That he wasn't quite as faithless as she feared.

'Shirley?' he whispered.

And it *had* to be wrong how deeply satisfied she felt that he even knew her name. Hayden Tennant wasn't a god; if he ever had been he was well and truly fallen now. But still her skin tingled.

She lifted her chin. 'Shiloh.'

His eyes narrowed. 'Shiloh?'

'It's what I go by now.'

The blue in his eyes greyed over with disdain. 'I'm not calling you Shiloh. What's wrong with Shirley—not hip enough for you?'

It killed her that he was still astute enough to immediately put himself in the vicinity of the secret truth. And that she was still foolish enough to admire that. 'I preferred something that was more...me.'

'Shirley means "bright meadow".'

Exactly. And she, with her raven hair and kohl-smudged eyes, was neither bright nor meadow-like. 'Shiloh means "gift". Why can't it be a gift to myself?'

'Because your mother already gifted you a name. Changing it dishonours her.'

Tendrils of unexpected hurt twisted in her gut and rolled into a tight, cold ball and pushed up through her ribcage. But she swallowed it back and chose her words super-carefully. 'You're criticising *me* for not honouring her?'

Surprise and something else flooded his expression. Was that regret? Guilt? Confusion? None of those things looked right on a face normally filled with arrogant confidence. But it didn't stay long; he replaced it with a careless disinterest. 'Something you want to say, Shirley?'

Suddenly presented with the perfect opportunity to close that chapter on her life, she found herself speechless. She glared at him instead.

He shook his head. 'For someone who doesn't know me, you don't like me very much.'

'I know you. Very well.'

He narrowed one eye. 'We've never met.'

Actually they had, but clearly it wasn't memorable. Plus, she'd participated secretly in every gathering her mother had hosted in their home. Saturday extra credit for enthusiastic students. Hayden Tennant had been at every one.

'I know you through my mother.'

His lush lips tightened. She'd always wondered if her own fixation with Lord Byron had something to do with the fact that in her mind he shared Hayden's features. Full lips, broad forehead, intense eyes under a serious brow… Byron may have preceded him in history but Hayden came first in *her* history.

'If you're suggesting your mother didn't like me I'm going to have to respectfully disagree.'

'She adored you.' *So did her daughter, but that's beside the point.* She took a deep breath. 'That makes what you've done doubly awful.'

His brows drew down. 'What I've done?'

'Or what you haven't done.' She stared, waiting for the penny-drop that never came. For such a bright man, he'd become very obtuse. 'Does *remembermrsmarr.com* ring any bells?'

His face hardened. 'The list.'

'The list.'

'You're 172.16.254.1'

'What?'

'Your IP address. I get statistics from that website. I wondered who was visiting it so often.'

'I…' How had this suddenly become about her? And why was he monitoring visitation on a website he'd lost interest in almost immediately after he had set it up? It didn't fit with the man she visualised who had forgotten the list by the time the funeral bill came in.

'I visit often,' she said.

'I know. At least three times a week. What are you waiting for?'

She sucked in a huge breath and ignored the flick of his eyes down to her rising cleavage. 'I'm waiting for you to tick something.'

An eternity passed as he stared at her, the sharp curiosity he'd always had for everything in life dulling down to a careful nothing. 'Is that why you're here? To find out why I haven't ticked some box?'

Pressing her lips together flared her nostrils. 'Not just some box. *Her* box. My mother's dying wishes. The things you were supposed to finish for her.'

His eyes dropped away for a moment and when they lifted again they were softer. Kinder. So much worse. 'Shirley, look—'

'Shiloh.'

'*Shirley*. There's a whole bunch of reasons I haven't been able to progress your mother's list.'

'"Progress" suggests you've actually started.' Okay, now she was being as rude as he'd been on her arrival. Her high moral ground was crumbling. She lifted her chin. 'I came because I wanted to know what happened. You were so gutted at the funeral, how could you have followed through on none of them?'

He shrugged. 'Real life got in the way.'

Funny. Losing your mother at fourteen had felt pretty real to her. 'For ten years?'

His eyes darkened. 'I don't owe you any explanation, Shirley.'

'You owe her. And I'm here in her place.'

'The teacher I knew never would have asked anyone to justify themselves.'

He pushed past her and headed for his house. She turned her head back over her shoulder. 'Was she so easily forgotten, Hayden?'

Behind her, his crunching footfalls on the path paused. His voice, when it came, was frosty. 'Go home, Shirley. Take your high expectations and your bruised feelings and your do-me boots and get back in your car. There's nothing for you here.'

She stood on the spot until she heard the front door to his little cottage slam shut. Disappointment washed through her. Then she spun and marched up the path towards her car, dress swishing.

But as she got to the place where the path forked, her steps faltered.

Go home was not an answer. And she'd come for answers. She owed it to her mother to at least try to find out what had happened. To put this particular demon to rest. She stared at the path. Right led to the street and her beaten-up old car. Left led to the front door of Hayden's secluded cottage.

Where she and her opinions weren't welcome.

Then again, she'd made rather a life speciality out of unpopular opinions. Why stop now?

She turned left.

Hayden marched past his living room, heading for the kitchen and the hot pot of coffee that substituted for alcohol these days. But, as he did so, he caught sight of a pale figure, upright and prim on his lounge-room sofa. Like a ghost from his past.

He backed up three steps and lifted a brow at Shirley through the doorway.

'Come in.'

Her boots were one thing when she was standing, but seated and carefully centred, and with her hands and dress demurely folded over the top of them, they stole focus, big time. Almost as if the more modest she tried to be, the dirtier those boots got. He wrestled with his gaze to prevent it following his filthy mind. This was Carol-Anne's kid.

Though there was nothing kid-like about her now.

'The door was unlocked.'

'Obviously.'

She pressed her hands closer together in her lap. 'And I wasn't finished.'

'Obviously.'

Less was definitely more with this one. The women he was used to being with either didn't understand half of what he said or they were smart enough not to try to keep up. It had been a long time since he'd got as good as he'd given. One part of him hankered for a bit of intellectual sparring. Another part of him wanted to run a mile.

'I think you should finish the list,' she said in a clear, brave voice.

Little faker.

'Start the list, technically.'

'Right.' She seemed nonplussed that he'd made a joke about it. Was she expecting him to go on the attack? Where was the fun in that when he could toy with her longer by staying cool?

Now that he looked at her, he could see the resemblance to Carol under all her make-up. *Mrs Marr* to everyone else, but he'd presumed to call her Carol the first time he'd sat in her class and she'd smiled every time and never corrected him.

It was Shirley's irises that were like her mother's—the palest khaki. He'd have assumed contact lenses if not for the fact that he'd seen them before on a woman too sensible and too smart to be sucked in by the trappings of vanity. Shirley reminded him of one of those Russian dolls-inside-a-doll things. She had large black pupils surrounded by extraordinary grey-green irises, within the clearest white eyeballs he'd ever seen, and the whole thing fringed by smudges of catwalk charcoal around her lashes. Her eyes were set off by ivory skin and the whole picture was framed by a tumble of black locks piled on top. Probably kept in place by some kind of hidden engineering, but it looked effortless enough to make him want to thrust his hands into it and send it tumbling down.

Just to throw her off her game.

Just to see how it felt sliding through his fingers.

Instead, he played the bastard. The last time he'd seen her she'd been standing small and alone at her mother's funeral, all bones and unrealised potential. Now she was... He dropped his gaze to the curve of her neck. It was only slightly less gratuitous than staring at her cleavage.

Another thing he hadn't touched in years. Curves.

'Looks like you've been on good pasture.'

The only sign of that particular missile hitting its target was the barest of flinches in her otherwise steady gaze. She swallowed carefully before speaking and sat up taller, expression composed. 'You really work hard at being unpleasant, don't you?'

A fighter. Good for her.

He shrugged. 'I am unpleasant.'

'Alcohol does that.'

His whole body froze. *A dirty fighter, then.* But his past wasn't all that hard to expose with a few hours and an Internet connection. 'I don't drink any more.'

'Probably just as well. Imagine how unbearable you'd be if you did.'

He fixed his eyes on her wide, clear ones, forcing his mind not to find this verbal swordplay stimulating. 'What do you want, Shirley?'

'I want to ask you about my mother.'

'No, you don't. You want to ask me about the list.'

'Yes.' She stared, serene and composed. The calmness under pressure reminded him a lot of her mother.

'How did you even know it existed?'

Her steady eyes flicked for just a moment. 'I heard you, at the wake. Talking about it.'

He'd not let himself think about that day in a long, long time. 'Why didn't you add your name?'

She shrugged. 'I wasn't invited.' Her eyes dropped. 'And I didn't even know she had a bucket list until that day.'

Did that hurt her? That her mother had shared it with strangers but not her? A long dormant part of him lifted its drowsy head. Empathy. 'You were young. We were her peers.'

She snorted. 'You were her students.'

The old criticism still found a target. Even after all this time. 'You weren't there, Shirley. We were more like friends.' He had hungered for intellectual stimulation he just hadn't found in students his own age and her mother had filled it.

'I was there. You just didn't know it.'

He frowned. 'What do you mean?'

'I used to hide under the stairs when you would all come over for your extra credit Saturdays. Listen in. Learn.'

What? 'You were, what, fourteen?'

'Actually, I was eleven when you first started coming. I was fourteen when you stopped.'

'Most eleven-year-olds don't have a fascination with philosophy.'

She licked her lips, but otherwise her face remained carefully neutral. Except for the tiny flush that spiked high in her cheeks. And he knew she was lying about something.

'Ask me what you really want to know.' *And then go.* His tolerance for company was usually only as long as it took to get laid.

She leaned forward. 'Why didn't you even start the list?'

Oh...so many reasons. None of them good and none of them public. 'How many have *you* done?' he asked instead.

'Six.'

Huh. That was a pretty good rate, given she had been a teenager for the first half of that decade. The old guilt nipped. 'Which ones?'

'Ballooning, horse-riding in the Snowy Mountains, marathon—'

He gave her curves a quick once-over. 'You ran a marathon?' She ignored him. With good reason.

'—abseiling, and climbing the Harbour Bridge.'

The easy end of the list. 'That's only five.'

'Tomorrow I swim with the dolphins.'

Tomorrow. The day after today. Something about the immediacy of that made him nervous. 'Won't you eviscerate if you go in the sun, or something?'

She glared at him. 'I'm pale, I'm not a vampire. Stop hedging. Why haven't you done a single one?'

She was going to keep on asking until he told her. And she wasn't going to like the answer. 'I've been too busy besmirching my soul.'

She frowned. 'Meaning?'

'Making lots of money.'

'That should make it easier to do the things on the list, not harder.'

'Success doesn't make itself. You have to work hard. Put in the hours.' So many hours...

Her lips thinned. 'I'm well aware of that. But this list was your idea. To remind you of the importance of feeding your soul.' His own words sounded pretentious on her dark-red lips. 'To honour my mother's memory.'

The distress she was trying to hide under her anti-tan crept out in the slightest of wobbles.

There it was again. The weird pang of empathy. 'They're meaningless, Shirley. The things. They won't bring her back.'

'They keep her alive. In here.' Pressing her long, elegant fingers to her sternum only highlighted the way her dress struggled to contain her chest. And the way her chest struggled to contain her anger.

'That's important for *you*; you're her daughter—'

'You were her friend.'

His gut screwed down into a hard fist. He pushed to his feet. Forced lightness to his voice. 'What are you, the Ghost of Christmas Past? Life goes on.'

Those eyes that had seemed big outside were enormous in here, under the fluorescent glow of her sorrow. The silence was breached only by the sound of her strained breathing.

'What happened to you, Hayden?' she whispered.

He flinched. 'Nothing.'

'I believed you, back then. When you sat at my mother's funeral looking so torn up and pledged to honour her memory.'

She stared at him. Hard. As if she could see right through him. And for one crazy moment he wished that were true. That someone could drag it all out into the open to air. Instead of festering. But the rotting had started long before he'd begun to go to her house on Saturdays.

He clenched his fists behind his back. 'That makes two of us.'

'It's not too late to start.'

He needed to be moving. 'Oh, I think the time for me to make good on that particular promise is long past,' he said, turning and walking out of the room.

She caught up with him in the kitchen, grabbed his arm and then dropped it just as quickly. Did she feel the same jolt he had?

Her steady words gave nothing away. 'Come to the dolphins with me tomorrow.'

'No.'

She curled the fingers she'd touched him with down by her side. 'Why not? Scared?'

He turned and gave her his most withering stare. 'Please.'

'Then come.'

'Not interested.'

The smile she threw him was tight, but not unattractive. 'I'll drive.'

He glanced down at her boots. 'You're just as likely to get your heel speared in the accelerator and drive us into—'

At the very last moment, his brain caught up with his mouth. She didn't need a reminder of how her mother had died.

Silence weighed heavily.

She finally broke it. 'I'll pick you up at dawn.'

'I won't be here,' he lied. As if he had anywhere else to be.

'I'll come anyway.' She turned for the door.

He shouted after her. 'Shirley—'

'Shiloh.'

'—why are you doing this?'

She paused, but didn't turn back. He had no trouble hearing her, thanks to the hallway's tall ceiling. 'Because it's something I *can* do.'

'She won't know,' he murmured.

Her shoulders rose and fell. Just once.

'No. But I will.' She started down the hall again. 'And so will you.'

CHAPTER TWO

'COME on, Hayden,' Shirley muttered.

She banged the door with the heel of her hand to protect her acrylics. She paused, listened. Stepped back and leaned over to look in the window.

Which bothered her more? The fact that he'd actually left his home before dawn to avoid having to see her again or the fact that she could have turned around a dozen times on the drive over here—maybe should have—but she'd decided not to.

Because she wanted to give him a chance. The old Hayden.

No one could be *that much* of an ass, surely. She stared at the still silent door.

Looked as if he was the real deal.

'Ass!' she yelled out to the empty miles around them, then turned and walked away.

The front door rattled as her foot hit the bottom step on his porch.

'Is that some kind of greeting ritual in your culture?'

By the time she had turned, Hayden was leaning on the door-frame. Shirtless, barefoot. A pair of green track pants hanging low on his hips and bunched at his ankles. Looking for all the world like he wasn't expecting a soul.

One hundred per cent intentional.

He was trying to throw her.

'Good. You're ready,' she breezed, working hard to keep her breathing on the charts and her eyes off his bare chest. She'd spent years as a teenager secretly imagining what her mother's star pupil would look like under all his loose bohemian layers. The sudden answer may not have been what her teenage self would have conceived, but it didn't disappoint. No gratuitous muscle-stacks, just the gently curved contours up top and the long, angular lines down lower that showed he kept himself in good, lean shape.

And he knew it.

She fixed a brave smile on her face and turned to make room for him on the steps. 'Shall we?'

'You don't actually think I'm going like this?' he drawled.

No. She hadn't. But she'd be damned if she'd play his games. She kept her face impassive. 'Depends if you have swimmers on beneath the track pants.'

His grin broadened, dangerously good for this early in the morning. 'Nope. Nothing at all under these.'

Her pulse kicked into gear. But she fought it. 'Well, you'll have to change.'

'Easily offended, Shirley?' He dropped his chin so that he peered up at her across long, dark lashes. It was possibly the sexiest thing she'd ever seen. More theatrics. She took a breath and remembered who she was. And who Shiloh had dealt with and bested in the past.

'The dolphins.' She lifted her chin. 'Wouldn't want them to mistake you for a bait fish.'

An awful tense silence crackled between them and Shirley wondered if she'd gone a step too far. But then he tipped his head far back and laughed.

'Give me five...' he said, still chuckling, and was gone.

She let her breath out slowly and carefully. That could easily have gone the other way. Maybe the last ten years hadn't thoroughly ruined him, then.

Only partly.

When he returned he was more appropriately clothed in a T-shirt, sports cap, board shorts and sockless runners. The covered-up chest was a loss but at least she could concentrate on the road with him fully clothed. The T-shirt sleeves half covered a tattoo on his biceps, but she'd been able to read it briefly as he stretched his arm up the doorframe earlier.

ΜΩΛΩΝ ΛΑΒΕ. Classical Greek.

She turned for the street.

'I'm not getting in that.' His arms crossed and his expression was implacable.

'Why not?'

He eyed her car. 'This looks like the floor might fall out of it if you put a second person in it. We'll take my Porsche.'

Nope. 'Wouldn't be seen dead in it. This is a '59 Karmann Ghia. Your Porsche's ancestor.'

'It's purple.'

'Well spotted. Get in.'

'And it has Shiloh plates.'

'And here I thought your mind was more lint-trap than steel-trap these days.'

He glared at her. 'I'm not driving this.'

She snorted. 'You're not driving at all.'

'Well, you're sure as hell not.'

She swallowed the umbrage. 'Because…?'

'Because *I* drive me.'

'You had a chauffeur.' She'd seen him in enough Internet photos falling out of limos or back into them.

'That's different.'

'You're welcome to ride in the back seat if it will make you feel more at home.' *And if you can dislocate your hips to squeeze in there.*

He glared at the tiny back seat and came to much the same conclusion. 'I don't think so.'

He folded himself into her low passenger seat and turned to stare as she tucked the folds of her voluminous skirt in under the steering wheel.

'Not the most practical choice for swimming, I would have thought,' he challenged.

'It won't be getting wet.'

His eyes narrowed. 'Because we won't or because you have something else?'

She glanced at him, then away. 'I have something else.' A something else she never would have worn in a million years if she'd had more than a few hours' notice that he was coming along. In fact, she would have chosen a totally different box on her mother's list if she'd thought for a moment that Hayden would actually join her. Something that didn't involve taking anything off. She'd only asked him along to shake him out of the unhappy place she'd found him. And to get him started on the list.

But parading around in swimwear in the presence of the man who'd made such a crack about her curves—yet who was apparently fixated by them—was not high on her list of most desirable things.

The thirty-minute drive would have been a whole heap more enjoyable if she'd been able to sing to the music pumping out of the phone docked to her stereo. It did prevent much in the way of conversation—a bonus—though it contributed to Hayden's general surliness—a minus—even after she'd pulled into a coffee drive-through for him. He'd leaned across her to take the coffee from the drive-through window and the brush of his shoulder, the heat of his body and the scent of early-morning man had stayed with her for the rest of the drive. She left her window wound down in the vain hope that the strong salty breeze would blow the distracting masculine fog away.

When they arrived at the beach, Hayden found himself a comfortable spot in the shade to resume napping and she wandered off to change in the public changing rooms.

She peeled off her dark red skirt, top and sandals, stored them carefully in her temporary locker and glanced critically in the mirror at what remained. Black one-piece, sheer wraparound skirt—also black—purple and black striped stockings to her mid thighs.

Swimwear for the undead. If the undead ever went to the beach.

She piled her hair high, smoothed thirty-plus-plus-plus foundation where her neck was suddenly exposed and turned to the mirror.

Pretty good. Nothing she could do about the Boadicean body.

She'd had it since she was sixteen and had learned by necessity to love it, even if it wasn't apparently to the taste of a man more used to size zero. But she still looked like Shiloh. And Shiloh could definitely walk out onto that beach and spend a morning in the water with Hayden Tennant.

Even if Shirley wasn't certain she could.

Today wasn't about how good or otherwise she looked in a swimsuit, and it wasn't even about the man waiting outside the changing rooms. Today was about living another experience that her mother had never had the chance to.

Making good on her promise to her fourteen-year-old self.

She swung away from the mirror and stepped through the door into the light.

'What were you doing, sewing the—' His impatient words dried up when he saw her, his mouth frozen half-open. The fascination in his gaze should have annoyed her, not made her pulse jog.

Not everyone appreciated her fashion sense. She understood that. And she got *that* look a dozen times a day. But somehow on Hayden it rankled extra much.

She walked towards him and retrieved her towel. 'Ready to go?'

'You can't… Can you swim in that?' he muddled.

'I'm not expecting to swim, just wade. The dolphins will come to us.' A blessing, because waist-high water would disguise her worst assets and highlight her best. And the dolphins below the water wouldn't care about her sporting thighs.

It didn't take Hayden long to recover his composure and he followed her down to the water's edge, glancing sideways at her and smiling enigmatically. She kept her chin high the entire way, ready for another crack about her body.

None came.

She smiled at the girl working at the edge of the water and breezed, 'Hi, I'm—'

'I know who you are,' the teenager gushed, ticking off her name on her register. 'I couldn't believe it when I saw who was in today.'

Hayden glanced from her to the young girl and back again. Confused. Small revenge for how off-kilter he'd tried to keep her yesterday.

'I'm looking forward to it.' Shirley smiled. 'What do we do?'

The girl stammered less when she was in official mode and so their instructions were quick. Head right out into the low tide, where a distant volunteer was waiting for them, and then stand still when the dolphins come.

Simple.

But not for Hayden. He stood rooted to the spot as she waded ahead of him into the surf, stockings and all.

She turned and looked back at him, the slight waves buffeting her. 'Coming?'

Or was he going to bail?

His eyes narrowed and he slid his sunglasses down against the glare of the water, then followed her out.

His longer strides meant they reached the volunteer at the same time. The man launched straight into a security drill, although the only emergency they really ever had was if the dolphins got too boisterous and knocked someone down. Then he opened a pouch on his side and retrieved a defrosted treat.

'Bait fish,' he announced as he held it under the surface and shook the morsel.

Shirley glanced sideways at Hayden, who was concentrating in the same direction as the volunteer. Except he had the tiniest of smiles on his lips. Exactly the same size as hers.

Within minutes, they found themselves circled by three curious dolphins.

'They come in every day about this time,' the man told them. 'And in the afternoon too, in summer. Three, sometimes more.'

Shirley held her footing against the repeated close buffeting of the soft warm mammals. Hayden did the same.

'They're well trained,' he commented.

'Not trained. They come in because they want to. We just make sure we're standing in the right spot when they come.'

Hayden's snort could have been a puff of air as one of the

larger males ran up against him. 'It has nothing to do with the fish you were waving around.'

Shirley glanced at him. *Really?* He was going to be like this? When they were here in her mother's name?

'We only use one fish to encourage them over. We don't want them to get habituated,' the man said.

'Yep. That would be awful for your business,' Hayden murmured below his breath.

'They stay because they want to.' The volunteer held his own. 'They find us interesting. This is their routine, not ours. We just bring people here to meet them.'

'Yet you charge for the privilege?'

'Hayden,' she muttered. 'Do you remember why we're here? Can you contain your cynicism for a few minutes, please?'

But the volunteer didn't need her help. He stood taller. 'Twenty-eight dollars of your entry fee goes directly to cetacean research. The other two dollars helps pay our wildlife licences and fees. All our staffing is volunteer-based.'

'What would stop me from walking up the beach this time tomorrow and waving my own fish?'

Shirley pressed her lips together.

'Nothing at all,' the man confessed. 'Except that here you'll learn a whole heap more about these amazing creatures than just how much they like fish.'

Hayden stood straighter and considered that.

Heh. *Volunteer: one... Bitter, twisted cynic: nil.*

'What sort of things?' she asked, moving the man on and giving him her best Shiloh.

Amazing things, was the answer.

He plied them with stories of dolphin intelligence and resilience and sentience and even unexplainable, extra-sensory experiences, and all the while the dolphins wove in between them, trying to trip them up, playing with each other.

'My colleague, Jennifer, had worked here four years and then one day Rhoomba, the big male—' he pointed at one of the dolphins '—started to nudge her mid-section. Every day he'd shove his snout just under her ribs and stare there intently. He got quite obsessed. One of the old fishermen who knows these waters told her to go for tests. They found a tumour behind her liver. She was away from the beach for over a year with the surgery and her chemo but on her first time back Rhoomba nudged her once, just to check, and then never did it again.'

Hayden lifted just one eyebrow over the rim of his sunglasses. Shirley hurried to fill the silence before he said something unpleasant.

'How is she now?'

'Good as gold. No further problems.'

They spent fifteen minutes out in the water, even after the dolphins swam off to re-join their pod. Volunteer talking, Shirley questioning, Hayden glowering. But the chill coming off the water finally got their attention.

'Make sure you give us a good rap, Shiloh,' the volunteer said, winding up.

'No question,' she assured. 'It was amazing, thank you so much.'

He turned for shore. So did Hayden.

He had taken a few steps before he realised she wasn't following. 'Shirley?'

'I'll be a sec.' She let the onshore breeze carry her words back to him and she stared out into the sea where the dolphins now swam deep. The rhythmic slosh of the waves against her middle was hypnotic. Hairs blew loose from the pile atop her head and flew around her face.

'Another one done, Mum,' she murmured to the vast nothingness of the sea after a moment. 'I would have preferred to do this with you, instead of—' She cut herself off. 'But it's a start, hey?'

There was no response save the beautiful language of air rushing across water. It was answer enough.

Then right behind her, a voice spoke, cold and curious. And male.

'Why exactly are you so determined to make me start this list?'

* * *

I would have preferred to do this with you, instead of—

Him.

If there was any doubt in his mind as to what she meant, it evaporated the moment Shirley spun her horrified face to his. It was more ashen than usual.

'I thought you'd gone in.' Flummoxed. Discomposed. The only sign he'd had of the real person beneath the make-up since the barest eyelid flinch yesterday.

'I bet you did.'

But she didn't answer his question. She just started pushing towards shore, hurrying ahead of him. He gave her a few moments, mostly enjoying the view as the sea floor rose to become the shore and first revealed the curve of her sodden wraparound skirt and then those ridiculous stockings. Except they weren't entirely ridiculous; they were also one part intriguing. The way they clung just above her knee. It made the narrow strip of skin above the stocking but below the wrap into something really tantalising. Even though there was much more gratuitous flesh on show higher up.

This was forbidden.

This was private.

And, from the back, it was insanely hot, because even *she* didn't get to see that angle.

He took his time following her as his cells blazed.

Onshore, she retrieved her towel and turned back to him, clutching it to her body. It did a reasonable job of helping him focus.

Down the sand, the teenage girl who'd gushed earlier called out, 'Bye, Shiloh!', as if they were now best friends. Shirley threw her a dazzling smile in return and waved, making her day.

Gracious.

He should have expected that of a Marr.

The brilliant smile looked out of place with lips coloured like black blood, but he realised that somewhere between yesterday and today he'd forgotten his first impression of her, standing over him with those forever boots, and she'd just become Shirley. Quirky and courageous and fast with a comeback.

She spun back to him and the dazzling smile died.

'Was she that easy to forget, Hayden?' Hurt blazed in her pale eyes. 'Or was it just some kind of dramatic, absinthe-fuelled gesture for an audience? And you expected everyone else to do the hard yards?'

He *had* pledged. He *had* vowed.

Then he had done nothing. Not one thing.

But he wasn't about to cop to it. 'Why are you so concerned about what I do? How do my choices mean anything at all to you?'

'Because she gave you her life. She gave you all her days teaching and her nights assessing your work and her Saturday afternoons giving her star pupils extra credit.'

'Instead of being with you? Is that what you mean?'

She shook her head. But she also flushed. 'She gave you everything, Hayden. But when she died you just...shrugged and moved on?'

He hadn't worked at the top of his field without learning a thing or two about subtext. This wasn't really about him... He just wasn't sure yet exactly what it was about.

'Every square next to your name is empty. Others have made progress, or at least a start. They've made an effort.'

She was going to ride the denial train right to the end of the line.

'Shouldn't you have let it go by now?' he asked.

She blew air out from between dark lips. 'Yes, I should have.'

The moment of honesty took them both by surprise. She frowned. 'If you told me that you'd been busy building orphanages in Cambodia for the last decade I think I could accept that. But you haven't. You have no excuse.'

He swallowed back what he really wanted to say. 'I don't need an excuse, Shirley. I'm not answerable to you.'

She clutched the towel closer to her pale skin. Her eyes flicked away and back again. 'I just thought you might...'

She didn't want him to do it because she'd make him feel guilty. She wanted him to do it because he was an all-round great guy deep inside. Secretly. 'Hate to disappoint you further, Shirley.'

Her shoulders rose and fell just once as she filled her lungs and moderated her exhalation. Just like her mother used to do before starting a tutorial. Her piled-up hair swung around her face in surf-dampened strands like Medusa's serpentine locks. 'At least take your name off the list. If you're not going to do any.'

So that the world didn't have to look at his disinterest? 'Why don't you add yours? To balance out my lousy effort. Show everyone how it should be done.'

'Maybe I will.' She turned to go, disappointment at his sarcasm patent in the drop of her shoulders.

Honey, I've done a lot worse in my life than let down someone who's been dead for a decade. Your silent judgement can just get in line.

Then she spun back around. 'Molon Labe.'

That threw him. 'What?'

'Your business name. Your tattoo. Why Molon Labe?'

He shrugged. 'Military defiance. When the outnumbered Spartans were called to surrender arms they said Molon labe—"Come and take them".'

'I know. I saw the movie. But *why* that phrase?'

His entire body tightened. 'Because I have a thing for the Spartans. Their courage.' Their defiance in the face of death.

'You don't find the irony exquisite?'

The breath thickened in his lungs. 'What irony?'

'You named your business after it. You branded your body with the Greek letters. Yet, in life, you laid down arms at the first hurdle. You dropped totally off the radar.'

She turned and walked towards the changing rooms. Away from him. Away from the disappointment. Away from the crater her verbal detonation had caused.

He forced his lungs to suck in air and his fingers to open and close again. Forced himself to remember she had absolutely no idea what she was dismissing.

How could she?

But he had enough fight left in him not to let that go unchallenged.

'Shirley,' he called.

She stopped. She turned. She looked ridiculously natural standing there, dripping wet and defiant. But also so very young.

'I understand deflection better than most,' he said without raising his voice across the space between them. Knowing she heard him. 'Attacking me takes the focus off you. But given there's only the two of us here and you clearly don't give a rat's what I think or feel—'

Her extraordinary eyes flickered.

'—you might want to ask yourself what you're trying to take the focus off. And for whose benefit.'

'Cos it sure as hell wasn't his.

Her gaze widened and then dropped to the sand. He turned away from her to climb the dunes up to the road, to find his own way home. He wasn't stupid. No way she was letting him back in her car. No way he'd get in there, even if she did.

Today had been a huge error on his part.

He'd been stupid to think that he could make good on any of his past failings. That just didn't happen.

And something else he knew.

Her stupid purple and black stockings pressing through the beach sand... That was the last of Carol-Anne Marr's crazy, high maintenance daughter that he'd be seeing.

CHAPTER THREE

'You went to Antarctica.'

Not *Hello?* Not *Is Shirley there?* Not *Sorry I was such an exceptional ass.* Shirley took a long slow breath and released it away from the mouthpiece of the phone.

'Hello, Hayden.' She'd know that deep, disparaging voice anywhere.

Instantly.

She'd flown back in yesterday evening and initialled the website just before collapsing exhausted into bed.

Commune with penguins.

Tick.

'That was a big one,' he opened.

'Certainly was,' she closed.

He didn't miss the frost in her tone. 'Listen, about the other day—'

Three months ago.

'—I'd like to apologise.'

Too late. She leaned back in her writing chair. 'No need. I had no right to judge you.'

A long pause from him. Was he trying to decide if she was genuine? 'I could have been more…diplomatic that day. I'm sorry if it hurt you.'

It had hurt but not because he'd slapped her down. Dredging it all up again had hurt. Sifting through her reasons had been hard.

She shrugged. 'The truth does sometimes hurt.'

A long, empty pause. Then, 'I climbed the bridge.'

Shirley's hand froze on the phone. The Sydney Harbour Bridge was on the list. The tiniest of flames puffed into existence deep inside her.

He'd started the list.

'I was there for a stockholder meeting. Thought I might as well.' The flame snuffed out again. Did he add that especially so she'd know how little effort he'd made?

'You didn't tick it off.'

'No, I…' Another pause. But she could hear his breathing. He cleared his throat. 'I thought I'd get a few under my belt before updating the site.'

A few? Did that mean he was going to honour his promise? But she wasn't ready to trust him yet. 'What are you going to do, work your way down the list?'

'The top is as good a place to start as any.'

Sorrow welled up inside, from somewhere deep and dark. 'Well, that should take you about a fortnight, then.'

This time the pause was laden with confusion. His. That was fair enough; she herself barely understood the bitterness creeping through her voice. 'I thought that we could team up for a few of them,' he persevered. 'Two birds, one stone kind of thing.'

Because this was such a massive inconvenience? 'The list is not really a team sport…'

'I enjoyed the dolphins.' A single strand of pleasure twisted through the darkness at his admission. 'The experience I would have had on my own was different to the one I had with you there.'

That was certainly true. 'You would have ended up in a fist-fight with the volunteer.'

'He was smug. And showing off for your benefit.'

'He was passionate. And proud of the work they do. You belittled him.'

'I tested him. Big difference.'

Why did that surprise her? He'd always been interested in breaking people down to see what made them tick. 'Not to the person on the receiving end.'

That shut him up. For almost half a minute.

'So, is that a no to partnering up? I already have reservations.'

She hated doing this by phone. It was all too easy to imagine vulnerability in his tone. If she was looking him in the eye he'd never get away with that. But his tone changed hers. She sighed. 'Tickets to what?'

'The symphony.'

'The Australian Symphony doesn't have Beethoven on their line-up for this year.' She'd already checked.

'Not the ASO. The Berlin Philharmonic. They're in town for a limited season. Three concerts.'

'Those tickets were expensive.' She'd checked that, too.

'So?'

'So throwing money at it is a fast way to get the list out of the way.' And off your conscience.

'Really? I suppose you walked to Antarctica, then?'

'No. I took a work opportunity. There was a media call to promote the hundredth anniversary of the end of Scott's expedition and I qualified. The only thing I paid for was my thermals.'

'Nice junket,' he snorted.

'Sure. If you don't count all the freezing-your-butt-off and hauling yourself up rope nets on and off an ice-breaker.' That had nearly killed her. Although it had helped her get fit preparing for it.

'So how were you planning on getting to Everest without money?'

She tossed back her hair. Maybe it would translate in her voice. 'I don't know. Work on a cruise ship to earn passage. Then make my way to Kathmandu by bike.'

She was nothing if not an idealist.

'It would take a lifetime to do the list that way.'

She stared at the wall. Suddenly something important clicked into place for her. Something she'd been missing.

'"*Full effort is full victory*",' she murmured. Satisfaction lay in the effort, not the attainment. Gandhi knew it. It was just a pity Hayden—the student of human nature—had forgotten what that felt like.

'What?'

She refocused. 'The list was supposed to be about honouring my mother's memory. Buying your way down the list does the opposite.' Almost worse than doing nothing at all.

His pause grew dangerous. 'So, now you *don't* want me doing the list?'

I want you to care. And she had no idea why that was so important to her. 'Not if it means you put in the minimal amount of effort or outsource it to someone to make you up an itinerary.'

Silence descended as he considered that.

'What if I didn't pay for the tickets?'

She blinked. 'Then I assume you'll be arraigned for theft when the curtain rises.'

'Ha ha. I meant that I contra'd them. Does that change how you feel?'

Did it? Last week, if someone had given her a month off work and a cashed-up credit card she would have zoomed through the list knocking things off, too. But she felt sure that there'd be no sense of achievement. Not like the year of preparation for the marathon, or learning to horse-ride well enough to tackle the Snowy Mountains, or working for months on the Antarctica proposal and her ice fitness.

Could she even enjoy the victory if it came so easily?

'Using your influence is like using your money—'

'It wasn't influence. I bartered a friend for the tickets. Good old fashioned labour.'

Labour? Those hands? 'What for?'

'I give you my word it's nothing that wouldn't honour the intent of Carol's list.'

She turned it over in her mind. And over. And then looked under it and really tried very hard to find something reasonable to object to. But her curiosity was piqued, too. What exactly did one trade for tickets to a performance that exclusive?

'Front row?' Okay, now she was just picking a fight.

'Centre.'

'When?' Did he just assume she'd be available?

'Tuesday night.'

Damn. She was.

Somehow it being an evening thing made it feel more like a date than a business arrangement. Which was ridiculous. Two birds, one stone, he'd said. The deal was made. The tickets arranged. Why shouldn't she benefit from whatever hard manual labour he was going to have to undertake to pay them off?

She sighed. 'Okay. I'll see you then.'

'Really?'

Lucky he couldn't see her, because she completely failed to hide the tiny smile that broke at the surprise in his voice. *Too cool for school* was kind of his thing back when she used to watch him from the stairs. It was nice to know that someone who had been that jaded at nineteen was still capable of surprise at thirty.

'Really.'

'Great.' *Awkward.* 'See you Tuesday, then.'

Her chest squeezed tighter at his parting words. But nineteen year old Hayden would never have been a good choice for her and she suspected thirty year old Hayden was even less so.

Lucky this wasn't a date, then.

'Is that a cape?'

Hayden stepped around her in the concert-hall foyer to check out the back of the indigo cloak that Shirley had put on over her simple black dress. The shoulders formed a reverse V that left her décolletage bare and met at an ornate black clasp that closed like fingers around her throat.

'Cape*let,* according to the label,' she informed him.

Whatever it was, it did amazing things to her eyes. And the dress for the rest of her, too.

'You're early,' she announced.

'I wanted to pick up the tickets. You're earlier.'

'I wanted to people-watch.'

At least *Shiloh* did.

He should have twigged when she'd first told him her new name, except that he'd been out of action for so long his connection to the living world had dwindled to what he read in the newspaper and saw on television the few times he turned the thing on.

The fawning of the girl on the beach that day was his biggest clue. That had sent him hunting on the Internet and it took no time at all to realise that *his* Shiloh was *that* Shiloh.

The people's princess.

Blogger extraordinaire.

Queen of snark and acute social awareness.

Possessor of a two-million-plus social network and a list of subscribers that contained every major news journalist, politician's aide and celebrity in the country. No one wanted to be the one *not* following Shiloh's eloquent posts, even if they didn't always like them. Or understand them.

He found the dolphin story—beautifully researched and filled with example after example of people whose lives had been changed following an encounter with a cetacean. Hundreds more in the reader comments. The dolphin that sensed the tumour. Or a pregnancy. A whale that monstered a swarm of sharks away from a flipped catamaran long enough for its passengers to scramble onto the upturned hull. Even a shy manatee that nudged an unconscious boy repeatedly to the surface until help arrived. She'd given the many people who volunteered with wildlife a nod through the voice of that man they'd stood with in the shallows. Yet she'd taken care not to identify the beach location or the animals, protecting them, too.

She knew her boundaries. And her power.

So he'd followed her blogs these past weeks to get a feel for the woman he'd only ever known as a child. She didn't disappoint. Astute. Acerbic. Fearless.

'The symphony's not really the sort of place you'd expect to encounter intriguing story leads.'

'You might be surprised at what people will talk about under cover of a crowd.'

She didn't even blink that he knew who she was. She tossed her hair and a waft of amberwood hit him, provocative and sensual. His breath thinned.

'Are you a regular at the Concert Hall?'

Not really the place he'd bring most of the women he'd dated. 'I've been a few times, but I usually sit up the back.' Right up the back, in the control box with Luc, generally. 'This will be my first front row.'

Her carefully shaped brows folded.

He stepped closer as someone squeezed past them, then looked down on her. 'That surprises you?'

She did her best to step back. 'You don't really strike me as an up the back kind of guy. I thought you'd want to be seen.'

'But you don't know me at all.' Despite what she thought. 'Come on, this way…'

He set off in the direction of the bar, not waiting for her to follow. Ordinarily he'd have found some way by now to touch a woman he'd invited on a date, multiple times if possible while shepherding her through the assembling crowd. But not only was this very much *not* ordinary, and *not* a date and *not* leading to anything further after the instruments were all back in their cases, but he thought Shirley might bite his hand off if he touched her. And he knew for sure she'd object to being corralled like some fragile thing.

She was anything but.

They passed the handful of patrons who'd turned up earlier than they had and crossed to the back area of the bar that served the exclusive members' lounge, past the shelves of expensive drinks. All his old friends lifted their hands in salute, trying to catch his eye. Johnny. Jack. Remy. MacCallan.

He pressed on past them all.

'Luc?'

It took a moment before anyone responded, but then his oldest friend appeared from a pair of doors behind the bar, carrying a sheaf of papers. He clapped forearms with Hayden and did a credible job of not looking at Shirley for more than the time it took to smile politely. Though he knew he'd get hammered for details later.

'Mate, good to see you,' Luc said.

'Is it all arranged?' Hayden asked. Keeping things businesslike.

'Good to go.' Luc reached into his pocket and produced two tickets. He held them aloft. 'These weren't easy to come by. There'll be no reneging?'

Please... 'When have you ever known me not to be as good as my word?'

'I've never asked something like this of you, though.'

Shirley *and* Shiloh both grew interested in that.

He handed over the tickets and Hayden pumped his hand. 'Cheers, mate. I owe you one.'

Luc laughed. 'You know what you owe me.' Then he disappeared back into the bowels of the Concert Hall. Hayden could feel Shirley's gaze branding the back of his head, so he took his time turning around. When he did, her immaculately made-up eyes were narrowed.

'What did you trade?'

He let a cautious nothing wash over his face. 'Oh, just a favour for a mutual friend.'

'What kind of favour? If I'm going to be party to a fraud, I'd like to know exactly what I'm buying into.'

'You're not buying into anything. This was my trade.'

'What was?' Her hands balled on her hips. 'I'm not moving until you tell me the truth.'

Air hissed from between his drawn lips. 'I'm helping out with a party Luc's sister is throwing in a few weeks.'

Her eyes narrowed. 'You mean you're paying for it?'

'No. I told you this wasn't a financial transaction.'

'I didn't realise event coordination was your bag.'

'I'm not organising it, either.'

'Catering?'

He glared at her.

'Not the alcohol, I hope?'

The glare intensified. 'It's not that kind of party. It's for Luc's nephew. He's...' *God damn her snooping.* 'He's nine.'

She blinked at him. A child's party...? Then the tiniest of smiles crept onto her lips. 'Please tell me you're dressing as a clown.'

He threw his arms up and walked across the room from her.

'Do you seriously think that a garden-variety clown would be the best I can do?'

'No, I expect you'd be a miserable, creepy clown.'

He paused, uncertain whether he'd just been insulted. 'Right. Exactly. Thankfully, Tim's not into clowns.'

'What is he into? And why are you trying so very hard not to say?'

He huffed a long breath. 'Warriors.'

Those expressive brows folded again. 'Soldiers?'

He guided her from the bar again without touching her. 'Old school. Swords and shields type of warriors.'

Out of the corner of his vision he saw her press her lips together to stymie the smile he was sure was wanting to burst forth. 'A boy after your own heart, then?'

'That's what Luc said.'

She walked beside him. 'Okay, so for the princely sum of one child's birthday party we now have front row access to the Berlin Philharmonic?'

He shrugged. 'That should give you an idea of how not a big deal this trade is for Luc.'

Her eyes narrowed. 'Or how very big a deal a kid's birthday party is for you.'

He grunted and pushed through the doors back into the foyer, holding it open for her. The noise from the mounting audience surged and washed over them.

'Are you coming or staying?'

It wasn't too late to scalp the tickets out front for a profit.

She let the smile loose, finally. Smug and a little bit too appealing. 'And forgo the chance to make you have to get your Spartacus on?' She pushed past him and spoke into the crowd. 'Not on your life.'

Shirley shuffled in her seat as the applause for the conductor finally died down. She had no idea who he was but every other person there clearly did, judging by the adulation. The white-haired man turned his back on the audience and sorted his music in the descended hush. The perfect acoustics of the venue meant that everyone heard it. Even the shuffling of music sheets sounded good.

Of course, her mother would have chided. *Beethoven wrote it.*

It was hard, as it always was, not to regret her mother's absence. How she would have appreciated this special moment. Then again, if she'd been alive, would any of them have thought of doing it? She'd barely gone to the movies in all of Shirley's childhood, let alone anywhere this special.

That was the awful irony about bucket lists.

'Ready?' Hayden leaned in and whispered. His shoulder brushed hers and the heat pumping off him surged.

The final murmurs from the rows of seating behind and above them stopped and, though nothing in particular was said, the orchestra locked their eyes on the white-haired man in front of them the moment he raised both arms and held them there.

Shirley's breath held, too.

And then they came... The first distinctive notes of Beethoven's Fifth symphony.

Da da da dum...

Da da da dummmmm.

This close, the music was virtually a physical impact. Its volume. Its presence. The hairs curling around her face blew and tickled in the breeze generated only by the synchronised speed of the string section as they commenced their furious playing.

She still hadn't breathed.

Hayden glanced sideways at her as the galloping, excitable violins grew in pitch and strength and she sat up straighter. It wasn't until the trombone had its momentary solo that she heaved in her first breath.

And still he looked.

Amazing, this close, this live. The passion of the performers poured off the stage and washed over her. The drama of the conductor's jerky directions, the rolling synergy of their notes.

Her eyes fell shut.

The music fluttered against her face as it entered the gentle, lyrical interlude which grew and grew.

This was what Beethoven must have experienced when he could no longer hear his music.

And then it came… The discordant counterpoint.

Her eyes opened and she glanced to her right. Hayden was still looking at her. She took a deep breath and returned her full attention to the hammering orchestra. Minutes passed, planets orbited, the poles melted. The music softened for a momentary reprieve. The poignant, forlorn aria of a lone oboe—she wondered how she'd never noticed it before when her mother cranked up her *Best of Beethoven*.

And then the tumbling notes, the controlled descent before returning to the power of the full orchestra for the climax which ended so very like it had begun. Her chest heaved, her heart beat in synch with the strokes of the musical genius. Her body flinched with the explosive closing notes, and she pressed her lips together to stop from crying out.

And then…nothing.

Silence.

The conductor lowered his baton. The orchestra breathed out as one—long, slow and silent.

Shirley turned, breathless, to Hayden. She couldn't clap because no one else was. She couldn't leap up and shout for more, though it seemed ludicrous that music like that wasn't supposed to be celebrated loudly. She could only look at him and hope that her excitement and appreciation were written in her eyes. Her fingers curled around his, hard, as though she could press her thoughts straight through his skin.

His return gaze was complex. Curious. As though she were an alien species he'd just discovered under a rock. But mostly laden with an unexpected quality.

Envy.

Someone behind them coughed. Someone else murmured as the orchestra quietly turned to the next piece. To them this was just another performance. Seven minutes of top-shelf proficiency.

To Shirley it was one of the most extraordinary things she'd ever done.

The audience murmuring grew loud enough that she risked a whisper. But while she might have been able to coordinate her lungs to push air through her voice box, she couldn't quite make the sounds into a meaningful sentence.

'Hayden…' she got out.

He seemed to understand, but his eyes glanced to the stage and then back at her as the conductor called his performers to order with a dramatic flourish and a man she hadn't been aware of stood and walked to a piano she'd barely noticed.

And then it happened…

The first sombre note of the Moonlight Sonata. It wasn't called that on the programme so she was taken unaware. Her eyes were still locked on Hayden's when recognition hit. The music that had played when they'd carried her mother's coffin out of the chapel. The emotional elation of just moments before plunged dramatically as the first haunting notes filled every crevice in the concert hall. She gasped.

Sorrow held her rigid and all she could do was hold Hayden's eyes, his fingers, as the warmth leached slowly from her face.

That horrible, horrible day.

His eyes darkened and his fingers curled around hers in support. She might have cried alone at her mother's funeral ten years ago but this time Hayden Tennant was here with her. Holding on to her. The only other person in the room who knew what this music meant.

Her chest heaves increased as she fought back the tears she could feel forming.

In vain…

Her eyes welled as the beautiful music unfolded in isolation of every other instrument on the stage. The rich, saturated tones of the expensive piano formed a thick private blanket of sound to hide her grief beneath. From everyone but Hayden; he had an unexpected stage-side seat to her pain.

She let her lashes drop to block even him out.

From the sublime to the tragic in the space of two beats of silence. He'd been captivated by Shirley's ecstasy in the face of the music. It had been so long since he'd felt anything, he was quite prepared to feed off her evident joy—her total absorption—like some kind of visceral vampire. He'd been able to stare at her for seven whole minutes unmolested as she reached some place high above the real world.

Buffeted and carried by the music.

Her eyes, when the first famous piece came to a powerful crescendo and she'd gifted him with her focus, had looked as they might in the throes of passion.

Bright, exhilarated, fevered.

And for one breathless heartbeat he'd imagined putting those expressions there, of inciting this strong, unique woman to cast aside the veneer of control that she always wore.

Possession had surged through him, powerful and unfamiliar.

But now those same eyes were off-limits to him, a fat tear squeezing out from under her long dark lashes and rolling down blanched skin. He knew what this music meant and he remembered how Shirley had looked—so small and bereft—the last time he'd heard it.

Her fingers tightened in his as if, by letting go, he'd be casting her adrift on a sea of remembered misery. He curled his other hand over the top and shifted forward so that she might feel his support.

The music turned more melodic, less mournful, and her lids fluttered open to reveal watery, sad eyes, a thousand miles from where they were, lost somewhere in memory. They looked right at him but he knew she wasn't seeing him at all. She was seeing through him.

Exactly as he feared she might if she looked too closely.

That was why she'd never get this close again. After today.

Today she was just a fourteen-year-old girl who needed her mother, and the harder she fought the expression of her feelings, the more he wanted to hold her as she bled her grief out onto the Concert Hall's plush carpet.

He shuffled his arm around behind her and pulled her gently to his shoulder.

The fact she came so very willingly told him a lot about how she was feeling.

They passed the whole piece like that, him curled protectively around her, giving her the privacy she needed, his eyes pressed closed against the evocative music. And against the warmth of the woman in his arms. He felt a few glances from the people around them but he didn't care.

He pressed his lips to her hairline and left them there.

The final notes lingered, eddied around them and then rippled out through the venue and were gone. The audience was completely silent, the hard thrum of blood past his ears the only sound in the place.

The conductor lowered his baton and turned, the pianist stood and bowed, and the audience responded to his cue by bursting into loud fevered applause.

'Shirley...' Hayden said over the din.

Her arm curled around his neck and held him close, her shudder half-swallowed. He gave her a moment, lent her shelter, lent her his strength.

Surprised to discover he had any left at all these days.

But eventually one of them had to move. He cleared his throat. 'Shirley...'

This time she withdrew—in body and in spirit—snaking her arms back into herself and pushing back in her seat. A furious flush stained her pale skin.

'Are you okay—?'

She pushed to her feet, swiping at her eyes. Enough of the audience were on their feet to celebrate the brilliant piano interpretation that their departure wasn't too shocking.

All anyone saw was an overwhelmed woman. They would have no idea what this evening meant to her.

'Are you okay?' he repeated the moment they were in the comparative silence of the empty foyer. A new piece began in the auditorium behind them.

'I'm fine.' She swiped at her eyes with a napkin she'd snatched from a foyer table and kept her eyes off his. 'I just...' She took a deep breath. 'I wasn't ready for it.'

'It's okay to miss her, Shirley.'

Her laugh was harsh. 'It's been ten years. You'd think I'd have a handle on it by now.'

What could he say? 'Would that we could all be loved that much.'

She shuddered in a deep breath and appeared to revive before his eyes. 'Thank you.'

'What for?'

'For arranging this. For her.' She smiled, watery but strengthening, and he realised for the first time how very many smiles she had. And how differently he felt about each one of them.

'I didn't do it for her, Shirley. Or for me.' Her delicate brows flickered. 'I wanted you to have this.'

Not that he had a clue why. It wasn't going to get him anything in return. Nothing she'd give him in a million years, anyway.

Her expression turned awkward. 'You don't think I'd have made it to the symphony unassisted?

'You would have been halfway up the back. You would have heard the music but not…' His fingers grasped for the words he couldn't find.

She lifted her eyes. 'Lived it?'

'Breathed it. She was a wise woman, your mother.'

Shirley sagged. 'I wish I'd known her as an adult, the way you did. To me, she was just my mum. She nagged me about homework and told me to clean my room and what not to wear in public.'

'You took that last one to heart, I see…'

She threw him her fakest smile and he laughed. It felt odd to have run the full gamut of emotions with her in just a quarter of an hour. Exhilaration, devastation and now humour. An intimacy trifecta.

'I would love to have just one adult conversation with her,' she murmured.

He plunged his hands into his pockets to stop himself from touching her. From stroking the sadness from that flawless brow. 'I think she would have been proud of what you do,' he said. 'Of the way you speak for some parts of the community and challenge others. Of how fearless you are. How provocative.'

She shrugged. 'That's Shiloh.'

He stared at her. 'I'd like to meet Shirley some day.'

Shirley lifted her gaze to Hayden's. 'I don't think she'd be a match for your sarcasm.'

The tic of his eye was almost a wince. 'But Shiloh is?'

She lifted her chin. 'Shiloh most definitely is.'

They stared each other down as music thumped, muted, from behind them. Two equals, perfectly matched.

'So the next one is yours,' Hayden finally said.

'Excuse me?'

'Our next adventure. Your choice. Your challenge. See if you can top this.'

'I didn't realise we were taking turns.' Or doing it again.

'Seems equitable,' he said. 'You're all for equity, I know.'

'You picked a pretty easy one.'

'How about you dress up in a loincloth and brave a house full of nine year olds, then tell me how easy this one was.'

She stared at him. Thinking. 'All right.'

'All right, what?'

'All right, I'll be your warrior sidekick. For the party. Since I enjoyed half of the reward today, it seems only fair that I should pay half the price.'

'You want to come to the kids' party with me?'

Yes. Inexplicably. Maybe it had something to do with seeing how he was with children? You could tell a lot about a man from how he interacted with animals and kids. Maybe she was just looking for the kiss of death to her lingering question marks about Hayden Tennant. To put them to the spear once and for all.

'I'm willing to do my part. In the interests of equity,' she said.

'You'll have to dress up. Or down in this case.'

'Not a problem.'

'You're serious?'

'Completely. Just tell me who you're going as and I'll match you.'

'You even have to ask?'

'Leonidas.' Of course; the Spartan king who'd first uttered those defiant words. *Come and take them.*

She could well imagine Hayden leading a dwindling army into certain death with defiance on their faces and blood-mingled sweat in their eyes. Barefoot, wild, determined.

Half-naked.

She shifted her eyes away from him as warmth suffused her. Perhaps the party wouldn't be entirely without reward, then. And just like that, she'd decided. Even though saying yes to this was a de facto agreement to undertake more of the list with him.

Her breath thinned. 'When is it?'

'Two weeks Saturday. I'll text you the address.'

She flicked her hair back over her shoulder. 'Great. In the meantime I'll get to work on our next tick off the list.'

How subtly *my* had become *our.* Had she made the mental shift when she'd agreed to come to the symphony with him? Or he'd agreed to go to the dolphins with her? Or was it implicit in the moment she'd curled her fingers so tightly in his during the Moonlight Sonata and she'd not objected when he'd pressed his lips to her forehead?

Maybe he'd branded them *they* with that one gentle action?

Certainly he'd branded her. She could still feel the place his mouth had lingered.

Shirley snorted inwardly. Or was she just a whole lot easier and a whole lot more female than she'd believed? One promise of a bit of gratuitous flesh on show and she totally caved in.

But some concessions were more tingly than others, it seemed. She took a deep breath. Finishing the list was now a combined effort. She had a point to prove about the real meaning of her mother's unfulfilled wish list and she suspected he had his own agenda, his own dark reasons for wanting to prove her wrong.

Yet, somehow, tackling the list with someone else—even if it was a someone else with a vested interest in not succeeding—made it seem less lonely, more achievable. More rewarding.

Even if it was also entirely foolish.

'Okay, see you two weeks Saturday, then.'

He glanced at the large auditorium doors. 'You don't want to go back in?'

Did she? They could walk back in after the first intermission. But how could she top either of those pieces for sheer impact? She looked around for an usher, caught his eye and called him over.

'Hi—' she smiled, one hundred per cent Shiloh '—I've got a sudden migraine and we were front row centre. I'm wondering if you could fill the seats for us? So that the Symphony aren't staring at a hole in their front row?'

The young man smiled. 'Yes, thank you for letting us know.' He started to move away.

'Actually, do me a favour. Could you find someone way up the back—someone who would die for those seats—and give them to them?'

The man's entire body language changed. 'That's awesome. Yes, I can. I have just the couple in mind. Thank you.'

'You're welcome.' He departed and Shirley turned. Hayden's expression was a mixture of bemusement, curiosity and something else. Something she couldn't quite define. 'What?'

'That was nice.'

'I'm frequently nice; don't look so surprised.'

'No, I mean that was *nice*. I wouldn't have thought to tell them, let alone offer them to someone who was missing out.'

She studied him for a moment. 'I think that says more about you than me, don't you?'

He thought about that. 'Maybe.'

'So... You'll text me?'

'I will.'

'Okay. See you then.' She crossed to the lifts.

'Who will you be coming as?' he called after her. Almost as if he were forestalling her departure.

'I'll let that be a surprise.'

'I hate surprises.'

She turned her head back over her shoulder and gave him

a blast of Shiloh. 'A bit of delayed gratification might be good for you.'

And then she walked out. And left him and his gorgeous suit standing in the foyer all alone.

CHAPTER FOUR

IF HAYDEN'S mouth gaped any further, one of these rampant nine-year-olds was just as likely to mistake it for a bouncy castle and run into it.

'Leonidas—' Shirley bowed '—Boudicca, Warrior Queen of the Iceni.'

She didn't have to worry about how low she bowed; the suspension in the get-up that Andreas had helped her with would have kept Dolly Parton fully immobile. The bodice was more strapping than bra, swathes of earthy fabric wrapped tight around her torso in the manner of the Celts and then flying back over her shoulder to form a cape.

'How did you even get into that thing?' he breathed.

'Andreas helped me.'

'Andreas?'

'My neighbour.'

He quirked an eyebrow, not that she could be certain under his ornate beaten-copper face-shield, which left only his eyes and lips visible, but it tipped slightly and his tone left her in no doubt that it would be lifted beneath the tin.

'Your gay male neighbour?'

Seriously, Hayden? 'My straight seventy-year-old, ex-opera-wardrobe-master-who's-great-with-a-toga neighbour.' The relief on his face was comical. And confusing. 'What does it matter who helped me dress?' she quizzed.

His eyes grew vague. '*Un*dress. Do you think that's appropriate to wear around young boys?'

She glanced down to make sure everything was still where she'd put it. With her long flowing skirts, the only part of her bare was a strip of midriff and her arms and shoulders, which Andreas had carefully decorated with eyeliner tribal tattoos. And her feet, which surely could not offend anyone.

Her laugh was ninety per cent outrage. 'That's rich coming from a man in a miniskirt.'

A thoroughly hot and distracting miniskirt and not a lot else. Leather thong sandals and wrought-copper leg guards protecting his shins—possibly handy if things turned ugly with the nine-year-olds—and some kind of metallic breastplate that accentuated the breadth of his shoulders. Spear with a cork stuck on the dangerous end. Battered shield. And the battle-mask which supported the mother of all mohawks above his head.

That was about it.

Nothing more gratuitous than she'd seen in the water three months ago but somehow infinitely hotter in the suburbs.

What was it about a man in a skirt?

'What did you do to your hair?' he accused.

Had holding that long blunt spear turned him into a caveman? 'I died it. Henna.'

'I liked the black.'

'Strangely enough, your preference didn't really influence my decision. Boudicca had flaming red hair.'

'And she was a brutal warrior. Again, maybe not appropriate for children.'

'Unlike Leonidas, who just carried his spear to pick up litter?'

Luc wandered past them with a steaming bowl of mini red frankfurters in one hand and a family-sized tomato ketchup in the other. 'Come on, you two, the fighting is supposed to be fictional.'

Shirley snapped her mouth shut with a click.

Hayden looked her over once more for good measure, shook his head, then turned and strode away from her. The turning caught his little skirt and gave it extra lift as he marched ahead of her and gave her a better look at his strong thighs.

Would Boudicca have busied herself with the undersides of the Roman tunics? she scolded herself.

A tiny smile crept onto her warrior lips.

I'd like to imagine so.

'You are the best army I've ever led!' Shirley whispered to her seven young boys, hunkered down behind a barrier of rubbish bins and a play house. Every one of them grinned, wide-eyed and excited, through the tomato ketchup now painted on their faces in a replica of her Celtic swirls.

Shirley doled out more fist-sized ammunition.

'I think it's time for a strategy change...' she whispered, laying on a thick accent that was somewhere between Scots and Welsh. And almost certainly nothing like Icenian. 'An army is never as strong without its leader so this time I want you to hurl everything you've got at Leonidas. Take. Him. Out!'

'Yeah!' The boys pumped their fists in the air and took up positions in the cracks between their protective barricade. Across the garden, she could see the erect mohawk of Hayden's Spartan headdress poking up above a hastily constructed shelter made of a deflated paddling pool and some upturned garden chairs and waving as he gave an inspirational battle speech of his own. Then half a dozen little faces peered up over the shelter with their own improvised headdresses on. A cut-down bucket, a foil headpiece, a dustpan brush taped to a head...

It made them easier to find than her stealthy, sauce-smeared Celts.

'Ready...' she whispered, and then surged to her feet, yelling, 'Leonidas!'

'Boudicca!' Across the lawn, Hayden leapt the barrier, thrusting his spear skywards and shouting.

Two mini armies exploded in opposite directions and both let the other pass to run to their real targets. Shirley backed away from the bucket-foil-and-brush-wearing Spartans. As one, they let their missiles fly and she curled her arms up over her head and turned side-on to the assault. Fifteen fat little balloons hit her and burst into a watery mess. High, low, middle. She had to admit, the Spartans were pretty well-coordinated little fighters, whereas her Celts missed more than they hit, then dashed off to pick up the unburst balloons and try again, giggling.

Hayden made much of his watery death, eventually falling flat in a blaze of glory on the suburban lawn. The Celts piled on, cheering. Then the Spartans piled on top.

'Okay, warriors...' Tim's mum intervened loudly, plucking the first of the children off a beleaguered Hayden. 'You have restored peace to this land and now a mighty feast awaits the victors in the kitchen.'

The boys and their bottomless energy fled into the house on a chorus of cheers.

Shirley plucked at her saturated bindings and dragged the wet fabric away from her legs. Her hair and the beaded Celtic inserts she'd woven in dripped more water onto her.

Hayden sauntered towards her, grinning. 'Quite the battle.'

Her pulse sky-rocketed. 'You were annihilated; dead men can't speak,' she puffed.

'You took a few mortal wounds yourself, judging by all that blood.'

It wasn't red but it dripped off her like the real thing. It dawned on her then that she hadn't really thought through the rest of this day. Or brought a fresh change of clothes. She'd imagined she'd be getting back into her car in the same state she'd got out of it.

Spot the one with no experience with children!

'They're amazing. So much energy.' She peeled her skirt from her thighs again but it returned, limpet-like, and so she gave up. 'I need a rest.'

She crossed to the Spartan camp and flipped both chairs upright and then dragged one into the sun. Half-in, half-out. Hayden flopped down next to her and thrust a tube of wet wipes at her.

'Here... Your face seems to have worn most of the carnage.'

Given how heavily tattooed it was with eyeliner, that didn't surprise her. She pulled a couple of the wet wipes out and set to work erasing the evidence of her slaughter, while the rest of her body slow-dried in the afternoon sun. But wiping off the Celtic make-up also took her regular make-up with it.

Still, no real choice unless she wanted to sit here looking shambolic.

Hayden lay stretched out on his lawn chair in his full Spartan glory, practically glistening from the paraffin added to the water balloons to stop them from popping too easily. Shirley stole a couple of peeks as she methodically removed every trace of make-up from her face.

'Leonidas suits you,' she said absently. Golden. Lean. Strong. Not bad for a hermit. Or a CEO.

He tipped his head sideways. 'I have to admit feeling very much like I could have been in his army a hundred lifetimes ago.' He didn't go back to studying the sky. 'You missed a bit.'

He tapped his nose but that wasn't terribly helpful without a mirror.

'Here...' He swung his legs over the edge of the lawn chair, plucked a fresh wipe from the container and slid his sunglasses up onto his head. 'Sit still.'

The move brought him closer than he'd ever been. Breath-stealingly close. He methodically removed the last of her make-up, gently turning her face side to side to make sure he missed none. When he was done, his eyes came back to hers. Her chest squeezed.

'And there she is...' he murmured, a half-smile twisting his lips. 'Nice to finally meet you, Shirley.'

The intensity of his gaze was infectious. Her breath struggled for function. 'We've met, actually.'

The smile grew. 'Not like this. Not formally.'

'You don't remember?'

He lowered his fingers, frowned. 'At the funeral?'

She shook her head. 'Before that. Long before that.'

He stared, his busy mind working furiously. 'I don't remember. I'm sorry.'

No. 'I wouldn't expect you to. It was nothing, from your point of view.'

But it had changed her life. She'd hit puberty on the spot. At eleven.

He sat back but didn't lie down again. He held her trapped in his gaze. Silence fell between them.

'Seriously, how long before your black hair comes back?' he blurted.

She laughed. 'For a man who's only ever been photographed with blondes, you certainly have a fixation with my hair colour.'

'I don't hate the red but I really liked the black.'

That brought a very different colour to her cheeks and she knew that he'd clearly see it, sans make-up. 'Actually it's called "Raven". The colour.'

He laughed. 'Of course it is. Very Edgar Allan Poe.'

Luc emerged with two tall glasses of iced water and he passed them one each. 'You guys should hire yourselves out as a double act,' he said. 'That was awesome.' Then he reached out and passed something else to Shirley. 'I got these from your bag for you, I hope you don't mind. It's bright out here.'

Sunglasses! As good as a face full of make-up when they were the size hers were. She slid them on. It was like sliding a mask back into place.

'Thank you, Luc. And thanks again for the other week at the Concert Hall; it was so wonderful.'

His eyes dragged quickly over Shirley's still drying, still snug form. She felt much more exposed when Luc looked at her than when Hayden had, but when Hayden looked she felt *naked*. In a good way. A dangerously good way.

Hayden glared pointedly at his friend.

'No problem,' Luc said, oblivious. 'You more than paid it off today.'

'I told you, it's going to be hard to top,' Hayden joked. 'You haven't forgotten that the next one is yours, have you, Shirley?'

She turned her focus more fully back to him, sitting perched on the chair still facing her. Seriously, had a man ever looked more ridiculous or more comfortable in a short skirt? Or more gorgeous?

'Not only have I not forgotten, but it's all arranged. I was going to tell you about it today.'

His eyes grew keen. Warmed with challenge. 'How? You've either done everything else already or it's overseas...'

She stared at him.

He frowned. 'We're going overseas? On no money?'

'Okay, this one is on *some* money, but not much. About one hundred dollars each way.'

His eyebrows lifted.

'And...' she said, readying to deliver her *coup de grâce* '...we get to tick off two things from the list.'

'For one hundred dollars?' Disbelief saturated his voice.

She smiled and turned her un-made-up face to the sun for some rare vitamin D. 'You'll just have to trust me.'

'Dangerous words, bro,' Luc said, standing, and looking at Hayden. 'Now, you need to throw some clothes on before all the mums start arriving and drive through my sister's hedges in distraction,' he said with a smile, then turned to her, 'and you need to cover up before Hayden tips right off that lawn chair. I have the important job of distributing the party bags.'

She glanced at Hayden, who busied himself studying the underside of the eaves.

Luc sauntered back into the house and an awkward silence fell. Until that moment she'd really not been all that bothered by the suction of her clothes to her curves, but it bothered her now. Luc's suggestion bothered her.

As in hot and bothered.

She stared at the *ΜΩΛΩΝ ΛΑΒΕ* tattoo on his shoulder. Shoulder seemed suitably modest.

'I think you should stay as you are,' she joked. 'And go out onto the street to welcome the mums.'

Even white, teeth sparkled. 'You're evil.'

'I'm a student of human nature. Isn't that what you once said?'

'Luc's right; I need to cover up.' He pushed to his feet and peered down at her. She lifted her hand to screen the bright sun.

He was gloriously broad in silhouette but it meant she couldn't see his face.

'And he's right about why you need to cover up, too.'

'So what's her story?' Luc said from behind him as Shirley's purple monstrosity drove away. With a still dripping Boudicca in it.

'No idea,' he murmured, still following her departure until she turned the corner. Then he dragged his eyes back to his friend. 'She's just a girl. The daughter of one of my lecturers.'

Luc laughed. 'She's not *just* an anything.'

He turned back to the empty road where her car had just been. *No.* Not even close.

'I assume you know what you're doing?' Luc went on as he thrust two party bags in the hands of the last departing nine-year-olds.

Hayden looked up. 'Meaning?'

'First the symphony, now Tim's party? That's not your usual playbook. And she's a total deviation from your usual type. I assume you're working an angle?'

Really? That was Luc's first assumption when his mate brought a nice girl over. Not that he didn't deserve the suspicion. 'No angle. I'm helping her with something.'

'Yeah, you're a regular Sir Galahad,' Luc snorted. 'You're hot for her. It's obvious.'

'That's not why I'm helping her…' Not that there wasn't a lot to be hot about. 'It's just a chance to get to know her.' That generated a modicum of stunned silence from his usually unflappable mate. Hayden turned. 'What?'

Luc masked his surprise. 'Nothing. Just never thought we'd have this moment.'

'Me standing in a skirt on your sister's verge?' No doubt.

Luc wasn't deterred. 'You admitting to interest in a woman.'

'I've had a lot of female interests. Far more than you, mate.'

Luc wasn't biting, either. 'Not like this, Hayds. Not someone normal.'

A laugh shot out of him. 'Shirley is far from normal.'

'You're doing stuff together, getting to know her, flirting…'

He turned for the house. 'That wasn't flirting. I was just entertaining myself.'

'Please. It was practically foreplay. If you're just amusing yourself then you might want to think about what that will do to her. She's not in the same league as the other women you've dated.'

Luc's words produced a fiery, blazing desire to be sure Shirley wasn't tarred by the brush of the many women he'd been with. Which in turn produced the confusing question—*why?* So of course he said the exact opposite of what he thought. 'She seemed up for it. She's stronger than she looks.'

'Steel's strong, too, until the moment it's not.'

Time for a new conversation. He swished back towards the house, Luc in tow. 'It's not going to be an issue. She's far too switched on to have a bar of me.'

'You might surprise yourself, Hayden. If you let someone in, they might want to stay.'

A dark, thick pool deep inside burped up a puff of uneasiness like a boiling tar pit. 'Maybe I should leave you my skirt, mate. If you're going to get all huggy on me.' He snagged up his sports bag full of street clothes. 'I do this for a living, Luc. For entire corporations. I think I can read one twenty-four-year-old woman, don't you?'

'I'm not worried about whether you can read *her,* Hayds,' he said. 'I'm worried that you don't read *you* all that well sometimes.'

Yeah, he did; better than his friend thought. Well enough to recognise when he had no idea what he was doing. Yet. But being in the dark wasn't the same thing as being oblivious. Leonidas would have agreed. Even if you didn't know exactly how many were in the opposing force or what weapons they were carrying, just knowing they were over the horizon was a huge advantage.

Forewarned was forearmed.

CHAPTER FIVE

'You realise the next time you say "Trust me, Hayden" I'll just laugh and remind you of this moment.'

They stood, suitcases in hand, on the dock of the port. The wrong side of the dock. The bright white, multi-storey cruise liners all lined up on the far side. On this side the dirty barnacle-encrusted freight liners slummed it.

Hayden stared at the hulking great vessel in front of them, with its towering patchwork of sea-containers. 'When you said pack for a sea voyage I had something very different in mind.'

Beside him, Shirley smiled. 'What did you expect for a hundred bucks each way?'

He sighed and closed his eyes. What had he expected? He'd had vague dreams of crewing on a maxi-yacht, or working for their passage on one of the leisure behemoths on the far side of the port. 'Not this.'

'I have a friend at the port authority. She gave me the tip about this vessel. It comes in fully laden and then offloads half its cargo and crew for shore leave before heading on to New Zealand to drop the rest and return half-full. Then they pick up their shore-rested crew and new cargo.'

She was staring at him with such enthusiastic expectation. He just kept staring at the vessel.

'So they have room for passengers there and back,' she went on. 'The catch is that you only get one day in New Zealand. But that's all we'll need.'

He nodded slowly. How else were they going to get to New

Zealand for the bungee jumping or Venice for the gondola ride, or the base camp of Everest? The list wouldn't have been easily achievable even for her mother. Some parts of it they had no hope of delivering.

This was pretty clever. But he wasn't about to give her that just yet.

'I hope they're not expecting me to haul containers?'

She nudged him bodily. 'Come on, Leonidas, I've seen your muscles.'

And that was all it took. An unexpected bit of full body contact and he was totally on board with this crazy plan. He stared at the *Delphi Paxos* and worked hard to ignore the tingling place in his arm where the curve of her breast had just brushed. 'As long as I can get a satellite signal then I can keep the shareholders happy for the week I'll be away.'

She glanced up at him. 'I know it's not the Ritz—'

Oh, honey, it's not even The Ritz's off-site warehouse.

'—but it's a virtually free ride to New Zealand and it puts two ticks in boxes.'

Ticks in boxes. Right. Everything was about the boxes with her. How had he forgotten?

She set off across the dock tarmac, pausing to let a kamikaze forklift whizz by. They reached the bottom of a long skinny gangplank. Shirley ground to a halt just in front of him. He peered around her to check her expression.

'I just...um...' she muttered.

He stepped around her and looked at her front-on. 'You okay?'

She took a deep breath. 'It's stupid...'

This whole thing was stupid but it meant something to her so here they were. 'What is?'

'I've never been on a boat. It looks so much bigger from here.'

Uh-oh. 'Never?'

She shook her head. 'Only river ferries.'

'Well, that's exciting then.' God loved an optimist. Yet the hint of vulnerability certainly wasn't *un*appealing.

She chewed her lip and raised her eyes up the side of the enormous hull. 'I hope so.'

'Once you're up there it won't look so big. I promise.'

But he couldn't promise what a novice would make of the pitch and roll of the Tasman Sea. Her clever solution wasn't going to look too great when she was face down over a toilet bowl for four days. Or the bow of the ship.

He took her hand and drew her upwards. Took a step. Then another. She followed him up the long skinny gangplank. They were met at the top by a smiling man who greeted them in heavily accented English.

'Welcome to ship!'

He glanced around at the heavy fittings, the utilitarian paint job. Yup, definitely a working vessel. But it did at least look solid. And clean. And much less daunting from on deck for his suddenly nervous novice.

Their crew member told them in broken English that Immigration would come through before the ship was cleared for departure and to have their passports ready, and to stay in their cabin until they'd been cleared.

Amongst so many mispronunciations, that little one slipped him right by.

At least until the man flung a small door wide and cheerfully announced, 'Room!'

The cabin was tiny but it had two neat beds in it. Skinny single beds. Shirley looked at the seaman sideways. 'Whose room?'

'Yes. Your room.'

'But which? Mine or his?'

The lines on his weathered face multiplied. Shirley grew dangerously still and the man started babbling in his own tongue. It was Greek. Greatly evolved from the ancient Greek Hayden had studied during his classical units, but close enough.

He stepped in and fumbled his way to offering to help in classical Greek. The man instantly refocused on the closest approximation to his own language in the room.

'How many cabins did you book?' he said quickly to Shirley.

'Two. Of course, two.' Furious colour crept ever higher.

He did his best to communicate the dilemma. The crewman nodded and shot back in rapid-fire Greek.

'I think he's agreeing with you.' The man held up two fingers. 'Two.'

'Damn right he is...' Shirley started to fan her hot face with her passport.

The crewman picked up Hayden's suitcase and placed it on the foot of the bed and then he picked up Shirley's and walked out of the room with it, crossed the tiny hallway and opened a door there to a room the twin of the first. He dumped her suitcase on the end of a bed in there. And then turned to check her understanding. Baffled but optimistic.

'Okay...?'

'Okay,' she said through a tight smile.

On the bright side, the distraction seemed to have made her forget all about her sea nerves.

She moved into her cabin.

'There are worse things in this life than sharing a room with me,' he joked. 'Women have cage-fought for less.'

She threw him her most withering glare. He loved that one.

'Seriously,' he probed carefully. 'Why are you so angry?'

She pressed her lips together. 'Because it was shaping up to be a stupid situation and I'm not accustomed to doing stupid things.'

He snorted. 'By contrast, I'm delighted to discover that you're fallible.' Way too pleased to be bothered at the thought of sharing a room. In fact, one tiny part of him was disappointed. The part that liked her best off-kilter.

She frowned at him. 'I didn't want you to think... It looked like...'

She fanned more furiously.

Oh... She didn't want him to think she'd planned it that way. Accidentally on purpose. 'You know you don't have to come up with convoluted excuses to sleep with me, Shirley. I'm easy. Or haven't you read the papers?'

She had roughly the same number of glares as smiles and he enjoyed them just as much.

'Easy? Hardly.'

But she kept her distance, he noticed. He flopped down on one of the tiny beds.

Her startled face returned to him. 'What are you doing?'

'Waiting for Immigration. We might as well save them some time and wait together.'

She grunted and set about transferring the contents of her suitcase into the stand-up locker in the austere room. He watched her crossing back and forth across the tiny space. Her movements were fluid, graceful. More dancing than walking. The items she was unpacking were mostly dark and plain. Not at all what he'd become used to her wearing.

'What?' she challenged on her third pass.

'I was expecting something more…nautical.' And how strange that he felt genuine disappointment at its absence. He'd grown used to her particular brand of fashion.

She straightened and turned. Considered him. 'Not really practical at sea. Most of what I've brought is supremely suburban.'

He stared at her. 'Does that mean no make-up?'

'*Pfff*. Don't be ridiculous.'

He tucked his hands behind his head. 'What if I challenged you?'

She frowned. 'To what?'

'You challenged me to do the list on a budget. What if I challenge you to do it in civvies with no make-up?'

'Why would you?'

He couldn't think of a clever answer to that so he went for honest. 'Because I got such a short glimpse of Shirley at Tim's party. And because that way we're both out of our comfort zones.'

And because I'm dying to know what colour your lips really are. He stared at them now, stained with dark lipstick, and imagined wiping it off with his thumb.

She stared him down. Thinking. 'All right.'

He knew her too well to imagine she'd just capitulate. All they'd done since meeting was trade—insults, tasks, looks—this wasn't going to be any different. 'But…?'

'I'll ease up on the make-up while we're on this trip if you'll answer a question. Honestly.'

The keen glint of her eye should have been warning enough. But he was too dazzled by it to recognise it straight away. 'Okay.'

'What was your fascination with my mother?'

His gut tightened up immediately, the bad old days still not his favourite pre-dinner conversation. But he'd agreed to be honest. 'She was a great teacher.'

Those eyes so very like her mother's narrowed. 'Every Saturday for three years?'

He stood. This conversation just didn't feel right with him stretched out on the tiny bed. Shirley crossed her arms, taking the leggings she was still holding with her. They bunched across her torso.

'She knew so much. She gave us one hundred per cent of her focus.' Which was a bit rough when that left nothing for her daughter, he suddenly realised. But at the time he'd simply craved a motherly connection. Anyone's mother would have done.

'I didn't have...access to my own mother. Spending time with yours was good for me. She helped keep me grounded. Her expectations. She set a high bar.'

'Tell me about it,' Shirley muttered, then cleared her throat and said, louder, 'You were pretty cut up when she died.'

He had been. Everything he'd shoved way down deep to survive his mother's death had come bubbling back up at Carol's. Except he had found something to console him, eventually. A series of somethings: pills, women, alcohol, in that order. And they'd got him through that loss and out the other side. And then they'd propped him up well into the next decade. Until he'd gone cold turkey on all three a few years ago.

Saved his life.

'Nothing compared to your loss, I imagine,' he murmured.

She shut that line of conversation down with the not very subtle zip of her empty suitcase. 'I always wondered where you'd gone for your knowledge fix after that.'

'I didn't. It was never about the knowledge for me.' It was about having a mother figure in his empty life.

She glanced back up at him. 'Then why do it?'

He shrugged. 'I was good at it.'

She turned back. 'I'm sure you were good at a lot of things.'

Not if you'd asked his father. Or his other lecturers. 'Really? What else? Cutting up the athletics track? Musical accomplishment? Do you think a masterful maths mind lurks in here?' He tapped his forehead.

'Masterful enough to run a successful business. Even more successful recently.'

He stared at her, a warm realisation leaching through his body. She'd been checking up on him. 'Someone else has been busy on Google, then.'

She stiffened, but ignored him. 'I thought you walked away from your business for a reason.'

Her green eyes bored into him, towards the truth that lurked deep within. 'I realised it was easier to change the business than myself.' And who he'd become was so tightly enmeshed with what he did. He'd needed some healthy distance in order to untangle it all.

'Changed it to what? From what? It's so hard to tell from your website.'

Why not? She'd find out eventually. It might as well come from him. 'I did my Masters in Influence.'

Her snort was the least ladylike and most sexy he'd ever heard. This woman just didn't care for the slightest pretension. 'Did you make that up?'

'No. It's made me rich.'

'You have some massive clients. That much I could tell.'

'Clients who paid generously for a look into the hearts and minds of their future customers.' She frowned and her eyes grew keen, and he remembered who he was also talking to: Shiloh. But—inexplicably—he also trusted her. 'Their businesses revolve around knowing where to target likely customers and what will get their buy-in.'

She stared at him. 'That's…'

'The word you're looking for is "lucrative".' It wasn't, but it was true.

'Which doesn't make it any more palatable.'

He tipped his head and granted her that. It was no more than he'd eventually come to think. The day he'd realised how closely all those 'somethings' that he consoled himself with were linked to his profession.

'Show me.'

He looked up. 'Show you what?'

'How it works. On me.'

'Oh Shirley, I don't think you're the same as everyone else. I wouldn't begin to claim I understand how your mind works.' Disappointment stained her already dark lips. He thought fast. 'But I can show you how you did it to me.'

Show her how it was inherent in everyone—even the virtuous Shiloh. Bred into the human species.

She sat on the edge of the second bed and folded her hands on her lap. It was entirely demure and insanely provocative.

'Influence is all about buy-in,' he started. 'Once you can get someone to say yes to something small they make a mental commitment to that thing and transitioning them to something bigger is more straightforward. If I want you to buy my car I get you to sit in it. If I want you to borrow money from me as an adult I give you a money box when you're a child. If I want you to accept my faith I get you to accept something smaller from me first.'

Her eyes slowly rounded as he spoke.

She might as well know who she was dealing with. 'You wanted me to do the list. You got me to let you into my house first.'

'Actually, I let myself in.'

'But I didn't throw you out. In the exact moment I accepted your intrusion, I bought-into your quest. I gave you something small—my attention—then you incrementally asked for more.' His eyes fell to her lips, which had parted softly. 'A few hours of my time to do the dolphins. Then a commitment to spend a lot more of my time working out how to do it on the cheap. Then you triggered my natural competitiveness and got me to buy in even further. And now we're sitting on a freighter getting ready to go to another country.'

'All because you let me into your house?' she breathed.

'All because you got me to commit a tiny part of myself to this quest. And the moment I made the mental shift there was no turning back.'

'I didn't mean to do any of that.' Heat rushed up her cheeks.

'Yes, you did, you just didn't name it. No one does.' He shrugged. 'I've made my business out of naming it.'

Out of selling his soul. For top dollar.

She watched him steadily. Read him correctly. 'So why do you still do it?'

The million-dollar question. The answer would be worth that if anyone could give it to him.

'Because I can?'

'Is that a good enough reason?' she murmured. 'Just because you can?'

'And because someone else would if not me.'

'Why don't you just leave them to it?'

'Because they won't do it as well as me.' He'd chosen that profession and he was good at it. The best. It was about the only validation he got these days.

Her curious green eyes dug deep. Trying to figure him out. There was more he could say, things that would only add to her confusion. But he didn't because they would only smack of justification.

'Anyway. That's how it's done. In life. In love. In everything.'

'Not love—surely?'

'Love isn't special. Or different. You just have to find the in-point. Something small.'

'That makes it sound very calculated.'

He shrugged. 'What is seduction if not entirely calculated?'

'We were talking about love, not seduction.'

'What's the difference?' Then it hit him. 'You don't believe that love is something that just happens without effort?'

She frowned and colour pricked at her cheeks.

'How can Shiloh operate on the sharp edge of the sword when it comes to every other aspect of contemporary life, yet still buy into the whole romantic love myth?'

'You don't believe in falling in love?' she bristled.

'That implies some kind of uncontrolled accident of fate. Love is a steady, intentional climb towards a goal.'

'You speak from experience?'

'I speak from centuries of experience.' Other people's experience. Myriad lives across time.

She lifted one brow. 'And the centuries tell you that seduction and love are the same thing?'

'They're symbiotic. Seduction is the best part of love.'

'Spoken like a true man,' she grunted. 'Somehow, I thought you'd be a devotee of the meeting of intellects being the purest form of love.'

He looked down on her. 'You think Plato or Socrates didn't consider mental sparring as a kind of seduction?' She wanted to deny it—he could see it in her troubled expression.

'Surely there has to be a physical attraction?' she pressed.

'It's a bonus but not essential.'

Keen green eyes fixed on him and he could see her sharp brain taking hold exactly as it had at the dolphins. Her mind was engaged. Great, he could work with minds.

'So how would you start a seduction of a complete stranger?' she asked. 'If I brought the question to Molon Labe as a business hurdle?'

He folded his arms and pretended to consider it. He didn't need to. This stuff came so naturally to him after all this time. In fact, even before that, human nature had always been so very obvious to him. The links between people, their motivations and drivers. It had taken him years to realise the rest of the world was more or less oblivious to that.

'You have to start with the ultimate goal. Do you want to feel desired? Get married? Be loved?' He locked his eyes on hers. 'Or do you just want to scratch that itch that burns like fire-ants under your skin?'

She swallowed hard, but her pupils grew bigger. 'Let's keep this tasteful. Let's say married.'

So Shirley Marr blushed like a schoolgirl at the thought of

sharing a room with him and wanted to be desired and loved but wasn't saying so.

Interesting.

He thought about it for a few moments, for effect. 'Marriage is a commitment. So your first step is to find a way to get a man to commit to the idea of commitment itself.'

'How?'

He searched the air for ideas. A hundred came to him immediately. 'Start a project together. Travel. Buy a puppy. Put a vegetable patch in. Get him to give you a space for your toothbrush at his place. Anything that requires him to lock a part of himself into something.'

The dark hair mounded on her head tipped as she considered that.

'Once he's made the mental shift towards commitment, then it's just a series of incremental rises until he's totally on-board with the idea of a permanent commitment.'

She stared at him. 'No wonder you're so cynical. If that's what you believe people do.'

'I'm not saying it's conscious, necessarily.'

'Surely being aware of it means it wouldn't work?'

He laughed. 'You wanted me to commit to the list and I did. Knowing what was happening didn't stop it from working.'

She chewed her lip. Suddenly two hundred per cent of his focus centred there.

'A demonstration, perhaps?' he murmured.

Her eyes darkened and widened within their kohl smudges as she stared up at him warily.

'I find myself very interested in the shape and taste of your lips,' he said theatrically. 'And I'm declaring that to you so you're aware of the direction of my thoughts and so you can plan to resist when the moment comes.'

And because success will be so much more satisfying that way.

He reached down and pulled her to her feet. She rose to stand before him.

Shirley had to push extra-hard to get words past her suddenly tight chest. 'This is hypothetical, I assume?' Hayden's smile reminded her of the Huntsman-wolf in Red Riding Hood. *All the better to eat you with...*

'If that makes you feel better about your chances of resisting,' he said.

He pulled her a little closer. Closed his arms around her, hot and strong. Her heart went berserk. 'So the question is, Shirley...knowing what I'm doing and knowing what my goal is—' he breathed down on her '—are you any less inclined to let me kiss you?'

She licked her lips. Struggled for air. 'You're assuming you already have my buy-in?'

Hayden blinked, slow, confident. That caused Shirley's own lids to follow suit, growing heavier. She tried to glance away to break the contact.

'A kiss is the touching of flesh on flesh. You started to buy into me touching you months ago...the first time you let my glance rest on your porcelain skin. Then later, when you let my fingers graze your hair. Then take your hand. Even now...my eyes are roaming where my lips cannot and you're allowing it.'

Sure enough, his veiled gaze browsed her mouth and made it part in breathless anticipation. She forced it closed.

'And now, even knowing what I plan to do and why, you're still in my arms. I think I'd call that buy-in.'

'Pretty clever,' she breathed, desperate to preserve some dignity. 'Assuming it's going to be any kind of kiss at all.'

His teeth flashed white and dangerous. 'And there it is. Full commitment.'

He took her weight on his arm and leaned her back into it, his mouth pressing down confidently onto hers, sliding against it, still half-smiling in his victory. She held firm against the heavenly feel and smell of him so close, refusing to give in.

She would have loved to stand, unmoved, in his hold. To let him kiss her senseless and then to emerge untouched. Indifferent.

But that wasn't going to happen.

Not in this lifetime.

The moment she resisted, holding her own—barely—against the breathless spin of her mind, he upped the ante. Plying her with the technique that must have unzipped many a skirt in its time. His mouth glided over hers, alternating pressure, his tongue teasing the firm line she maintained where her lips met. His flesh blazing against hers. Her head spun wildly.

He pulled back a little, breathed words against her flaming skin, and something about the shift of colour in his eyes told her he wasn't playing a game any more. 'I'm going to kiss that dark gloss off until I reveal what's underneath it.'

A sudden erotic lance speared way down deep inside. He set to work doing just that, pressing himself more fully into her, binding them close and kissing the living daylights out of her. Her fingers, pressed against his chest to stop him getting closer, curled, of their own accord, into the fabric of his shirt. Her feet, which she'd positioned to help her push against Hayden, subtly shifted weight so that she leaned more fully into him.

Into his kiss.

Her head, which should have been screaming resistance, swam uselessly in the wash of scent and sensation pumping off the human hormone holding her up.

And her mouth opened.

Instantly he was in, his triumph punctuated by the thrusts of his tongue and the heaving breaths they both stole between kisses. Her whole body flamed with desire and she speared her fingers up into his hair, keeping him close. He backed her up against the wall.

'Witch,' he pressed into her hungry lips. 'There was never any other avenue for us.'

Something about speech. Something about the incendiary way the two of them had burst to flame the moment they touched and the way the oxygen they sucked in only fuelled it more. *Something* finally drew her attention to what they were doing and where.

She pulled back, chest heaving. 'You assume that was all your doing,' she whispered the moment her lips were free. 'What if I've been angling for a kiss since the beginning?'

His eyes darkened, dropped. Then his hands followed suit. Then he stepped away.

'That's the other key principle of influence,' he heaved, dragging his wrist across his lips. 'Convincing the subject it was their idea all along.'

And then he was gone, back across the hall to his own room, leaving her half sagging against the cold steel wall of the cabin.

Damn you, Hayden Tennant.

It was minutes before she had the strength to lever herself upright away from the wall long enough to sag down onto the little bed.

Had she ever before wanted something as badly and resented it so thoroughly as that kiss? She hated the fact that she was no more a match for his seduction than any of the other women he'd targeted and overpowered. And she *really* hated the fact that he'd been so supremely confident of her capitulation. Was he that sure of his own prowess or did he think her so lacking in resolve and character?

Quite accurately, as it turned out. On all fronts.

Should she cut herself some slack that it was—without question—the best kiss she'd ever received? That it jammed electrodes into parts of her that usually slumbered happily and forced them into sparking, buzzing animation until they lurched to life like the Frankenstein of body organs. It was as surreal and unforgettable—and futile—as being snogged by some handsome movie star who kissed for a living. What hope did she have?

Yeah, that was satisfactory. No personal responsibility required at all, then.

'Ugh.' She bounced her head a few times on the neat pillow in its faintly diesel-smelling coverslip.

Of course she was responsible.

She'd been on slow simmer since the day of Tim's party, having filled her imagination and the weeks since with images of an oil-slicked, half-naked Hayden sprawled so comfortably on that lawn chair. Yet strangely, it had been his comfort—not his state of undress—that had particularly appealed to her that day. She'd stretched out alongside him, dripping and smiling, and felt such an astonishing sense of amity for the man she'd only sparred with until then. Fellowship made a nice change from the thin edge of conflict or the dangerous high-wire of attraction. The best parts of being with Hayden were just…being.

But she knew which part got her pulse racing hardest.

She lifted her fingers to her lips.

So he'd kissed her. So what? He was just making a point. It just happened that he was as good a point-maker now as he had been when he was younger. Thorough and convincing. And she'd been well convinced by his kiss.

Right up until the moment he'd taunted her that it was fake and walked out of the room.

She rubbed the puffy skin of her bottom lip. Ridiculous. It was *not* still tingling. It was projection. It had just been a really spectacular kiss from someone self-proclaimed in the art of seduction. And she was generally hormone-deficient, so hitting a charisma bomb like Hayden was bound to have an impact.

Not *deficient;* that was hardly fair to a body that was capable—more than capable, apparently—of simmering. Perhaps *suppressed* was a better word. If you denied something long enough, your body eventually stopped expecting it.

Shirley blew air slowly out through still-pulsing lips.

She needed fresh air. Perspective.

She needed to get away from his lingering scent and the breath-stealing memory of him bending her back in his arms and plundering her mouth. Like the pirate he was. The stealer of kisses. And of dignity.

Half an hour in the bracing air of the Tasman Sea would do her wonders.

It might even help distract her from the all-encompassing desire to find Hayden and to pick a fight with him again, just to keep her arousal levels up. Up where he'd left them dangling so helplessly. So wasted.

If she couldn't kiss him, she could shout at him a little bit and release tension that way.

CHAPTER SIX

HE'D made his point but he didn't feel particularly good about it. Hours later and far out to sea, Hayden was still rattled by that kiss. The kiss he'd initiated then rapidly lost control of.

He'd lost control before, but it was always a carefully reined surrender. Even letting himself go came with some strict rules and recovery solutions. At all times.

With Shirley he'd literally lost it. His body participated in direct defiance of his will. On its own agenda. Nice little karmic reward for being a bastard and bending her to his will.

Just because you can...

He released his fingers from the punishing fists he'd made standing there at the bow of the *Paxos,* resting his arms on the aperture in the high wall which protected the crew and cargo from potentially high seas. Other people clenched their teeth when they were stressed, he clenched his fingers. To the point of pain.

It was unconscious but it made his dentist happy.

'Hayden.'

Shirley spoke, soft and tentative, behind him. Knowing he was the cause of her uncertainty only infuriated him more. He turned slowly and faced the music.

She was in black from head to toe but it was just a T-shirt and leggings and she'd toned her make-up right back to a translucent foundation. Closer to what it had looked like the day she'd wiped Boudicca from her skin. Hayden stared at her and she shifted uncomfortably under his scrutiny. When he wasn't being distracted by dramatically highlighted eyes and burnished coffee lips it was possible to appreciate the fine texture of her skin. He'd attributed its smoothness to her make-up. But it looked as if it was all natural.

He cleared his throat. 'You honoured our bargain.'

One elegantly plucked brow arched. 'You thought I wouldn't?'

'I thought I might have voided it.' *By kissing you.*

She glanced away briefly. 'I asked you a question and you answered it. It wouldn't be reasonable to protest.'

'Most people would.'

'I'm not most people.'

No. She wasn't.

'Anyway, I came to get you. There's something you need to see.'

'Where?'

'Towards the back of the ship.'

A mosaic of sea-containers? He could see those from here. But what else did he have to do with his time other than humour her? Even a half-hour in the stuffy little cabin had done his head in.

'Lead on.'

She led him down the length of the ship and then stopped as she slipped one shoe on from its resting place against a giant blue sea-container. It was only then he realised she'd come to him barefoot. It seemed so comfortable on her he hadn't stopped to think how out of place it was on a working freighter.

'I worried I might not find it again,' she said, her face strangely alight, turning down a gap between the high-rise of stacked containers.

'For someone who takes things so seriously you seem unnaturally delighted by shipping containers.'

She laughed but didn't turn, continuing into the man-made valley. 'Just wait...'

They turned at her next shoe and he began to understand why she'd needed markers. Without the horizon to keep you oriented, this was a maze. She marched onwards then peered to her right—straight into another container from where he stood—

paused and turned back to him, looking for all the world like a delighted child.

Was it a coincidence that he'd only been able to remember her after she'd shed the Shiloh mask?

She grinned at him. 'What's the thing least likely to be around this corner? In the whole world?'

The rapid mental shift that question required took him a moment to adjust. He thought of the craziest and most unlikely thing he could conceive. 'My parents having high tea.'

The delight fell from her face just slightly and her slim fingers rested gently on the edge of the container as she frowned at him. She wouldn't know—about *them*, about why that was such a ludicrous concept, whether they were at sea or not—but she was smart enough to read between the lines.

'I assume it's not that,' he said to cover the silence. To mask his sudden pain.

She straightened and backed up, holding one hand out as though to take his across the emptiness between them, keeping her eyes firmly locked on his. Warm. Beckoning.

A true Siren...

It was only as he stepped towards her that he realised it wasn't a solid wall of sea containers to her left; it was another turn. A turn which opened out to—

'What the—?'

Her face split into a radiant smile and he stumbled to a halt, utterly and genuinely dumbfounded for the first time in his entire life.

A giraffe.

It stood, munching happily on straw and staring at him with a general sort of curiosity as he stood gaping at it. It was housed in the biggest animal crate he'd ever seen, with an opening large enough for it to stretch its long neck and head out of and get a whiff of the sea. A large sort of container clearing had been built around it at the heart of the ship to shelter it from rough weather but give it some sense of air and space.

The strangest sense washed through him—alien and long-forgotten.

Wonder.

Had it really been that long since something had amazed him? Moved him the way those enormous thick-lashed, liquid mercury eyes did. This extraordinary creature standing in this extraordinary place.

Maybe so.

'Back again?' A blonde woman stepped out from behind the crate and murmured quietly to the giraffe before turning her attention to Shirley. She was dressed casually but had the boots and tan of someone who worked outdoors for a living.

'Hayden, this is Caryn,' Shirley said next to him. 'And that—' she nodded at the enormous chomping head fifteen feet above them '—is Twuwu. She's en route to a new home in New Zealand.'

Shirley greeted the woman as he still struggled to find words. En route to a zoo. Of course she was. He'd never had occasion to think about how else you got an animal as big as a giraffe across an ocean.

Shirley went straight into Shiloh mode, asking what were clearly not her first questions of the day, examining the box, leaning back on a tower of containers and just…contemplating. He watched her do her thing but mostly he watched Twuwu. She was so very unconcerned by what was happening around her, content to merely munch on her hay.

'Is she sedated?' he asked.

Caryn turned to him and gave him a winning smile. She was every bit a daughter of nature. Golden-haired, tanned, fit. And interested. Instantly obvious.

'She was lightly sedated for the drive down to the port, and the loading. But she's fully recovered now.'

'She's placid.'

'She's spent a lot of time in that crate preparing for the journey. It's become like her stable.'

He glanced around at the multicoloured wall of containers that surrounded the crate on all sides. 'What would happen if she saw the ocean?'

Again the brilliant smile. Caryn sank on one hip and looked up at him. 'Hopefully we won't find out.'

Shirley rejoined them. 'Will you stay out here for the whole journey?' she asked tightly.

'Most of the day, monitoring her condition, but I'll sleep up in the cabins with everyone else.'

Did she just flick him a glance? Yes, she did.

Well, well...

Shirley continued with her questions and, before long, they knew everything there was to know about international wildlife transactions and the toiletry habits of giraffes. He watched Shirley work—drawing conclusions, filing away every answer for a future story. Eventually all the questions were asked and all the good reasons to be hanging around evaporated.

'You should come back and visit Twuwu during the trip,' Caryn said to Shirley but her eyes flicked to his again. 'She likes company.'

Shirley thanked her and they retraced their steps back through the maze of containers from the heart of the ship to the edge.

'You seem very relaxed.' Just when he thought he liked her best off kilter. Mellow Shirley made him think about long, lazy summer sleep-ins. Naked.

Not appropriate.

'There's something about this ship... Maybe it's the gentle sway... But it chills me out. I find myself relaxing.'

'Maybe it's me?'

Her immediate laugh ricocheted off the containers. 'It's not you.'

Right. Then again, his first instinct on getting her alone in a room with a bed in it had been to paw her. So...

'The giraffe then?' Twuwu had certainly done wonders for his blood pressure.

'Maybe.' They turned out of the massive load of containers at the edge of the ship. 'I'll certainly be visiting again. What an awesome bonus.'

Their next steps passed in silence. Until he couldn't take it any more. 'What do you want to do now?' he blurted.

She turned and blinked at him. 'What do you mean?'

'Us. What will we do now?' And for the next four days.

She laughed and started walking again. 'Don't know about you, but I'm going to start a story for next week.'

He frowned. 'You're working on this trip?'

'Of course. So are you.'

He was supposed to be. But… 'We're in the middle of the ocean. Surely that demands some down time?'

'You've had two years of down time. Are you really so hungry for more?'

No. But he was hungry for something and he couldn't quite put his finger on it. It was an odd kind of…emotional famine. Then it dawned on him.

He wanted company. *Shirley's* company.

'I'm bored. Sea life is interminable.'

She laughed again and jogged ahead of him up the functional steel staircase. He lagged back to appreciate the view. 'We've only been out of the harbour for a couple of hours, Popeye,' she said.

'Entertain me.'

She threw him an arch look back over her shoulder. 'Entertain yourself.'

He thought about Caryn. Then dismissed it. Prodding at Shirley was so much more fun. 'You can write your story when it's dark.'

'I plan to be sleeping when it's dark.'

'Really?' He followed her from the deck into the long corridor that their cabins were in. 'That's a lot of cabin time. What will I do?'

She paused at her door. 'Whatever you want. I have work to do.'

Seriously? She was ditching him? 'Will I see you in the mess room?'

She turned back from unlocking her door. 'Seven p.m. sharp.' She stepped into the room, faced back out at him and leaned on the door. Smiling the way you did to door-to-door salesmen you wanted to get rid of. 'See you then.'

And then she was gone and Hayden stood staring at the flaking paint on the timber, speechless for the second time in a day.

Blonde.

Of course she was. And, in case Hayden hadn't noticed her golden locks, Caryn had tossed them around unmissably. Her skin as tanned as Twuwu's markings and with lashes just as long, too. And all the while *she'd* hovered off to the side, ignored, with her thick hair hauled back in a sea-sensible ponytail and her face virtually make-up-less.

Shirley lay back on one of the two beds in the room and glared at the ceiling. Could it be any more grey or uninspiring?

Could she be any grumpier?

She'd liked Caryn just half an hour earlier. They'd chatted for ages about her work and destination. Then she'd introduced Hayden, picked up on the none too subtle vibe pinging between the two of them and rapidly gone off her.

Not that it was Caryn's fault. She was blonde, gorgeous and willing. Exactly Hayden's type, even if she was wearing steel-capped boots and serviceable shorts and not something slip-thin and expensive. And she herself had been the genius to go and find him and hand him, gift-wrapped, to the only blonde on the freighter. It was entirely self-inflicted.

She sighed.

She'd just… She'd wanted him to have the experience she'd had. The discovery. Coming around that corner and seeing that beautiful animal, so misplaced and unexpected. And she'd enjoyed giving it to him. Everything had gone slow motion just then, as she'd fixed her eyes on his and stepped backward to bring him out into the giraffe's eye line. His face had transformed in that moment, practically glowed, and she had—for precious seconds—a glimpse of the old Hayden. The young man who'd found every aspect of life a revelation. She remembered that face from when she'd hidden under the stairs and watched him through the door crack on Saturdays.

And she'd given him that today.

And then his eyes had refocused on their target—a blonde, the only kind of woman he ever dated—and they'd hardened back into the new Hayden. The Hayden she'd met that very first day at his cottage. The Hayden who was bored with life and out to wring its riches. He hadn't done much else—he hadn't needed to, really, because Caryn seemed happy to carry the burden of the flirting—but her implication was clear.

Come back and visit...

Yay.

She pushed herself onto her side and sat up. Work. She'd said it to get a clean break from Hayden, but suddenly it did seem like a reasonable distraction from her unsanctioned thoughts about *the kiss*. First, unpacking had been a good excuse to stay in here long enough to lose him to his curiosity about how freighters worked. Then roaming the deck and the Lego-stacks of containers.

Now work.

Caryn's chat had triggered a blog idea. About the unseen challenges of international livestock transactions. Zoo animals, racing horses, stud bulls. How many other unique passengers were sitting in crates on ships, planes and trucks around the world right at this moment? It was as unsung as travelling the world on passenger freighters.

She sketched out the preliminary outline of a story and jotted down some research ideas. That neatly took care of…oh… minutes.

'Ugh.' She threw herself backwards and stared again at the offending ceiling. Had they not painted this vessel at all since it was commissioned?

Hayden was responsible for this off-balance mental mess. His incendiary kiss. It had been as unexpected as the giraffe. Though, like the giraffe, once discovered, it was a hard thing to put out of your mind. She'd had to work hard out there on the deck not to keep staring at his mouth. Remembering.

No doubt Caryn the zookeeper would be discovering it very soon.

She'd never met anyone as cynical and miserable as Hayden. That he believed love was a challenge you negotiated rather than something that just struck you... And that he thought it so pathetic that she believed otherwise. That he developed plans for big businesses to better exploit the community.

That was not the boy she'd hidden in the shadows to watch.

The man he'd become might have a full bank account but his moral account was sadly lacking.

Judging him made her feel vaguely better about letting him kiss her.

She forced herself up, back to her laptop, back to the outline of the story she could feel burbling, and verbalised it to tell herself she really meant it.

'Enough.'

A knock at the door ripped her out of the concentrated place where she'd lost time.

'Shirley? It's Hayden.'

Seriously? Could the man not amuse himself for an hour? She had that thought even as her chest tightened around the anticipation. She hit 'save' on her work, stood and yanked the door open. 'Yes?'

He stood there, casually but gorgeously dressed. A clean shirt and well-fitting trousers. Shaved, even. And smelling pretty much like ambrosia.

'Are you coming up for dinner?' he said. 'I thought we were meeting up there?'

She blinked. Half at his appearance and half at what him being showered and shaved meant. 'Now?'

'It's past seven.'

'Right!' How many hours had she lost in her story? That was always a good sign for an engrossing read but not great for saving face in front of Hayden. 'Coming.'

Every instinct called her to put on Shiloh's face—eyes, lips, pallor, carefully chaotic hair—because she'd be meeting strangers, but she remembered her commitment to Hayden and she was determined not to be the one to break faith. On principle. She slipped on her shoes and untwisted the elastic holding her hair back. Sea or not, if tumbling masses were good enough for Caryn…

She raked her fingers through the waves to give it body and then smiled at Hayden. 'Sorry. Let's go.'

Mistake number one.

The wind conditions buried below deck—or even behind a wall of sea containers—and the wind conditions at the top of a freighter were not the same thing. Immediately her hair whipped like silken razors around her face in the gusts, tangling and flying. She wrangled it down as best she could and twisted it in her hold until they reached the outer door of the *Paxos*'s galley. Hayden held the door for her from outside and she stepped through.

Six people turned to look at her—five crew and one zoo-keeper.

Awesome. Nothing like a subtle entrance.

She blew loose strands from her sea-whipped face and plastered on a smile. 'Sorry I'm late, everyone. I got absorbed in my work.'

She summed up the seating arrangement at a glance. Two empty seats on opposite sides of the table and the one next to Caryn had a half-drunk bottle of Hayden's favourite non-alcoholic beverage in front of it.

Okay...

She moved towards the second vacancy, flanked by the ship's crew.

Introductions were brief, given most of the crew spoke only Greek, but a man she hadn't yet met had good English and proved himself an admirable translator. He was the *Paxos*'s Captain. Just as Greek as the rest of them, just as old and weathered, but somehow more…striking.

Or maybe it was just the uniform.

Hayden sank back into his seat next to Caryn, who immediately drew him back into conversation.

As dinners went, it wasn't the worst she'd had. The food was unexpectedly good and the mood at the table was genial. In fact, the buzz of tension between her and Hayden was the only thing marring it. He glanced up often, inspired by the booming laugh of Captain Konstantinos or the smiles of the crew, or to frown at something one of them said to the other in Greek. And she did her best to follow along between sips of Australian wine. Caryn was outstripping her in that regard, putting away two glasses to her one.

The wine brought immediate colour to Shirley's cheeks in a Mrs Claus way rather than the appealing slash of colour up the jaw like it did on the vivacious blonde.

Typical.

Caryn talked and Hayden listened, apparently rapt, and responded on cue. Brief but sufficient. She was certainly doing all the talking in that little relationship. But then Caryn's conversation was not what he was interested in. Fortunately, it looked as if she was equally prepared to let body language do the real talking. She turned three-quarters in to him and leaned forward to brush or touch him, *a lot*.

Eventually the night and the meal drew to a close and the crew retired to their bunks or to their shifts. Shirley stood as the man next to her did and smiled at him. 'Thank you, Captain. That was lovely.'

He murmured in Greek and then kissed her hand in a sweeping gesture and told her, in English, that the ship's cook had something suitable for breakfast or lunch at any time they cared to visit the mess room but that everyone dined together nightly.

'Tomorrow night, then,' she said smiling.

Hayden stood and gave Caryn his arm to help her to her feet. 'Tomorrow night, then,' he echoed brightly.

Maybe if she'd had less wine under her belt Caryn wouldn't have let the stab of confusion actually show on the outside, but Shirley saw it as Hayden turned to shake the Captain's hand. She allowed a momentary pang of sisterhood sympathy; Hayden had given Caryn his undivided attention for over two hours now suddenly it was 'goodnight'? She shot her a smile she hoped would be equal parts sympathetic and confederate.

Shirley moved to the door and Hayden crossed to stand behind her, reaching over her shoulder to push it open.

'Batten down the hatches,' he murmured as it gusted open.

The wind had picked up in the time they'd been in the warmth of the Captain's table, so her hair immediately exploded into a tangle around her face. Hayden moved to her other side to help shield her from the worst of it, but all she could do was move as fast as possible back along the deck and down to the floor below where the cabins were, her arms curled around the billowing mess.

She practically fell through the door into the accommodation corridor and he tumbled in behind her. They occupied the few metres to their doors by exclaiming relief at the sudden drop of the elements and then they stood, facing each other, at their respective thresholds.

'I'm coming in,' Hayden announced.

She studied the trace of anger at the corners of his lips. But there was no point fighting it and, truth be told, nine o'clock was rather early to be going to bed, even for her. She opened her door and stood back to give him access and prepared for an onslaught.

'Please, speak to me of something of consequence,' he declared, tumbling like a felled tree onto the second little bed in her room.

The door hung open. It saved her mouth from having to similarly gape. She gently clicked it shut and released the handle. 'You've had nothing but conversation all night.'

'No.' He slid his hands behind his head to replace the pillow she'd stolen to stack on top of her own. 'I've had nothing but yammer all night.'

'She was talking of her home. Her family. Things that were important to her.'

'How could you hear through all the Greek on your side of the table?'

Because she'd been motivated to eavesdrop. And because she'd always been a good lip-reader—a skill she'd perfected under the stairs. 'It was a small table.'

'Longest two hours of my life.'

'That's not fair. If you weren't interested you could have changed the subject.' By the moment, her loyalty was swinging back Caryn's way. Poor woman. She spent all day in the company of a giraffe and he begrudged her a little verbal offload. 'Or gone wild and contributed to the discussion a little.'

He snorted. 'You think the conversation lacked momentum? She talked for two hours solid.'

'It wasn't a conversation. She was doing all the work and you just sat there being enigmatic and mysterious.'

'I wasn't striving for enigma. I was striving for polite.'

Oh, really? 'Was it polite to skip out immediately the food was taken away?'

'You were about to.'

'I didn't have an offer so clearly on the table.' She balled her hands at her hips and glared down at him. Suddenly the flirtatious Caryn had taken on Everywoman status. And Hayden had assumed the wrongs of every man who had ever done womankind a bad turn.

He stared at her for heartbeats. She struggled to rein in the inexplicable heaving of her lungs.

'I wish you could see yourself right now,' he murmured, his eyes dark and keen.

Her hands immediately went to the disaster that was her hair and she hated that they'd acted of their own free will. It shouldn't matter what she looked like. Kiss or no kiss.

'Don't,' he warned. 'You'll ruin it.'

Her fingers paused a breath away from contact, trembled just slightly. 'Ruin what?'

'All that colour. All that chaos. It's perfect.'

She dropped her hands. 'You think windswept shambles is the right look for me?'

'I think anything that brings life into your eyes is a good look. But that one particularly.'

She narrowed her eyes. 'Why?'

He grinned and wriggled in more comfortably. 'If I told you that, Shirley, you'd throw me out. So how about a new subject?'

A clamp tightened around her organs way down deep inside. 'What if my conversation also fails to meet the rigid standards of Hayden Tennant?'

'Impossible. You could speak of the weather and I'd find it interesting.'

She stood firm. 'Shall we test that theory?'

The grin graduated into a full smile. 'No. Let's talk about the list. About how we're going to get ourselves up to Queenstown.'

The list. That was safer, yes.

'I don't know.' She shrugged. 'It's an adventure. Let's just see how we go.'

She *should* know. Flying by the seat of her pants was not how Shiloh usually rolled. She really needed to start getting her mind around what would happen beyond the four days with Hayden.

'And so we get there, jump, and then come back to port and these cabins? Seems rather a shame. New Zealand's very beautiful. And romantic.'

'We're not going for the romance. We're going for the adrenalin rush of leaping off a bridge.'

'This doesn't strike me as something Carol would have been into. Needlessly scaring herself witless.'

She sat on her own bed and tucked her legs up next to her. 'I don't think it's about the fear; I think it's about the sensation. The free fall. She might as easily have picked skydiving.'

'I don't see her as a sensation-seeker, either. She was so…'

Shirley lifted a brow. 'Serious?'

He shook his head. 'Cerebral.'

'So bright people trade their right to feel for intelligence? You, of all people, think that?'

He looked up. 'Why "of all people"?'

'Because you're the ultimate sensation-seeker. Or you were.' The photos online showed that.

'Are you saying you think I'm bright?'

She'd thought so once. As brilliant as a polished gem. 'Don't fish for compliments, Hayden. It belittles you.'

'I'd like to know. I know you think I'm disparaging and mean-spirited and idle. It might help balance things out a little if I thought there was any positive in there at all.'

She hadn't called him any of those things out loud so it must have leaked through in her attitude. Natural justice made her confess, 'You were always brilliant, Hayden. And ten years hasn't done anything to diminish that, it seems.'

He considered her. 'For what it's worth, the feeling is mutual.'

She tossed her hair back further from her face. 'It's worth nothing. I don't care what you think of me.'

'Oh, that's clearly not true, or you wouldn't be sitting here twitching to comb your hair.'

Again her fingers betrayed her. She curled them into her fist.

He didn't miss it. His eyes darkened and grew sharp. 'Ask me what I meant when I said this look particularly suits you.'

'No. I don't care what you meant.' And the *thump thump* of her heart was a powerful motivator to silence.

'Yes, you do. You're just too scared to know.'

She glared at him silently.

'I meant that you look like you've just crawled out of a particularly warm and sensual bed.'

Heat instantly returned to her cheeks.

'There it is again. The splash of passion.'

Damn him. She tightened her fists. 'If you'd wanted to play with someone's emotions you should have stayed upstairs.'

'Why can't I just be commenting on fact? You're usually so impeccably presented, so seeing you like this is...stimulating.'

'You should have stayed upstairs for that, too.'

'Are you trying to force me to go knocking on Caryn's door?'

Tension cranked up her spine. 'Actually, no, I don't think she's done anything to deserve the heartbreak you'd inevitably bring.'

One dark blond brow lifted. 'Harsh words, Shirley. You doubt she would understand the concept of a one-night stand?'

'I doubt she'd ever have conceived of what a one-night stand with a man like you might mean.'

The suavadore act dropped. Immediately. The air turned dangerous. 'Meaning?'

Her heart thumped for a different reason then. But she'd started it... 'Meaning it might not be enough for you just to have her and leave. You'd have to break her first.'

He stared. '"Break her"? Is that what you think?'

'It's what you do, Hayden. You take people apart. And you don't always take care to reassemble them again.'

His jaw flexed. 'Have I done that with you?'

He'd done it to year after year of idealistic students on Saturdays. 'I won't give you the chance,' she vowed. 'Ever.'

'Forever's a long time.'

'Fortunately, I have outstanding discipline.'

His smile deepened. 'Oh, yes, you do. But don't you see what that is to a *man like me*?'

She watched him, critically aware that they were alone, in a room full of beds and not much else. And critically aware of what had happened between them the last time they were here. He twisted his body into a seated position, facing her. Closer.

'It's a red rag.'

She lifted her chin. 'I still have free will.'

'I think we've seen how far your free will got you, just this afternoon.'

'I'm not interested in a one-night stand.'

His brow lifted. 'You'd be interested in something longer?'

'No, but that's a moot point. You'd never want something longer.'

'You think not?'

'I know not. If you did you'd have shacked up with any one of those women years ago.'

'What do you have against them? They were all perfectly nice women.'

'Give me one single name.'

He blinked at her.

'Just one, Hayden. If they were so lovely.' She waited. 'I think there's a reason you're so sold on the idea of a love that's intellectual, because it means you can explore the physical with no risk of attachment. Keep the two firmly separate.' She stood. 'But I'm not interested in being your intellectual intimate any more than your physical one.'

Liar!

His face hardened. 'Why not?'

'Because you're too much like hard work. And too risky.'

Blue eyes narrowed. 'What are you risking? Not your heart, which you've firmly stated is inviolate. And not your body, which you protect behind layers of sod-off. So what's left?'

My soul.

'Is this the conversation you were looking for when you came in here tonight?' she gritted.

'No. But maybe it was overdue. I certainly appreciate knowing how you really see me.'

Guilt niggled. 'Hayden, I wouldn't be here with you at all if I thought you were a horrible human being. You're not. But you're not someone that a woman should be backing, emotionally. Not once she gets to know you.'

He reeled back on the bed.

Then he stood. 'Right.'

She stood behind him, stepped towards him. 'Hayden—'

Hayden stopped her with an upheld hand. 'I'll see you in the morning, Shirley.' He got through the door and pulled it shut behind him before breathing again.

Not pity. Not on top of the mouthful of reality she'd already delivered. Just when he thought he didn't have anything soft and squishy left inside, along came Shirley in her metaphorical commando boots and ground what little was left into pulp.

Not once she gets to know you.

Not that he hadn't long suspected it—or could even disagree with it—but something about having it spelled out quite so dispassionately...

By her...

Well, he'd wanted conversation. And one thing he knew about Shirley was that any time spent with her would never go where he thought it would. He'd imagined himself a cosy little scenario that involved the two of them talking long into the night, sharing. Bonding. He'd not let himself imagine anything beyond that, but her wild and dishevelled state over dinner had teased and taunted and distracted him for most of the evening as he'd pretended to listen to Caryn but in fact fantasised about ways of getting Shirley that mussed up himself.

She'd been happily engaged in a long conversation with their trusty Captain about piracy on the high seas—though, given a chance and despite his age, he'd bet his life that the charming Captain Konstantinos would have proven just as untrustworthy with his passenger—and he'd had the double assault of endless monologue on one side and the Shirley Marr show on the other. Complete with seamen who didn't know he understood some Greek discussing with much hilarity the comparative merits of tanned blondes versus sultry brunettes.

The brunettes won.

It wasn't fair to blame Caryn for not being as interesting as the only other woman in the room. The two were completely different people. Night and day. Except he'd spent his entire life indulging in bright, obsequious day when deep down inside he was all about the cool, mysterious night. The cover of night disguised so many more faults.

Shannon. Courtney. Louisa. Dominique.

He had as many names as Shirley could possibly want to hear. It wasn't a struggle with recall that had kept him silent; it was the implication of her words. That he should have started a life with one of them by now. That he was late to some kind of party and that it was his personal failing.

Did she not see the irony?

Shirley had more shields around herself than any man could possibly negotiate. She'd be single and stoic until her last breath, despite her great faith in the random lightning-bolt strike of love.

Who was she to judge his choices?

He reached into his room and grabbed his coat, then headed for the wind storm outside. It was too early to sleep, even if he believed he could. But there was a lot of unexplored ship out there yet.

And a lot of disquiet to burn off.

He wandered the entire circumference of the freighter, staring out through the occasional slot in the bulky siding into the vast nothing of the ocean and up into the vast everything of space. So far from the visual pollution of land, and despite the floodlights at the front of the ship and the glow of the full moon, the stars seemed to blanket the dark sky. Together they were more than ample to see by.

But one circumference was complete and he wasn't yet ready to return to the solitude of his cabin, which was insane because the past two years had been all about solitude. He turned into the heart of the sea-containers massed in the middle of the vessel.

He heard Twuwu's contented rumination—a kind of chew and snort combo—before he turned the corner into her clearing. A bit of time in the company of a female with no expectations, no opinions and no judgements to cast. That was what he needed.

'Hayden?'

Hell. Awful timing on his part.

'Out for a walk?' Caryn asked. The caution in her voice was immediately obvious and his mind went straight to Shirley's defence of the woman. He sighed.

'Caryn, I think I owe you an apology...'

They talked for quite some time as Caryn finished her checks on Twuwu and settled her for the night. She accepted his fumbled explanation and his assurances of regret for his hasty departure earlier in the evening.

'Is it Shirley?' she asked, wiping her hands on her jeans.

His denial was instant. Too fast. Like his pulse at the mere suggestion of something more going on with him and Shirley. 'It's such a short trip, Caryn...'

She called him on that deflection. 'You don't really strike me as a man who would have a problem with something short-term.'

'I'm not.' At least he wasn't. That thought got him frowning.

'I thought we had a spark.'

And a spark might once have been enough. More than enough. The truth—and the outrage of what it signified—burned. 'It's me.'

She stared at him long and hard. But what could she say, really? Other than the obvious. 'Fair enough. Your loss.'

Maybe so. And given how tightly wound he'd been after storming from Shirley's room, *definitely* so. 'Come on, I'll walk you back.'

'Oh, God, chivalry? You really aren't interested.' She fell in beside him.

It felt good to laugh. And it felt strangely pleasing to have treated this woman with respect. This woman who loved her family and her homeland and was happy to talk to a stranger for hours about them.

'Can I ask you something, Caryn?'

'Shoot.'

'Is your wildlife park anywhere near Queenstown?'

'About four hundred kilometres away.'

Oh. It was worth a shot.

She took pity on him. 'But we go right through Queenstown on the way.'

He lifted his head. 'Will you need any help with Twuwu on the journey?'

She laughed. 'No. There'll be a whole transport team meeting us at Invercargill. Why? You need a lift?'

'It's a long story, but yeah.'

'Let's see what happens. There're always multiple vehicles.'

He held the door of the accommodation deck for her and dropped his voice. 'Thanks. We'll even ride in with Twuwu if we need to.'

'Are you kidding? No one gets to do that.' She stopped a few doors down from Shirley's room. 'This is me.'

He shoved his hands into his pockets, carefully away from her. He wasn't used to negotiating his way *out* of a woman's room. 'I appreciate your understanding, Caryn,' he whispered. 'Considering.'

She laughed in the silence and unlocked her door. 'I think I understand a lot better than you do.'

'See you tomorrow.'

'Yep. Bright and early.' She stepped into her room.

''Night.'

Her door clicked shut. Hayden leaned on the corridor wall and looked diagonally down the hall at Shirley's door. Would she have given him points for that? For extricating himself with care and leaving Caryn's pride intact?

He gave himself a few. And that was rare.

He pushed off the wall and his expensive shoes took him silently down the hall. He opened his door gingerly to avoid waking Shirley. It closed just as quietly.

The entire time he'd paced the ship's deck he'd been working himself up to the decision that he would sleep with Caryn just to show Shirley he didn't care what she thought. To do something with the useless tension resonating through his body and maybe to prove himself as heartless and soulless as she clearly believed. If he was going to burn, it might as well be justified.

Yet here he was, heading to bed solo.

So, all those points he gave himself for treating Caryn with compassion...?

He ripped them off again for being so damn weak.

CHAPTER SEVEN

'SO, LOOKS like we're giving you a lift when we head north.' Caryn looked up as Shirley slid into a seat across from her.

'Sorry?'

After a night with no sleep in that tiny dark cabin, she'd been desperate to get out of the confined space that had started to feel like a coffin. Hence her early breakfast. She thought she might have seen some of the crew but she hadn't expected either Caryn or Hayden. Not at this hour. Not after what she'd heard in the hall.

A deep, familiar masculine murmur. A throaty, carefully muted feminine chuckle.

The stone in her stomach settled in further. What had she expected? It wasn't reasonable to tell a man he was worthless and then be shocked when he went out to find someone to prove otherwise.

'When we hit Invercargill,' Caryn clarified. 'Our convoy will go right past Queenstown.'

A ride. She tried to muster up some enthusiasm. 'Oh, great. Thank you.'

'You don't look like backpackers,' she hinted.

So Hayden hadn't told her why they were heading for New Zealand. Shirley didn't know whether to be grateful for his discretion or appalled at his form. He *still* hadn't made actual conversation with her?

What a prince.

A confused jumble of anger and hurt curdled her hastily downed cup of tea. 'We're kind of on a...challenge.'

'You against him?'

Most of the time. 'No. Together.'

'Shame. I could have arranged to leave him behind. We girls have got to stick together.'

Shirley lifted her heavy head. The hint of solidarity confused her. 'He'd only get his wallet out and hire a chopper and be standing there, smug, when we arrived.'

Caryn's eyes grew keen. 'He's loaded then?'

'You could say that.'

She grunted and went back to her eggs. 'Well, that figures.'

'Ladies...'

The man of the moment walked through the door and slid into a seat next to Shirley. Caryn said a cheerful good morning through a mouthful of eggs and Shirley gave a tight smile as the ship's cook came out with two more plates of breakfast and placed them next to each other on her side of the table.

'How did you sleep?' Caryn asked casually.

Shirley reached for the salt and pepper, desperate to be doing something as this conversation happened around her. She concentrated on breathing.

'Actually, like a log,' Hayden said. 'Must be the sea air.'

'Or the late night exercise,' the blonde offered.

Shirley's hand closed hard around the salt shaker. Any harder and it might shatter. 'I'm surprised to see either of you up this early,' she hedged.

'Twuwu has to have checks every four hours overnight,' Caryn said. 'Ten, two and six. So here I am.'

'You went out again after I left you?'

'The line of duty,' Caryn said, wiping her hands and mouth on her napkin. 'I can sleep all I want when I get home.' She stood. 'That said, I'm going to head back down to her now for her six o'clock check. Remember to come on down and say hi. She's bored already.'

'I know the feeling,' Hayden grunted.

Was that why he'd pursued Caryn—*ennui?*

And, ultimately, what did it matter why he'd done it?

You didn't want him, Shirley...

Shirley smiled as Caryn departed, then let it fall from her lips. She focused on pushing her scrambled eggs around the plate.

'You working on a masterpiece, there, Picasso?'

She lifted her eyes to Hayden's. They were lighter, by far, than they had been when she'd last seen him. Maybe his good mood was symptomatic. Unfortunately for him, she'd had no sleep and no…stress relief to enhance her mood. She hit him with full-frontal sarcasm.

'Does arrogance come naturally to you, Hayden, or do you have to work at it?'

His frown doubled. 'Shirley…?'

'Late night exercise. Caryn.'

Duh!

Right at the back of his deep blue eyes a little light bulb illuminated. His answer was measured. 'I walked around the deck and I ran into Caryn on her way back from checking on Twuwu.'

'Unplanned, of course.'

'Yes.'

'Because you know nothing about planning seductions.'

Ha. Hoist with his own petard. And other nautical metaphors.

'There was no seduction.'

'I guess there wouldn't need to be if she was willing enough.'

'There was no sex.'

She pushed her plate away. 'Spare me the details, Hayden. I don't know why I'm so surprised.'

'Given *the kind of man I am*, you mean?'

She rounded on him, guilty heat surging forth. 'Well, was I wrong?'

'Actually, yes, you were. I have nothing to apologise for. And no requirement to, come to think of it. I'm a free agent.'

'So all those murmurings I heard last night were just hallway chit-chat, were they?'

'I have no idea what you heard, but yeah, they would have been.'

A strange kind of earnestness tinged his expression. She frowned. 'You didn't sleep with Caryn?'

'I did not.'

The overhead radio crackled out music but the silence from the kitchen suggested the cook had tiptoed out or was listening in avidly to the raised voices in the mess room. Probably the latter. Maybe he had more English than he let on.

'Right. Okay then.'

Awkward...

His lips twisted but she couldn't honestly call it a smile. 'Apology accepted.' His voice lowered dangerously. 'Now you can tell me something, Shirley... Exactly what business is it of yours what I do? Or with whom?'

She pressed her lips together. 'I... It's not.'

'Insufficient.'

Of course he wasn't going to let her just walk away from having made a colossal ass of herself. He was Hayden. She hissed out a breath. 'You'd just finished telling me how she'd yammered at you all night. So the thought that you'd go straight to her from...' She ran flat out of steam. And courage.

His eyes grew keen. 'Straight to her from you?'

She sat up straighter. 'Straight to her from our argument.'

'No. From you. That's what's bothering you.'

All right, fine. 'You kissed me half to death yesterday and just hours later you were kissing her.'

'Only I wasn't.'

'I didn't know that.' She took a breath. 'It...disappointed me.'

His eyes narrowed. 'I'm sure I disappoint you daily. That's nothing new.'

She didn't answer.

'I have no obligation to you, Shirley. We're friends.' He glanced away. 'If that.'

Ouch. That hurt, unexpectedly. 'We're friends,' she confirmed.

'Then how have I broken faith with you?'

'I just...' What? She had no idea why she had such massive

expectations of him. She sank back in her chair. 'I don't know. I don't know how. I'm sorry.'

The silence in the kitchen slowly returned to the sounds of cooking. Their conversation had apparently become less riveting. Hayden's eyes went from thoughtful to slightly abashed.

'You don't need to beg my forgiveness any more than I need to explain myself to you.'

Friends apologised to friends. Friends explained things to friends.

Not owing him an explanation was a careful way of double reinforcing the fact that they barely even made friend status. As if she'd been clinging to some kind of illusion.

Maybe she had.

Silence resumed.

'How did you go for Internet signal yesterday?' he asked, finally breaking it.

'Good. The ship has a router on the accommodation deck. The Wi-Fi is good.'

'Great.'

Awesome. Talking about Internet signal strength. Only marginally less pathetic than talking about the weather.

'Does that mean you're going to be working today?' she checked.

'I think I might. Up here in the recreation area. See what I can get done.'

Was she surprised he was in no hurry to hang out with her? Or even near her. 'Okay. Good luck with that.' She stood. 'I'm going to head off for a shower.'

'Catch you later, then.'

And less enthusiastic words had never been spoken. She noticed the careful way he studied the watery horizon.

Lord.

It was going to be a long four days.

CHAPTER EIGHT

THE CONVOY pulled away and rumbled off into the distance, leaving Hayden and Shirley standing on the edge of the Gibbston Highway, daypacks in their hands. Twuwu's massive head poking out the back of the trailer grew smaller and smaller in the distance until she pulled it back inside her crate.

Shirley did a slow three-sixty, taking in the dramatic view around them. This part of New Zealand's South Island was a topographer's delight, all ancient ranges and green river valleys with turquoise water lying far below. On the horizon, snow-capped mountain peaks were protected by a layer of white cloud.

'So, here we are,' she breathed.

'They're expecting us?'

'They know we're coming today, just not when.'

And thanks to Caryn and Twuwu being the first piece of freight off the *Paxos*, they were hours ahead of what she'd forecast.

They started walking towards a distant car park to check in. Beyond that was an old steel and stone suspension bridge that forded the river rushing by fifty metres below. And dotted all over that were people. Everywhere. Even though it wasn't yet mid-morning.

A long scream punctuated the serenity like the cry of an eagle soaring overhead, chased, moments later, by cheers and whistles.

She sucked in a breath.

Hayden glanced at her. 'Nervous?'

Until that moment, she hadn't been. She'd been way too busy

being distracted by Hayden's emotional withdrawal. But given how her body reacted to simply walking up the *Paxos*'s gang-plank, she suddenly doubted whether she'd be able to step out into the nothingness of open space at all.

Cord or no cord.

Fear was not a good way to get something like a bucket list achieved. She blew the breath out carefully. 'I guess we'll find out.'

The organisers slotted them in after the present batch of jumpers had gone through. They waited for the first hour on the observation deck, which hung out high above the gorge, amongst the friends and families of those taking the leap. As the morning wore on, the deck got more and more slippery as those taking the plunge climbed back up the side of the valley, wet, and then joined the spectators to vicariously relive their experience.

'That's a good sign,' Hayden murmured close to her ear. 'If it was traumatic I doubt people would stick around to watch others going through it.'

Trauma. Something else she hadn't thought about. She'd been so focused on how she was going to get out there at all she hadn't really thought about whether or not she'd ever recover from it.

The growing spectator crowd pressed them closer together and Hayden slid an arm around behind her to keep the soggiest of them back. Soon enough they were funnelled out of the crowded area to the two ornate stone towers that anchored the bridge to the land at both ends. A production line of safety instructions and advices began there and Shirley busied herself with taking them very seriously and making an endless stream of decisions.

'Single or tandem?' the young man in the bright T-shirt asked.

'Single,' she said. Just as Hayden said, 'Tandem.'

She looked at him. He lifted an eyebrow. 'Do you seriously think you're going to be able to do this alone?'

She glanced over the edge of the bridge at the sparkle of blue water so very far below. Not as far as in the movies, but far enough to kill you if you got it wrong. There was a couple jumping together as she watched and it wasn't…intimate…in the way tandem skydives were. They just stood next to each other.

Until they plunged, of course.

She dragged her eyes back to the young man. 'Tandem. Thank you.'

'Bob, touch or full immersion?'

'Uh…' It was like ordering a pizza. Mozzarella or feta? She glanced at Hayden, lost.

'You want to get wet?' he translated.

No. She didn't want to do this at all, as it turned out. But her mum would have wanted the full splash-down experience. 'Full immersion?'

Hayden smiled at her uncertainty and murmured, 'That's my girl.'

They shuffled forward. Only one station from the one with rubber ropes involved. Oh Lord…

A girl met them this time, even younger than the first and with a heavy Welsh accent. She took them through the safety talk again and outlined the procedure for getting out of the water at the bottom.

'Relax,' Hayden murmured in her ear.

Her tight throat translated into a squeaky voice. 'This place is run by child backpackers…'

He laughed and shuffled her forward, right to the opening on the side of the red iron bridge. It wasn't glamorous—far from it—but the men doing the tying on at least did look as if they'd been shaving for longer than a year.

Ahead of them a young woman jumped, and then a fifty-something man.

Surely if someone with silver hair could do it then she could do it?

A heavily tattooed arm waved them forward.

Her feet locked to the bridge as surely as if they had been bolted there. 'I can't do it.'

Hayden looked back. 'Yeah, you can. Look how much trouble you've gone to getting here.'

She pressed back against the side of the suspension bridge. 'It doesn't matter. I can't do this.'

Behind Hayden, the man lowered his arm and started towards them. She instinctively curled her fingers into Hayden's shirt in case the big guy just picked her up and threw her over. His arms immediately curled around her. 'What about you just step out there with me. Take a look?'

She'd been looking all this time—what was going to change about it out there? She shook her head.

'Come on, gorgeous.' The operator smiled, reaching them. 'It's not as bad as it looks. You've got a fourteen-year-old behind you.'

She turned to check on the veracity of that. Sure enough, a toothy kid smiled back at her.

'Is this your first time?' she asked.

He shook his ginger hair. 'Fourth. It's cool.'

She looked back to Hayden. 'There you go,' he said. 'It's cool.'

She didn't want to be cool; she wanted to be alive. Then, right hard on the heels of that thought, came another one—they were doing this in the first place to *feel* alive. To experience life in all its forms.

Including its terrifying ones.

Her foot peeled off the deck.

'That's the way,' the operator said and whistled for his compatriot, who hung two large white lengths of rubber rope on their bollards.

Hayden curled his fingers through hers and led her forward.

'Aren't you scared?' she whispered up at him.

'Yep. But I'm not about to let you see that. On principle.' He winked at her. 'Anything Shiloh can do, I can do.'

Shiloh. She could do it.

She let herself be shuffled out onto a platform fixed to the side of the bridge and she let the safety lesson wash over her. Something about the little yellow boat that would come for them when they were done and about keeping your feet together.

As she heard the words, someone snapped two thick blue straps around her ankles like fabric handcuffs, forcing them together. Then they did Hayden's. It meant they could shuffle but not walk out onto the timber dive-boards that got them clear of the bridge. One was skinny, the other wider. For two.

Hands guided her out onto the wide one and Hayden shuffled up next to her.

'Okay?' His glance held genuine concern. 'Ready?'

Her chest tightened so hard she could barely get a word out. 'No.'

'To which?'

'To both.' The blood rushed past her ears the way the river below them roared down the gorge.

'Take a second, Shirley,' he whispered close to her ear. 'Appreciate where we are.'

She forced her head up, away from the milky-blue water deep below, forced herself to think about where they were and what they were doing. How extraordinary it was. How stunning the landscape was.

'Look at me...'

She brought her eyes back to his. They were the same blue as the tumbling water below. For one fanciful moment that actually made all this better because falling from a great height into Hayden's eyes was something she could easily imagine. And not imagine hating.

Her pulse settled just a fraction.

'This is for your mum,' he said. He lifted the hand that she hadn't realised he still had clasped in his. 'We're doing this because she couldn't. And I really can't imagine a time or a place that we could possibly be closer to her than here, doing this crazy wrong thing. Look around and tell me that gods didn't carve these mountains, that angels don't roost amongst those trees.'

She did, and she couldn't.

'We're going to step out together, Shirley, into this magical, mysterious air. And it's going to glide us down safely to the boat below like God's breath.'

She stared up at him, her icy fingers clenched tightly in his, breathing as fast and shallow as she had after their kiss. Every single thing she knew about him and his past evaporated in that moment and he was just a man she trusted, a man she admired. A man heavy with flaws but so very heavy with brilliance, too.

A man who could get her through this and any other challenge she ever had in life.

She smiled, even if it did wobble. 'You're so full of it, Tennant.'

His head dropped and his smile broke sunlight across the whole valley. 'But did it work?'

She looked inward. Her pulse had leveled out, her breathing had eased and even the distance below them seemed to compress into something survivable. This was just like jumping off the high board back in school.

A really, really high board.

She turned and faced outwards, keeping her hand curled in his. 'It worked.'

Behind them the tattoo guy counted down.

Five...four...

When he got to three, Hayden turned suddenly, bent and pressed his mouth to hers, hot and hard.

One.

Gravity tore their lips apart as they fell forward, free and fast, and her stomach heaved. The sound coming out of each of them was much the same, just harmonised. Then the straps around her ankles tightened into a fabric vice and her free fall arrested and she was dunked bodily into the Kawarau River before being yanked out again and hurled back into the air like a rag doll.

Her smaller size meant she bounced in opposition to Hayden, laughing and sobbing and crying out to the gods that she'd just defied by surviving such a fall. Life coursed through her veins like the drug it was, and she simultaneously felt the exact position of every cell in her body. Every decision in her life suddenly grew acutely clear—the wrong turns and the right. Above her dangling self she saw the yellow pickup boat moving into position and the pressure of her full weight on her ankles started to bite. Her hair pointed in long, straight, drenched shards to the earth.

'Oh, my God!'

She turned to face Hayden, hanging upside down like Spiderman next to her. He reached out a hand, stretched out a finger and snagged one of hers, pulling her close as the pickup guys hooked her bungee with a boat hook. It took only a minute to pull them down into the boat and release the ankle boots. She fell, as heavy and inelegant as a load of fish from a dragnet, into the base of the boat. Hayden sprawled in next to her. Their cords vanished back up into the sky.

There were no words.

There was no past and no future.

There was no one in the world but them.

She twisted in the puddle on the floor of the boat and threw her arms around Hayden, overcome. Their wet, heated bodies fused together along with their lips. His hands bunched in her wet hair and pulled it out of the way so that his mouth could raze her own. She sucked in his air and his smell and the very flavour of him and pressed herself more fully against him, desperate for more. Wondering how she'd survived this long without ever feeling this.

Her head spun more now than during her free fall.

He twisted her into him and dragged her across his lap as the little boat began to move to the edge of the gorge. She fed off his heat and gasped at the furnace of his touch.

It was the gasp—or maybe the touch—that drew a tactful throat-clear from one of the two men running the boat. 'Adrenalin,' he volunteered. 'We get this a lot.'

She immediately stiffened and went to pull away but Hayden simply lifted his lips and pulled her back to lie in the soggy bottom of the dinghy, staring at the sky. Together. His heart hammered right below her ear where she rested on his chest. Hers matched it. It hadn't stopped pounding since she'd first stepped onto the bridge all the way up there, and it was still repeating as hard as their outboard motor now.

As she lay there using Hayden as a pillow, the cadence of the thumps and the punctuation of his breaths formed a hypnotic blanket. Slowly...so slowly...her pulse eased, her breath returned and her mind was quiet.

'Land ho,' one of the two men said as the dinghy bumped against the edge of the gorge. She would have scrambled out anyway but it was doubly tough in saturated clothes that clung and inhibited her progress.

What was it with her and Hayden? She seemed to be forever plucking sodden garments from her body when he was around. This time she didn't bother. If he wanted to stare at her wet butt as he followed her up the long, steep trail back to the top of the gorge he could knock himself out.

It wasn't as if they were strangers any more. Not after that kiss. Or the one before it.

'Retinas intact?' she asked, back over her shoulder, when she should have been apologising for launching herself on him.

He laughed through the puff of scaling the gorge wall. 'So far so good.'

The climb became torture, so close behind the chemical rush of the jump and the muscle collapse of recovery, and took all her strength and air. Conveniently, it also excused her lapse into silence.

She used the time to think.

What had just happened?

He might have kissed her briefly at the top of the jump but it had been more of a solidarity kiss, a kiss for courage. What they had just shared splayed out in the bottom of the boat, despite the audience, was something else altogether. Something far more dangerous.

And she'd started it.

The adrenalin, of course. The skipper of the pickup boat had excused it as much. In that moment she'd needed nothing more in the entire world than someone to connect with. But would she have done that with some stranger that she'd just met?

No.

This was about Hayden.

She'd felt it when she'd first walked up to him at his cottage and he'd looked at her with such sultry interest. She'd felt it surrounded by children, crouched across a suburban battlefield from Leonidas, and doubly so when they'd lain in the sun drying. She'd definitely felt it when he'd kissed her half to death to make his point just a few nights ago.

All of those moments were just leading to the one they'd just shared in the boat.

And he knew it.

You started to buy in to me touching you months ago...

He'd warned her. He'd told her how his vision of strategic seduction worked. Why should she be surprised, now, to discover his manipulations were working?

Except...was it manipulation if you really wanted it?

If you started it?

Then again, wasn't that one of the key principles of his theory? Convincing her it was her idea all along.

She emerged at the top of the gorge slightly ahead of him and didn't wait. She struck out across the car park, shaking her head briefly at the staff member waiting at the top to upsell a second jump.

Seriously? People could do it again after just a short break?

'Shirley...'

She kept moving.

'Are we jogging back to the ship?'

That slowed her. Where exactly did she think she was going? She had to face him sometime.

'Stop.' A strong hand curled around her upper arm and drew her to a halt.

She let him pull her into a standstill, smack bang in the middle of the car park out here in the middle of nowhere. Halfway back to the locker that held their daypacks.

She spun on him. 'What?'

'We kissed. It's not the end of life as we know it.'

Not for him, maybe. The chances of her ever forgetting how she'd felt with her skin merging with his? Not high. 'It wasn't what I wanted.'

'You kissed me.'

'I know!' That was what was so infuriating. And confusing.

'It doesn't mean anything.'

Again, not for him, maybe. She lifted her eyes. 'It means your stupid games worked.'

He wasn't about to pretend he didn't understand. A tiny part of her acknowledged the respect that hinted at. 'I thought it was a pretty good way to cap off an amazing experience.'

'That's because it wasn't your mother we were doing this for.' She frowned. How had her mother come into this all of a sudden?

'No. We're a decade too late for my mother. And she never had a bucket list. She was too busy surviving.'

A car tooted politely behind them and Shirley realised they were standing in the middle of the vehicular thoroughfare. She stepped back, away from Hayden, and he did the same. The car progressed through.

'What do you mean?' she asked when he stepped back up next to her.

His eyes stayed fixed on the building their lockers were in. But he avoided her question. 'You can't use your mother as a shield every time we start getting close.'

She stiffened. 'I don't.'

'Yeah, Shirley. You do.'

'Then we see it differently.'

He hissed his frustration and she turned and kept walking. 'I'll tell you how I see it,' he said, catching up with her. 'We have massive chemistry but, instead of indulging it and working it out of our systems, we go head to head constantly and leak it out that way.'

'Speak for yourself,' she muttered.

'I am speaking for myself. I just stand near you, Shirley Marr, and my cells start twitching. If that little boat had been slower and emptier and if what I wanted was the only thing that mattered, then you and I would be having sex right now instead of standing up here getting our kicks verbally.'

'You make a lot of assumptions, Tennant.'

'You're lying if you say you don't feel it.'

She spun again. 'I don't *want* to feel it.'

He snorted. 'I get that, loud and clear. It must infuriate you to find yourself attracted to *a man like me*.'

'Oh, will you let that go? I was angry.'

'You're always angry, Shirley. And it's getting pretty old.'

She stared at him, shuffling through all the words available to her and none of them seemed adequate. Except maybe the truth.

'You're not safe, Hayden,' she whispered, pressing her fingers to her left breast. 'For me.'

The rapid change of direction had him shaking his head. He took a moment to choose his words. 'Life isn't safe, Shirley. But you have to live it or you might as well not bother.'

'Like you haven't been for the past few years?'

His eyes didn't waver. 'Yeah. Exactly like that. I was just taking up air.'

Her lips pressed together. But on some level she recognised his use of the past tense. 'Why?'

'No.' He shook his head. 'You don't get to have it both ways, Shirley. You can't keep me locked at arm's length but then expect me to share myself with you.'

'Is that why you never have close relationships? So you don't have to share yourself?'

His jaw tightened and his skin seemed to drop colour. 'The bus is coming.'

She followed his eyes and, sure enough, the hourly shuttle bus back to Queenstown was trundling over the traffic bridge that spanned the Kawarau River.

They turned for the locker area and retrieved their property. Shirley checked in briefly with the owner and got a contact for a later interview on the history of this insane sport, then jogged across the asphalt and climbed onto the waiting bus.

Hayden sat three-quarters of the way back, staring out of the window. Expression closed. As she approached, she saw that his bag occupied the empty seat next to him.

Right.

She pivoted on her feet and returned to a seat immediately behind the driver and promptly engaged him in a conversation long enough to pass the entire trip back to Queenstown.

The driver radioed ahead and arranged with the departed Invercargill bus to slow its progress long enough for them to intercept it on the highway. They did a quick roadside bus-swap and found themselves heading south. This time Hayden left the seat next to his open and she sank into it wordlessly. She pulled out her notepad and made some fast notes from her discussion with the driver and then busied herself admiring the stunning scenery as they travelled south to the coast. Out of the window, away from Hayden. But the whole time he dominated her thoughts. Him and the heated moments in the boat.

They cleared port immigration and headed for the waiting *Paxos*.

'Welcome back,' the crewman they'd first met said as she hurried up the gangway. Not because the ship was waiting to leave but because she couldn't wait a moment longer to get a nice solid door between herself and Hayden.

So much hung, unsaid. Yet they'd also said too much. How could both be true?

He led them back up to the accommodation corridor and turned to them with a flourish.

'Two rooms,' he announced in passable English, clearly pleased with himself.

They'd had to surrender their rooms on arrival for immigration reasons but their bags sat waiting neatly in the hallway outside their previous accommodation. Shirley stared at her bag as though she were seeing it for the very first time.

Hayden's words back up at the gorge whooshed through her head.

Life isn't safe.

She could spend the next few months running from the feelings that were growing more confusing and more intense by the day, or she could turn and face them. On her own terms. Maybe she could control it if she was driving it.

Or die trying.

'One room,' she heard herself saying past a dry mouth.

The crewman's lined face wrinkled further. Hayden's eyes swung her way.

'One room?' the two men said together.

She locked eyes with Hayden. Shock filled them. And that was pretty rare in the Master of the Impassive. She lifted a brow. Took a breath. 'Any objections?'

Five little syllables that changed so very much.

He stared at her, a question live in his blue eyes. The crewman glanced between them, still uncertain.

'One room.' Hayden nodded.

In a flourish of reproachful Greek, the crewman collected her bag and Hayden's and swung the door to his old room open and placed the suitcases inside. Then he turned and stomped off. Shirley followed Hayden in, her heart wringing every single drop of blood out of its tight chambers. He spun around to face her as soon as she clicked the door shut behind them. And locked it.

'You have to live life or you might as well not bother,' she quoted, bolder than she felt.

Suspicion lined his handsome face. 'You didn't want this.'

'I still don't.' He frowned. She swallowed slowly, dampened her lips. 'So why do I? So very badly?'

Then she was moving. And so was he. They came together in the middle of the tiny room, all hands and lips and tongues and clumsy haste. Hayden pressed her up against the locked door and plundered with his tongue, forking his fingers into her hair and yanking it roughly out of its elastic band. She did the same with his T-shirt from the band of his shorts. It was still damp from their river dunking and bus travel. But freeing it meant she could slide her hands around his searing flesh and mould the refined, lean contours of the back she'd glimpsed when he was Leonidas as he pressed into her hard from the front.

'It's like the surf at night,' he murmured, nuzzling his face into the dark waves of her hair and breathing fire into her ear. She smiled at the poet still in him, knowing well what it must really look like after their adventures today, and tipped her head back as far as the door behind her would allow so that he could suck and bite his way across her throat.

Then he returned to her mouth, pressing short and long kisses into her receptive flesh as he ground his hips into hers. 'I've wanted to do this since you first sat in my living room all prim and proper and with boots fastened up to your knees.' His hands left her hair and traced a path down to her waist. 'I wanted, then, to unlace you one eyelet at a time. This will have to do.'

Her dark maroon shorts were a surf brand, tied at the top for effect. He impatiently yanked each lace free of its eyelet and then pulled her backwards towards the two tiny beds. He released her only long enough to get behind one while she got behind the other and they pushed them together, the momentum flinging them back into each other's arms as they met in the middle.

She kneeled on her side of the bed, stretching up to find his mouth again, breathing heavily. Gasping as she had in the boat. Overwhelmed by her own audacity. And need.

He fisted his fingers in her hair and tipped her head back, away from his lips, until her heavy glance lifted and focused on his.

'Are you sure, Shirley?'

She was sure that she'd never felt this swirling, uncontrollable need in her life. She was sure this moment would never come again if she stopped it now. She was sure that people had survived entire lifetimes on a single glance, a touch, and that just wasn't going to be enough for her.

Was she sure…?

'No,' she breathed. 'But I'm doing it anyway.'

He circled her with his arms and twisted her below him, lying at right angles across the rift between the twin beds, pressing down hard and hot on top of her and gently finding her lips with his. If he'd come on heavy just then—seducer Hayden—she might have baulked, the intensity of feeling soft mattress below her and solid man above just a little bit too real. But he didn't; he timed his switch to explorer Hayden just perfectly—long, leisurely, lazy—and it sucked her into a place where the room spun gently and her breath shallowed out, and the only thing that wasn't spinning or stealing oxygen was right in front of her.

Hayden.

Heavy and protective lying across her. Stroking her hair back from her damp face, taking his time, getting to know her, his blue eyes creating an anchor for her out-of-control emotions. He levered himself up onto one hand and stripped his shirt off with the other, watching her closely the whole time. Waiting for her to freak out and change her mind. Waiting for her to follow suit.

She lay there, breathing heavily as his eyes raked her body. Flat out refusing to back out now. Just when she was getting everything she didn't know she wanted.

'You want some help getting those off?' he whispered, his eyes darkening dangerously and his fingers tracing down her shirt to her unlaced shorts.

'What?' She gasped at his fingers low against her belly and forced herself to focus.

'Your shorts. Your shirt.'

She sucked her lip between her teeth and breathed, 'You want them...?'

His body answered for him. His eyes darkened. 'I want what's inside them.'

She locked eyes on his and smiled—determined, desire-heavy, defiant—and then purred two magical words into the air between them.

'*Molon labe*.'

CHAPTER NINE

COME and take them.

Boy, had he. He'd practically torn them in his haste to get them off her, to strip off all the final trappings of Shiloh and get back to the raw essence of Shirley.

Raw.

The right word. That was how they'd been long into the evening. They'd missed the captain's supper—*bad passengers*—and he'd had to sneak up to the galley late that night to guilt the cook into bundling together a few things for them to eat. To refuel.

A few hours later they'd fallen asleep, slick and spent and wrapped in each other's scent in the pushed-together bed.

And now it was morning. And Shirley was stirring.

Hayden used the last precious moments of her oblivion to scan her face once more. Free of make-up, free of stress, free of any kind of judgement. Greedy, guilty, stolen moments. He lifted a single lock of dark hair from her face with his little finger.

Her eyes fluttered open, confused. But they cleared again a heartbeat later as she remembered what they'd shared the night before.

He put on his game face. 'Good morning.'

She stretched like a cat under the sheets. Winced. Then blushed at the reason for the wince. Then smiled.

A smile. *Could've been worse.*

'Morning,' she murmured.

'Hungry?'

'Ravenous.'

'Want to head up to breakfast?'

'In a bit.'

He nodded. 'Want first run at the bathroom?'

She shook her head. 'Let me wake up first.'

'Want to talk about what changed between Queenstown and the docks?'

He didn't mean to say it, didn't even know he wanted to ask it until the words tumbled off his lips. He wasn't in the habit of questioning—or pushing—his luck.

She watched him steadily. 'Other than the scenery?'

'Ha ha.'

She sat up and kept the sheet tucked carefully under her arms. That seemed a crime now that he knew from first-hand experience what was under there. The memory of her skin sliding against his was still so fresh.

She shrugged. Slowly. 'I just decided that casual sex shouldn't be merely a male prerogative.'

His gut tightened. 'Casual as in one-off?' It hadn't felt very casual as she'd writhed under him and clenched her long fingers into his flesh.

She arched a brow. 'I think we're already over our quota for that, don't you?'

Point.

'Casual as in...casual,' she went on. 'Not a big deal. Something nice to do when we see each other.'

Nice. He stared at her, not letting the twist in his belly grow into anything harder. 'Those might just be the last words on the planet I ever expected to come out of your mouth.'

She leaned back against the wall and kept her eyes guarded. 'Maybe I've found myself at sea.'

Or lost yourself. And he had a nasty feeling he might have been responsible for that.

Shouldn't he be celebrating now? He'd got to have sex with Shirley. Shirley-the-untouchable. She'd let him touch her wherever he wanted last night. Repeatedly.

A man like you...

Had he dragged her down to his level?

Her scowl returned and that, too, was a crime after the ecstasy that he had seen stamped on her features last night. 'Relax, Hayden. You haven't corrupted me. I'm here because I wanted to be.'

Had she meant to use the past tense?

And…by the way…could he *be* more of a teenage girl about this?

He gave himself a mental punch. *Come on.* This was what he did. He had sex with beautiful women, enjoyed them in the moment, kissed them goodbye and moved on. Occasionally he came back for round two but never round three. On principle.

Moments like this were not new to him. But this…disquiet certainly was.

This felt all kinds of wrong.

He glanced at naked, make-up-less, alabaster-skinned Shirley. Carol-Anne's little girl. But he would totally have hit on her way back when she'd sat in his living room like a gift from the gods of sensuality if he'd thought he had a chance, and he'd known *then* who she was. So it couldn't just be about her genes.

This was about her.

He was uncomfortable because it was *her*.

Shirley. The person. The woman. The soul.

He pushed to his feet. 'I might just grab a shower.' It was down the hall. A decent physical separation so that he could think.

Khaki eyes tracked him silently as he pulled on jeans and a T-shirt over his nothingness and bundled up some clean underwear and a towel. That beautiful mind turning slowly over. It made him nervous. But he made himself turn back and smile. Just because he was wigging out didn't mean he had to show it.

'Back in a tick.'

She nodded and he was gone. The one bathroom on the floor was small but serviceable and, given how few of them there were on this skeleton-crew voyage, it was in reasonable condition. He stripped off again and stepped under the spray before it was fully warm.

Shirley hadn't responded to him as if she was caving under

pressure. On the contrary, she'd taken the lead. She'd been more than decisive at his door yesterday afternoon. Far more than he'd managed. All he'd done this trip was moon around feeling misunderstood. Last night Shirley had been a wake-up call. A healthy reminder that short, passionate affairs were his past and his future. And roughly what he had a right to expect, given the kind of man he was. If she'd gone on being enigmatic and chaste and so bloody *uninterested* he might have started getting unhealthily obsessed. Clouded and off-track. Started doubting the lessons of his life.

He was a man who did best with his emotions firmly holstered.

She was a woman who had impeccable timing and a sense of the dramatic. Just because she played him better than most didn't mean it wasn't still a play. Hell, he admired her all the more for it. That kind of sense for people would do very well at his firm. Below the intrigue and the professional disguise, Shirley was a woman just like any other—infinitely less inhibited as the night wore on and she let herself open to him—and hard to walk down the hall away from. But basically made of the same cloth.

And, frankly, he was relieved.

If she'd been cut from any other fabric he might have had a much harder time walking away from her. Not just down the hall to the shower but *away*.

He built himself a decent soap lather and then slopped it everywhere that mattered. Rather more roughly than was warranted.

Again—why wasn't he celebrating? He had a gorgeous, flammable woman in his bed offering him a no-strings out, and the significant pleasure that he gleaned from being right. Last night had been in their future from the first time she had let him touch her.

So why would he really rather be wrong?

Shirley let her breath out slowly and evenly as Hayden's footsteps diminished with distance. She sagged back against the wall.

What was she doing?

Had she truly gone all *friends-with-benefits* on him? Hayden? The man who'd made an art form of the one-night stand? As if there was any other way of doing things in his head. She might just as likely wander up to the bridge of the *Paxos* and tell Captain Konstantinos the difference between port and starboard.

Part of what she'd said was true—she was here because she wanted to be. But he'd looked so earnest when he'd asked her what had changed after Queenstown, and then so *sick* when she had assured him how much she wanted to be here.

Way to play all your cards at once, Shirley.

But done was done. And there were worse outcomes, for her, than having him believe none of this was a big deal. Though it was. A very big deal. She might have made her decision suddenly but she hadn't done it lightly. She knew exactly what she'd be sacrificing by being with him. But she hoped her dignity would be partially salvaged by making it clear that them being together was not because of any *influence* he'd applied, but because it was her choice. What she wanted.

And was it ever.

She'd stood there in the corridor and tried to imagine them going to their separate rooms and maintaining a careful distance all the way back to Australia, the way they had on the way out. And she couldn't do it. Too much had passed between them.

She'd hung, upside-down, from that old bridge and curled her fingers around his as he pulled her into his strong orbit and she'd known there and then that they would be together one way or another.

Her subconscious just hadn't updated the rest of her until the last moment.

And maybe it had been wise not to if it had had a clue of the ferocious charge that would surge between them once she opened the proverbial floodgates. The moment her decision had been made and his lips had touched hers…she'd been lost.

Lost enough to still feel it now.

Lost enough to want more the moment he got back.

But sane enough not to let it show.

Ever.

Four days back seemed to take half the time of the journey east. Maybe it had something to do with the ocean currents or trade winds, or the way time altered when she was with Hayden. And how it lagged when they were apart. Which wasn't often. They slept together, they ate together, they walked together, they worked together.

A whole lot of together considering they were two very un-together type people. But having no right to claim on someone was strangely liberating. Either of them could walk out of the door at any moment and the other would have no fair cause for complaint.

But something kept them tethered to each other like they had been up at Kawarau gorge.

Maybe it was knowing that as soon as the boat docked in Sydney—this moment, now—their relationship would be over. Their *thing*. No legitimate reason to be with each other any longer. Until next time. A few more precious, extraordinary days.

Shirley turned and peered up the vast hull of the docked *Paxos*. She waved back at Captain Konstantinos on the bridge. Funny how rapidly friendships formed when you took meals together.

Going back to eating alone was going to be tough.

She turned back to Hayden, standing on the dock. Funny how rapidly friendships formed when you took pleasure together, too. The past four days had been the shortest and longest of her life. He'd liberated parts of her she'd never met before and let her get closer than she could ever have imagined getting to him. Not all the way in, but part way.

For him, she sensed, that was a lot.

'So...' He swung around to face her once they were clear of the busy port activity.

She smiled up at him brightly, determined not to let anything show. 'So...'

'I guess that's it then?'

Did he have to sound so relieved? 'Guess so.'

'Until next time?'

Right. The list wasn't done yet. That meant neither were they. 'The next one's yours,' she breathed. And that meant the ball was in his court. If he didn't want to see her again then he only had to drag out organising the next list item.

She wasn't going to beg.

He looked away, watched a dispute between forklifts nearby. Then he brought his eyes back to her. 'I really enjoyed New Zealand. The journey. Our time together.'

Lord… Were all casual things this awkward to walk away from? 'Yeah, it was fun.'

And intense and challenging and scary and deeply moving all at the same time. But 'fun' just seemed safer to go with under the circumstances.

'Thank you,' he finally said. The first honest thing to come from his mouth.

'What for?' Throwing herself at him or not making a scene about their parting?

'For letting me come on this journey with you.'

'I know you probably would have been more comfortable on one of those.' She nodded at yet another cruise liner berthed across the harbour. And suddenly she was imagining being with him in an opulent suite with a spa bath and a king-sized bed and a really plush, really comfortable carpet.

'Maybe, but it wouldn't have been nearly as memorable. Actually, I was thanking you for letting me in on this whole journey to fulfil the list. It's been—' he struggled for the right word '—good for me. To have direction. Purpose.'

That was such a profound thing to say twenty seconds before they parted ways.

Unless…

It wasn't too profound for a goodbye statement. It would be just like Hayden to seek closure with some grand gesture. Maybe he wouldn't follow up with the next list item after all.

She stretched up and kissed him on the cheek. Ridiculously chaste. Determined to save him the trouble of ending things.

'Goodbye, Hayden. I'll see you—' *Soon? Later? In my dreams?* She didn't have control over any of them, so she just settled for, 'I'll see you.'

'I'll be in touch.'

Which was just one step removed from *'I'll call you.'*

She had no experience with the whole friends-with-benefits thing. What was the protocol here? Cool, aloof and *take it as it comes?* Or warm, open and *on like Donkey Kong the next time I see you?* She was almost certain it wasn't *throw your arms around him and beg him to stay.*

That burning urge couldn't be good for anyone. And, as she'd once bragged, her strongest trait was supposed to be her self-discipline.

She turned for the long-stay parking and reached for her bag. He bent for it at the same time and their fingers tangled on the handle. He straightened, his eyes locked on hers. He relinquished the bag.

'I'll be in touch,' he repeated. Somehow his intense eye contact was like an elaborate signature at the bottom of a legal document. So she knew he meant it.

She smiled. Turned. Left.

Walking away was even harder than stepping off the platform up in the gorge. At least then she'd had the press of his hot, urgent lips to distract her.

Now she had nothing.

CHAPTER TEN

'I AM almost certain this is not what my mother had in mind.'

Six weeks. Six weeks after the *Paxos* had berthed in Sydney and swapped her half-empty cargo for a full complement and left two passengers standing on the dock.

Six long weeks without seeing Hayden.

But she wasn't about to betray her excitement.

The two of them wobbled horribly in a dug-out canoe ten feet from the jetty sticking out from the immaculately crafted but soulless canal suburb feeding off the Georges River.

'Where did you hire this…?' She hesitated to call it a boat.

'This gondola.'

Her laugh was immediate. It was partly fuelled by sheer joy at sitting across from him again. She hadn't realised until she'd opened the door to him earlier today how not-fully she'd been breathing in the previous six weeks. She sucked in the fresh air now and her body exulted. 'This is not a gondola.'

He ignored her. 'We're not going to get to Venice on a freighter and even hiring a gondola here was more costly than I thought was appropriate, given the no-money restriction.'

'This was the best you could steal?'

He tutted, offended. 'Make, actually.'

'You made this?' She stared at the most cerebrally talented man she knew. 'With your hands?'

He flushed overtly. 'I had help, but yes.'

In that light, it wasn't all that bad. But it still wasn't a gondola. 'Why isn't it finished?'

He stared at her. 'Because I'm impatient.'

Her heart flip-flopped. Had he been eager to see her? He could have picked up the phone at any time. Then again, no, he couldn't, not without saying much more than he would have been comfortable with. 'Impatient to finish the list?'

His eyes darkened and one side of his mouth quirked as he concentrated on keeping the little boat upright. 'No.'

Oh. But she wasn't brave enough to ask further so she worked her way around to what she really wanted to know. Crafty as a fox. 'Who helped you make it?'

'Russell.'

Should that mean something? 'Russell who?'

His dark brows folded down. 'Actually, I don't know. Russell from the dolphin place.'

She sat back hard in the canoe. 'The guide?'

'Yeah. He's a carpenter in his day job.'

Not a very good one, it seemed. But, since it was better than either of them could have done she wasn't going to judge. 'How do you know? You only said two words to him.' And neither of them were polite.

'We've been...working together.'

'What? Since when?' Not cool, that high-pitched squeak in her voice. She moderated it.

'Since about a month after we went out into the surf with him.'

She gaped and then grabbed at the sides of the boat as it rocked perilously again.

'He got me involved with the Dolphin Preservation Society. They're a client now.'

Umbrage broiled up fast. 'You hit them up for business?'

His lips thinned. 'Yes, Shirley. I figured they must have millions hidden beneath the moth-eaten nothing they appear to have and I wanted my cut.'

She let the rest of her confusion out on a hiss. 'I don't understand.'

'I work with them *pro bono*. Help them to position themselves in the market, to find contributors for their cause and customers for the beach experience. Building their capacity.'

A strange kind of mist rose on the water, swirled around their boat and then sucked up into her body, making her feel light and fluid. 'You helped them?'

'I am capable of random acts of kindness from time to time.' His words were half defensive.

'I… Yes, of course.' She'd seen that gentle side at work. Up close and personal. 'Why didn't you tell me?'

'I just did.'

'No, months ago… Why keep it to yourself?'

'I knew you'd carry on like this. Make a big deal of it.'

'I'm not carrying on, I'm curious.' She sat taller. 'And it is a big deal.'

'Well, far be it from me to fail to assuage Shiloh's fathomless curiosity.'

Super-hedge. And then it hit her. Her breath tripped over the skipped beat of her heart. 'Did you… Was it because of me?'

Ridiculous, surely. He wouldn't care what she thought of him. Beyond what she thought of him in the sack. And he knew the answer to that. Because no one could fake the responses he elicited.

'No, it wasn't for you.' Immediate. Slightly urgent.

Okay. 'So it was for you?'

He rushed to address that misconception, too. 'No, it was not. It was for them.'

She smiled as he realised he'd been snookered. Whether for her, or them or himself, it didn't change the facts. 'That's a pretty significant philosophical shift, Hayden.'

'You think I'm only interested in money? Ever?'

'Based on the evidence, yes.' Except now the evidence had changed. Now he'd thrown a massive curve-ball into her neatly stacked up preconceptions. And she knew she'd never be able to stack them the same way again.

Which meant it had just got a whole heap harder to keep her feelings at arms' length. While he was a man who would use his skills to exploit and manipulate others it was possible to maintain a rigid defence against the attraction and intrigue that battered on the door of her resolve.

But if he was a man who helped those who helped others. A man who'd carve a boat to please her. Or jump from a bridge...

She needed to move things back onto a safer footing. 'So this is our gondola?'

'And this—' he cast his arms wide at the ultra-modern canal lined with expensive houses '—is our Venice.'

It was a bit of a cop-out, but then again Venice was a very long way away, and he had *built something*—with his hands—for her. That was a turn-on in a very caveman kind of way.

Okay, Venice it was.

She settled herself more primly in the bow of the boat and tucked the folds of her skirt around her. 'Shouldn't you be poling us along? And singing in Italian?'

'Nobody needs to hear that,' he joked. 'But...*Ecco!*'

He drew a tall, brightly painted pole from along the floor of the canoe. The boat wobbled horribly as he rose to his feet, balancing the timber across him like some kind of trainee circus performer and then lowering it into the water on one side. Somehow they stayed upright.

'Is it long enough? This channel looks awfully deep.' It had to be for some of the enormous pool toys moored to every jetty.

He slid it into the water. 'We'll find out.'

It was, though Hayden's prowess in the field of gondoliering left a lot to be desired. Fortunately his prowess in other fields more than made up for their slow progress. They splashed on in silence for a few minutes and Shirley let herself enjoy the view. Both in the boat and out of it. Hayden's muscles bunched under his T-shirt as he propelled them along, his locked thighs holding him steady in the little boat.

She let herself look her fill. Everything around them went kind of...glazy.

'Don't look at me like that, Shirley,' he warned after a silent moment. 'It's just a canoe.'

Whoops. What had she failed to disguise? She caught his

eyes. Held them. 'You built it with your hands.' *For me.* 'That's not nothing.'

His snort was about as graceful as his boat. 'I did that to get laid. I knew I couldn't show up empty-handed and expect you to invite me back into your bed.'

No. She knew him well enough now. The defensive tone stood out in mile-high fluoro. He'd done it for her. To please her. A warm rush started at her toes and worked its way upwards. But pressing the point wasn't going to help matters.

'How kind that you were willing to wait for an invitation,' she teased.

He smiled, infuriating in its confidence and seat-squirmingly uncomfortable in its sexiness. 'Lip service. I know how I affect you.'

Yes, he did. More fool her. And he was affecting her right now. To the point that she wanted to do something about it. Something they weren't going to be able to manage in his terrible gondola.

So she changed the subject instead. Big time. Desperate times, desperate measures.

'How old were you when your mum died?'

Hayden dropped his chin, didn't answer, just kept punting them along. For the longest time. 'What makes you think she died?' he eventually said.

She shook her head. 'What you said just before you met Twuwu, about your parents sitting there together being the least likely thing you could ever imagine. And then at the gorge, you said that we were a decade too late for her.'

'It's not really something I talk about,' he said.

None of your business, in other words. She'd been telling other people straight for long enough to recognise *from the hip* when she saw it. And to accept it. It wasn't reasonable to be offended by it. Even if it also hurt.

'No. Okay.'

Splash, splash... They drifted on, a dark, heavy cloud suddenly hanging over Hayden. She distracted herself looking at the McMansions lining the canal side.

He cleared his throat. 'There was a reason I was so gutted when we lost your mum.'

We. She would have liked that sentiment at the time; it would have made her feel less alone.

'It hit me extra-hard because I was grieving for two mothers.'

Her stomach tightened. 'Did yours go that same year?'

'Three years before. Just before I started coming to your house on Saturdays.'

Shirley realised what a jerk she'd been, assuming his anguish at the funeral had all been for effect. 'You hadn't grieved?'

'Not properly. There were…reasons for that. But it all kind of caught up with me at Carol's funeral.'

Where did a girl begin to undo that kind of mistake? 'I'm sorry that I judged you for not starting the list.'

He shook off the dark cloud. 'Their deaths motivated me. It reminded me that you can't rely on anyone but yourself. I set up Molon Labe the next year. Started small, building a client list, making my own way.'

She stared at the darkening waters that rolled in huge swells past the boat. 'And your father?'

'He's still around. I see him about once a year when he wants money.'

Her chest squeezed as tight as his voice. 'God, Hayden…'

'It's a small price to pay. Literally.' He glanced at her sideways. 'What about yours?'

Her father? The man who'd left them when she was small. 'No idea. I don't remember him.'

Didn't let herself, anyway. Though she'd found a photograph amongst her mother's things and kept it. Just because.

'Carol only spoke of him once. Sounds like a man unsuited to settling down.'

A man just like Hayden? Was she really that much of a cliché? Falling for a man like her father? 'I wouldn't know.'

'You've never tried to find him?'

She looked up. Her chest pressed in. 'He knew where we were all that time. He lived there, too, when I was a baby. Until he left. And we were doing fine. Mum finished her PhD at night, then she went back to work as soon as I was at school full-time. We got by.'

'What about her funeral. You didn't send word?'

'I sent word.' She dropped her eyes. 'He just didn't come.'

'That's…' A lost-for-words Hayden was a rarity. 'He had no contact after he left?'

The pressing against her lungs became crushing. 'He'd made his choice. He left because of me; he was hardly about to ask for weekend visitation.'

Hayden stopped, turned towards her. 'Who says he left because of you?'

She studied the sparkling water. The poling stopped.

'Shirley?'

'He wasn't ready for fatherhood. And I wasn't a quiet baby.'

'But who *says* that?' He pushed them along again. 'If you were so young, how do you know that's true?'

She blinked at him. 'Mum said. Now and again. When she was mad or upset.' Or wanting to dent Shirley's embryonic spirit. 'Sometimes she'd talk about how much she loved him. Other times she'd talk about how he wasn't cut out for parenthood. Or how maybe if I'd been quieter…happier…'

'She blamed you for his leaving?'

'She *attributed* his leaving to me,' she said carefully. 'There's a difference.' But when you were six years old, the difference wasn't very distinct. 'It took her a long while to get over him.'

He shook his head. 'She never remarried?'

Shirley raised her hand. 'Guilty again. It was hard to find love with a toddler in tow.'

Hayden frowned. 'Where are these words coming from? They're not yours.'

She actually had to think about it. Though she knew exactly where the ideas had come from—and the words—when she let herself acknowledge it. 'My mother wasn't quite so prosaic when it came to her own emotions as she was when discussing Nietzsche or Socrates or Demosthenes.'

'And you were how old?' His words were as unexpectedly gentle as his touch late at night.

She shrugged. 'Depends; she said some more than others.'

But enough that she'd received the message loud and clear. Enough that Shirley had spent her young life trying to make up for crimes she hadn't even meant to commit.

He stared at her. 'My mother was far from perfect, but everything she did she did for me. I can't imagine her ever putting her own needs ahead of mine like that.'

The intense desire to excuse her mother overwhelmed her. That was straight from the ancient part of her brain. 'She was brilliant and focused and hardworking and totally dedicated to her job.'

To the exclusion of all else.

He turned and looked at her. 'I guess all that focus had to be coming from somewhere.' She glanced away. 'I'm really sorry it was from you.'

She shrugged. 'It's not your fault she wasn't better at the personal stuff—'

'It wasn't your fault either, Shirley.' He moved them onwards, visibly battling with something. He lifted the pole out of the water and sat down in front of her, with it lying flat across the gondola. 'I'm sure there are things in your childhood you *did* do and you can feel all the guilt in the world you want over those, but don't take on your father's abandonment. That's a reflection on him, not you. And if your mother let you be the reason she never tried to build a new family for you, then that's on her. Plenty of single mums build new families. Their kids are only an impediment if they're looking for one.'

'Why would she seek out reasons not to find love again?' Who *didn't* want to be loved? Other than Hayden.

'Maybe she couldn't find it and it was easier to blame something external for that.'

She stared.

'I'm just saying you shouldn't carry guilt for her issues,' he finished.

She sat up straighter. 'I'm not.'

'You're carrying something. Why else would you have this burning desire to finish her list?'

'To honour her memory.'

'Why does it need to be honoured?'

'Because I loved her.' Even if it wasn't a perfect love. She was the only mother—the only parent—she'd had.

'You don't need a bunch of activities to love her. Why the list?'

She stared at him. Utterly at a loss. How had their nice day on the water turned suddenly so very confrontational?

He wobbled back up onto his feet and moved them along again. 'That's a rhetorical question, Shirley. You don't have to answer to me. Only to you.'

They rowed in silence, the *splish-splash* of the pole becoming quite hypnotic.

'Amazing we turned out such a balanced pair, really,' he murmured into the warm air.

His smile was contagious. Then it turned to a chuckle and a full-out laugh and the gondola rocked. Neither of them could really claim any prizes for mental health. Not if you scratched below the surface. Not even far below.

Maybe misfits were drawn to each other.

'Take me back to the jetty, Hayden,' she breathed.

Jetty, car, her place. It was a one-hour trip, minimum. The sooner they could be in each other's arms, the better. And the list clock was ticking.

'Does that mean you don't want to see my place?'

She lifted her head. 'What place?'

'The house behind the jetty. It's mine.'

She twisted to peer down the canal the way they'd come. A huge beige monstrosity stood beyond an immaculate field of heavily reticulated turf.

'That's yours?'

In her periphery, she saw him nod. Watching her closely.

She turned back and folded her hands in her skirt and stared somewhere over his shoulder. 'I like the cottage better.'

He stopped poling. Stared at her. Then he slowly started up again and muttered, 'Me too, actually.'

'Though it is pleasingly close,' she teased, and plucked at the front of her peasant blouse. Loving the way his eyes instantly refocused.

'You want to see it?'

'You made me a boat—' she shrugged, all absent concern '—I suppose that deserves some reward.'

He turned the gondola and punted double-time back towards the jetty. Following the strong movements of his muscles gave Shirley a thoroughly good mental distraction from his innocent question.

She'd never asked herself why the list had become her obsession virtually the moment she'd discovered its existence. Why she'd ridden it hard through the past decade. Why she'd built her life around accomplishing it.

For a woman used to asking the hard questions, this simple one her stumped.

Why the list?

'Home sweet home,' he said, sliding the patio door open and letting her into the ultra-white, ultra-clean living area.

'No, it's not. You don't live here.' A house full of props selected by a stylist, maybe, but nothing *his*. No mess. No plants. No books. It was the latter that gave him away most—his cottage was overflowing with books. Stuffed into every available crevice. 'You probably bring women here. Maybe you stay here when you have late meetings. But you don't live here.'

'I did,' he murmured, reaching into the enormous stainless-steel refrigerator for bottled water. She got glimpse enough to know the only other thing in there was a long-life milk carton. Unopened. 'For quite a few years.'

She slid onto a white leather stool. 'When did you move out to the cottage?'

His hand paused on the steel lid of the ornate designer water bottle, then flicked it off carelessly. Its tumble clattered and echoed in the big house. 'Couple of years ago. When I scaled back at the office.'

'Why was that?'

'I needed time to reassess.'

Their lives were so different. The idea of just dropping off the grid for two years to *reassess*. 'And how did everyone at the office feel when you recently reappeared?'

'I took the front-of-house team to lunch. Made their managers sit on reception.'

She grudgingly smiled. 'I'm sure that was popular.'

'It got their attention. One coped just fine and the other knows where his knowledge gaps are.'

'And the receptionists?'

'Had a lovely lunch, got sloshed and betrayed everything that was really going on while I was away.'

Away. As if he'd been off travelling. Maybe that was what they thought. 'Their existence should be hellish once you start firing people,' she murmured.

He slid a glass of water towards her.

'No one's getting fired. I'm not going to punish anyone for something that was my doing. I was too focused on keeping the clients happy; I neglected the team. The people who helped me deliver it. So that's my mistake, not theirs.'

She stared at him for long moments, unease at discovering these new aspects to him fuelling her confusion. Working with NGOs, owning his mistakes, hand-making boats.

What was he doing—*trying* to be irresistible?

She shook her head. 'Who are you?'

'Maybe a better question would be "who *was* I?"' He leaned back on the kitchen island, tall and strong, his hips turned squarely towards her, ankles crossed. 'And the answer was "blinkered and self-involved".'

'Past tense?'

'Somebody helped me to see things a little differently. To widen my lens.'

'Would that someone be me?' She dropped her eyes, then glanced up at him.

He winced. 'See, *somebody* is bound to get full of themselves and become unbearable if I answer that.'

A smile slipped past her careful barriers. 'Not that you'd recognise the signs of that.'

His own lips parted in a reciprocal smile. 'Not at all.'

'Huh. Shame,' she said, leaning back as far as she could on her white stool and matching his body language. 'I find self-confidence extremely appealing.' He paused with the glass of water halfway to his lips. 'Almost as appealing as that whole bad-boy thing you have going on.'

But only because she was starting to understand it was just a mask he wore. Maybe only another mask-wearer would notice.

'I didn't realise the bad-boy thing was part of the attraction.' He placed his glass on the spotless benchtop and moved towards her. 'Being a jerk will certainly save me a heap of time and effort.'

She laughed and tipped her head up to face him. 'You've exposed yourself as a decent guy now. Damage is done.'

His grin turned feral. 'It's only just gone noon. I have hours yet to disappoint you.'

God, she adored this man's brain. She knew plenty of smart men who left her cold, so it wasn't just an IQ fetish. Hayden did intellectual foreplay like no one else on this planet. He barely had to try. No wonder she'd fallen for him.

She spluttered her first sip of water.

Realisation and despair flooded her in equal measures.

Hayden relieved her fingers of her own half-drunk glass and Shirley used the moment to curl her other hand around the leather top of the seat and steady herself while her world rocked. Like balancing in the gondola in stilettos. She kept her eyes fixed on him, convincing herself that if he wasn't stumbling then the intense rocking couldn't be real.

Fallen for him? Was she that stupid?

He helped her down off the stool and led her across the lower floor of the property. 'Where are we going?' she murmured past the tight choke in her chest.

Love. The one thing she'd promised herself she would not do. Not with him.

He turned back to her, oblivious to her crisis. 'I thought you might like to see the view from the bedroom.'

She forced air back over her lips and into her tight lungs,

determined to give nothing away as his fingers curled more securely into hers and they stepped onto the central stairway. 'That's subtle. Has that worked for you in the past?' She forced another breath in.

That was the key—in, out, in, out. Until breathing felt normal again.

'It's working for me now. You're still moving.'

She made herself laugh. Light and casual. Nothing like she actually felt. 'It's in my best interests to follow you. We don't have much time together. I wanted this.'

But she didn't want to love him. She hadn't meant to.

'See. You're an influence natural. I should recruit Shiloh.'

That actually achieved the impossible, distracting her slightly from the momentous bad news of just a moment before. The one starting with L…

She stopped midway up the stairs and stared at him. He turned back and looked down at her.

'It hasn't dawned on you yet, has it?' he said. 'How similar our jobs are.'

'They're nothing like each other.'

'Come on,' he challenged. 'You didn't write that article on Russell's group to get him a swag of new supporters? To raise awareness about dolphins?'

'I informed people…'

'You influence them.'

She stared. He pulled her into movement again, up onto a landing as immaculate and show-homey as downstairs.

'You appealed to their compassion or their intellect, you targeted it and you used it. Admit it, we're in the same game.'

'No, we're not.' He seemed way too pleased with that idea.

'I shouldn't be surprised; we were taught by the same woman.'

Fortunately, he stopped to open two enormous doors into an equally enormous suite. That saved her the trouble of having to plant her feet again.

'What?'

'Your mother was the queen of influence, Shirley. She knew

how to get the best from her students, the top grants out of her institution, the best office from her Dean.'

She had sure as hell known how to get her daughter to toe the line.

'Is this really your best effort at foreplay, Hayden? Talking about my mother?' But even that was better than the way her thoughts had been headed downstairs.

He swung her around in front of him to stand at floor-to-ceiling windows that looked out over the sparkling canal. 'No, this is...'

He pressed a button and they darkened just slightly. He moved up behind her and leaned her into the glass.

'One-way tinting,' he murmured, reaching around both sides of her to loosen the ribbons of her blouse. 'We can see out, no one can see in.'

Anticipation robbed every thought from her brain. And an empty mind was exactly what she needed right now.

An empty mind, a fully occupied body and strong arms to hold her.

Together, they might just be enough to outrank a heart gone rogue.

CHAPTER ELEVEN

HE'D finally got his fantasy moment there in his pristine white bed, unlacing Shirley hook by hook as though she were some medieval maiden, burying his hands in layers of fabric and stripping it back. Kissing the colour right off her mouth and revealing the pink, pure lips beneath.

The whole gondola thing had been a travesty. It had seemed like such a good idea at the time but he'd come across as a sap and a soft touch, telling her about his work for the dolphin mob. Thank God she hadn't pressed him regarding the growing list of others.

How would he explain that he had besmirched his soul in seducing her and now he scrubbed it clean again helping a raft of new clients? They bought him perspective. And balance.

A good balance.

He still struggled with the lingering sense that there was something extra *wrong* about the time he spent with Shirley; that it had just been too fast for him to believe she wanted this as much as he did, so it was probably just as well that weeks passed between them seeing each other. And it was probably just as well that the list was nearing an end for her.

A dark shadow took him.

He stared at *www.remembermrsmarr.com* on his laptop, at his own listings and at hers she'd added back when he'd challenged her to. Shirley had had a seven-tick head start even before he'd started trying.

He ticked off 'Hunt for a dinosaur fossil' on the live site. That only left the three unachievable ones. Everest, a grandchild and being touched again. It was odd imagining that his mentor—the woman who'd insisted that Plato's intellectual love was the purest—had secretly wanted to be loved again. Touched again. And all the while she'd had a small, vulnerable girl right there just *begging* to give her as much love as she needed. And to receive it.

But this dinosaur trip into the desert meant their achievable list was done. No more list, no more reason to be together. No more together, no more sex. No more sex, no more precious glimpses deep inside the mind and soul of the most intriguing woman he'd ever known. And if he was getting intrigued and habituated...

Probably just as well it was over.

'Hey.' Shirley pushed into their tent, two coffees in hand, looking earthy and radiant.

Nearly over.

He had one weekend. One last opportunity to be greedy. He wasn't going to wish that away until he absolutely had to. He hastily unchecked the box.

She sank down, cross-legged, next to him and passed him a steaming mug. 'Freshly brewed.'

Coffee only came one way on this expedition—hot and strong. But it had been months since he'd craved something fancier. Barista-made had lost its charm. Plain and strong would do him just fine.

'Thank you.'

She was back to being Shirley again, regular make-up and a more moderate selection of clothes without a buckle or hook in sight if you didn't count her laced-up trainers. He loved to spend time with this Shirley. Though he couldn't say he didn't love it when Shiloh made an impromptu appearance in their limited together time, too. The wilder the better.

'What are you doing?' She leaned over to glance at his screen.

He tipped the screen towards her. 'Visiting the list. You haven't updated.'

Her eyes briefly flicked to the corner of the tent. 'No. I'm keeping track in my notebook.'

He tipped his head. 'Privately?'

She studied the floor and then lifted green eyes to his. 'I think it should always have been private. It should never have mattered what everyone else was doing.' She took a breath. 'I'm sorry I pressured you into it. That was unfair.'

Her unrealistic expectations seemed like eons ago. And totally irrelevant now. He wanted to say *without that we never would have met*, or something equally corny. Wanted to, but he didn't. He reminded himself that the past months had probably been all the better for being temporary.

'Are you kidding?' He kept it light. 'If not for you, I would never have detached my retinas or frozen my butt off in the desert.'

She smiled. 'It's lovely out here, though, despite the cold. So incredibly vast. Can you imagine how much life is buried in ancient sediment here?'

The ancestors of eagles, enormous wombat third-cousins, a sea-floor full of marine fossils from back when the desert plain they'd pitched their tent into had still been ocean floor. The team had uncovered lots of ancient bones, but none of them dinosaur.

Yet.

The museum had willingly taken on two unskilled assistants for the long weekend and even been kind enough to find them tasks to do that felt meaningful. They weren't. Everyone seemed to know that but they were entirely prepared to fake it out of consideration for their guests. This time, no one knew she was Shiloh and no one knew that he was loaded. As far as the museum team was concerned, they were just hopeless enthusiasts.

We can always do with enthusiasm, the project director had kindly told Shirley when they'd applied. And she'd glowed. There was a lot to be said for kindness.

And for Shirley glowing.

'What time are they heading out?' he asked.

'As soon as everyone's caffeine ratio is optimum. Mornings seem to be expedition time and afternoons are for analysing results.' She rummaged around, tossing things onto her air mattress. *Their* air mattress, since it was a double and since they were back in 'list time'. Short grabs of heaven every few weeks. Little contact in between.

The perfect set-up.

Shirley's mattress pile grew. A spare shirt, camera, notebook, drink bottle, insect repellent, sunscreen. Everything a girl could need for a day in the desert.

'Be right back.' She bent and crawled out of the tent and he took the chance to watch. He'd grown really fond of that rear end really fast. He hooked the fly sheet with his boot and pulled it back to see where she went as he sipped his coffee. The latrine tent. Dug way out in the distance, necessarily.

His own pack was already loaded up so he grabbed hers and started stuffing the piled-up items into it as well as taking a couple of snack bars from the container she kept perpetually handy. The notebook slipped off the pile as he packed and fell open at an oft-thumbed page.

Her list.

He stared guiltily. Cross-through after cross-through mocked his still poor effort. She had thirteen of the fifteen items. Worse than he'd realised. She'd even crossed the dinosaur one off already.

His belly looped back on itself.

Hang on... Thirteen? When only twelve were achievable?

He traced the page with his finger and then slid to a halt at the mystery tick-box. He stared.

Be transported by a touch.

His first reaction was an insanely powerful surge of self-satisfaction. His touch had transported her. *His* touch. Impossible to know exactly when she'd ticked that but there'd been a whole lot of touching going on since their first night on the *Paxos*. Then the gondola day. And the previous two days.

And then...right behind the conceit came a wave of dread.

That wasn't the tick of someone who was casual about their time together. That wasn't the tick of someone who was content to let weeks pass between encounters. Or who'd be unfazed about moving on when the time came.

The wave of dread solidified.

That was the tick of someone for whom their encounters had been meaningful. Enough to tick a box on a list that had taken on religious significance for her. That tick meant something.

Not something...*everything.*

He shoved the notebook and pen in on top of the snack bars and zipped the pack up, then sat back and stared at the brown swirl in his cup. Was it a mistake to have let himself believe she was in the same class of woman as the others in his past? Easier, faster women. Or was it just blind wishful thinking on his part? Maybe he'd just seen what he wanted to see?

Wouldn't be the first time.

'Taking up reading coffee grinds?' she joked, ducking back into the tent. She saw her packed bag. 'Oh, thank you.' She threw it over her shoulder, bent and kissed his cold lips and ducked back out again. 'I'll see you by the truck.'

Confusion roiled.

Her demeanour was relaxed enough. Her kiss, easy. She wasn't fawning or clinging. In fact she'd just ditched him for more interesting people, as far as he could tell. Nothing about her actions betrayed the glaring tick in that very significant box.

Unless... Was she so desperate to finish the list that she'd thrown in a near-enough-is-good-enough tick? Or maybe she was a good compartmentaliser: *transportational* sex in one department and the real world in another. Or maybe she'd only slept with him in the first place to get the tick.

No.

Just...no.

He took a deep breath and tossed his remaining coffee out of the tent door. *Maybe* he was making much more of this than it was worth. Her actions had to mean more than what she wrote down in private.

In her notebook...

Which was virtually a diary...

He straightened outside the tent, and intercepted Shirley's

glance from across the campsite. It was a smile, small and private, much like any other she'd tossed at him on any of their adventures. Yet it suddenly took on so much extra meaning.

Was it the smile of someone harbouring a secret?

Was it the smile of someone trying very hard not to liberate a much bigger, more gushing one?

Was it the smile of a woman who knew that their time was very soon to be over? A weaning-off kind of smile.

Or was it just the smile of someone quietly excited about the day and trying to be cool in front of the experts?

Hell.

He snagged his backpack and hauled it out of the tent after him.

And *this* was why ignorance was bliss.

It might have been one of the coolest things she'd ever done but it was also one of the dullest. As one half of the least experienced duo on the expedition, Shirley couldn't have expected to be in charge of anything exciting and, to be fair, the scientists alone were doing their fair share of grunt work, too. They stood as a group at the base of sheer rock face in an ancient eroded gully.

'This was once a cave system,' the head palaeontologist told them, 'before it all tumbled in and wore away to become the plateau we see today. So there's a decent chance of finding a few bits of interest.'

Hopefully that was palaeontologist-speak for 'dinosaur'.

That helped motivate her as the hours passed and teams of them spread out over parallel search vectors and combed the desert floor, literally, for anything of note. At first the pressure of not knowing what might be 'of note' and missing something significant crippled her, but as hours passed with no one calling for professional opinions Shirley relaxed and let herself just drift, eyes firmly down, looking for anything that just didn't look quite right.

It gave her lots of time to glance at Hayden one vector over and worry about what was wrong with him.

He'd barely spoken to her the entire drive out here. Lots of smiles—carefully neutral and thin—but not a whole lot of substance. And they never reached his eyes. She'd surveyed the past few days in the same way they surveyed the ancient cave floor, segment by segment with a mind for the smallest out-of-place detail. He'd been fine for the first two days, as chatty as Hayden ever got, and focused on the stories told by the museum team of their past trips.

But come the dawn of day three and he had become a different man altogether, distracted, uncommunicative, hollow.

Anxiety burbled close to the surface. Why was her go-to response to assume something was wrong? That *she'd* done something wrong? Perhaps he had some kind of threshold for living rough and he'd reached it. Or three days was too much living out of tins and gas cooker coffee. Maybe he was more accustomed to finer comforts than he'd realised.

Those were all much better options than the lingering concern that it might be her.

Or *them*.

'Nothing?' she asked, loud enough that he could hear.

He glanced up. Shook his head. Then went back to studying the earth. Clearly still distracted.

She swallowed the little hurt and the frown and redoubled her efforts on the earth as she walked forward at a speed akin to continental drift.

Rock. Tussock. Earth. Rock. Earth. Bone… She stopped and bent lower, examined it. Nope—too bleached and surface dwelling for something older than a year. That much she had picked up from the professionals.

Tussock. Earth. Rock. Odd-shaped rock…

She paused again, bent. Gently dusted some dirt away from the edge of this particular rock. Rocks, she'd discovered, tended to be roundish or sharpish. A sharp rock with rounded bits in it was noteworthy. A rounded rock with a sharp bit in it—like this one—was equally interesting.

'Eric?'

She called their floating expert over. He finished marking a site several vectors away and jogged over to her. 'Whatcha got?'

She pointed to her feet. 'Weird rock.'

‘Excellent,’ he murmured, forgetting her presence already. ‘We love weird.’

He dropped a circular frame around the rock and stabbed a small red flag into the earth nearby. He pulled out a sand sieve and started to trowel the dirt around the rock into it, shaking the balance free off to one side.

Her job was to continue onwards.

She glanced up and caught Hayden’s sideways look. He returned his gaze to the earth.

‘Is everything okay?’ she suddenly asked, surprising herself as she started forward again.

‘Yep.’ He raised his eyebrows. ‘Good.’

‘Hayden, you’re way too surly a human being to pull off a convincing “chipper”.’

He paused to stare intently at the dirt and Shirley got the feeling it was faked. He struggled with something.

‘This is our last list item together.’

Her heart emulsified into soggy goo. That he was keeping track. And that he cared. ‘Yeah, it is. I didn’t think you were aware of it.’

A dark flush stole up his neck. ‘I have a numbered list to keep me aware.’

Oh. Right.

He cleared his throat. ‘So what happens now?’

God. What a horrible place to be having this discussion. Forced to remain ten feet apart and surrounded by others with varying degrees of good hearing, including Eric, who was only a few feet behind her, albeit fully absorbed with the excavation of her rock.

She took a breath. ‘What do you want to happen?’

‘We sort of fell into it,’ he said. ‘I’m not sure how we fall back out of it.’

Fall back out.

She did her best not to stumble on the disappointment. He wanted to end things. Just when she thought they might have moved past the whole friends-with-benefits thing. Of course he did. Why had she expected any differently? Tightness in her throat translated audibly in her voice, but she'd be damned if she'd let him see how deeply she was affected. 'How do you usually extricate yourself from unsatisfactory relationships?'

He looked up.

She looked down.

'It's not unsatisfactory, Shirley—'

'Sorry.' She smiled thinly. 'Maybe I should have said "past their use-by date"?'

His lips thinned. 'Ordinarily, we'd have established that up-front.'

'So this must be awkward for you then. Most inconvenient.'

'Shirley—'

'Though we kind of did, right?' she barrelled on. 'While the list was ongoing we could be…ongoing.'

He frowned. 'And you're fine with that? Now that the achievable list is over?'

She tossed her head back. 'Sure.'

'Meet my eyes when you say that.'

She forced them to his. Glared. Could he hear Shiloh in her tone? 'Get over yourself, Hayden.'

His own narrowed slightly, clouded. 'Okay then.'

'You don't think this would have been a better conversation to have tomorrow? We have tonight to get through yet.'

'We've managed worse.'

True.

Behind her, a throat cleared. She turned and stared at Eric, confused. How could she have forgotten he was there? He held a partially hacked away chunk of rock in his hands.

'Shirley, I'm going to take this back to Dave at the van. I think you might have something here.'

Really? 'Okay. Bye. Should I just keep going?'

What an inane thing to ask. And why wasn't she more excited? Maybe she'd just found a species no one else had ever identified.

'Yeah, you should keep going—' the bearded Eric laughed '—maybe you'll find more.'

He whistled through two fingers and one of the team marked

their progress in the ground, then stopped scanning the dirt to meet him just outside the search zone and examine the rock. They hurried together to the van.

She turned back the way she'd been going. Hayden stared at her. 'What did you find?'

She shrugged. '*Dinosaurus shirleii*.'

He smiled despite himself and despite the tension of moments ago. Then it turned into a wry chuckle before he returned to ground-scanning, shaking his head. 'You're impenetrable, Shirley. Nothing touches you.'

Not if she didn't let it, no.

The day stretched out with a few promising finds, and then dinner stretched out with more than a few fascinating discussions around the fire afterwards. Her weird rock turned out to be more fossil than rock—a fifty-thousand-year-old middle toe of something called a Thunderbird.

'*Dromornis stirtoni*,' their project leader helpfully added. 'The biggest bird in Australia. Three metres tall.'

'Rare?' she asked hopefully.

'Reasonably common.'

Of course it was. 'And not a dinosaur?'

'About one hundred million years too young for that. But Stirton's Thunderbird was a contemporary of the woolly mammoth, if it's any consolation.'

Shirley was struggling to feel consoled by anything much at all this evening, but that piece of news did at least rouse a comment from Hayden, who'd been silent for the best part of the night.

'Are you saying that Big Bird and Mr Snuffleupagus were hanging out even in the pleistocene?' he said.

His dry question caused a moment of stunned silence amongst the learned group who would have been forgiven for believing up until now that he was mute, but then they burst into laughter. Even Shirley had to fight the twitch of her lips.

She didn't want to find him funny. She didn't want to find him clever or witty or sharp. Or still the most interesting brain in the room even when it was full of bigger brains. She did better when he was being surly and stand-offish. It was easier then not to love him.

She lifted her eyes and sighed. She didn't quite manage to cover the appreciation in her glance. Hayden's lips thinned.

Great.

She turned back to the conversation.

The moon climbed higher and then between one conversation and the next it seemed to cross half the sky.

'It's late,' the project leader finally said, tipping the last of his coffee in the fire. 'I'm to bed.'

Shirley glanced at their distant tent again and knew she'd have to return there eventually. Staying up all night had occurred to her, but she was already wearing every layer she'd brought with her and it wasn't keeping the cold out any longer.

She shivered even in front of the fire.

'Come on, Shirley. Let's get you warm,' Hayden said.

Let's... How cosy that sounded.

'I'm fine.'

''Course you are. For a snowman.' He stood. 'Come on.'

They left the lingerers to deal with the fire and headed slowly back to their tent. Every heavy footstep bought her seconds of reprieve. At last the moment of truth...

She turned to face him. 'So, now what?'

His brow furrowed as he lifted his eyes. 'Now we sleep?'

'Is that all?' Or was it just a euphemism?

He grew cautious. 'Do you want that to be all?'

No. But it had to be. 'You sound surprised.'

He stared at her thoughtfully. 'I believed you when you said you knew we'd be over after this trip.'

'I do know.'

'So I didn't expect our final night together to hold anything other than a vague poignancy of parting.'

Vague poignancy... That was something, right? She took a breath. 'It doesn't.'

Blue eyes challenged her. 'Liar.'

'I'm not lying.'

His gaze grew acute. 'Then why is tonight any different to any other night we've shared if it has no other meaning? Why can't I draw you into the warmth of that bed, the warmth of my arms and body, and farewell you slowly and thoroughly, like a goodbye should be?'

It literally hurt to push words past her constricted larynx. 'Because we're done. We decided that out at the ridge, today.'

'We confirmed this trip would be our last,' he allowed. 'We're not done until I drop you back at your front door.'

She stared. 'Seriously? Down to the wire? Just so you can get one more roll in the hay?'

'This isn't about sex.'

She snorted. 'Of course it is.'

'This is about *us* meaning more to you than something casual. Because if you truly didn't care then you wouldn't have any concerns about sleeping with me now.'

Every muscle squeezed. He was way too close. 'No. This is about you wanting to milk a good thing for every drop.'

And she'd been beyond foolish to ever set herself up for this.

His expression grew dangerously blank. 'You think I'm hard up for female company, Shirley?'

She'd never asked him if he was seeing anyone else. She'd never wanted to know. Because asking meant trusting his response and somewhere way deep down inside that she never looked she feared she couldn't trust him. Not with her heart.

'I'm sure there's a queue waiting for their chance at a rich, handsome man, no matter how damaged.'

He pursed his lips and nodded. Then he spoke. 'Casting stones, Shirley?'

To look at him—his casual stance, his even colour—you'd think he was supremely unconcerned by this awful discussion. But the vein pulsing high in his temple said otherwise.

He was bothered.

She just didn't know by what.

She held her ground. 'I'm not damaged.' Not to the same degree.

'Oh, please... Look at the extremes you're going to in order to please a woman who's been dead for a decade. Your career choice. Your choice in men.'

'What men?'

'Exactly my point. And when you did finally relent to one, it's casual and commitment-free. You're hiding from the entire world one way or another.'

'Pot, meet kettle.' Shirley glared. 'For someone who hasn't left his cottage in two years or had a steady relationship *ever* you're very fast to spot deficiencies in others.'

'I know why I went underground. Can you say the same? Why hide behind the job? The crazy outfits?'

Really? Now even her clothes were a crime? She threw her hands in the air. 'It's fashion, Hayden. It doesn't mean I dally in self-harm or dance around naked in a circle of stones when the moon is in its zenith.'

'It's a mask. And it fits you so well you've forgotten you're wearing it.'

She locked eyes. 'I'm having *no problem* right now understanding why commitment-free seems attractive…'

'Come on, Shirley, ask yourself. Why do you do all of this? What are you protecting yourself from?'

She stopped, dead. 'What?'

'How many close friends did you have growing up?' he challenged.

The rapid subject change threw her. 'A few.' *Two.* Two tenacious girls who never had been able to recognise subtext. They stayed with her, no matter what.

No matter what you did to ditch them, a voice whispered.

Or maybe test them.

She frowned.

'What do my friends—' or lack thereof '—have to do with anything?'

'It's indicative of you avoiding opening yourself up to people. What is it that you think they'll find if you let them in?'

Insufficiency. Her mind immediately filled in the blank. Someone who is somehow sub-par.

Her bunching muscles forced her to shove that away and focus on the man in front of her. 'I'm confused, Hayden. A few minutes ago you were the champion of keeping things light, now you're criticising my lack of commitment. You can't have it both ways.'

Like white blood cells rushing in to swamp an open wound, excuses clustered around her vulnerable heart, making a prickly shield for it. She wanted to be sorry she'd ever agreed to sleep with him in the first place. But she couldn't. He'd moved her in too many ways. But she certainly could be damned sure it never happened again.

'This whole conversation is only reinforcing my decision to end things now,' she said as she started stuffing her belongings into her two backpacks.

'What are you doing?'

'Packing. I'm not staying here.' *With you.*

'Where exactly do you plan on going? We're in the middle of the desert.'

He had a point. She hardly knew the museum crew well enough to crawl in with one of them. The back seat of the troop carrier was looking pretty good at this moment. 'Not your problem.'

'Shirley—'

She spun around on him. 'I found a dinosaur fossil.' Or close enough. 'So the achievable list is now complete.' She flat-lined her hands in front of her. 'We're done.'

'You'll freeze out there.' His voice dropped. 'You can't leave.'

Damn him for being right. Her hand stopped, mid-stuff. 'I can't stay.'

'Why?'

Her chest rose and fell with alarming regularity. Why couldn't she be more like the women in his past? Why couldn't she just enjoy a good physical send-off? Why did she want tomorrow to never come?

'Because it feels wrong,' she whispered.

'You offered a no-strings, casual relationship, Shirley. I just took you up on it.'

Yeah, well…that was before her feelings had changed. Although… maybe they hadn't changed at all. Maybe she'd had them all along and just saw them clearly now. Because even though she had all the reason in the world to despise him right now, she couldn't help but be drawn to his sheer presence, still. It was galling.

Lord. Had she fallen for him that very first day? Or had she just never got him out of her system from when she was fourteen?

She lifted her chin. Tired of subterfuge. 'Are you really that much of a machine, Hayden? You have no other feelings complicating things at all?'

His face became a mask. 'That's not what we were about.'

'And so you won't miss me? You won't wonder what might have been?'

He didn't answer. But he looked like he wanted the answer to be *nope*.

'And will you still be doing that in twenty years? Thirty?' she prodded, desperate to even up the emotional score. 'Is that how you plan to end your days? Alone?'

His tan turned slightly sallow under the lamplight. 'If I play my cards right.'

'You don't want that.' Surely?

'Not everyone wants the picket fence.'

'Or do you imagine you don't have to worry about forever?' she persisted. 'Do you truly think that you'll exit this world early in a blaze of glory? Like Leonidas? Or will you just avoid any kind of emotional connection until the end?'

'That's the plan.'

She stared at him, utterly lost. Heartsick. 'Why?'

'Because it's what I want.'

No one wanted to be alone. Not really. Then a thought popped into her mind. 'You said you knew why you went underground a few years ago. Is it connected?'

'I said I knew. I didn't say I was planning on sharing.'

Her confidence shrivelled. She could have argued that, Lord knew she wanted to. But she was too tired. Tired of thinking about him. Tired of hurting. Her soul ached.

She went back to stuffing her bag.

'Shirley. We're adults. I'm sure we can share a bed without mauling each other.'

'That's not what I'm worried about.' She'd take his arm off if he made a move on her. 'Given how I feel right now, I can't promise not to suffocate you in my sleep.'

He laughed. He actually laughed.

Maybe he *was* a machine.

Her badly packed belongings weren't fitting in as they had on the journey out. She kept shoving them down into unseen air pockets. Jerky and strong.

'Okay,' he said. 'You stay here and I'll go sleep in the truck.'

She turned heavy eyes up to him. 'You think your freezing point is lower than mine?'

'Oh, there are people who would assure you that I'm already sub-arctic.'

'Here. You'll need this,' she grunted, and tossed a sleeping bag at him. He stumbled backwards half out of the tent to catch it like a marked football and then lifted bemused eyes. Had he not expected her to agree? She lifted her chin. 'Unless that was just lip service?'

A curious expression crossed his face and he backed fully out into the cold. 'Thanks.'

'See you in the morning, then.' She smiled brightly and then zipped the tent closed in his face.

And then sagged down onto the air mattress.

He was right. They were as damaged as each other.

To please a woman who's been dead for a decade.

Harsh, ugly words. But were they true? Was that what she was doing? Pleasing her mother? She thought back on how desperate she'd been to cling to something stable in the awful, disruptive weeks right after the funeral. The list had been like an anchor then, giving her something tangible to focus on. As though as long as the list endured so did her mother.

Then, as she'd crossed from child into young woman, as she'd trained for the gruelling marathon, she'd realised that it [illegible] more about *honouring* her—just as Hayden had pledged [illegible]se months before. The list wasn't going to bring her, or

Shirley's old life, back. It was just something she could do. And had continued to do to completion on principle.

At least she'd believed it was principle.

To please a woman...

She'd certainly spent the better part of her childhood pleasing her mother. Studying hard, doing all her chores without reminder, keeping out of the way when she had students around. Making sure her mother never had cause for complaint. Because she held enough things against her daughter as it was: her father's departure, her failure to find someone else in her life—

Shirley frowned.

—her inability to apply for exciting jobs overseas, her inability to move to a more upmarket district outside Shirley's school zone. Now that she thought about it. She'd cried-poor Shirley's whole life, despite having a crowded wardrobe and the best magazine subscriptions. She'd rarely gone out to dinner or the theatre or even a movie with friends. *I can't afford it* she would say on a sigh. *Not with Shirley's school fees.* Yet they'd been able to afford cable TV and a gardener and cleaner once a week.

She'd been fourteen when her mother had died. She'd only ever seen her through a child's eyes. And of course she saw an accomplished, popular, beloved teacher and mother. Maybe she would have seen a bad money manager if she'd been old enough to understand what she was seeing? Maybe her mother had actually been lousy at friendships and that was why she'd surrounded herself with a revolving door of students who adored her, but she'd rarely gone out with any of her peers. Maybe she'd been loath to give up the stability of tenure and her home to chase new experiences but hadn't been able to admit that to her colleagues. Maybe her husband had left because their marriage had failed, not because Shirley had been born.

Shirley stared at the fabric wall of the tent.

Maybe a whole lot of things weren't as they seemed. How many times had her mother used the single-mother excuse to disguise her own failings? And how many times had she willingly let those excuses settle onto tiny, anxious shoulders?

More important, how much of her mother's denial had she inherited?

Her stomach churned, just like it had when she was little.

She *was* still trying to please her mother. Every time she worried about the list, about doing it right, about doing it fast enough or slowly enough, about doing it the way *her mother* would have wanted, it was as if she were still here, judging Shirley's performance. Finding her wanting.

And she was still six years old, trying to make up for all the trespasses she sensed but barely understood.

Her mother hadn't been a saint or a legend or an oracle. She had just been a flawed human being who'd had trouble with friendships and taking risks and who'd used the nearest justification to excuse it. At the expense of her daughter.

Something shifted deep down inside her, clicked into place so perfectly and comfortably it could only be *rightness*. And, as though in shifting it had uncovered a tiny drain hole in her soul, years of hurt and bewilderment started to drip away, leaving a lightness behind.

Damn Hayden Tennant.

What else was he right about, then?

Did she hide behind Shiloh so that no one could reject *her* or find her thoughts and opinions wanting? Did she avoid forming relationships? She had a raft of online acquaintances and faces to nod and smile at when she met them at public events. Media she knew. Contacts she cultivated. People she liked to sit with at tables who all knew her as Shiloh. But no real confidantes. No one she'd feel comfortable calling up for a chat. Or drinks. Or a movie.

No one to call to wail that her time with Hayden was over.

No one she'd let see her without make-up.

Her father had left because she cried too much.

Her mother had blamed her for *everything* wrong with their lives. And then she'd died.

Trouble making friends.

Abandonment and judgement of one sort or another everywhere she looked.

Had she come up with as many clever life strategies as her mother to avoid having to engage with people? To avoid taking personal risks?

Had it made her crawl inside herself and let nothing out?

Shirley forced herself to her feet, turned off the lamp and crawled onto the airbed, still dressed.

But she had let something out. She'd fallen for Hayden, unwound for him, incrementally. Given him a space for his toothbrush in her heart. She'd found, in him, her intellectual match and maybe her spiritual match too. Two damaged people grasping each other in the darkness.

Only she hadn't realised it was dark.

And he wasn't so much grasping as holding her at arm's length. Long, rigid, determined arms.

Deep sorrow congealed in her gut. And now he wanted out. Whatever he needed to make him want to stay, she lacked it. She'd thought this connection they had would be enough to ride out the obvious disconnect between them.

But it wasn't.

The high-tech properties of the sleeping bag did their job, slowly forming a warm blanket of air around her. Her muscles relaxed. Her goose bumps eased. Her eyes grew heavy.

Yet they didn't close. Not quite.

She stared into the thick black of the night around her and waited for morning.

CHAPTER TWELVE

Ziiiiiip.

The sound morphed, in her dream, into the long, teasing tug of a dress zip lowered by warm, exploring fingers. She wriggled against the pleasant sensation.

But then came a rummaging, a huff, a sigh, and those sounds struggled to find a logical place in her subconscious.

She stirred. Turned.

A dark shadow sat hunched in the camp chair in the corner of the little tent silhouetted by the high moon outside.

'Hayden?' It was only as she whispered his name that the memory of their conversation just hours ago returned. She stiffened.

'I'm sorry, Shirley,' he whispered. 'It's freezing out there. The truck's door seals are shot. I'm going to wait out morning here.'

In a chair? Wrapped in a sleeping bag? Watching her sleep?

She rolled back over. 'Suit yourself.'

Silence.

Then a heavy breath.

She rolled back over. 'Were you hoping I'd relent and let you in?'

His low voice smiled. 'Kind of, yes.'

If he'd denied it she would have left him there to freeze. But the smile she could hear in his voice said so much about his amazing ability to compartmentalise his emotions. He was who he was. It wasn't his fault he was built differently inside to everyone else. He hadn't invited her affections or been dishonest with her. He was just a leopard with very definite spots. Not at all interested in changing them. Not for her.

Plain and simple.

He'd only called things as he'd seen them.

She rolled away from him again but spoke softly. 'Fine. Get in.'

The bed lurched before she'd even finished the sentence and Hayden tossed the second sleeping bag over them both, taking care not to touch her. But his cold radiated every bit as much as her warmth and she felt it across the gulf of inches between them. She slid her leg across to touch him experimentally with her toe.

'Oh, my God, Hayden…!' She lurched up.

He was ice-cold. Hypothermic kind of cold. He flinched as though *he'd* touched *her*.

'I'm sorry…' he slurred.

She turned. 'You're freezing.'

'This is like some bad porno,' he said, his laugh constricted by the spasms of his chest. He'd gone past shivering to a place of rhythmic, full-body muscle contractions.

'You need to get warm.'

His shaking head rustled against the sleeping bag he'd hiked up to his face. 'I don't think that would be a good idea for either of us.'

She wasn't in a hurry to have him pressed up against her, either.

'Take the underneath layer,' she ordered, 'and wrap it around you like a cocoon. It's got my warmth.'

He did it and the shifting and tucking let in a whole lot of cold night air. Her goose bumps returned. But then he was done and he curled onto his side and let her remnant body heat do its job.

'You're so warm,' he murmured as her toasty thirty-seven degrees centigrade soaked into him from the high-tech fabric.

Her lips quirked and she rubbed at the gooseflesh. 'I was.'

He roused. 'Now you're cold.'

She pushed him back down. 'I'm not hypothermic. I'll make some more heat. Don't worry. Go to sleep.'

She turned away from him and scooted as best she could to

her side of the double bed. It really wasn't big enough for much separation, especially with him curled. But she understood why he needed to be. His body was protecting its vital organs.

In the silence, the time between his convulsive muscle clenches slowly lengthened. Then eased altogether. His pained sigh was a kiss of cold air on the back of her neck.

'Better?' she whispered back over her shoulder.

'Getting there.'

It wasn't tawdry. He was about as protected from any accidental contact as he could be, wrapped in a full-body sheath of goose down. But she wasn't going back to sleep either. He was way too close for that.

'Thank you,' he whispered into the darkness.

'You're a jerk, but you don't deserve to freeze to death.'

'No...' His breaths drew out and his words sounded close against her ear. 'Thank you for finding me. That day.' He breathed again. 'Thank you for saving me.'

Every muscle in her body paused to listen.

'I was on a path nowhere good when you pulled up to my cottage that day. I'd quit drinking but the whole downward spiral hadn't really changed. You forced me back out into the world and made me engage with it again.'

A deep ache started up in her chest. What could she say to that?

'I love doing what I do, but I don't always *like* what I do,' he murmured between tremors. 'I don't like the expression I imagine on my mother's face when I think of her looking down at me from above and seeing who I've become. I didn't like the look on your face when you found out. The judgement.'

She opened her mouth to apologise.

'That's not a criticism of you,' he whispered against her back. 'It's me. It's my choices. But you've shown me a way forward that I think I can live with. The road ahead is no longer a dark abyss.'

She lay in silence, understanding that he needed to do this. Fearing he'd stop if she spoke. Greedy to understand him better, even if it was their last night together.

'My parents split when I was sixteen,' he breathed into her hair.

Just *split*? That was less dramatic than she'd imagined.

'My mother finally found the courage to leave. He wouldn't let her go before that. Or me.'

Her heart squeezed. Domestic violence. Closer to what she'd imagined.

'My father told her she could only go if I stayed. Knowing she'd never leave me behind. That's what he traded on. Our love for each other. If she stayed, I was powerless. If I stayed, she was. But with her gone…' He swallowed. 'I made her go. I was nearly sixteen, close enough to independent. By then I could play him like a piano, keep myself safe. But I couldn't keep both of us safe at the same time.'

His cold-slurred speech tapered off and she wondered if he'd fallen asleep.

'She left you with him?' she risked, not wanting to break the spell.

'And set up on her own across town. But she didn't get all her bone breaks treated professionally. One of them grew an abscess and leached toxins into her system over a couple of years. Irrevocable.'

Shirley swallowed around the sudden lump in her throat.

'Those years of freedom were the best of her life, even though they were still so imperfect. I avenged her every day, manipulating my father and learning to despise how easy he was to play. I had him in the palm of my hand and absolutely no inclination to take care with what I had. Everything bad I learned about human nature I learned from him, one way or another. As education went, it was powerful.'

So were his words, confessed to the night and suddenly so close to her ear. A tremor skittered down her flesh.

'She died about the same time you started coming to my house?'

'Registering for your mother's class was the best thing I ever did. Without her, I would have assumed all people were like my father. But I did it because I thought she was someone else

I could play. A great brain I could challenge and best. A whole class full of students to be smarter than. That's who I was.'

She pressed her lips harder together in the shadows.

'Except she saw immediately who I was and she never let me best her. She was always a step ahead, in a way that lifted me up to her level. It challenged me to be better, not smarter.'

Would he admire his mentor so much if he knew what she'd done rather than face her own flaws?

'I'm hurting you, Shirley, and I can't forgive myself for that.'

'Because I am her daughter?' she whispered.

He stroked her hair. 'Because you are you. But I can't be who you want me to be, I can't turn myself into someone who can do forever. Not even for you.'

She wanted to rail, to point out that she hadn't asked him to. But this was goodbye; fighting it wouldn't change it.

'And I *would* hurt you again, eventually. I would take what I know about you and your feelings for me and use them against you. Because that's what I do as automatically as breathing. I exploit people's natures. You are so much better off far away from me.'

She smiled into the tent wall. Hollow and empty.

'"If you love until it hurts, there can be no more hurt, only more love."' This time it was his turn for silence. 'Mother Theresa,' she finished weakly.

'You don't love me, Shirley,' he breathed after a long nothing. Tight. Uncertain.

She forced a smile to her lips, even though he couldn't see it. 'Do I get any points for not meaning for it to happen?'

A slight crack on the last word betrayed the tears that had started to roll in the darkness.

'Shirley...' He scooted forwards, pressed hard up against her. 'Please don't cry. Please.'

'I'm not crying—' she laughed '—I'm leaking.'

'I am *so* not worth your tears.'

'You have a very low opinion of yourself,' she whispered when she had control of her voice again. 'Or a very high one of my tears.'

He pressed his lips to the back of her ear. 'They're diamonds to me.'

The diamonds tumbled free like a spilled bag of gems, then. And Hayden held her as they fell. Hours passed that way, a lifetime. Or maybe only minutes. But, when she next opened her eyes, early fingers of light stole through the fabric of their tent and he was still there, curled into an S behind her. Still awake, breathing steadily into her hair. Stroking her.

'Open your cocoon,' she murmured. 'I need a skin memory.'

He did, silently. She pulled off her shirt. He stripped off his. And she squirrelled back into his embrace, his hot, hard chest against her back, his arms draped securely across her. They lay there like that until the camp started to rouse around them. She tucked his arms more firmly around her, so he could never leave. He pressed his lips to her shoulder and they'd warmed back up to his usual blazing-hot furnace.

'I love you,' she whispered to the morning.

Admitting it felt like the healthiest thing she'd ever done in her life.

He kissed her neck. Stalled. Then said gently, 'You deserve to have that love returned.'

Ache coiled up into a serpent in her belly. He found her lips and pressed his there, hard and desperate. She clung to them, far beyond caring what he might think or what that might say about her. Or how much it would hurt later.

This was their last kiss.

Deep inside, her heart tore away from the sheath holding it suspended in her chest cavity and it split open as it tumbled down to lie, askew, against her diaphragm. She pushed out of his arms and wobbled to her feet, clutching her shirt to her bare chest, unwilling to be as physically vulnerable as she was emotionally.

She stumbled across the tent. 'I have to finish packing.'

Hayden let her go. Watched her silently as she dressed and then stuffed some final items into her bag. Her pain reached out to him and twisted around his gut in eloquent agony. But, no matter how much she hurt now, this was still better than what he might do to her if he stayed. What he'd done to his father.

How he'd twisted him up in psychiatric knots. Until the day he'd walked out of the front door of the family home he would never see again, leaving his father cowed and intellectually broken.

Every woman he'd been stronger than, he'd controlled. He tied them up emotionally too, to keep them away. Just because he could. Because that was what he knew.

He'd gone on to ruin his monster of a father a hundred different ways through the clients he took on. To continue besting a man who could cause him and his mother no more pain. He greedily hoarded the fantasy that his finance clients would be foreclosing on Trevor Tennant, the insurance companies he consulted for would tie the monster up in loopholes, and the pharmaceutical company would have his father desperate and reliant on their products.

That fantasy made everything he'd done doable.

But it hadn't stopped him becoming the creature he'd fought. Controlling. A monster. Just like his father. Just in a better suit.

Behind him, Shirley spoke. Her voice was still hoarse from her tears. It rasped on his conscience like sandpaper. 'You're not packing?'

'I'll pack while you're at breakfast,' he lied. Hating himself just one more bit. Just when he thought there was nothing new left to despise.

She nodded sadly. Combed her hair. Left.

He let his head drop back against the mattress, let himself drown in her fast-fading smell on the pillow. The sweet, innocent smell of honesty.

No one had ever given him their love. Despite—desperately—not wanting to love him, she still did. One long-buried part of him held that to his gnarled chest like something precious.

He was loved.

Surely that was only a heartbeat removed from being able to love himself? Somehow? Some time? But letting her go now was emotional euthanasia. So much kinder in the long run, rather than prolonging her suffering.

Maybe it was something good he could finally do for someone.

Even if it felt bad.
Really, really bad.

'Hayden? The truck's warming up.'

Two vehicles were going back to the city that morning and two were staying to carry on the dig—the ones for whom being out here digging *was* their day job. Shirley's bags and equipment were loaded up in the first vehicle.

But their tent was still up. Surely Hayden wasn't going to just leave it for someone else to take down? She poked her head through the entrance.

He was back in his corner chair. Hands pressed to his thighs, waiting. The inside of the tent was otherwise exactly as she'd left it when she'd gone for breakfast.

Her heart lurched, then kicked into a hard rhythm as the penny dropped. 'You're not coming.'

Did the tent suddenly echo or was it just her ears?

'I think it would be better if I stayed a few more days.'

She'd been working herself up to the long silent drive back to the city, planning out her coping mechanisms, trying hard not to imagine how that final moment between them would go.

And here it was…happening live, in 3D. And she was totally unprepared.

Pain tore at her. 'So that's it? Goodbye?'

He stood. Stepped closer. 'I'll miss you, Shirley.'

She wanted to be brave. She wanted to be as strong and resilient as Boudicca. But she also wanted to curl up in a ball and die.

'No, you won't.' She knew that down to her marrow. 'You'll close the door on our time together before the dust plume has even settled on the horizon. That's what you do with things you don't want to deal with. You bury them.'

He said nothing. As though he would stand and take any emotional flaying she cared to dish out. As though that was what he was used to doing. That should have made it less satisfying, but it didn't. After everything they'd been through, all the excitement and clashes and intimacy, *this* was how they were going to part? So very civilised and…beige? In a tent?

No way.

'Say it, Hayden,' she gritted.

He stared at her.

'Say that I mean absolutely nothing to you. Say you don't love me and you never ever could. I want to hear it.'

His throat lurched. His eyes glittered. He didn't make a sound.

'Speak, Hayden!' she shouted and shoved at his hard chest, but a choked sob totally undermined her. 'I need to hear the words.'

His head tilted, his eyes creased. He gathered her hands into his and held them, hard, pressing his lips to them and speaking into her fingers.

'I will never be able to love you, Shirley.'

The air sucked out of the tent. She stared up at him, frozen. He held her eyes. He took her pain. He remained unmoved.

Outside, the truck horn honked.

Hayden gently released her hands and stepped back. She stumbled against his chair and glanced down to right herself. When she lifted her eyes he'd turned, robbing her of a final connection with those deep, expressive eyes. Gave her his back.

'Goodbye, Hayden,' she whispered.

She got out of the tent with much more aplomb than she felt. She didn't stumble once on the way to the truck, or as she hauled herself up into its backseat, or as she defied her shaking hands and shoved her seat belt into its fastener.

And she didn't look back.

Because she didn't want to know if he'd turned around. If he'd followed the truck with his eyes.

She wanted to remember the exact girth and shape of his turned back.

It would help her to hate him. And as long as she hated him, she couldn't love him.

The truck rumbled away and she sought refuge in the steady stream of conversation from the other passengers. But deep inside she was reliving her own conversation—the conversation from last night and early this morning. Their last.

Mother Theresa had it all wrong.

There was *always* more hurt to be had in love.

CHAPTER THIRTEEN

www.shiloh.com.au—An open letter to my mother, 19th September.

Dear Mum,
I've done as much of your bucket list as I could. I've skidded down a hillside clinging to a sure-footed stock-horse, I've trembled with exhilaration atop the Sydney Harbour Bridge and I've thrown myself off a perfectly sound one in New Zealand. I've felt his music as Beethoven must have, and the extraordinary mercury-leather brush of dolphin skin against my body. I've dropped down the side of a building and floated high above the world. I've been marched across by penguins as I lay enraptured on an ice-sheet and moved to tears by a touch more reverent and gentle than I had ever imagined could exist.

I couldn't do everything on your list, but perhaps that was always the point. That life fully realised is something you strive for but should never attain. Because once you tick off that final box, what is left to do, then, but wait for your allotted heartbeats to run out?

Somewhere in my childhood I learned that love is earned, not bestowed, and believing myself unworthy of it—yours, my father's, even my own—has shaped my life. But it has made me more determined than ever to believe that there is a love out there—somewhere—that strikes like lightning. Because surely if love demanded perfection then none of us would ever find it. And if it is no more than a thing to be won via strategic campaign, then who amongst us would ever have the heart to try?

It has taken me weeks to accept that I am the apple fallen from your tree. I have avoided risk in my life every bit as much as you did and I've let the excuses become truth, every bit as much as you did. In protecting myself I've damaged myself.

Therefore, today, I step out of the shadows into full sunlight, naked and exposed. I hope and trust that the respect and commitment my reading community has shown to Shiloh they'll extend to the real me.

I am the silent child watching, breathless, under the stairs. I am the girl with no parents. I am the blogger behind the mask. I am the woman who loved.

I am...and always will be...your daughter, Shirley Marr.

CHAPTER FOURTEEN

A YEAR ago she could never have conceived of standing here, swathed in thermal clothing and yak furs, gasping for breath, minutes from the base camp of Everest.

Yet here she was.

She'd outed herself publicly a month after getting back from the dinosaur trip and published her mother's list, along with the letter to her. The outpouring of support—from readers and media and sponsors alike—had blown her away and, not long afterwards, a ticket had arrived courtesy of a local travel agent who wanted to help her finish the list.

I can't help with both of the final things on your list, the agent had written, referring to her mother's desire to hold her grandchild, *but I can get you to Nepal.*

Ten days of flights, buses, yaks and hiking later and here she was… Staring at the bright wind-tattered prayer flags so typical of Nepal and the scattered synthetic tents of the climbers. Being practically carried by her patient, serious-faced guide.

Five thousand metres above sea level, all uphill. And they called this 'base' camp?

She lifted her eyes to the peak of the mountain. 'Holy Mother' to the Tibetans. Despite being more than halfway up it already, Everest only got bigger. Less imaginable. Getting to base camp had nearly killed her, even with the compulsory acclimatisation days midway. No roads, no tracks, just vague, invisible trails lined with rocks. She couldn't begin to understand what scaling to Everest's summit would be like.

The tents in front of them looked like acne—bulbous and out of place on the spectacular natural landscape. She laughed out loud at the image and her guide threw her the latest in many concerned looks.

'Rest,' he ordered and then thrust a flask of hideousness at her. An iron-based drink. Good for blood cells, good for altitude sickness. Bad for taste buds.

She could have gone to North base camp. That was accessible by road. But no, she'd had to do it the old-fashioned way. Ready or not.

And, in her case, definitely not.

She looked around as her guide saw to their trusty yak. She'd become quite fond of the matted, stinky thing that tootled along under the very small burden of her backpack, tent and food supplies. It finally dawned on her, halfway up the trail to base camp, that the yak was actually for her, if she passed out, so that her Sherpa could get her back down again without having to carry her himself.

She might have been wobbly but she was still, at least, on her feet.

And she was here. The entrance to Everest base camp.

Tick.

Something about being halfway up this mountain made her feel very close to her mother. And to God, though she was not a religious person, generally. Here, it seemed, she was.

Her breath came as shallow and tightly as ever, thanks to the altitude, and she did her best to only half-fill her lungs the way her Sherpa had shown her. But she'd grown accustomed, now, to dizzy spells and dark patches at the edges of her vision and to slowing her pace to accommodate the lack of oxygen in her blood.

'Shirley?'

She spun at the sound of her name. Pure instinct. Visions were something else she'd grown used to as her oxygen-starved brain played tricks on her but that was her first aural mirage.

Except that it wasn't.

Hayden stood in front of her, bright orange trekking gear, tan even darker than normal.

Her breathing escalated. The dark patches swarmed.

She reached for her guide on instinct.

And then she passed out.

Gentle fingers stroked her back to consciousness.

She opened her eyes a crack and stared at Hayden.

The real one. Not the Hayden of her walking daydreams. Or her fevered night dreams. Her brain wasn't so oxygen-starved that it had forgotten how to deduce.

She sagged. 'You sent the ticket.'

Played again.

'I saw your blog,' he said. 'I wanted to do something to reward your courage. It was the only thing I could do.'

'Most people would send flowers.'

He smiled and quoted her. 'I'm not most people. I had to find something far more dramatic and convoluted.'

Her wind-cracked lips turned up at the corners just a little. 'Figures.' She looked around. 'Where am I?'

'Medical tent.'

'Did you carry me?' Lord, please no. As if passing out in the first place wasn't unseemly enough.

'You had a yak.' He laughed at the horrified expression she couldn't mask. 'The altitude hit me hard too; I wouldn't have been able to carry you here.'

She struggled to sit up. 'So you slung me over the yak, butt waving in the air?'

'Pretty much,' he conceded. 'You're going to be fine, by the way. You just hyperventilated.'

'I don't care why I got here. I care *how* I got here.'

'Shirley...' He smiled, reaching out and tracing a loose strand of hair. The soft expression on his face spoke volumes.

Her outrage dried up. Her smile died. How was *he* even here? She asked him.

'I've been waiting for you.'

'You knew I was coming?'

'I knew you'd use the ticket. I hoped you hadn't decided on a lengthy tour of Nepal first. I nearly died when I discovered there are two base camps. Who knew?'

Anyone who'd done the slightest bit of planning? 'What if I'd gone to the other one?'

'I had spies along both trails. I knew word would very quickly spread of a lone woman trekking towards base camp. Besides,' he added, 'I figured you wouldn't do the easy one.'

So he did know her, just a little bit. She narrowed her eyes. 'How did you get here ahead of me? Chopper?' She knew him a little bit, too.

A dark flush crept above the pinched neck of his trek gear. 'Yeah. From halfway up. Greatly jeered at as I landed by the climbers.'

'So that's "how" taken care of.' She swallowed. 'Now *why* are you here?'

'I needed to see you.'

'You have my address.'

'I needed to see you far from home, somewhere magical.'

Her breath started to thin out. Was it the air again, or just her usual reaction to Hayden's presence? She took what passed for a deep breath in the highlands of Nepal.

'Why?'

He stared, glanced around to see if they were alone. 'Because…'

She waited. The first month of being away from him had been pure misery. Knowing he didn't love her. Knowing he didn't even *want* her enough to just tell her what she wanted to hear. The second month, marginally better and by the third month she'd made some decent progress on getting her life back on track.

Hence the Everest trip.

'Were you overdue to throw my life back into turmoil?'

His eyes softened. 'Is it turmoil—seeing me?'

She swung her legs off the side of the stretcher and sat up. Her head spun. She breathed back the nausea. 'Nothing I won't survive again.'

His gaze changed. 'I don't know whether to be proud of your courage or ashamed of myself that you need to call on it.'

She held her tongue. 'Why are you here, Hayden?'

'I missed you.'

Was he serious? 'Couldn't find a blonde?'

'Not sex, Shirley. I missed *you*. The moment you left the dinosaur campsite, the moment you climbed out of bed that day.'

'You turned your back on me that morning in the tent, Hayden. The message was pretty clear.'

'I didn't want you to see my face. And I couldn't look at yours again. At the pain.'

The first part stopped her cold. But the last part rankled. 'Don't pity me.'

He took her hands where they'd bunched into fists. 'I don't pity you, Shirley. I pity me.'

What?

'I'd convinced myself that the pain I felt that day was yours. That I was simply responding to hurting someone I cared about.' He resettled himself on his haunches. 'But it went on. And on. And it finally dawned on me that it was *my* pain. I'd never been in pain before.'

'Everyone feels pain.'

'Not if you've numbed yourself to survive. I'd never let myself care enough, be engaged enough, be emotionally invested enough to care if something was taken away from me. Not since I was a boy. I'd shoved it right down deep inside out of sheer survival. I'd forgotten what loss felt like.'

Every humane cell in her body responded to that, totally overruling her anger.

'I don't want to be like him, Shirley. Controlling others to make up for something in myself.'

'You're not like him.'

'Two years ago it finally dawned on me what I was becoming. The socially acceptable version of him. So I dropped out and tried to get myself sorted. I thought I had it beat. And then you looked at me that day in the tent the way my mother used to look at him. That awful mix of pain and love and resignation. And I knew I was kidding myself thinking I could manage it alone.'

Alone. Was he looking to her to be some kind of salvation?

'I'm getting professional assistance now.'

Nothing he could have said—nothing—could have surprised her more. Not if he stood on the top of Everest and declared undying passion for her yak. 'You're in therapy?'

'He's an idiot—' he brushed it off, shifting the angle of his crouch by her stretcher '—but he seems to know some things. We're making progress.'

Given his budget, he probably had the best the country had to offer.

'But I didn't need Sigmund Freud to tell me why I was hurting. I missed you, Shirley. In my life. In my arms. In my business.'

He smiled, but she couldn't match it. This was all too monumental.

Seriously, if she woke up on the side of some pebbly track with her Sherpa and the yak staring down at her she was going to just...walk off the edge of the nearest crevasse. And have a very unfriendly discussion with the God she was starting to get a sense of up here.

She got to her feet and he pushed himself up to stand in front of her. She stared up at him. Made herself say it. The bitterest pill.

'You told me you could never love me.'

He dropped his eyes. 'I told you I'd never be *able* to love you. Not the way you deserve. Not the way it is supposed to be.'

It was impossible to know whether it was just *her* air that got tighter or the altitude. 'You let me believe it was me.'

'I thought that was what you wanted to hear. Needed to hear.'

He was right. She had. She'd needed to hate him. She lifted her eyes and took a breath. 'It's too late, Hayden. I've moved on.'

His dark brows dropped. 'On? To what?'

That was the problem with lying; ideally, you needed to have put thought into it. 'On to...getting over you.' *Ugh. Lame.* 'I'm going to hold out for someone who can love me the way I need, the way I deserve.'

His colour dropped slightly. But then his eyes narrowed. 'No. You fainted when you saw me.'

Confident words, but they weren't matched by his tone.

'It was the—'

'No, it wasn't.' Stronger. Surer. He shuffled closer. 'It was me. You still care.'

She clamped her lips together.

'Shirley, you're not that inconstant. And you're too moral. You might have been *trying* to get over me, but you're not.'

Pfff... 'You're so arrogant.'

He smiled. 'Yet you still love me.'

She dropped her head and when she lifted it she left behind all her masks, all her pretensions. 'Is this fun for you, Hayden, tormenting me? Is the ego stroke worth flying across the world for?'

His smile evaporated, his eyes darkened. 'No, Shirley. This is not about my ego. This is about my...feelings. My heart.'

The discomfort was what gave him away. It showed in every crease and fold in his handsome face. Talking about this was excruciating for him.

He was serious...

'Just say it, Hayden.' Whatever he'd come here to say.

He looked around them again. 'Not here. This is not how I imagined it.'

'No. Here, or not at all. You don't get to orchestrate every moment to your personal satisfaction.' Not when it hurt this much.

Indecision flitted across his features. 'Please, Shirley. Just step outside. Only a few feet.'

The plea was so honest and so earnest, it was hard to ignore. *Fine.* 'Just outside. No further.'

He led her out into the bright daylight. After the darkness of the tent, the electric-blue sky half blinded her. She raised her hands to let her eyes adjust more slowly. It didn't help when he turned her so that she was looking at him against the backdrop glare of the main peak of 'Holy Mother'.

'I need sunglasses—' she started.

'God, woman, you're making this very hard.'

His tone clamped her mouth shut. He'd never, *ever* snapped at her like that, hissing with frustration. Even when they were fighting. But, for once, she didn't immediately assume responsibility. Not everything was her fault. And that was a massive mental shift for her.

'Just let me do this,' he gritted. He paused, composed himself and then lifted his eyes back to hers. 'Shirley… You were never going to be just casual for me. I was a fool not to see it coming. I was way too fascinated and intrigued by you.'

Everest disappeared. Her entire vision right now—her entire world—was Hayden Tennant.

'I pushed you away and threw the gift of your love back in your face rather than face my own demons.' He blew out a long breath. 'I was terrified that I would hurt you even more if I stayed in your life. I even justified it that way to myself and felt quite the hero for doing the hard thing. I couldn't have been more patronising if I'd tried. The truth is…'

He frowned and struggled with what came next but she couldn't move for all the oxygen bound up in the snow-caps.

'The truth is, I was scared to let myself feel. To care. Love and I don't have a particularly good track record; my father's obsession with my mother destroyed her, my love for her imprisoned me with him. I have no idea what loving someone safely entails. I was frightened that I would stuff it up if I tried. That I'd fail and you'd end up hating me. But you ended up hating me anyway—'

'No, I didn't,' she murmured.

'You must have.'

'I wanted to, believe me. I couldn't forgive you but I couldn't forget you, either.' She sighed. 'And I couldn't hate you.'

His Adam's apple bungeed a few times. 'Then I saw your blog and what you said about not having the heart for a love that was like a military campaign—'

'Actually, that was—'

'Will you stop interrupting?' he barked. 'I'm trying to tell you I love you.'

Oxygen-less air whooshed into her lungs.

Hayden snapped his mouth shut, and then his lips tightened. 'Though I was hoping to do it more romantically than that,' he muttered.

She didn't dare breathe out in case there was nothing left to take back in. The dark patches appeared in her peripheral vision again. 'More romantic than at the foot of Everest? Having flown halfway around the world and paid off half of Nepal and Tibet to find me?'

His lips twisted. 'Yeah. More than that.'

She finally inhaled. A ridiculous lightness—totally different to what she'd felt coming up the mountain—suffused her.

His eyes darkened. 'This is what I came to. Love liberates, it doesn't entrap. It's not something you can plan for or manage. It's like stepping off a bridge into nothing.' He took a deep breath. 'But it's so much less terrifying when there's someone there, stepping off with you.'

She swallowed back tears. She'd done enough blubbing in front of Hayden for a lifetime. He took her hands.

'If this isn't love,' he said, threading his fingers through hers and boring into her with the intensity of his gaze, 'then it should be.'

So much for not blubbing. Tears spilled, heedless of her will, over her lashes and ran down her wind-whipped, make-up-less face. Lord, what a picture she must present. But she didn't care. She'd bare her whole soul if he asked her to.

And then—despite every fear and doubt and heartbreak and agony of the past months—they were kissing again. The sensation she'd believed she'd never have access to again, the rush of adrenalin that came from just touching him, coursed through her blood where the oxygen couldn't go.

She clung to his strong frame, weakened, and he gathered her more tightly in to him, worshipping her mouth with his. There was barely enough oxygen to go around for one, let alone keep two hearts pumping. They fell apart, panting.

'I am good enough for you,' she gasped. It felt important to make that clear.

He blinked, confused. 'I agree.'

'I mean that I'm through with doubting myself. Believing myself unworthy. I want a strong, equal relationship.'

'Princess, you're preaching to the choir…'

'And I want you to admit that this wasn't strategic. Neither one of us *made* the other love us.'

His eyes softened. 'Everything about you made me love you, Shirley.'

She glared at him.

'You want the lightning bolt?'

'I want you to admit that something special happened here. Something bigger than both of us.'

'How about I tell you when it happened, instead?'

She stared.

'I first bought in to loving you when you stood on my porch and called me an ass that day. No one had challenged me like that, ever.' He stepped closer. 'Then when your ridiculous stockings at the beach forced such lightness into the darkness inside me.' His hand twisted up into her hair. 'Then when you gave up your seats at the symphony for some strangers way up the back and you revealed your soul.'

Her eyes brimmed over again.

'But I still wavered. Then you were so natural and good with the boys at Tim's party and all I could think about was what a spectacular mother you would make.'

A tear wobbled free.

'But if you want the thunderbolt. The moment I knew I was screwed?'

Only from Hayden would she take *screwed* as a compliment. She nodded and shook another tear loose.

'The giraffe. That moment surrounded by sea containers and diesel fumes when you held your hand out to me, your eyes filled with such magic and mystery and drew me into your fantasy. No-one had ever given me the gift of joy before. Unconditional generosity.'

And there was the magic word.

Unconditional.

'I don't ever want to have to earn your love,' she whispered.

He stepped back and regarded her gravely. Then he sank to one knee, on the rocks and shale underfoot, just as he had inside the tent. It wasn't a proposal. It was older and more classic than that. It was a Spartan honour pledge.

'I give it to you. As a gift. Whether you want to keep it or not, it doesn't change how I feel. My love is yours, unconditionally.'

She sank down onto her knees to join him. The stones cut into her skin. She ignored it. 'I accept. And I love you. Every part of you.'

They fell forward into each other's lips, kissed as if it were their first time. Then they pulled back and stared at each other, lost. Panting.

'I caught up to you on the list,' he got out between breaths.

She leaned against him. 'In just a few weeks? How?'

'I cheated.' He laughed. 'We're neck and neck now that we're both here.'

She smiled. 'You know what? That list doesn't seem so important now.'

He curled his arms around her. 'Typical. Just as defeat is on the horizon.'

She chuckled. 'We have something much more impressive on the horizon.'

They stared up at the Himalayan peaks together. Awed.

'This really hurts,' Shirley finally admitted.

'You're not kidding.' He pushed to his feet and then pulled her carefully up with him off the sharp rocks.

'You know you're hiking down off the mountain with me, right? I won't be seen in your chopper.'

'And miss all those nights in a tent with you?' He kissed her again. 'I wouldn't have it any other way. You still owe me from the dinosaur dig.'

'We can't do anything.' She giggled. 'We'll have a guide sleeping just feet away.'

He pushed back and stared at her. 'Did you just...giggle?'

Truly unmasked now. Exactly how she wanted to stay. 'That's just one of a range of ordinary-person sounds I make when I'm not on guard,' she joked. 'And you're going to get to discover them all.'

He swooped down to kiss the side of her throat. 'That's not going any way to preserving the modesty of your guide. Now all I can think about is getting you in a tent and eliciting all those sounds.'

'Truly,' she said, curling her head and seeking out his lips for more oxygen deprivation. 'They can't be any worse than the sound of the yak on the way up.'

EPILOGUE

Two years later

EXACTLY as Hayden had promised her all those adventures ago at Everest, it *was* so much less terrifying when there was someone there, stepping out into the nothingness with you.

He hadn't left her side, not for one overwhelming moment of the birth.

She lay curled around their tiny baby boy, throbbing with love for this precious, precious gift. She'd thought it impossible to feel more love than she already did for her complex, brave Hayden but this little bundle had come out with masses more all ready to go.

She stroked his tiny cheek and glanced at her sleeping husband.

Hayden had pulled a chair up to the side of the bed and leaned forward to watch his son nurse with all the pride and amazement and trepidation of a first-time dad. Then he'd fallen asleep there, totally destroyed by the past forty hours, with one hand on her and one on his new son, draped on the side of her bed. Even the visiting nurses worked quietly around him so that he could sleep.

Then again, he had charmed every one of them. They would have done anything for him. She bundled Leo up more tightly in her hold and looked up and around her, too shattered—too happy—to sleep.

'Mum,' she whispered to the night. 'This is your grandson,

Leonidas. I'm sorry you can't hold him yourself but Hayden and I will hold him for ever for you and keep him safe.'

She stroked his flushed little cheek with her index finger. 'I get it now, Mum. How unprepared we all are at this moment. How much we want to be the perfect parent for our babies. But it doesn't change us. It can't make us perfect, or even better. We can only do our best.'

She gently extracted the sleeping baby from under Hayden's touch, bundled him more securely and curled him into a hold close to her body.

And then she rocked him and told him all about his grandma.

Tick.

* * * * *

The Devil and the Deep

Amy
ANDREWS

Amy Andrews has always loved writing and still can't quite believe that she gets to do it for a living. Creating wonderful heroines and gorgeous heroes and telling their stories is an amazing way to pass the day. Sometimes they don't always act as she'd like them to—but then neither do her kids, so she's kind of used to it. Amy lives in the very beautiful Samford Valley, with her husband and aforementioned children, along with six brown chickens and two black dogs.

She loves to hear from her readers. Drop her a line at www.amyandrews.com.au.

For Halle Anne Baxter.
Much loved.

PROLOGUE

Lady Mary Bingham had never seen such a fine specimen of manhood in all her twenty years as she held out her hand to her unlikely saviour so he could aid her aboard. Pirate or not, Vasco Ramirez's potent masculinity tingled through every cell of her body. And even had it not, his piercing blue eyes, the exact colour of warm, tropical waters that fringed the reefs he was rumoured to know like the back of his hand, touched a place inside her that she'd never known existed.

A place she could never now deny.

She supposed, if she were given to swooning, this would be as good a time as any. But she wasn't. In fact she'd always found the practice rather tiresome and refused to even allow her knees the slightest tremble. Women who had fits of the vapours and cried for their smelling salts every two seconds—like her aunt—were not the kind of women she admired.

Her breath hitched as sable lashes framing those incredible eyes swept downwards in a frank inspection of every inch of her body. When his gaze returned to her face she was left in no doubt that he'd liked what he'd seen. His thumb lightly stroked the skin of her forearm and she felt the caress deep inside that newly awakened place.

Looking at the bronzed angles of his exotic face, she

knew she should be afraid for had she not just gone from the frying pan straight into the fire?

Yet strangely she wasn't.

Not even when his gaze dropped to the pulse beating rapidly against the milky white skin of her neck. Or lower to where her breasts strained against the constrictive fabric of her bodice. His lazy inspection of the agitated rise of her bosom did not elicit fear even when what it did elicit was reason for fear itself.

Her uncle, the bishop, would have declared him an instrument of the devil. A man willing to lead unsuspecting ladies to the edge of sin but strangely she'd never felt so compelled to transgress. The thought was titillating and she sucked in a breath, annoyed that this buccaneer had caused such consternation after such short acquaintance.

After all, was not one pirate just like the next?

Mary looked down at the insolent drift of his thumb. 'You will unhand me immediately,' she intoned in a voice that brooked no argument.

Ramirez's smile was nine parts charm one part insolence as he slowly—very slowly—ceased the involuntary caress.

'As you wish,' he murmured, bowing slightly over her hand, his fingers tracing down the delicate blue veins of her forearm, whispering over the fragile bones of her wrist and the flat of her palm as he released her.

Lady Mary swallowed as the accented English slid velvet gloves over already sensitised skin. 'I insist that you return me to my uncle forthwith.'

Vasco admired her pluck. The girl, who he knew to be barely out of her teens, may well be staring him straight in the eye but he could smell her fear as only a veteran of a hundred raids on the high seas could.

Lord alone knew what had happened to her in the two

days she'd been at the mercy of Juan Del Toro and his ruffians. But something told him this pampered English miss could certainly hold her own.

And virgins fetched a much higher price at the slave markets.

'As you wish,' he murmured again.

Mary narrowed her eyes, suspicious of his easy capitulation. 'You know my uncle? You know who I am?'

He smiled at her. 'You are Lady Mary Bingham. The bishop commissioned me to...retrieve you.'

For the first time in two days Mary could see an end to the nightmare that had begun with her abduction down by the wharfs a mere forty-eight hours before and she almost sagged to the damp floorboards at his feet. She'd heard her former captives talking about slave markets and had been scared witless.

Alas, falling at the feet of a pirate, whether sanctioned by her uncle or not, wasn't something a young woman of good breeding did. 'Thank you,' she said politely. 'I am most grateful for your speedy response. Juan Del Toro's men do not know how to treat a lady.'

'Do not thank me yet, Lady Bingham.' He smiled with steel in his lips. 'There are a lot of miles between here and Plymouth and by the end of it my *men may well care less about you being a lady and more about you being a woman.'*

Mary raised a haughty eyebrow, hoping it disguised the sudden leap in her pulse. 'And you would allow such fiendish behaviour amongst your crew?'

Vasco smiled his most charming smile, his dark tousled hair giving him the look of the devil. 'Amongst my crew? Of course not, Lady Bingham. But captains do enjoy certain privileges...'

STELLA MILLS sighed as she closed down the document on her desktop and dragged herself back from the swashbuckling seventeen hundreds to the reality of the here and now. She could re-read the words that had flowed effortlessly out of her last year and made her an 'overnight' sensation until the cows came home but it didn't change the facts—one book did not a writer make.

One book did not a career make.

No matter how many publishing houses had bid for *Pleasure Hunt* at auction, no matter how many best-seller lists it had made or how many fan letters she'd received or how much money competing film companies had thrown at her for the film rights.

No matter how crazy the romance world had gone for Vasco Ramirez.

They wanted more.

And so did the publisher.

Stella stared at the blinking cursor on the blank page in front of her. The same blinking cursor she'd been staring at for almost a year now.

Oh, God. 'I'm a one-hit wonder,' she groaned as her head hit the keyboard.

A knock on the door interrupted her pity party and she glanced up. Several lines of gobbledygook stared back at her as the knock came again. She grimaced—it seemed she was destined to write nothing but incomprehensible garbage for ever more.

Another knock, more insistent than the last, demanded her attention. 'Coming,' she called as she did what she'd done every day for the past year—deleted the lot.

She hurried to the door and was reaching for the knob as a fourth knock landed. 'Okay, okay, hold your horses,' she said as she wrenched the damn thing open.

Piercing blue eyes, the exact colour of warm, tropical waters that fringed the reefs she knew he knew like the back of his hand, greeted her. She blinked. 'Rick?'

'Stel,' he murmured, leaning forward to kiss first one cheek then the other, inhaling the familiar coconut essence of her.

She shut her eyes briefly as the smell of sea breezes and ocean salt infused her senses the way they always did whenever Riccardo Granville was close. When she opened them again Rick had withdrawn and her mother came into focus, hovering behind his shoulder. Her eyes were rimmed with red and she was biting on her bottom lip.

Her mother lived in London and Rick called the ocean his home. Why were they here? In Cornwall. Together?

Stella frowned as a feeling of doom descended.

'What's wrong?' she asked, looking from one to the other as her pulse wooshed like a raging torrent through her ears.

Her mother stepped forward and hugged her. 'Darling,' she murmured, 'it's Nathan.'

Stella blinked. Her father?

She looked over her mother's shoulder at Rick, his face grim. 'Rick?' she asked, searching for a spark of something—anything—that would bring her back from the precipice she was balanced upon.

Rick looked down at the woman he'd known almost all his thirty years and sadly shook his head. 'I'm sorry.'

CHAPTER ONE

Six months later...

THE cursor still blinked at her from the same blank page. Although Stella rather fancied that it had given up blinking and had moved on to mocking.

There were no words. No story.

No characters spoke in her head. No plot played like a movie reel. No shards of glittering dialogue burnt brightly on her inward eye desperate for release.

There was just the same old silence.

And now grief to boot.

And Diana would be arriving soon.

As if she'd willed it, a knock on the door heralded Stella's closest friend. Normally she'd have leapt from her seat to welcome Diana but not today. In fact, for a moment, she seriously considered not opening the door at all.

Today, Diana was not here as her friend.

Today, Diana was here as a representative from the publisher.

And she'd promised her chapter one...

'I know you're in there. Don't make me break this sucker down.'

The voice was muffled but determined and Stella resigned herself to her fate as she crossed from her work area in the window alcove, with its spectacular one-eighty-degree views of rugged Cornish coastline, to the front door. She drew in a steadying breath as she unlatched it and pulled it open.

Diana opened her arms. 'Babe,' she muttered as she swept Stella into a rib-cracking hug. 'How are you doing? I've been so worried about you.'

Stella settled into the sweet sisterhood of the embrace, suddenly so glad to see her friend she could feel tears prick at the backs of her eyes. They'd only known each other a handful of years since meeting at uni, but Diana had called most nights since the funeral and this was her tenth visit.

'Pretty rubbish,' she admitted into Diana's shoulder.

'Of course you are,' Diana soothed, rubbing her friend's back. 'Your dad died—it comes with the territory.'

Diana's parents had passed away not long before they'd become friends so Stella knew that Diana had intimate acquaintance with grief.

'I want to stop feeling like this.'

Diana hugged her harder. 'You will. Eventually you will. In the meantime you need to do what you need to do. And I think that starts with a nice glass of red.'

Diana held up a bottle of shiraz she'd bought at an off-licence in Penzance on her way to the windswept, cliff-top cottage her friend had taken out a long-term lease on after her strait-laced fiancé, Dreary Dale, hadn't been able to handle the success of *Pleasure Hunt* and had scuttled away with a stick jammed up his butt.

Sure, Stella had insisted her reasons had more to do with the historic coastline's rich pirate history stimulating her muse but, given that no book was forthcoming, Diana wasn't buying it.

Stella looked at her watch and laughed for the first time today. It was two in the afternoon. 'It's a bit early, isn't it?'

Diana tutted her disapproval. 'The sun's up over the yardarm—isn't that what you nautical types say? Besides, it's November—it's practically night time.'

Diana didn't wait for an answer, dragging her pull-along case inside the house and kicking the door shut with her four-inch-booted heel. She shrugged out of her calf-length, figure-hugging leather coat and unwound her Louis Vuitton scarf from her neck—all without letting go of the bottle. She wore charcoal trousers and a soft pink cashmere sweater, which matched the thick brunette curls that fell against its pearlescent perfection.

Diana was *very* London.

Stella looked down at her own attire and felt like a total slob. Grey sweats, coffee-stained hoodie and fluffy slippers. A haphazard ponytail that she'd scraped together this morning hung limply from her head in an even bigger state of disarray.

Stella was *very* reclusive writer.

Which would be much more romantic if she'd actually bloody written anything in the last eighteen months.

'Sit,' Diana ordered, tinkling her fingers at her friend as she headed towards the cupboard where she knew, from many a drinking session, the wine glasses were housed.

Stella sat on her red leather sofa if, for nothing else, to feel less diminutive. Diana was almost six feet and big boned in a sexy Amazonian, Wonder Woman kind of way. She, on the other hand, was just a couple of centimetres over five feet, fair and round.

'Here,' Diana said, thrusting a huge glass of red at her and clinking the rims together before claiming the bucket chair opposite. 'To feeling better,' she said, then took a decent swig.

'I'll drink to that,' Stella agreed, taking a more measured sip. She stared into the depths of her wine, finding it easier than looking at her friend.

'You don't have the chapter, do you?' Diana asked after the silence had stretched long enough.

Stella looked at Diana over the rim of her glass. 'No,' she murmured. 'I'm sorry.'

Diana nodded. 'It's okay.'

Stella shook her head and uttered what had been on her mind since the writer's block had descended all those months ago. 'What if I only ever have one book in me?'

The fear had gnawed away at her since finishing the first book. Dale's desertion had added to it. Her father's death had cemented it.

Vasco Ramirez had demanded to be written. He'd strutted straight out of her head onto the page in all his swashbuckling glory. He had been a joy, his story a gift that had flowed effortlessly.

And now?

Now they wanted another pirate and she had nothing.

Diana held up a hand, waving the question away. 'You don't,' she said emphatically.

'But what if I do?'

Stella had never known the sting of rejection and the mere thought was paralysing. What if Joy, her editor, hated what she wrote? What if she laughed?

She'd had a dream ride—from a six-figure auction with a multi-book contract to *New York Times* best-seller to a movie deal.

What if it had all been a fluke?

Diana stabbed her finger at the air in her general direction. 'You. Don't.'

Stella felt a surge of guilt mix with the shiraz in her veins, giving it an extra charge. Diana had championed her crazy foray into writing from the beginning, encouraging her to take a break from being an English teacher and write the damn book.

She'd been the first to read it. The first to know its potential, insisting that she take it to show her boss, who was looking for exactly what Stella had written—a meaty historical romance. As an editorial assistant in a London publishing house Diana had been adamant it was a blockbuster and

Stella had been flabbergasted when Diana's prediction of a quick offer had come to pass.

She smiled at her friend, hoping it didn't come across as desperate on the outside as it felt on the inside. 'Will you get sacked if you return to London empty-handed?'

Almost a year past Stella's deadline, Joy had pulled out the big guns to get her recalcitrant star to deliver. She knew how close Diana and Stella were so she'd sent Diana to do whatever it took to get book number two.

Diana shook her head. 'No. We're not going to talk about this tonight. Tonight, we get messy drunk, tomorrow we talk about the book. Deal?'

Stella felt the knot in her shoulder muscles release like an elastic band and she smiled. 'Deal.'

Two hours later, a storm had drawn night in a little earlier than usual. Wind howled around the house, lashing at the shutters, not that the two women cosied up by the fire were aware. They were on their second bottle of wine and almost at the bottom of a large packet of crisps and were laughing hysterically about their uni days.

A sharp rap at the door caused them both to startle then burst out laughing at their comic-book reactions.

'Bloody hell.' Diana clutched her chest. 'I think I just had a heart attack.'

Stella laughed as she rose a little unsteadily. 'Impossible, red wine's supposed to be good for the heart.'

'Not in these quantities it's not,' Diana said and Stella cracked up again as she headed towards the door.

'Wait, where are you going?' Diana muttered as she also clambered to her feet.

Stella frowned. 'To open the door.'

'But what if it's a two-headed moor monster?' Even through her wine goggles Diana could see the rain lashing the window pane behind Stella's desk. 'It is the very definition of a dark and stormy night out there, babe.'

Stella hiccupped. 'Well, I don't think they knock but I'll politely tell it to shoo and point out that Bodmin is a little north of here.'

Diana cracked up and Stella was still chuckling as she opened the door.

To Vasco Ramirez. In the flesh.

Light from inside the cottage bathed the bronzed angles of his jaw and cheekbones, fell softly against his mouth and illuminated his blue eyes to tourist-brochure perfection. His shoulder-length hair, a relic from his tearaway teens, hung in damp strips around his face and water droplets clung to those incredible sable lashes.

He looked every inch the pirate.

'Rick?' Her breath stuttered to a halt as it always did when he was too close, sucking up all her oxygen. The recalcitrant memory of an almost-kiss over a decade ago flitted like a butterfly through her grey matter.

Rick smiled down at a frowning Stella. 'Now what sort of greeting is that?' he teased as he moved in for his standard double cheek kiss.

Coconut embraced him. Nathan had bought Stella coconut body products every year for her birthday and she'd faithfully worn them. Still was, apparently.

Stella shut her eyes and waited for the choirs of angels in her head to start singing *hallelujah* as the aroma of salt and sea enveloped her. He was, after all, so perfect he had to be heaven-sent.

She blinked as he pulled away. 'Is everything okay?' she asked.

Her heart beat a little faster in her chest. Which had nothing to do with the erotic scrape of his perpetual three-day growth or the brief brush of his lips, and everything to do with his last visit.

Rick didn't just drop by.

Last time he'd arrived unannounced on her doorstep looking bleaker than the North Sea in winter, the news had not been good.

'Is Mum—?'

Rick pressed his fingers against her mouth, hushing her. 'Linda's fine, Stel. Everything's fine.'

She almost sagged against him in relief. Certainly her mouth did. He smiled at her as he withdrew his hand and she smiled back, and with the wind whipping around them and flurries of raindrops speckling their skin it was as if they were kids again, standing on the bow of the *Persephone* as a storm chased them back into harbour.

'So…not a monster from the moors, then?' Diana asked, interrupting their shared reverie.

Rick looked over Stella's shoulder straight into the eyes of a vaguely familiar, striking brunette. She looked at him with frank admiration and he grinned.

God, but he loved women.

Particularly women like this. The kind that liked to laugh and have a good time, enjoyed a flirt and some no-strings company.

'Honey, I can be whatever you want me to be,' he said, pushing off the door jamb, brushing past Stella and extending his hand. 'Hi. Rick. I think we've already met?'

Diana smiled as she shook his hand. 'Yes. When you were here for the funeral. Diana,' she supplied.

'Ah, yes, that's right,' Rick said, stalling a little. He'd been so caught up in his shock and disbelief and being strong for Stella and Linda that he'd not really taken anything in. 'You work for Stel's publishers?'

Diana grinned, her eyes twinkling, not remotely insulted that Rick had struggled to remember her. 'Took you a while.'

Stella watched her bestie and her…whatever the hell Rick was—old family friend? deceased father's business partner?

substitute brother?—flirt effortlessly. Now why couldn't she be more like that? The only time she'd been comfortable, truly comfortable, with a man had been with a fictional pirate.

Even her relationship with Dale had been lukewarm by comparison.

A blast of rain spattered against her neck, bringing her out of her state of bewilderment, and she realised she still had the door wide open. She shook her head at her absent-mindedness.

'To what do we owe the pleasure?' she asked, shutting the weather out and joining the chatty twosome in the centre of the room.

Rick looked down at Stella's cute little button nose. 'Well—' he winked at her before returning his attention to Diana and running his finger around the rim of her glass '—I heard a whisper there was a party going on.'

Diana laughed. She looked at Stella. 'You never told me he had ESP.' Then she scurried to the kitchen to get another glass.

Rick watched her for a moment before returning his gaze to Stella. She stared up at him and the familiar feeling of wanting to wrap her up swelled in his chest. 'How are you doing, Stel?' he murmured.

Rick had felt the loss of Nathan Mills probably even more profoundly than his own father. Nathan had been his guardian and mentor since Anthony Granville had got himself killed in a bar fight when Rick had been seven. The man had been the closest thing to a father he had, had curbed all his hot-headed brashness and he felt his loss in a hundred different ways every day.

He could only imagine how Stella must feel.

Stella shrugged, feeling again the mutual despair that had added an extra depth to their bond. She fell into the empathy that shone in his luminescent gaze. Sometimes it was hard to reconcile the impulsive, teenage bad-boy of her fantasies with the hardworking, responsible, compassionate man in front of her.

'I hate it,' she whispered.

The truth was Stella hadn't seen her father regularly since she'd started university and joined the workforce.

Become a grown-up, as her mother would say.

A flying visit at Christmas, the arrival in the mail of a single perfect shell he'd found on a beach somewhere that always made her smile, an occasional email with pictures of him and Rick and some amazing find at the bottom of a sea bed.

But just knowing he was out there doing what he loved, following his wild boyhood dreams of sunken galleons, had kept her whole world in balance.

And now he was gone, nothing was the same.

'I know,' he murmured, putting his arm around her shoulder and pulling her into his chest. 'I hate it too.'

And he did. He hated doing what he did without the one person who truly understood *why* by his side. He hated turning to tell Nathan something and him not being there. He hated the absence of wise words and Nathan's particular brand of bawdy humour around the dinner table.

Rick shut his eyes against the loss he still felt so acutely and sank into her, enjoying the familiarity of having her close. He liked how she tucked into him just right. How her head fitted perfectly under his chin and how his chest was just the right height to pillow her cheek and how she always smelled liked coconut.

As kids he'd been the pirate and she'd been the mermaid and they'd played endless games revolving around sunken treasure. Not very politically correct these days, he supposed, but they'd amused themselves for countless hours and forged a bond that he still felt today.

Of course there'd been times, during their teenage years, when their games had taken a certain risqué turn and while they'd never indulged, they'd diced pretty close.

Holding her like this reminded him just how close.

'Okay, okay, you two,' Diana teased, pushing a glass of red

wine into Rick's hand. 'No maudlin tonight. That's the rule. Eat, drink and be merry tonight.'

Rick forced himself to step away, grateful that Diana was here to ground them in the present. He'd thought a lot about Stella since Nathan had died, more than usual.

And not all of those thoughts had been pure.

He accepted the wine. 'Good plan,' he said, clinking glasses with them both.

Stella indicated the lounge chairs huddled around the fireplace and watched as Rick shrugged out of his navy duffle coat to reveal well-worn jeans that clung in all the right places and a thick turtle-neck, cable-knit sweater.

Even off the boat the man looked as if he belonged at sea.

Diana lounged back against the cushions, inspecting him dispassionately, her wine goggles making the job a little difficult. She pointed at him over the rim of her glass.

'There's something familiar about you,' she slurred.

Stella didn't like the look of speculation on her friend's face. She'd seen that dogged look before and didn't want to give Diana too much latitude.

'Yes, you met him at the funeral,' she said, hopefully redirecting her friend's thoughts that tended to fancy after several glasses of red.

Diana narrowed her eyes. 'Nope,' she said as she shook her head. 'I have this feeling I know you beyond that.' Even at the funeral all suited and polished he'd looked vaguely familiar to her but now, looking all lone-wolf-of-the-sea, there was definitely something she recognised about him.

Was it his eyes? Or maybe his hair?

Rick chuckled. 'Maybe I look like your great uncle Cyril?'

Diana burst out laughing as she sipped on her drink and Stella even envied her that. She had a jingly laugh that sounded like Tinkerbell waving her magic wand. Stella had no doubt that red wine would be pouring out of her nose had she tried that same manoeuvre.

Diana wagged her finger. 'Good try but *you* don't look like *anyone's* great uncle Cyril.' She narrowed her eyes again and nudged the side of her nose three times with her index finger. 'Don't you worry. I *will* remember. I may just need—' she looked at her almost empty wine glass '—a while.'

Rick saluted. 'I look forward to the final outcome.'

Diana nodded. 'As well you should.'

Rick looked over at Stella sitting quietly watching the byplay. The firelight spun the escaping tendrils of her long blonde hair into golden streams and he was once again reminded of their childhood games when she'd been the mermaid singing his ship onto the rocks. How many times had he snorkelled over reefs with her, her long blonde hair flowing behind her just like the mermaids from ancient mythology?

'So,' he said when the silence had stretched enough. 'Did you get it?'

Stella frowned at him. 'Get what?'

'Your half.'

'My half of what?'

Rick grinned. 'The map?'

Stella shook her head. 'What on earth are you talking about?' she asked.

Rick's eyebrows drew together in a frown to match hers as he placed his half-empty glass on the coffee table. 'You should have received it early last week. I posted it ages ago.'

Diana rolled her eyes. 'She probably has. She's just not been responding to any correspondence.'

Stella blushed at her friend's astuteness as Diana made her way to the hall stand. Unopened mail oozed all over the edges of the sturdy eighteenth-century oak and Stella felt her cheeks grow warmer. She'd been avoiding any attempt at communication with the outside world—particularly from her editor. She didn't open her mail unless it had a window. She screened all her calls. She didn't go to her inbox.

Diana quickly riffled through the mound of mail, letters

and other miscellaneous items that had made it through Stella's front door, some of it spilling haphazardly to the floor. She pulled out a large flat yellow envelope with enough stamps to start a collection.

'This it?' she asked holding it up.

Rick nodded. 'Arrr,' he said in his best pirate accent. 'That be it.'

It was Stella's turn to roll her eyes. Rick had perfected the pirate vernacular as a child, lending an authenticity to their imaginary games.

Diana laughed as she rejoined them, thrusting the envelope at Stella. 'Ooh, you speak pirate?'

Rick grinned. 'Aye, my lovely.'

'Forget it,' Stella murmured absently as she turned the envelope over and over in her hands. There was a variety of colourful postal stamps and airmail stickers adorning the front. 'Diana's a Jack Sparrow fan. You're wasting your time.'

Rick look affronted. 'Are you saying I'm not Captain Jack material?'

It was on the tip of Stella's tongue to say that he was a thousand times sexier than the iconic film character. He was broader and taller with better oral hygiene and more scruples.

'Hmm, I don't know,' Diana mused. 'I'm sure a little more scruffed up…'

But Stella wasn't listening. Her father's distinctive handwriting had drawn her gaze and she touched the letters with great reverence as if they could somehow bring him back.

Rick glanced at Diana as Stella's continuing silence fell loudly around them. She shrugged at him hopelessly and he could tell that Stella's grief touched her too.

'Where did you get this?' Stella asked.

'I finally got around to cleaning out Nathan's desk. It was in a drawer. There was one for me as well.'

Stella nodded absently at his response. It was strange receiving something from her father six months after his death. Like a hand extending from the grave.

'Aren't you going to open it?' he asked quietly.

Stella looked up at him through the blonde stripes of her half-up-half-down fringe. 'Do I want to?'

He grinned and nodded. 'If it's what I think it is you do. You really do.'

Stella doubted it but she turned the envelope over and neatly sliced open the back. A sheath of loose papers lay within and she pulled them out after another encouraging nod from Rick. A brief note from her father was paper-clipped to the front.

Stel,
Inigo's treasure is there, I just know it.
You and Rick go find it.
Make me proud.
Daddy.

Stella swallowed hard and for a moment the bold vertical slashes blurred in front of her eyes. Finding out on autopsy that her father had been riddled with cancer and wondering if the scuba-diving *accident* had really been an accident had been hard to come to terms with.

But this seemed to confirm that he'd known his days were numbered and chosen to go in his own way doing what he'd loved most.

She glanced at Rick. 'You got the same?'

He nodded and she looked back at the documents, leafing through the rest. A hand-drawn map was at the very back.

Or half a map to be precise.

'What's this?' she asked, not quite comprehending her father's frenetic squiggles around the margins.

'The other half of this,' Rick said, pulling out a folded page from his back pocket, unfolding it and laying it on the coffee table.

Diana sat forward. 'Is that a…treasure map?'

Rick grinned. 'Sort of. It shows the potential resting places of Captain Inigo Alvarez's ship, *La Sirena*.'

Diana scrunched up her face, trying to remember her schoolgirl Spanish. 'The…?'

'The Mermaid,' Stella supplied.

'Oh my,' Diana said. 'How exciting! Inigo Alvarez…' She rolled the name around her tongue. 'He sounds positively dishy.'

Rick laughed. 'He was. A late-eighteenth-century pirate known as the Robin Hood of the seven seas. Robbing the rich to give to the poor.'

Stella blasted Rick with a *down-boy* glare. 'Robin Hood of the high seas,' she tisked, shaking her head in disgust. 'That's all just anecdotal and you know it. Do not encourage her.'

'Drat,' Diana mused.

'Okay, maybe he was as bloodthirsty and marauding as the rest of them but there's heaps of historical documents citing his and *The Mermaid*'s existence,' he said calmly. 'You used to believe,' Rick reminded her.

They both had. Everyone in the salvaging industry seemed to have a story about the mysterious Captain Alvarez and as children they'd listened to each one until he'd grown large in both their imaginations. Rick picked up the papers that had accompanied the map, the same ones that had been in his envelope. Years of Nathan's research into a character that had captured them both.

'What happened to him?' Diana asked.

Rick looked at a captivated Diana. 'He just disappeared off the face of the earth. There were rumours at the time that *The Mermaid* went down laden with stolen booty during a vicious storm.'

'Where?' Diana whispered, sucked in even if Stella was sitting back in her chair, refusing to be drawn. 'Here somewhere, right?' she asked, picking up Stella's half of the map and joining the two pieces together on the coffee table.

Rick shook his head. 'Nathan obviously thought so. He's drawn this up from his research over the years so I guess it would be hard to be sure. But he was the best damn intuitive treasure hunter I've ever known and if he thinks Inigo's ship is here somewhere, then I'm willing to bet it is too.'

'So why didn't he go after it himself?' Stella demanded, getting up off the chair and heading for the kitchen sink. When she got there she tipped out her almost-full glass of wine. She was suddenly angry with her father.

If he'd known he was dying, why hadn't he told her? Why hadn't he got treatment? Why hadn't he come home?

'When did he have the time, Stel, with so many other projects—sure things—on the books?'

Stella looked up at the reproach in his voice, feeling suddenly guilty. They'd both known Nathan's plans had always involved finding Inigo's treasure…one day…when he retired…

'Why on earth did he give us half a map each? He must have known I was just going to give you my half and let you have at it.'

She'd loved her father and he had given her a magical childhood filled with sunken treasure and tropical waters but it had been a long time since she'd been a little girl who believed in pirates and mermaids. And the romance of that world had always warred with the realities of her life—divorced parents, divided loyalties.

Rick stood and walked towards her. He could tell she was struggling with the same emotions he had when he'd seen Nathan's handwriting again and the memories it had stirred.

'I think he knew his time was drawing to a close and maybe it was his way to keep us connected? I think he wanted us to go and do this together and I think it would be a great way to honour his memory. What do you say? The long-range weather forecast is good. You want to come on a treasure hunt with me?'

Stella glared at Rick as his not-so-subtle guilt trip found its mark. Well, it wouldn't work. 'Are you crazy? I can't go gallivanting around the bloody ocean. My editor would have apoplexy. My book is way overdue and I have probably the worst case of writer's block in the history of written language, don't I, Diana?'

She looked at her friend for confirmation, who did so with a vigorous nod of her head.

'Well, this is exactly what you need.' He grinned, unperturbed. 'Nothing like the open ocean to stimulate the muse.'

Stella stared at him askance. 'Don't you have other salvage jobs on the go?'

Rick shrugged. 'Nothing the guys can't handle. Besides, it won't be a salvage job, just a recon mission, see what we can find. A few weeks, four at the most. Just you and me and the open ocean. Salt, sea air and sunshine. You could get a tan,' he cajoled as he took in her pallor. 'It'll be just like we were kids again.'

Stella shook her head against the temptation and romance of yesteryear, which appealed to her on a primal level she didn't really understand. She dragged her gaze away from his seductive mouth.

They weren't kids any more.

'I can't. I have a book to write.'

'Come on,' he murmured, feeling the longing inside her even if she couldn't. 'You know you want to. You always wrote like crazy whenever you were on the *Persephone*. Remember? You were always scribbling away in that writing pad.'

She remembered. She'd either had her head stuck in a book or she'd been writing something. He'd teased her about it mercilessly. She should have known back then she was destined to be a writer. 'I can't. Can I, Diana?'

Diana looked at Stella. Then at Rick. Then back at her

friend. If anyone needed a change of scenery it was Stella. These four walls were obviously becoming a prison for her despite the view—maybe mixing it up a little would get the juices flowing again.

And if the open ocean was where she was most creative…

Joy would have a fit but Diana had a hunch that this was just what her friend needed. She bloody hoped so because her head would be on the chopping block if Stella returned tanned and still bookless.

She stood and joined them in the kitchen. 'I think you should go. I think it's a great idea.'

Stella blinked. 'What?' she said as Rick's grin trebled.

'*This*,' he said, slipping his arm around Diana's shoulders, 'is a wise woman.'

'Thank you.' Diana beamed at him.

'Come on, Stel. *I dare you.*'

Stella rolled her eyes. As kids their relationship had thrived on dares and one-upmanship, Stella hell-bent on proving she could keep up with a boy.

Dare you to swim through that hole in the wreck. Something expressly forbidden by her father. *Dare you to bring a coin up from the bottom.* Also forbidden. *Dare you to touch that manta ray.* Just plain stupid.

It was a wonder they'd both survived.

She remembered when the dares had stopped. That evening on deck when she'd dared him to kiss her. She wondered if he remembered. His eyes glittered back at her—all bad-boy blue—and she *knew* he remembered.

'Tell you what,' Rick said as he pulled himself back from that ancient memory that still resonated in his dreams, 'don't decide now. Sleep on it first, okay. I bet it won't seem as crazy in the morning.'

Stella was willing to bet that in the cold light of day *and* stone-cold sober it would not only seem crazy, it would actually *be* crazy.

Utterly certifiable.

He leaned forward and kissed her forehead, then winked at Diana. 'Can I crash here?'

Stella felt like a child between two grown-ups. 'What, no girl in this port, sailor?' she asked waspishly. The man had never lacked for company on shore.

Rick chuckled. 'Not one who can make pancakes like you.'

'Ah,' she said, realising she was being churlish and making an effort to get them back to their usual repartee. 'So you only want me for my pancakes.'

'And your half of the map.' He grinned. 'I'm beat. I need a shower. Then I need to sleep for a week. Towels still in the same place?' he asked as he left them, not waiting for an answer.

Diana watched him go. 'Wow.'

Stella nodded. 'Yes.'

She turned to face the sink, leaning her elbows against the cool steel as she looked out of the large bay window into the bleak dark night. Diana joined her, still sipping at her wine.

'Does he wear contacts?' she mused. 'It's quite striking to see a man with such dark colouring have such blue eyes.'

Stella nodded again. She'd been captivated by them for as long as she could remember. 'Yes, it's really quite mesmerising, isn't it?'

'Which room are you in, Diana?'

Both women started guiltily as the voice from behind them had them straightening and whipping around to face Rick. He was naked except for possibly the world's smallest towel around his waist, clutched at the side where it didn't quite meet. His blue eyes looked even bluer with less of anything much to detract from them.

'The one on the left,' Stella confirmed after a quick glance at a gawking, mute-looking Diana.

'Great, I'll doss down in the other.' He smiled at both of them. 'See you in the morning, ladies.'

Stella and Diana watched him as he swaggered away, the towel slipping as he gave up on trying to keep it on. They caught a glimpse of one naked buttock just before he disappeared around the corner.

A buttock adorned with a very sexy, perfectly round, dark brown birthmark, right in the middle of a very sexy dimple.

Diana gasped as suddenly everything fell into place. Bronzed colouring, piercing blue eyes, long shaggy hair, a mouth made for sin and a very cute blemish in a very specific place.

'Oh, my God!' She looked at Stella. 'That's why he's so familiar. It's him—he's Vasco Ramirez!'

CHAPTER TWO

STELLA blushed furiously. 'Shh,' she hissed. 'Don't be preposterous.'

Diana laughed. 'Methinks the lady doth protest too much.'

Stella turned back to the sink, busying herself with washing out her wine glass. 'There are some similarities…' she admitted.

'Similarities?' Diana hooted. 'I *knew* I knew him…I just couldn't figure out where from. I mean, hell, let's face it, if I'd met him somewhere before I'd hardly be likely to forget him—the man's a total hottie. And, I have to say—' she nudged Stella '—looks like a total sex fiend.'

'Diana!'

She shrugged. 'In a good way.'

'Well, don't look at me,' Stella muttered. 'You know I've only ever been with Dale.'

Diana tisked. 'I can't believe you've never gone there… well, I mean you've obviously thought about it because you wrote an entire three-hundred-and-seventy-five page sexual fantasy about the man—'

'I did not,' Stella denied, picking up a tea towel and briskly drying the glass.

Diana crooked an eyebrow at her. 'Stella, this is me. Diana. Who knows you.'

Stella looked into her friend's eyes and could see that she

knew the truth. She sagged against the sink. 'Okay, yes,' she sighed. 'Rick was the inspiration for Vasco.'

Stella hadn't set out to write a book with Rick as the hero but Vasco had taken on Rick's features in a totally organic way. She hadn't even been truly aware of it until she'd written the first kiss.

And then it had been so blindingly obvious she'd wondered why it had taken her so long.

'Hah! I knew it!' Diana clapped delightedly.

Stella rolled her eyes. 'This is between you and me, Diana,' she said, placing a hand on her friend's arm. 'Promise?'

'Don't worry,' Diana said, waving a dismissive hand, 'your secret is safe with me.'

'Thank you,' Stella said, releasing a breath as she shuffled away from the sink and headed towards the fire.

'Well, there's only one thing for it now,' Diana said as she followed Stella and plonked herself down on one of the lounge chairs. 'You have to go with him.'

Stella looked up from her log poking. 'What?'

'The man obviously inspires you to write. You need inspiration. *You need to write.* Problem solved.'

'Joy doesn't want another Vasco Ramirez, Diana.'

'Yes, she does,' Diana said. 'That's exactly what she wants. Vasco sold like hot cakes. Vasco is king. Of course she wants you to do another Vasco.'

Stella gave her friend an impatient look. 'You know what I mean.'

Diana sighed. She didn't want to pull out the big guns. 'Babe, things are going to start to get nasty. And trust me, you don't want to be with a publishing house that plays hard ball. There'll be lawyers. It's time to quit the whole writer's block nonsense and write.'

Stella felt Diana's words slice into her side. 'You think it's nonsense—that I'm making it up?'

Diana shook her head. She knew Stella's instant fame had

compounded her already entrenched second-book syndrome and her father's death had just aggravated everything further. She totally got that Stella's muse had deserted her. But…

'The lawyers will think it is, babe.'

'I just need a little more time,' Stella muttered.

Diana nodded. 'And you should take it. Absolutely. Go with Rick, get inspired. Come back replenished.'

Stella glanced at her friend. She made it sound so easy. She shook her head. 'It's crazy.'

'Why?' Diana challenged. 'Because you have a thing for him?'

'I do not have a thing for him,' Stella denied quickly. A little too quickly perhaps. 'He's an old, *old* friend,' she clarified, not bothering to keep the exasperation out of her voice. 'We've known each other *for ever.* There is no *thing.*'

Diana looked at her friend. Oh, there so *was* a thing.

Even better.

Lord alone knew, if she hadn't had sex for almost a year on top of fairly pedestrian sex for the previous five she'd be looking at a way of fixing that pronto. And if it so happened that the man of Stella's fantasies was there at the precise moment she decided to break the drought, then surely everyone won?

'So it shouldn't be a problem, then?' Diana asked innocently. She held up her hand as Stella went to speak again. 'Look, Rick's right. Just sleep on it. I know it's a lot to consider but, for what it's worth, I think you're mad if you don't.'

'But the book…' Stella murmured in a last-ditch effort to make Diana see sense.

Diana shrugged. 'Whatever you're doing here on good old terra firma ain't working, is it, babe?'

Stella went to bed determined to wake up in the morning and tell both Rick and Diana to go to hell.

But that was before the dream.

She dreamt all night of a mermaid following a pirate ship. No…

She was the mermaid and *she* was following the pirate ship. Inside the hull a lone, rich, tenor voice would occasionally sing a deep mournful song of lost love. It was a thing of beauty and she'd fallen in love with the man even though she'd never laid eyes on him. But she knew he was a prisoner and she knew with an urgency that beat like the swell of the ocean in her breast that she had to save him.

That he was the one for her.

Stella awoke, the last tendrils of the dream still gliding over her skin like the cool kiss of sea water. It was so vivid for a moment she could almost feel the water frothing her hair in a glorious golden crown around her head.

The urge to write thrummed through her veins and she quickly opened the drawer of her bedside table, locating the stash of pens and paper she always kept there. She brushed off the dust and started to scribble and in ten minutes she'd written down the bones of a plot and some detailed description of Lucinda, the mermaid.

When she finished she sat back and stared at the words in front of her. They were a revelation. And not just because she'd written something she didn't have the immediate urge to delete, but because it was a whole new approach.

Stella hadn't imagined for even a minute that the heroine's point of view would take precedence in her head. Vasco had been so strong and dominant, striding onto the page, demanding to be heard, that she'd assumed starting with the hero was always going to be her process.

All this time she'd been beating herself up about not being able to see a hero, getting her knickers in a twist because, no matter how hard she tried to visualise one, no hero was forthcoming.

And he still wasn't. But Lucinda *was* fully formed and she was *awesome*.

Lucinda excited her as nothing had since Vasco had arrived. Lucinda was no Lady Mary waiting around to be saved. The world had gone crazy for Vasco last time, this time they would go crazy for Lucinda.

She could feel it deep inside in the same place that had told her Vasco was special, but she'd been too inexperienced to listen.

Well, she was listening now.

God, Joy was probably going to have a fit at her kick-ass mermaid. She could hear her now saying, *But what about Inigo, Stella*?

Stella gasped as his name came to her. *Inigo.* Of course that was his name. *Inigo.* It had to be Inigo.

It was working.

The buzz was back. *The magic was here.*

Inigo would be strong and noble, a perfect match for Lucinda because a strong woman required a man to equal her. A man secure in himself. A man who would understand the divided loyalties she endured every day and wouldn't demand that she chose between the sea and land.

A subject that Stella could write about intimately.

God, why hadn't she thought to approach her story from this way before? It seemed so obvious now. She kicked off the sheets, reached for her polar fleece dressing gown.

She had to get out of here. Had to get to her computer.

She almost laughed as she tripped over her gown in haste. The revelation had come just in time. It had saved her. There was no time now for seafaring adventures.

There was a mermaid to write. A hero to rescue.

Lucinda was calling.

Inigo too.

Stella padded straight to her computer, notes in hand. She drummed her fingers on the desk as she waited for it to power up. As soon as she was able, she opened a new word document and typed *The Siren's Call* in the header.

She blinked at it. Her fingers hadn't even consulted her brain. The title had just appeared.

It was all happening.

Then the cursor winked at her from a blank page and the buzz and pulse inside shrivelled like a sultana.

What? No...

She took her hands off the keyboard, waited a moment or two, then placed them back on. She waited for her fingers to roam over the keys, pressing randomly to make words on the page. She consulted her notes and desperately tried to recall spunky Lucinda.

But nothing came.

'You're up early,' Rick's voice murmured in her ear as he plonked a steaming hot cup of coffee at her elbow and she almost leapt two feet off the chair.

'Bloody hell, Rick, do you mind?' she griped as she clutched at her chest. Had she been that focused she hadn't even noticed he was up, or smelled the aroma of coffee?

'Whoa there, sorry, didn't mean to startle you.' He grinned. 'What are you working on?'

Stella minimised the document, leaving only her screen saver to view. She glared up at him. Then she wished she hadn't. He was wearing long stripy flannelette pyjama bottoms and nothing on top. The drawstring was pulled low and tight on his hips, revealing way too much skin right at her eye level.

Suddenly Lucinda whispered in her head again, murmuring her story, buzzing through Stella's veins like an illicit drug. Flashes of her childhood felt sweet against Stella's tongue. Lucinda's despair over Inigo tightened Stella's chest.

This was crazy.

Stella turned back to the computer, the need to write an imperative even with Rick hovering. But as suddenly as it had come upon her the flow stopped. Stella blinked—was there a tap somewhere that somebody had just turned off?

Rick let out a long low wolf whistle, ignoring her silence—Stella had never been a morning person. 'Sexy cover,' he murmured, taking the other chair at the desk and straddling it. 'Great rack.'

Stella, still willing Lucinda to come back, took a moment to work out what Rick was referring to. She looked at her computer, the cover for *Pleasure Hunt* her screen saver. Lady Bingham's flowing scarlet dress with the plunging neckline made the best of her assets, pushing her milky breasts practically into the face of the leering Vasco Ramirez.

'Nice.' Stella glared at him as she reopened her blank page, obliterating the screen saver.

Lucinda? Lucinda? Where are you?

'I'm just saying, he seems to be enjoying the view and I can't blame him.'

It would indeed be hypocritical, Rick thought, considering how very much he enjoyed that kind of view himself. The kind of view that Stella was giving him right at this moment as her gown flapped open and the low-cut vest shirt she wore gaped a little to reveal a glimpse of soft female breast.

The view he was trying to ignore.

He'd had a lot of practice at ignoring Stella's breasts, given his treasured honorary position in the Mills family, but that didn't mean it had been easy—then or now. Witness the time he'd lost his head and succumbed to her kissing dare with a heady mix of trepidation, challenge and anticipation.

Anticipation that had been building since the summer she'd arrived on the *Persephone* with curves and a bra.

Being sprung by her father before he'd reached his target and Nathan's little *chat* with him afterwards had set him straight. And he'd never betrayed Nathan's trust.

Not consciously anyway.

'He's practically drooling,' he murmured, gaze firmly fixed on the screen.

Stella turned to Rick to defend Vasco. To say that her hero

was not a salivating pervert, but of course she couldn't because the man *was* a scoundrel of the highest order and she knew damn well he'd appreciated Mary's cleavage as he'd appreciated countless other women's cleavages before he'd met Mary and probably still was, out there in fiction land somewhere.

But it all died on her lips as Lucinda's sweet melodic voice started up a dialogue in her head again, talking about her father disowning her for following a whim and her mother's grief over their rift.

The implications stunk to high heaven.

Oh, God. Please no, not this, Lucinda. I'll do anything, I'll go anywhere else you want, but not this.

Just then Diana entered the room, negating the need for Stella to say anything, for which she was grateful. She yawned loudly and bade them both a good morning as she made her way to the kitchen in her clingy satin Hello Kitty pyjamas and poured herself a coffee from the percolator.

Rick whistled. 'Well, hello Kitty.'

Stella rolled her eyes. Diana grinned as she plonked herself down in a lounge chair.

'So?' she demanded. 'Are you going with Rick or what?'

'Good question, Miss Kitty.' Rick nodded. 'Well?' he asked, seeking Stella's gaze.

Even just looking at him looking at her, Stella could feel the story buzzing through her veins. She could feel Lucinda beckoning her like the siren she was, waving at her from the rocks, drawing her ever closer to her doom.

She looked back at the computer screen with its mocking little cursor and acres of blankness and got nothing.

She sighed as Lucinda won. 'Yes. I'm going.'

'Really?' Rick stood and punched a fist in the air at her curt nod.

How on earth was she going to share a boat with him when she hadn't had sex in ages and he'd always been her private fantasy go-to man?

They were friends.

They were business partners, for crying out loud!

'I've booked us two tickets to Cairns on a flight that leaves Heathrow early this evening.'

'Ooh, cocky, I like that,' Diana murmured, sipping her coffee.

Stella ignored her, as did Rick who, Stella knew from experience, must be biting his tongue to let that one go.

'Australia?' she squeaked.

Rick shrugged. 'The map's Micronesia and I haven't taken the *Dolphin* out since I bought her.'

Stella stood. 'You bought the *Dolphin*?'

Rick had been fascinated with the thirty-foot classic wooden yacht for as long as she could remember. They'd seen it in various ports over the years and it had always been a dream of his to have it for himself.

'When?'

He grinned. 'A few months ago. I finally tracked her down in New Zealand and had her refitted in Cairns. She's ready to go.'

Stella felt a little thrill that had nothing to do with Lucinda. Rick had talked about it so much over the years it had almost become her dream too. 'So we're going to take her?' she clarified.

He nodded. 'If you want to. I could always hire something bigger, whiter, more pretentious if you preferred.'

Stella smiled at the distaste curling his lips. The Mills and Granville salvage fleet was three big white, powerful boats strong and, while she knew Rick was proud of what her father and he had built up, his passion had always been the classic beauty of the *Dolphin*. 'Perish the thought.' She grinned.

Rick grinned back at her and felt a hum of excitement warm his belly. There was something different about Stel this morning. Last night she'd been the Stella he'd always known—slopping around, no airs and graces, no special treatment.

This morning she glowed as if she had a secret that no one else knew. Her olive-green eyes seemed to radiate purpose. Her cheeks seemed pinker. Even her scraped-back ponytail seemed to have more perk in it.

She looked like women did when they were pregnant, as if they were doing something truly amazing and they knew it.

She was *radiant.*

It was quite breathtaking and his stomach clenched inside in a way that, as a man, he was all too familiar with.

But not where she was concerned.

He looked at Diana, all sleepy and tousled with her knowing eyes and cute mouth, and waited for the twinge to come again.

He got nothing.

Hmm.

'Right.' He drained his coffee quickly. There were things to do and not being here for a while was a good option. 'Gotta go get some things sorted. I'll see you both later.'

Stella busied herself in the kitchen until Rick left the house five minutes later. 'How are you going to break it to Joy?' she asked Diana.

'Oh, forget that,' Diana said, waving the query away. 'I'll tell her you've gone off to be inspired. There are much more important things to discuss.'

Stella frowned. 'There are?'

Diana nodded vigorously, her shirt pulling tight across her chest as she leaned over the kitchen bench. 'You two should have sex,' she said.

Stella almost dropped her second mug of coffee. *Was she mad?* 'Ah no.' She shook her head. 'Bad. Idea.'

Diana raised an eyebrow. 'Okay, well, you're going to have to explain that one to me.'

Stella didn't even know where to start with how bad an idea it was. 'Because we're friends. *And* colleagues. I'm his silent partner, for crying out loud! And trust me, I know better than anyone not to get tangled up with a man of the sea. They never choose land. They never choose love.'

Diana rolled her eyes. 'You're just having sex with him, not marrying the man.'

'Which is just as well because men of the sea should not marry. My father chose the sea over my mother. Rick's mother left when he was a baby because his father wouldn't settle on land. We've both seen how that kind of life isn't compatible with long-term relationships.'

'You're. Just. Having. Sex,' Diana reiterated.

'Oh, come on, Diana, you know I'm not good at that. The last guy I was just having sex with I ended up engaged to.'

Diana nodded. 'And the sex was lousy.'

'Hey,' Stella protested. 'It wasn't lousy, it was…nice. Sweet. It may not have been…imaginative but it could have been worse.' Her friend didn't look convinced. 'He was a pretty straight guy, Diana. Not all men want to have sex hanging from the chandeliers. There's nothing wrong with sweet.'

'No, absolutely not,' she agreed. 'Except you did write a book full of hot, sweaty, dirty, pirate sex during your time with Dale.' She shrugged. 'I'm no psychologist but I think they call that transference.'

'*They*,' Stella said, bugging her eyes at her friend, 'call it *fiction*.'

Diana held up her hands in surrender. 'All right, all right. I'm just saying…you're going to be on that boat with him for long periods of time where there'll be nothing to do…it might be worth thinking about, is all…'

Stella shook her head at her incorrigible friend. 'I'll be writing.'

Diana laughed. 'Good answer.'

At two Stella hugged Diana ferociously and thanked her for locking up after them. She was staying on for another night to get some work done far from the distractions of London.

'I promise I'll come back with a book,' she whispered to her friend. 'The ideas are already popping. Tell Joy she's going to love Lucinda.'

Diana laughed. 'Joy will be overjoyed.'

Stella grimaced. She hoped so. She'd added a decade to her very patient editor's life and she *owed* Joy this. Not just a book, but a book to rival Vasco's. She scurried to Rick's hire car with her bag, hoping they made it out of Cornwall before another storm blew in.

Rick pulled up beside Diana and smiled at her. 'See ya later, Miss Kitty. It was nice spending some time with you,' he said.

Diana nodded distractedly, bobbing her head back and forth to see what Stella was up to.

Rick frowned. These two women were hard on his ego. 'I know Stel values your friendship and—'

'Yeh, yeh,' Diana said, cutting him off and dragging him back inside the cottage. She pulled her dog-eared copy of *Pleasure Hunt* from her handbag on the hall stand and thrust it at him. 'Take it. Read it. You won't be disappointed.'

Rick frowned down at the cover he recognised from earlier. 'Er, it's really not my thing.'

'Trust me. It's your thing.' She glanced over Rick's shoulder, knowing that Stella would kill her if she even had an inkling of what Diana was doing. 'It's really quite…illuminating.'

'Okay.'

He ran his fingers over the raised gold lettering that spelt out Stella's name. He felt a surge of pride that Stel had made a path for herself in the world—something that rocked her boat. He knew that Nathan had been immensely proud of his little girl's success.

'Thanks,' he said as he tucked it under his arm and backed out of the cottage.

'Stop,' Diana hissed. 'What are you doing?' She whisked

it out from under his arm, spun him around, unzipped his backpack and shoved it deep inside.

'She's sensitive about it,' Diana explained as Rick gave her a questioning look. 'Do not read it around her. And if she springs you—I will deny all knowledge of how you came by it. Capiche?'

Rick chuckled as he held up his hands in surrender. 'Sure. Okay.'

He took a couple of tentative paces out of the cottage, expecting to be yanked back inside again. It wasn't until he was halfway to the car that he started to relax.

He smiled to himself. *God, but he loved women.*

Five hours later they were airborne and Rick was busily flirting with the air hostess. Stella wasn't sure why she was so annoyed. After all, she'd seen Rick in action with women nearly all of her life.

Maybe it was just the relentless afternoon of it. The woman at the petrol station. The one at the rental desk. Another at the check-in lounge. Oh, and the coffee shop—and she'd have to have been in her sixties. It seemed there wasn't a woman in existence who wasn't fair game for his laid-back style of flirting.

Including her.

But she was used to his casual, flirty banter. She knew it was harmless and she could give as good as she got.

The women of the world were not.

'Champagne?' Rick asked her.

It was tempting but after last night her liver probably needed a break. 'No, thanks,' she said, smiling at the hostess, who she was pretty sure actually didn't give a damn if Stella wanted a drink or not.

Rick watched the swagger of the stewardess's hips in her tight pencil skirt as she left to grab his beer. Stella rolled her eyes at him and he grinned. 'So,' he said, snuggling down further into the comfortable leather seat. 'You haven't asked how the business is going.'

Stella pulled the blind down on her window. 'Well, we're in business class so I'm assuming it's all going okay.'

Rick nodded. 'It is.'

Stella sighed. 'Rick, I told you at the wake that whatever decisions you wanted to make were fine by me. That I only wanted to be a silent partner. You've been half of the business since you were fifteen. It's been *your* blood, sweat and tears that helped to build it to where it is today. Dad should have left his half to you, not me. It should be all yours.'

Rick looked askance, his blue eyes flashing. 'Stel, what is a man worth if he cannot provide for his family?' he said, his voice laced with reproach and sounding remarkably Spanish all of a sudden. 'The business was Nathan's legacy and he knew how much you loved it. Of course he wanted it to go to you. Of course he wanted to leave you with no financial worries.'

She raised an eyebrow. 'Do you have any idea how much money my book has made?'

Rick thought about the contraband copy of *Pleasure Hunt* secreted away in his backpack. 'No. But the business has a multimillion-dollar turnover annually and whether you need it or not—half of it's yours.'

'I know…I'm just saying, I can look after myself.'

He nodded. 'I know that. I've always known that.'

Stella's breath caught in her throat at the sincerity in his tropical eyes. His shoulder-length hair fell forward to form a partial curtain around his face and, with his slight sideways position, she felt as if they were cut off from the rest of the aeroplane.

'Your beer, sir.'

Stella glanced up at the stewardess and was surprised to feel Rick's gaze linger on her face. She looked back at him quizzically and they just looked at each other for a long moment before he smiled at her, then turned to accept the offering.

He started to chat with the stewardess again and Stella turned away. She shut her eyes, not wanting to hear the banter that fell so easily from those wicked Vasco lips.

It was a long flight. She might as well try and get some sleep.

She woke a few hours later feeling miraculously refreshed. Rick was stretched out asleep in his chair, his face turned towards her, those killer sable lashes throwing shadows on his cheeks.

For a moment she just stared at him, at his utter beauty. He'd always been good-looking but age had turned all that brash youthful charisma into a deep and abiding sex appeal.

The urge to push his hair back off his forehead where it had fallen in haphazard array almost trumped the urge to trace his lips with her finger. They looked all soft and slack in slumber but she knew, without ever having experienced it, that they would be just the right amount of hard at precisely the right time—like Vasco's.

She'd come perilously close to knowing it for real. Could still remember the way her pulse had roared, her eyes had fluttered closed as he'd leaned in to make good on her dare and fulfil all her teenage fantasies.

And, courtesy of a crush bigger than the United Kingdom, there'd been plenty of them.

Fantasies that had seen her tick each day down on a calendar as the holidays had approached, her foolish heart tripping every time she'd thought about those blue, blue eyes and all that bare, broad, bronzed skin courtesy of his Spanish mother.

All the time hoping that it would be this summer he'd see her as a woman instead of a girl. That he'd make good on the increasingly confusing signals he sent and act instead of tease.

And the eve of her sixteenth birthday all that breathless longing had come to fruition.

'Sweet sixteen and never been kissed,' he'd teased.

He'd been nearly nineteen and so much more experienced. She'd watched him flirt with girls since he'd been thirteen and been aware of his effect on them for much longer than he had.

She'd screwed up her courage. 'Maybe you should do something about that?' she'd murmured, her heart hammering.

She'd watched as his Adam's apple had bobbed and his gaze had briefly fallen to her mouth. 'Yeh, right,' he'd dismissed.

She'd smiled at him and said the one thing she'd known would work. 'I dare you.'

And it had worked. She'd seen something inside him give as his gaze had zeroed in on her mouth and his lips had moved closer.

Her father's curt 'Riccardo!' had been the bucket of water they'd both needed.

A reminder that there was a line between them that should never be crossed no matter how close they'd danced to it.

And she was glad for it now.

Glad that this magnificent man liked her and enjoyed her company and called her his friend. That he could drop by out of the blue and use her shower and doss down for the night and there was no awkward history, no uncomfortable silences.

Despite what Diana thought, a person didn't die of sexual frustration and she wouldn't sacrifice their friendship and mutual respect for a brief slaking of bodily desires.

No matter how damn good she knew it would be.

He stirred and she froze, hoping like crazy that lazy blue gaze wasn't about to blast her in tropical heat.

It didn't. But it was enough to spur her into action. She was not going to sit here and ogle him as if she were still in the midst of her teenage crush, watching him surreptitiously from behind her dark sunglasses as he went about the business of running a boat.

Without a shirt.

Always without a shirt.

She pulled out her laptop and powered it up.

An hour later the cabin crew came through offering a meal and Rick woke. He stretched, then righted his chair, glancing over at Stella busily tapping away. She seemed engrossed and he smiled at her.

'I thought you were blocked.'

Stella looked up from her notes. 'I've had an idea,' she admitted.

'Hah!' he crowed. 'I told you all you needed was a treasure hunt.'

'Yeh, well, all I'm doing is some preliminary planning, at the moment. It remains to be seen if I can actually write anything.'

Although she knew she could. In fact she itched to. Lucinda and Inigo's story was becoming clearer and clearer.

'So how does that work, then? Writer's block?' he asked.

She shrugged. 'I look at a blank page all day terrified that I'm not good enough, that I'm a one-book wonder, willing the words to come and when, on a good day, some actually do appear, they're all crap and I delete them.'

Rick nodded thoughtfully. He couldn't say that he understood exactly, but he could see the consternation creasing her brow and the look he'd seen in her eyes last night akin to panic. The same look he'd sometimes seen when she'd been a kid and Nathan had been late returning to the surface.

'Maybe you need to give yourself permission to be crap?' he suggested. 'Just get it all down, warts and all. Switch your internal editor off?'

Stella raised an eyebrow at him. 'Did Diana tell you to say that?'

Rick chuckled. 'No.'

'Well, it's easier said than done, believe me.' She sighed.

'I think if I'd had a whole bunch of books rejected before *Pleasure Hunt*, then I'd have known stuff like that. But this crazy instant success didn't give me any time to fail or any time to know who I am as a writer. I think I needed this time to figure that out.'

Rick nodded. 'So…' he said, looking over her shoulder, 'are you going to tell me what it's about?'

Stella shut the lid of her laptop. 'Nope.'

The last time a guy had realised what she'd written it hadn't ended well.

'Excuse me, Ms Mills?'

Stella looked up at a stewardess who had brought her some water earlier. 'Yes?'

'I'm sorry, I hope you don't mind—I saw your name on the passenger list and I just finished reading *Pleasure Hunt*.' She held it up. 'Would you mind signing it for me?'

Stella blushed. 'Certainly,' she murmured as she held her hand out for the book and proffered pen. 'Is there any message in particular you'd like me to write?'

'Just to me, Andrea.' The stewardess smiled.

Stella wrote a brief message to Andrea, then signed her name with a flourish before handing the book and pen back.

'Thank you so much,' Andrea said. 'I shall cherish it.'

'Thank *you*,' Stella replied. 'It's always nice to meet people who like what you do.'

Andrea nodded. 'I better go and serve dinner or my little band of travellers won't be happy.'

Stella and Rick watched her walk away. He turned to her. 'Wow. You're seriously famous, aren't you?'

Stella chuckled. 'Does that threaten your masculinity?' It had certainly threatened Dale's.

'Hell, no.' He grinned. 'I'm a little turned on, actually.'

Stella shook her head. 'If you're thinking threesome, forget it.'

Rick laughed. 'Well, I am now.'

CHAPTER THREE

STELLA had been seven and Rick ten when they'd first laid eyes on the *Dolphin* anchored at St Kitts. They'd both stood on the bow of the *Persephone* with their mouths open, staring at the wooden beauty. Teak, oak, cypress and the original brass fittings had given her an old-world charm hinting at an era when craftsmanship was everything and things were made to last.

Stella still remembered Rick's awed whisper. 'One day she's going to be mine.'

And as they stood on the wharf looking down at her now, the brass gleaming beneath a high Aussie sun, the wooden deck warm and inviting, she looked as grand and majestic as ever.

Lucinda sighed in her head.

'God, Rick,' Stella breathed, that same stirring in her blood she always felt with a stiff sea breeze ruffling her hair. 'She's even more beautiful than I remembered.'

Rick looked down at her, her hair streaming behind her, her pink lips parted in awe. She'd changed into a vest top and cut-off denim shorts and she was so tiny the urge to tuck her under his arm took him by surprise.

'Yes, she is,' he murmured, looking back at his purchase.

Stella looked up at him. The sea breeze whipped his long pirate locks across his face. His strong jaw was dark with stubble. 'She must have cost you a fortune.'

He shrugged. 'Some things are beyond money. And she's worth every cent.'

She nodded, looking back at the superbly crafted boat. 'Why now?' she asked.

He shrugged. 'I listened to your father talk about *The Mermaid* all my life. About how one day he was going to find Inigo's final resting place. And then he died without ever having seen it.'

Rick felt a swell of emotion in his chest and stopped. He slid an arm around her shoulders and pulled her gently into his side. 'I always thought Nathan was invincible…'

Stella snaked an arm around his waist, her heart twisting as his words ran out. She'd always thought so too. Always thought her father would be like Captain Ahab, *The Mermaid* his white whale. They both stood on the dock watching the gentle bob of the *Dolphin* for a few moments.

'I've dreamt about owning this boat since I was ten years old,' Rick murmured, finding his voice again. 'I didn't want to wait any longer.'

Stella nodded, feeling a deep and abiding affinity with Rick that couldn't have been stronger had they been bound by blood.

That wouldn't have been possible had they been lovers.

'Besides,' he grinned, giving her a quick squeeze before letting her go, 'the *company* owns it.'

Stella laughed. 'Oh, really, creative accounting, huh?'

'Something like that,' he laughed.

'So she's actually half mine?' she teased.

Rick threw his backpack on deck and jumped on board. He held out his hand. *'Mi casa es su casa,'* he murmured.

Stella's breath hitched as she took his hand. He spoke Spanish impeccably and with that bronzed colouring and those impossibly blue eyes he was every inch the Spaniard. He might have an English father and have gone to English schools but for his formative years he was raised by his Romany grandmother and she'd made sure her Riccardo had been immersed in the lingo.

As she stepped aboard she checked out the small motorised dinghy hanging from a frame attached to the stern above the water line. Then her gaze fell to the starboard hull where the bold gold lettering outlined in fine black detail proclaimed a change of name. She almost tripped and stumbled into him.

'Whoa there,' he said, holding her hips to steady her. They curved out from her waist and he had to remind himself that the flesh beneath his palms was Stella's. 'You've turned into a real landlubber, haven't you?' he teased.

She stared at him for a moment. 'You changed her name?' she asked breathlessly.

He shrugged as he smiled down at her flummoxed face. 'I promised you.'

Stella thumped his arm and ignored his theatrical recoil. 'I was seven years old,' she yelled.

She stormed to the edge and looked over at the six yellow letters, her eyes filling with tears.

Stella.

'You don't like it?'

She blinked her tears away and marched back to him and thumped his chest this time. 'I love it, you idiot! It's the nicest thing anyone's ever done for me.' Then she threw herself into his arms.

Not even her father had named a boat after her.

Rick chuckled as he lifted her feet off the ground and hugged her back, his senses infusing with coconut.

'I can't believe you did that,' she said, her voice muffled against a pec. She pushed against the bands of his arms and squirmed away from him.

'I told you I would.'

Stella had forgotten, but she remembered it now as if it were yesterday. Rick talking incessantly about buying the *Dolphin* that summer they'd first seen her and her making him promise that if he did he'd rename it after her.

'I didn't think you *actually* would,' she said incredulously.

'Anything for my favourite girl,' he quipped.

She ignored his easy line as she'd ignored all his others. 'You should have said no. I was a brat.'

He nodded. 'Yes, you were.'

She gave him another playful thump but smiled up at him just the same. He smiled back and for a moment they just stood there, the joy of a shared memory uniting them.

'Well, come on, then,' she said after a moment. 'Show me around.'

A spiral stairway led to a below deck that was far better than Stella had imagined in her wildest dreams. Polished wood invited her to run her hands along its surfaces. Brass fittings gleamed from every nook and cranny. The spacious area was dominated by ceiling beams, heavy brocade curtains over the portholes, oriental rugs and dark leather chairs.

It wasn't lavish—she'd seen plenty of lavish interiors in her time—but it *was* very masculine, the addition of Rick even more so. He looked completely at home in this nautical nirvana and for a moment Stella could imagine him in a half-undone silk shirt and breeches, sprawled out down here, knocking back some rum after a hard day's seafaring.

She blinked as Rick segued into Vasco.

'Saloon here, galley over there,' he said, thumbing over his shoulder where she could see a glimpse of stainless steel. 'Engine room…' he stamped his foot '…below us. Forward and aft cabins both have en suites. I thought you might like the aft cabin? It's slightly bigger.'

'Sure.' She shrugged, her pulse tripping madly at her bizarre vision. 'That sounds fine.'

Rick, who'd only seen photographs of the finished product himself, sat in a chair. He ran his hand over the decadent leather. 'Wow, they've done a magnificent job.'

Stella blinked again as she looked down on him for once. If ever there was magnificent it was him, sitting in that chair, captain of all he surveyed. It reminded her of the scene in *Pleasure Hunt* where Lady Mary finally capitulated to his touch. Where she realised, after a particularly harrowing raid, life was short and she didn't want to die without having known the touch of a truly sensual man.

She stood in front of Vasco in the privacy of his cabin as he sat, thighs insolently spread, in his chair, caressing the arm as if it were the breast of a beautiful woman. She looked down at him, waiting. When he leant forward and reached under her skirts she didn't protest, nor when he placed his hands on the backs of her thighs and pulled her onto his lap so she was straddling him, her skirts frothing around her.

'It's so much better than the photos,' Rick murmured.

Stella blinked as his voice dragged her back to the present. She took a step back as the vivid image of Vasco played large in her mind.

'It's amazing, Rick,' she agreed. 'Just...incredible.'

Rick smiled at her as his hand continued to stroke the leather. He was pleased Stella was here to share this moment with him. This boat, more than any of the ones they'd been on over the years, connected them in a way only shared childhood dreams could.

'Let's take her out,' he said, standing. The sudden urge to hoist a sail and go where the wind took him shot through his veins like the first sip of beer on a hot summer day.

'I know we should be provisioning her for our trip but we can do that tomorrow. Let's take her over to Green Island. Give her a good run. We can go snorkelling. We have the basics here...well, we have beer anyway...and we can catch some fish and anchor there for the night. I want to lie on the deck and look at the stars like we used to do when we were kids.'

'Sure,' she agreed readily. Anything, anything to get her out of this saloon and far away from the fantasy.

Where the hell was her filter? She did not fantasise about Rick.

Not in front of him anyway.

'Fabulous idea. Can I take her once she's out of the harbour?'

Stella had learned to sail practically before she could walk. Her father had seen to that. Hell, so had her mother, a keen sailor in her own right, but it had been a lot of years since she'd been on the open sea.

'You still remember what to do?' Rick teased.

She smiled at him. 'I'm sure it'll come back to me. It's just like riding a bike, yes?'

Or having sex.

Diana had assured her you didn't forget how to do that either.

'Don't worry, I'll be there to guide you. Do you trust me?'

Yep...exactly what Vasco had said to Lady Mary.

Do you trust me?

Stella swallowed. 'I trust that you don't want me to run your very expensive boat—sorry, the *company's* very expensive boat—onto a reef,' she quipped.

Rick laughed. 'You have that right. Come on, first mate, let's get this show on the road.'

Within half an hour they were under way, out on the open ocean, and Stella couldn't remember the last time she'd felt this alive. She'd waited patiently while Rick had used the motor to manoeuvre out of the harbour, then helped him with the still familiar motions of putting up the sails. She heard Lucinda sigh as they billowed with the moderate breeze and her pulse leapt as the boat surged forward, slicing across the whitecaps.

Rick, who had taken his shirt off—of course—stood behind her at the wheel for the first ten minutes, giving her a quick refresher. It wasn't needed. Her feel for the boat was instantaneous, like the familiarity of her own heartbeat, and even if it hadn't been they could easily have switched to the sophisticated autopilot system guided by the satellite technology that he'd had installed as part of the fully computerised upgrade.

But it was exhilarating to feel the pulse of the ocean beneath her feet again. She shut her eyes, raised her face to the sun as the big wheel in her hands felt like a natural extension of her being. In her mind's eye she could see Lucinda laughing up at her as she undulated through the waves, riding the bow with the dolphins.

Rick looked up from tying down a loose rope and caught her in her sun-worshipping stance. He'd worried that buying the *Dolphin* on a whim had been a mistake, an indulgence he didn't have the time to realise, a reaction to Nathan's sudden death.

But he didn't any more.

Nathan's *accident* had rocked him to his very core. He'd been there that day. Had seen Nathan's lifeless form, minus his breathing apparatus, bob to the surface. Had frantically dragged him aboard, puffed air into lungs that had been consumed by sea water too many minutes before.

Had demanded that he stay with him.

Stay *for* him.

Stay for Stella.

His own father's memory had faded to nothing over the years. He'd been too young when his father's regular bouts of drunken shore leave had caught up with him. Just a few faded photographs and the oft-repeated stories that got more and more fantastical late into the night after one too many beers.

Anthony Granville had occupied a legendary status amongst the men that knew him but he'd still got himself dead.

It was Nathan who'd been Rick's role model. His stand-in father. And Nathan who had taken on his full-time guardianship when he was a tearaway fifteen-year-old and his grandmother had washed her hands of him.

Rick had only ever wanted to be at sea managing his half of the business. And Nathan had facilitated it.

But he hadn't made it easy—oh, no.

Nathan had been a tough task master.

Rick had thought his days of schooling and routine were done but Nathan had been worse than his grandmother. Nathan had insisted that he do his schooling by correspondence. And when he was done with that for the day, he'd given him every lousy job possible.

Had worked him like a navvy.

And Rick couldn't be more grateful. In his own way, Nathan had given him a better grounding than if he'd grown up in a loving, two-parent secure home.

He'd been so angry with Nathan when he'd landed in the UK thirty hours after they'd given up trying to resuscitate him.

Angry that Nathan had left him to be the bearer of bad news.

Angry that he'd left full stop.

But he'd known the news had to come from him.

The thought of someone else telling Linda—telling Stella—had been completely unpalatable. Nathan would have wanted it to be him and he hadn't wanted it to come from anyone else.

How could he have let some faceless policeman tell Linda? She and Nathan might have been divorced but even Rick had been able to see the deep and abiding love she still felt for him.

And there was no way he'd have let anyone else tell Stella.

The autopsy results just prior to the funeral had made Nathan's death more palatable. Rick had understood, as a man of the sea himself, that Nathan had chosen the ocean over a hospital.

But it hadn't lessened his loss.

And his very impulsive purchase of the *Dolphin* was so

mixed up in the whole vortex of grief he just hadn't been sure of his motivations.

But, as she opened her eyes and smiled at him as if she were riding a magic carpet instead of some very tame waves, he was one hundred per cent sure.

The *Dolphin* was part of them. Their history. And whatever else happened over the years in their lives, it would always bond them together, always be theirs—his, hers and Nathan's.

It had been quite a few years since Stella had been snorkelling. But as they lay anchor a couple of hours later crystalline tropical waters the exact shade of Rick's eyes beckoned, and she was below deck and back up again in record speed.

'What on earth are you wearing?' Rick demanded as she appeared by his side while he was rummaging around in a storage compartment for some goggles and fins.

Stella looked down at her very sensible one-piece. 'You don't like the colour?' she asked.

He tisked to cover the fact that he didn't give a damn what colour it was. 'It's stinger season, Stel. There should be a wetsuit hanging on the back of your cabin door and a stinger suit in one of the drawers.'

Stella looked at the water, desperate to feel it on her skin with no barriers just as she had in her Lucinda dream.

'Oh, come on,' she protested. 'We'd be pretty protected out here on the reef, surely?'

'I'll be sure to tell them that's what you thought when they're giving you the anti-venin.'

Stella shrugged. 'I'm willing to risk it.'

Rick shook his head emphatically. 'I'm not.'

He worked in an inherently dangerous field—there were a lot of things in the ocean that could kill a man—and his reputation for safety was second to none. He certainly wasn't going to have to explain to Linda that he'd let her daughter die too.

He pointed to the stairs leading to the lower deck. 'Go,' he intoned.

Stella rolled her eyes. 'Yeh, yeh.'

'Don't make me come down there,' he threatened.

Stella felt the flirty threat right down to her toes. What would he say if she challenged him to do just that?

Rick smiled to himself as she slunk away, her one-piece riding up the cheek of one buttock. He looked away. When she reappeared a few minutes later she was zipped into light blue neck-to-ankle Lycra.

'I hate these things,' she complained as she pulled at the clinging fabric. 'I look like a dumpling.'

Rick deliberately didn't look. What Nathan's daughter did or did not look like poured into a stinger suit was none of his business. He was still trying to not think about that half-exposed butt cheek.

'Everyone does,' he said, handing her some flippers and her mask and snorkel.

Stella glared at him. No, not everyone did. Not size-zero six-foot supermodels. Which she wasn't. And certainly not him, half zipped into his, his thighs outlined to perfection, the narrowness of his hips a stark contrast to the roundness of her own. *He* looked like an Yves St Laurent cologne guy or James freaking Bond walking out of the Mediterranean in his teeny tiny swimming trunks.

She fitted her mask to her head and looked at him. 'Aren't you coming?' she asked, staring pointedly at his state of undress.

'Right behind you,' he said.

They snorkelled on and off for most of the afternoon. They stopped a couple of times to grab a drink of water and Rick found his state-of-the-art underwater camera but otherwise they frolicked in the warm tropical waters for hours as if they were kids again playing pirates and mermaids.

She'd forgotten just how magical it was with the sun beating on her back and her head immersed in an enchanted underworld kingdom. Where fish all the colours of the rainbow darted around her and cavorted amongst coral that formed a unique and fascinating underwater garden.

Where the dark shadows of huge manta rays and small reef sharks hovered in the distance.

Where the silence made the beauty that much more profound.

It was after five o'clock when they called it a day. Stella threw on her clothes from earlier; Rick just unzipped his suit to his waist and looked all James Bond again. They threw some fishing lines in to catch their dinner while they drank cold beer and looked at Rick's pictures on her laptop. They laughed and reminisced and Rick showed her the pictures from their latest salvage—a nineteenth-century frigate off the Virgin Islands.

They caught two decent-sized coral trout and he cooked them on a small portable grill plate he'd brought up from below. It melted in their mouths as they dangled their legs over the side and watched the blush of twilight slowly creep across the sky to the gentle slap of waves against the hull.

Stella could feel the fatigue of jet lag catching up with her as the balmy breeze blew her drying hair into a no-doubt completely unattractive bird's nest.

That was the one good thing about hanging out with a guy who'd known you for ever—he'd seen her looking worse.

Rick took her plate away and she collapsed back against the deck, knees bent, looking up at the stars as they slowly, one by one, appeared before her eyes. She could hear the clank of dishes below and by the time Rick rejoined her night had completely claimed the heavens and a mass of diamond pricks winked above them.

A three-quarter moon hung low in the sky, casting a trail of moonbeams on the ocean surface.

'Are you awake, sleepy head?' Rick asked as he approached.

She countered his question with one of her own. 'Is it waxing or waning?' she asked, knowing that a man of the sea knew those things without ever having to look at a tide chart—it was in their DNA.

'Waxing,' Rick confirmed as he took up position beside her, lying back against the sun-warmed wood, also staring towards the heavens. He'd taken his stinger suit off and was wearing just his boardies.

Stella sighed. 'It's so beautiful. I bet you never get sick of this.'

'Nope. Never.'

He'd spent countless hours on deck at night, with Nathan teaching him how to navigate by the stars. He supposed to some, even back then, it had seemed hopelessly old-fashioned with all the sophisticated GPS systems and autopilot technology that had been around in the salvage industry for decades, but it had got him out of trouble more than once when satellites had been down or equipment had failed.

And he'd loved listening to the awe in Nathan's voice as he'd talked about the heavens as if each star were a friend. He hadn't just known their shape or the positions in relation to the horizon, but he'd known all the old seafaring legends about them and told them in such a way that had held Rick enthralled.

Nathan's celestial knowledge had been encyclopaedic and Rick had soaked it up like a sponge.

And then he'd regurgitated it to an awestruck Stella, who'd hung on his every word.

How many hours had they spent as kids lying on their backs on the deck of a boat pointing out different constellations, waiting with bated breath for the first shooting star of the night?

Her arm brushed his as she pointed at the Southern Cross and he realised he'd missed this.

This…companionship.

The last time they'd done it was the summer she'd finished school for good. A year after that near kiss. She'd alternated between giddiness at the freedom of it all and distraction over her impending results. They'd lain together on deck and looked up into the diamond studded abyss and he'd told her if they saw a shooting star it would be a sign that she'd passed.

No sooner had he spoken the words than a white streak trailed its incandescent light across the heavens right above them. She'd gasped and he'd told her to shut her eyes and wish upon it and watched her as she did.

Yep. He'd missed this.

God knew he'd had a lot of women in exactly this position over the years but this was different. For a start he hadn't been remotely interested in looking at the stars with any of them. Although to be fair, as his relationship with Stella had teetered on the brink of something neither of them had been game enough to define during their teen years, he hadn't exactly had his head in the stars with her either.

But he did tonight. Stella somehow seemed to bring out the amateur astronomer in him.

And it was…nice.

No agenda. No pressure. No expectations.

Just two old friends relaxing after the perfect day.

'Hey,' Stella said, extending her neck right back as her peripheral vision caught a moonbeam illuminating a chunk of metal hanging off some kind of a fixed pole at the stern. She squinted. 'Is that a shower head?'

Rick extended his neck too and smiled. 'Yep. I've always wanted to be able to take a shower under the stars.' He grinned, relaxing his neck back to a more neutral position.

She laughed as she also released the abnormal stretch, returning to her inspection of the night sky. 'Well, you've thought of everything, haven't you?'

He nodded. 'I've been thinking about this boat for a lot of years.'

They fell silent for a moment, letting the slap of waves against the hull serenade them as their gazes roamed the magnificence of the celestial display.

Stella's yawn broke the natural rhythm. 'I'm beat.' She shut her eyes. 'All that sun and sea on top of the jet lag is a deadly combination.'

'You can't go to bed before we see a shooting star, Stel. Look.' He nudged her shoulder. 'There's Gemini.'

Stella's eyes flicked open and she dutifully followed the path of a perfectly formed bicep all the way to the tip of his raised index finger. She tutted. 'You always had a thing for Gemini.'

He grinned. 'What's not to like about two chicks?'

They laughed and just as he was lowering his arm it happened: a trail of light shot across the night sky, burning bright for long seconds.

Stella gasped and Rick whispered, 'Quick, make a wish.'

Stella thought about Lucinda and Inigo. And dear Joy with the patience of Job. She squeezed her eyes shut as the light faded into extinction and wished for another blockbuster.

Rick turned his head and watched her eye-scrunching concentration. 'What'd you wish for?' he asked.

Stella opened her eyes, her breath catching in her throat at their closeness. Even with the dark pressing in around them, his blue eyes seemed to pierce right into her soul. 'It's a secret,' she murmured. 'If I tell you it won't come true.'

He shook his head. 'You always were a romantic. I should have known you'd go on to write romance novels.'

His voice was light and teasing and not full of scorn as Dale's had been. Dale had been barely able to say the R word. She smiled. 'Says he who insisted I wait to wish upon a star,' she countered.

He laughed. 'Touché.'

His laugh did funny things to her insides and a part of her wanted to stay out with him all night and watch the sun come up, but her eyelids were growing heavier and she yawned again.

She sat. ‘Right. I’m off to bed.’ She stood and looked down at him lying on the deck of his boat wearing nothing but a pair of low-slung boardies and still somehow managing to look as if he ruled the entire ocean. ‘See you in the morning.’

He nodded. ‘I won’t be too far behind you,’ he murmured.

Stella turned away from him, padding her way across the deck, conscious of his eyes on her. She heard his faint ‘Night, Stel’ reach her as she climbed down the stairs.

She was too beat to reply as her legs took her past the galley, through the saloon to the aft cabin where Rick must have placed her luggage earlier. She didn’t bother to shower, hell, she barely bothered to undress, just kicked out of her shorts, pulled the sheets back and crawled under.

She was dreaming even before her head hit the pillow.

Dreaming of Vasco.

CHAPTER FOUR

IT WAS ten the next morning before Stella woke. The gentle rhythm of the waves had rocked her into a deep, jet-lagged slumber. She had a quick shower and threw on a sarong and T-shirt. Rick wasn't below deck but there was an incredible aroma coming from above and she followed her nose.

He was standing at the grill in his boardies—no shirt—and for a moment she just watched the broad bronzed planes of his back that narrowed the closer they got to his waistband.

Or perhaps hip-band might have been more salient.

But then her stomach outed her by growling loudly and she propelled herself forward. 'Sorry for sleeping so late,' she said as she approached him.

Rick turned and smiled at her. 'It's fine—jet lag's a bitch like that. I've only been up for half an hour myself. But, lucky for us—' his smiled broadened into a grin '—the fish have been up for a while.'

Stella inhaled. 'Hmm. Smells great.'

'Grab some plates—we'll eat, then get back to the marina.'

They ate quickly and were under way half an hour later, Rick again letting Stella take the wheel. It was early afternoon before they were finally on land again and alighting a taxi at Cairns Central Shopping Centre.

'So you think you can remember how to provision a boat for a few weeks?'

Stella nodded. She'd often gone with Sergio to buy supplies just prior to an expedition. Serg, a grizzled veteran of the merchant navy and stalwart of Mills and Granville, usually went out on the longer trips as chief cook and bottle washer. He cooked good plain food in bulk and pastry to die for.

'I checked out the galley properly so I know what storage capabilities there are. I assume we'll buy fresh food where we can along the way?'

'Yep.'

'So I'll get all the usual staples.'

He handed over the company credit card of which she was a signatory. 'Where are you going?' she asked as she slid the plastic into the back pocket of her shorts.

'I'm heading to the Boating, Camping, Fishing store to pick up a few things. Let's meet up back here at that coffee shop,' he said, pointing behind her, 'in about an hour?'

Stella checked her watch. 'Right. See you then.'

Shopping in another country was always a challenge. In Penzance she frequented the local supermarket and she knew what and where everything was. Far from home, it took her much longer to find the things she'd already put on a mental list in her head.

But at least Cairns had first-world shopping facilities and everyone spoke the same language. She and Serg had certainly shopped in much more rudimentary surrounds.

By the time the hour was up Stella had a trolley piled high with provisions and the credit card had taken a hit—if they were going to be limited in what they ate for the next few weeks, then she was going to make damn sure what they did have was of the highest quality. Good chocolate—for her anyway, Rick wasn't fussy—and the most decadent biscuits money could buy—for him.

Serg had told her when she was a teenager that Rick had a sweet tooth that was best kept fed. She hadn't been sure whether that had some double meaning or not, but it had certainly fed *her* hormone-fuelled imagination.

Stella pushed the uncooperative metal beast with two wonky wheels for what seemed like five miles in the giant sprawling shopping centre. She almost crashed into a shop window and earned the wrath of a mother who thought Stella was deliberately trying to run her tantrumming little angel down.

When she finally reached the coffee shop her abdominals, quads and biceps were cramped with the effort of keeping the damn thing on track. Her mood was not great. It didn't improve any to find Rick, with one shopping bag, chatting up a tall, dark-haired waitress who looked as if she were born dancing the Flamenco.

Of course.

The man had a perpetual hard-on.

'Hi,' she said, using the back of Rick's chair as a brake for the trolley.

Rick spun around as the impact interrupted him mid-flirt.

'Oops, sorry, damn thing is impossible to control,' she said, smiling sweetly at the waitress, who looked as if she was about to give Stella a piece of her mind for careening into a customer.

A sex-god customer.

Stella was pretty damn sure if someone had barged into her chair with a dangerous weapon, Ms Flamenco wouldn't have batted an eyelid.

'Hey, Stel.' He grinned. 'Have a seat. You want a coffee? Something to eat? Ramona says they do a mean nachos here.'

Stella smiled at Ramona. 'Nachos and a flat white would be great, thanks.'

Ramona nodded at Rick. 'I'll be back in a jiffy.'

I just bet you will, Stella thought uncharitably as she sat down.

'Whoa, you buy the whole shop?' Rick asked, examining the contents of the missile that had smacked into him.

'You have to cover every contingency,' she said waspishly.

'Ooh, Snickers,' he said, pulling out the packet of fun-sized chocolate bars. 'My favourite.'

Yes. Which was why she'd bought them.

'Can I take your order, sir?'

Stella looked up at another goddess smiling down at Rick as if he'd invented oxygen. Lord, where did this coffee shop source their staff from—www.lookgoodnaked.com?

'We've ordered,' she said tersely.

'Sorry.' Rick smiled and shrugged.

'No worries,' the woman said, her smile not wavering, her gaze not leaving his. 'If you need anything just yell. I'm Holly.'

'Thanks, I'll holler, Holly,' he said and she giggled.

Stella rolled her eyes. 'You're incorrigible.'

Rick grinned. 'I have no idea what you're talking about.'

Stella ignored him, instead choosing to go through the docket with him for anything she might have forgotten while they waited for their meal. It was going to be too late once they'd cast off in the morning. No less than two waitresses interrupted them while they did so.

Their meals finally arrived and Stella almost laughed as yet another woman, a leggy redhead, delivered them.

Were they drawing straws?

This one looked older—older than Rick for sure—and had the calm authority and predatory grace of a woman who knew what she liked. She introduced herself as the owner.

'Ramona was saying you're sailing north for a few weeks. I don't suppose you need a deckhand?' she joked as she placed Rick's meal in front of him.

'I'm the deckhand,' Stella intoned.

Was she invisible?

Was it that ridiculous to think that she could be his girlfriend? It seemed every female employee in the coffee shop thought so, if their quick dismissive gazes followed by their unabashed flirting were any indication.

She wanted to stand up and say, *Hey, I'm a famous author,*

don't you know. But then Rick looked at her and winked and she felt as if he'd just ruffled her hair and slipped her a few bucks to run along and leave him do his thing.

She felt like his kid sister.

'Do you know boats?' Rick asked.

The woman smiled. 'Oh, yes, my ex always owned classic yachts. I hear yours is a beauty.'

Rick nodded enthusiastically. 'You should drop by the marina and see her. The *Stella* is a true class act.'

Stella blinked.

Had he just invited a cougar back to the boat?

Oh, no, don't mind me.

The woman smiled at him. 'I may just do that.'

'Can I get some cracked pepper?' Stella asked.

The redhead gave her a cursory once-over and disregarded her in less than five seconds. 'I'll send Ramona over,' she said and she slunk away.

'God, this looks good, doesn't it?' Rick asked as he turned his attention to his meal.

Stella had suddenly lost her appetite. Sometimes she just couldn't work him out. The man knew he was attractive to women. She'd seen him work that to his advantage too many times to class him as clueless, but she didn't think he truly understood how effortlessly it worked in his favour.

Even when he wasn't trying, women flocked. And of that, he was totally unaware. She was sure of it.

She picked at her meal and was pleased when they managed to leave the coffee shop unmolested forty-five minutes later. He took the trolley, managing it like the flocks of women—effortlessly—and they caught a taxi back to the marina.

Once on board they stocked the galley with the supplies then sat at the dining table drinking beer and plotting their course. Stella felt the jet lag catching up with her again as Rick's deep English voice, sounding even more so in this land of different accents, laid out the first leg from Cairns to Port

Moresby, which would take them about two sailing days. The boat bobbed rhythmically to the melody of a hundred loose halyards clinking against their masts and she yawned.

It wasn't until a voice from outside disturbed them that Stella realised two hours had passed in a drowsy haze and she'd barely taken any of it in.

'Ahoy there! Anyone home?'

Rick frowned. 'Who's that?'

Stella's head cleared as she recognised the sultry tones of the coffee-shop owner. 'I'm guessing it's the leggy, red-headed cougar.'

Rick laughed as he took a swig of his second beer. 'Really? Oh…'

He seemed disappointed, which perversely made her both happy and annoyed and a lot more awake. 'Er…you invited her here. What did you expect?'

'Did I?' Rick frowned. He didn't recall.

Stella blinked. 'You said, you should drop by the marina. Women are literal creatures, Rick.'

He stood. 'That's cool.' He disappeared into the galley and came out with another beer. 'It's never a hardship to spend some time with a beautiful woman. Who appreciates a classic yacht.'

Stella rolled her eyes. 'She's a decade older than you.'

He shrugged, then grinned at her as he cracked the tops on the beers. 'So?' And then she watched him disappear up the winding staircase.

Great.

What the hell was *she* supposed to do while he dallied above deck with a woman about the same age as her mother as if he were some young buck in need of sexual tutelage?

God, no, he wouldn't…surely he wouldn't have sex with her up there where anyone could see him? Surely he'd at least bring her to his cabin?

But then the thought of him bringing her down here was

confronting on other levels. Stella didn't want another woman below deck sullying all that it meant to her—to them.

God, would she be forced to listen to them rocking the bloody boat all night?

Would they be loud?

She didn't think that Rick would be a silent lover. She'd always imagined he'd be quite vocal in his appreciation of a woman.

Just like Vasco.

She could only pray the jet lag still tugging at the peripheries of her consciousness would sink her completely under in a deep sound-proof abyss.

Stella could hear their muffled voices above her and could feel herself getting madder with each passing minute. She tried to concentrate on the weather charts and tide times on the laptop in front of her, but her eyes felt too gritty. She even pulled out her father's research papers and tried to immerse herself in them, but she was just too damn tired and the redhead's deep throaty laugh was just too damn distracting.

She could feel herself getting more and more tense.

How dared he entertain a lady and expect her to just meld into the furniture, stay below deck and pretend she wasn't even here?

It might be his boat but she wasn't going to feel ignored or non-existent. He had his whole life to be with as many women as he liked. To flirt and indulge in whatever hedonistic lifestyle he wanted.

But for the next few weeks he was on this boat with *her* with a job to do and he could bloody well take a break from being Mr Irresistible and keep his head in the game.

Stella was pacing when he joined her five minutes later, aware on some peripheral level she wasn't feeling particularly rational. 'That was quick,' she said testily.

Rick shrugged. Danielle's company had been pleasant

enough but he didn't feel like entertaining tonight. There was a lot of planning to do and he was aware of Stella below deck.

'Big day tomorrow,' he said as he made a beeline for the galley, throwing the empty beer bottles in the bin under the sink.

'You should have brought her down here and shown her around. I bet she was dying to see below deck—a woman with an eye for a classic yacht and all,' Stella said, sarcasm oozing from her pores.

Rick grinned as he washed his hands at the sink. 'Oh, she wanted to. But I told her you had a headache. You know, from the jet lag.'

'How considerate,' she said sweetly. 'She must have been devastated.'

'Nah...I don't really think she was *that* interested in the boat.'

Stella snorted. 'You don't say.'

Rick poked his head out of the galley to look at her. She seemed mad. 'You're bitchy when you're jet-lagged.'

'Yeh, headaches bring out the bitch in me too,' she snapped.

Rick saw a spark of heat turn her olive gaze to an ominous green, like a hailstorm. He knew he was in trouble, he just wasn't sure why. 'What's wrong?' he asked warily, approaching her.

Stella wasn't exactly sure why she was *so* mad all of a sudden, but she knew she was. She shook her head at him. 'You.'

'Okay...?'

'You honestly can't switch it off, can you?'

Rick frowned. 'Switch what off?'

'God, you should come with a flirt alert. How on earth are you possibly going to manage this trip, four bloody weeks, without a woman around to charm?'

Rick, who was used to spending lengthy periods at sea, wasn't worried about it. 'I think I'll manage,' he said dryly.

'Manage?' Stella snorted again. 'You can't go a day without trying to hook up.'

Rick laughed. 'I think you're exaggerating a little.'

Stella stopped pacing and glared at him. 'In thirty-six hours you have flirted with every woman who has crossed your path. Diana, the rental-car woman, the airline check-in chicky, the grandmother who ran the refreshment stall at Heathrow, several air stewardesses, the taxi driver, every waitress in the coffee shop today...'

She ticked off each conquest on a finger. 'And when we get on that boat tomorrow after about twelve hours you're going to start in on me *because you can't help yourself*,' she finished a little shrilly.

Rick blinked. Stel wasn't usually the nagging, hysterical type so it was either jet lag or PMS. Neither of which he was game to suggest, but he hoped it was the former because that surely couldn't last more than another day.

'But I always flirt with you.' He shrugged. 'It doesn't mean anything.'

Stella glared. 'Why the hell not?' she demanded, uncaring that she knew. 'Is there something wrong with me?'

Rick blinked, not quite able to believe he was having this conversation. 'That's not what I meant. There's nothing wrong with you. You're perfectly...' He groped around for a word that was flattering without saying all the things he'd desperately tried not to think about her over the years—curvy, sweet, bootylicious.

A Nathan-approved word.

'Decent.'

Decent?

Good God, she sounded as if she were someone's homely cousin who was all right at a pinch but was hardly likely to be picked to play spin the bottle at a party. Stella doubted she'd ever felt so underwhelmed in her life.

'Gee, thanks,' she snapped.

Rick pushed his hair off his face as he tried to comprehend how this night had gone so rapidly to hell. 'I don't understand… Do you…want me to mean it?' he asked.

Stella's breath hitched in her throat at the illicitness of the suggestion. What would *that* be like? To have all that deliberate blue-eyed charm turned on her? Like when they'd been teenagers and their banter had occasionally wandered into dangerous territory.

But grown up.

Diana's *you should have sex with him* slithered into her brain and she pushed it away.

'Of course I don't!' she said in her very best English-teacher-talking-to-a-student-with-a-crush voice. 'But I don't want you flirting with every other woman you come across either. It really is rather tiresome to watch and completely unproductive.'

Rick cocked an eyebrow. *He'd personally never found flirting to be unproductive.* But she was obviously accusing him of lack of control. 'You think I can't go a few lousy weeks without flirting with a woman?'

Stella crossed her arms. 'Oh, I'm sure of it.'

'Is this a dare?' he asked.

Stella felt the conversation suddenly shift gears. It should have taken her back to their childhood but the silk in his voice took her to another place entirely.

A very adult place.

'Sure.' She shrugged. 'I dare you. I dare you to go through this whole voyage without flirting with a single woman you meet along the way.'

Rick grinned, his gaze locking with hers. 'And what do I get?' he asked, his voice low.

The timbre of his voice stroked along all her tired nerve endings as he stared at her with his Vasco eyes.

What did he want?

Stella swallowed. 'Get?'

Rick held her gaze. 'If I win?'

Stella was lost for words for a moment. They'd never played for stakes before. Several inappropriate suggestions rose to mind but she quashed each one. She was too strung out to play games with him. 'How about my undying gratitude?' she quipped.

Rick shook his head slowly, dropping his gaze to her mouth. 'How about that kiss that we didn't quite get round to?'

Stella blinked as the teenage bad-boy looked back at her. It was a tantalising offer. One she knew he didn't expect her to take. But she'd never been one to back down from a dare and, frankly, the idea was as thrilling as it was illicit.

She smiled. 'Deal.' She held out her hand. He wouldn't be able to manage it, of course, but if the stakes were...interesting...maybe he'd at least try and comply.

Their gazes locked and Rick swallowed as he took her hand, cementing the deal.

Would she taste like coconuts too?

They cast off the next morning at eight o'clock, a good wind aiding their departure. The long-range weather forecast was favourable and Stella was feeling as if her body clock was finally back in sync.

Of course, she was also really embarrassed by her carry-on last night. She tried to apologise to Rick once they were out of the harbour and heading north.

'Are you trying to welch on the deal?' Rick teased. 'Because you know how much I love a challenge.'

She did. God knew how many times she'd come close to drowning while challenging him to a competition to see who could hold their breath underwater the longest.

He'd beat her every time.

Except for that time he'd let her win and she'd been so mad at him he'd promised never to do it again.

'Absolutely not,' she said, shaking her head. 'I stand by it.'

'Good.' He grinned. 'Now go write something.'

And she did. Sitting in a special chair at the bow of the boat, sun on her shoulders, breeze in her hair, laptop balanced on her knees, she found Lucinda flowed from her fingers onto the page. It was as if she frolicked and danced along the keys, slipping magically between Stella's fingers, informing every letter, controlling every mouse click.

The cursor no longer blinked at Stella from a blank page. Instead words, lovely rich words of a bygone era, filled all the white spaces up. When Rick brought her a snack and her hat she realised she'd been writing for two hours solid and the number down the bottom of the page told her she'd written thirteen hundred words.

Thirteen hundred glorious words.

The morning flowed into the afternoon; the perfect calm conditions continued. Rick occasionally called to her, pointing out a pod of dolphins or an island in the distance. She got up and stretched regularly and when she was grappling with a scene she'd take the wheel for a while and magically, like tankers on the horizon, the solution appeared.

By the end of the day she'd written three thousand words and she felt utterly exhilarated. And it wasn't all about the writing.

She'd forgotten how elemental sailing made a person feel. How it connected you to the earth on such a primitive level. How the feel of the waves beneath your feet and the push and pull of the tide drew you into the circadian rhythm of the planet.

How it connected her to her father.

She'd missed Nathan terribly the last six months, but out here he was everywhere. Every turn of the wheel, every flap of the sail, every pitch and roll of the hull.

They anchored just before sundown in the middle of nowhere. Just her and Rick bobbing in the middle of an enormous ocean beneath a giant dome blushing velvet and dappled with tangerine clouds.

Rick grilled steaks this time and Stella was pleased she'd kept a serving out of the freezer. She loved fish, but she knew by the time the voyage was over she'd be all fished out. And with three thousand words to celebrate, nice thick juicy steaks seemed like the perfect food. She tossed a salad and completed the meal with melt-in-your-mouth bread rolls.

It was utterly delicious and they savoured every morsel of the fresh food. Much later in their journey, when their fresh food had run out, the meals wouldn't be this exciting.

Of course, there would always be fish.

Stella took their plates while Rick cleaned the grill and she joined him on deck twenty minutes later after a quick shower. He was lying as he had the night before, flat on his back, stretched out beneath a vast canopy of black and silver.

Although tonight, at least, he'd decided to wear a shirt.

'Are we going to do this every night?' she asked, joining him.

He looked up at her. She was wearing a sarong tied around her neck in some fashion, the corners flapping in the breeze to show a little bare thigh. He looked back at the sky.

'Weather permitting,' he murmured.

Stella settled back, the slap of the halyard against the mast making a delightful clink. The stars seemed so close this far away from the light pollution of land.

'Well, I think I did very well today,' he said after they'd lain in companionable silence for a few minutes. 'Are you ready to concede yet?'

Stella laughed. 'There's only been me here.'

He smiled into the night. 'It won't make a difference.'

'Well, we'll see how it is when you're surrounded by all those Micronesian babes who want to be your own private deckhands.'

He chuckled then and Stella shivered as the delicious noise

slipped down her spine like a feather stroke. She raised her hand to distract herself, just as she had as a child, holding up her thumb to the moon and squinting, obliterating the glowing white orb from her vision.

She dropped her hand. 'They look like you could just pluck them from the sky, one by one, don't they?'

'And that's why you write romance novels,' Rick teased, rolling his head to the side to look at her.

Stella smiled and just as abruptly stopped. Rick seemed so laid-back about what she did.

He frowned. 'What's wrong?'

'Nothing,' she sighed.

'That's kind of a big sigh to be nothing. I thought you were ecstatic about your word count today.'

Stella let her head roll so she was facing him too. 'I am, I'm...beyond ecstatic. I'm just...'

'Just? Are you not happy with what you do?'

'No. I'm very happy with it. Especially now I have words,' she joked. 'I have a great publisher. An editor who's a saint, an agent who's a shark...'

'But?' he asked as she turned her head away to look at the sky. 'You should be proud of what you do. Nathan was. We're all so proud of you, Stel.'

Stella gave a light snort. 'Trust me, not everyone is so... proud of what I do.'

Rick frowned. 'Oh? Someone in particular?'

She looked at him again. 'Dale. He...broke off the engagement when he realised what I wrote.'

Nathan had told Rick about the break-up when it had occurred. Rick hadn't asked why, he'd just assumed it was the usual sort of stuff that broke relationships up. He did remember Nathan being secretly pleased. He'd always thought his daughter's long-term fiancé was a bit of a cold fish.

Rick had to admit to feeling a little pleased himself. He'd

never met Dale but Nathan's instincts about men had usually been spot on.

'He didn't know?'

She shook her head. 'Dale thought I was writing respected historical research on eighteenth-century pirates.'

Rick was confused. 'Didn't you tell him?'

'Of course I did, but he was never good at listening. He's an academic, one of those absent-minded professor types, and all he heard was historical and pirate…'

Rick suppressed a shudder. *He sounded like a total bore.*

'So,' he said, wanting to clarify the situation before he spoke ill of her idiot ex, 'he dumped you when he found out you wrote…'

Stella nodded. 'Trashy, smutty, dirty little books.'

Rick cocked an eyebrow. *He really had to read that book.* 'You write trashy smut?' What the hell was wrong with the man? Didn't he realise that was a really good reason to hang onto a woman?

Stella rolled her eyes. 'No. I write historical romantic fiction for women. Dale called them trashy and smutty.'

Rick sucked in a breath. *What a dufus.* 'How did he find out?'

'One of his students asked him if he was the inspiration for Vasco Ramirez.'

Rick rolled up onto his elbow and looked down at her. 'Was he?'

Stella laughed then. The irony of Rick, Vasco Ramirez personified, asking that question was just too much. 'Most definitely not.'

Rick grinned. 'Ouch.'

Stella felt instantly contrite—not everyone looked like an eighteenth-century pirate. 'No, I'm sorry, I didn't mean it like that. Dale's lovely…was lovely. In kind of a…self-absorbed way. He's just not…buccaneer material.'

'Well,' Rick announced. 'The man's clearly an idiot.'

'Not really...he has an IQ in the hundred and thirties.'

Rick fell back against the deck. 'He can't be too smart if his fiancée is writing smutty novels and he doesn't use that to his advantage.'

Stella burst out laughing. 'His advantage? How?'

Rick shrugged. 'Dress up in breeches and make you read it aloud to him.'

Stella laughed again. The very thought was as wicked as it was absurd. Dale would no sooner have done that than flown to the moon. 'Dale was a little too strait-laced for role playing. In fact I think he considered human desire a little beneath him altogether. Too...messy or something.'

There was just something about laughing with Rick in the night under the stars that encouraged confidences and she felt as if they were kids again, whispering their secrets to each other.

Rick couldn't believe what he was hearing. In fact he was pretty damn sure he didn't want to hear it. And not just because a woman like Stella, or any woman for that matter, should not be having mediocre sex. But because putting sex and Stella in the same sentence was something he'd avoided his entire life.

'Why on earth did you stay with him?' he asked.

Stella rolled her head to face him. That one was easy.

'Because he was a nice guy. A good guy. A kind guy. He made me laugh.' *Not in the ribald way Rick made her laugh but in a lovely, easy way that warmed her up inside.* 'He had a great job. On terra firma. He wanted to get married. He wanted kids.'

Rick almost yawned, it sounded so boring, but the way her voice softened was telling. He looked away. How could someone who had the swell of oceans running in her veins settle for such mediocrity?

'Well, it sounds like you're well shot of him to me,' he said after a few moments star gazing. 'A woman who writes smut needs someone to inspire her.'

Stella laughed. 'You're incorrigible.'

'That's what you like about me.'

She thumped him on the chest. Yeh, it *was* what she liked about him but she wasn't going to admit it.

'I'm going to bed,' she said, sitting up.

He sat also. 'I'm up for that.'

Stella looked behind her at his bad-boy grin and rolled her eyes. 'By myself.'

'I can do smut.'

Stella laughed. 'I bet you can.'

He held up his hand. 'Just saying. The offer's out there.'

Stella shook her head. 'I think this is called flirting, Rick.'

'Hey, you said, with women I meet along the way. I already know you. You're fair game.'

Stella guessed she'd walked right into that one.

'Besides I gotta put the flirt somewhere. It's not good to let it build up. Men,' he said, lowering his voice, 'should never let anything build up.'

Lucky for her she was used to Rick's teasing and was sufficiently over the jet lag to not let it push her buttons. She stood. 'Goodnight, Rick.'

'Sleep tight.' He grinned as he watched her walk away.

Then there were just the stars, the ocean and him, but not even they could keep him from the smutty book he had secreted in his cabin.

He gave her five minutes, then followed her down.

Six hours later, Rick read *The End* and knew he would never be the same again. Diana had been right. It was most illuminating. The hard-on he'd got in chapter two was still there and there was no way it was going away unless he did something about it.

Fortunately now he had plenty of images to help him in that department.

Two things were crystal clear.

Number one—Dale was an idiot of the first order. Hell, if he had a woman that had this sort of stuff in her head—the sheer eroticism of the beautifully scripted love scenes still clung to his loins—he wouldn't let her out of his bed let alone his life.

Number two—the most shocking of all.

She'd written the book about him.

He was Vasco Ramirez.

CHAPTER FIVE

Lady Mary stifled a gasp as Captain Ramirez rose from the tin bath tub with the fluid grace of a stallion. Water sluiced down the long lines of his body as the flickering lamplight gilded his bronzed skin, throwing it both into mysterious shadow and enticing relief.

The mucous membranes of her throat cracked as dry as parchment, her heart skipped frantically in her chest.

She should not be here.

She should not be spying on a man, a nude man, who was unaware of being watched.

But she simply could not stop.

The last time she'd seen flesh this magnificent had been at Lord Ladbrooke's stables and her nostrils flared as she remembered how all that leashed power had felt beneath her jodhpurs as she'd straddled and then ridden the Arabian beauty bareback.

Much to her aunt's chagrin.

Lord alone knew what she'd do now witnessing Mary's scandalous behaviour. There'd be smelling salts for sure.

But, alas, Mary could not take her eyes off the man.

Steam still rose in wisps around his calves as he stood waiting for the excess water to run off. She held her breath as her gaze roamed over the board-taut planes of his shoulders, obscured towards the middle by sleek wet strips of dark hair. Water trekked from the dripping ends and she followed the path of one errant droplet, gleaming in the light, as it slid down the furrow of his spine nestled between the well-defined muscles either side.

She lost it in shadow as it entered the dip of his back, bracketed by enticing hollows, but her eyes roamed south regardless to the rise of his buttocks. Two firm slabs of muscle, potently male even in his relaxed state, greeted her.

Her gaze was drawn to the left where an imperfection snagged her attention. There, in the centre of his left buttock, lay a large smooth brown birthmark.

It was utterly fascinating and Mary stared at it open-mouthed. It was a perfect circle as if some lover, for he looked to be a man who took lovers, had drawn it deliberately to brand him.

Mary's cheeks flamed at the risqué image and she felt the roughness of her breath as it quickened in her lungs.

Just when she thought he'd turned to stone he turned slightly, affording Mary a different view. Her gaze brushed along the flare of a bicep, the jut of a masculine hip, which seemed as savage as it did graceful, and the perfect delineation of a meaty quadricep that seemed to vibrate with barely leashed power.

And then there was his…

Mary swallowed. She had seen illustrations of the nude male anatomy in obscure texts in her uncle's library when she'd been fifteen but they hadn't managed to capture the sheer beauty of the real thing. The long elegant line of the male member in all its potency was a sight to behold.

It was more elongated and the girth more significant than she'd ever imagined. The curls at its base more enticing.

How magnificent would it look standing out proud as she'd seen on the midnight Arabian?

Mary felt a strange sensation take root deep inside her.

How on earth did it fit?

Captain Ramirez suddenly reached for a nearby towel, covering himself as he stepped out of the bath, his fascinating birthmark the last thing she saw before everything was obscured. Just as quickly he'd padded over to the door that led to his private bedchamber and disappeared through it.

Mary let out the breath she'd been holding. It stuttered noisily into the air around her. She knew she should move but she was utterly incapable.

Until now she'd assumed that pirates didn't bathe.

She would be grateful until the day she died that Captain Vasco Ramirez had shattered that rather high-handed illusion.

Vasco was breathing rather heavily himself as he shut the door to his bedchamber, leaning against it, his long sable lashes covering the smoulder in his devil blue eyes. Ever since he'd seen Lady Mary in the looking glass peeking out from behind the curtains he'd been determined to shock her.

But he hadn't been prepared for her thorough appreciation. Nor for his completely involuntary reaction to her fascinated scrutiny.

His fancy did not usually involve gently bred ladies but he'd seen those flared nostrils, heard that muffled gasp.

Maybe beneath all those prim petticoats and haughty eyes beat a passionate heart. Maybe she wasn't as indifferent to him as her demeanour suggested.

Maybe she could be persuaded to make this voyage a lot more bearable for both of them?

RICK shut the book as he finished chapter two.

Again.

He could hear Stella moving around above him and knew he had to get out of bed and get under way but he wasn't sure he could look her in the eye this morning.

And—he looked down at the tented sheet—he needed a little time to compose himself…

He ran his fingers over the glossy cover of *Pleasure Hunt*, the metallic letters boldly pronouncing her name—*Stella Mills*.

This *was not* the Stella Mills he knew.

What on earth had happened to her? The Stella who had played mermaid and pirates? Who liked to snorkel and scuba dive? Who liked to read and watch the stars at night? The Stella who hated carrots and could almost hold her breath as long as he could?

The one who had been devastated when her parents had divorced and had made him promise that whatever happened in their lives they would always be friends.

Of course that Stella had been ten years old.

Just the way he liked her.

Because otherwise he had to think of her as a very different Stella.

A grown-up Stella. Who got engaged.

Who had sex.

Who was twenty-seven and *not* the virgin her father had hoped she would be for ever.

Not if *Pleasure Hunt* was anything to go by anyway.

God, she probably didn't even hate carrots any more.

Rick threw the covers off. This was ridiculous. And not helping his situation down below.

He cut straight to the crux of the issue, or one aspect of it anyway.

She *was not* Lady Mary.

He let it reverberate around his head for good measure.

Lady Mary was a character she'd made up. In that vivid, hot, lustrous, dirty—*God, so dirty*—imagination of hers.

Just because Vasco was him, didn't mean that Lady Mary was her.

It didn't mean she'd been fantasising about him sexually. Or that she'd put herself into a character whose lust for his character bordered on pornographic obsession.

That was just plain crazy.

There was nothing remotely similar about Lady Mary and Stella—nothing.

So he needed to get over himself.

He needed to go and take a shower—a cold one—and get the bloody boat moving.

He was on deck twenty minutes later. And he was in big, big trouble. Suddenly the filter that had always been in place where she was concerned had been stripped away. Those teenage dreams he'd had about her and refused to let himself dwell upon were front and centre.

She was in teeny tiny denim shorts with a frayed edge and a shirt that barely met in the middle. A straw cowboy-style hat, the edges curled up, sat low over her eyes and held her tucked-up hair in place save for a few haphazard wisps that had escaped and brushed her nape.

The girl he always saw, the one he'd trained himself to see, ever since Nathan had sprung them about to kiss, was gone for ever.

Now he saw the ripe bulge of her breasts as the bra he could clearly see through the thin fabric of her shirt pushed and lifted in all the right ways. The wink of her belly button taunting him from the strip of bare skin at her midriff. The killer curve where her hip flared from the tiny line of her waist.

He'd never noticed how curvy she was before. Not consciously anyway. Consciously he'd always thought of her as short and cute.

Like an elf or maybe a munchkin.

But there was nothing cute about those curves—they should come with a yellow warning sign.

And he was stuck on board with them for the next few weeks.

'Well, about time,' Stella said as she caught Rick's advance in her peripheral vision. 'Another gorgeous day for sailing.'

Rick smiled, his gaze drawn to her mouth. The mouth that was nowhere near as innocent as he'd always thought. A mouth he tried and failed not to think about on his body the way Lady Mary's had been on Vasco's.

Stella popped the lid on a bottle of sunscreen and squirted some into her palm. 'If you get us under way,' she said, slapping it on her chest, 'I'll cook some bacon and eggs.'

Rick swallowed as Stella distributed the white liquid to her shoulders and upper arms and across the swell of her cleavage, dipping her fingers beneath the fabric a little.

Do not look at her breasts. Do not *look at her breasts.*

Too late.

He looked at her breasts.

'Sure,' he said distractedly as her hands continued to massage the crème until her cleavage glistened in the sun.

Stella frowned at him as he stood there looking at her. Was he…was he perving at her chest? There were times when they'd been younger, pre her sweet-sixteen debacle, when she'd caught him looking at her, when their gazes had locked and he'd smile at her with wolfish appreciation, but that had been a long time ago.

'Rick?'

Her voice brought him back from the fantasy of licking every inch of the crème off her. He blinked and quickly donned his sunglasses. 'Yes, absolutely, getting under way.' He saluted, turning from her gratefully, his hands trembling as if he were fifteen years old again and trying to undo Sharon Morgan's bra.

He really needed to get a grip.

By the time the sun was high in the sky Rick was half-way to crazy. The boat was travelling along at a steady clip, which left him nothing else to do other than stare at Stella. Even metres away from him in her low chair, doing nothing but writing, she destroyed his concentration. She was almost directly in his line of sight, her legs supporting her laptop, her shirt riding up her spine to reveal a good portion of skin, including the dimples at the small of her back.

With conversation non-existent, he was left with a lot of time to think. A lot of time for his mind to wander.

Standing at the helm, the wheel in his hand, the ocean at his command, it was a little hard not to think of himself as the all-conquering pirate Vasco Ramirez.

The Vasco who decided to turn his treasure hunt into a pleasure hunt. Who actively seduced Lady Mary after the bath scene and whose slow, deliberate dance with her was both clever and cunning.

Rick's mind wandered to those scenes of calculated seduction. Vasco washing Mary's hair on deck. Vasco removing a splinter from her finger with his teeth. Vasco cutting into the juicy flesh of a dripping pear with his jewelled dagger and feeding her slice after slice.

And the sexiest scene of all where Vasco had tied her spreadeagled in her under-things to his bed until Mary had admitted her desire for him.

That one had got Rick hotter than a summer day on the equator.

In fact just thinking about it now was getting him pretty damn hot. Not helped by the fact that she had abandoned her seated position and was doing a sexy little stretch, bending over and touching her toes, then arching her back as she linked her hands above her head and twisted from side to side.

Oh, Lord, kill me now.

She turned then and walked towards him and he was

pleased, as her breasts jiggled enticingly, for the secure placement of his very dark sunglasses.

'You fancy a cold beer and a bite to eat?' Stella asked as she approached.

'Sounds great,' he said.

Stella patted him absently on the arm. 'Be right back,' she said.

Rick stayed very still as the fleeting touch seemed to reach deep down inside and stroke something that it just shouldn't have. Since when had a perfunctory touch from her had such an effect? But he suddenly understood Ramirez's puzzlement over the sensations that Lady Mary had created when she'd clung to his sleeve briefly during some choppy weather.

Rick shook his head at the direction of his errant thoughts. *Bloody hell, had he been emasculated overnight?*

When Stella rejoined him ten minutes later with some ham and salad rolls and two beers, he'd found his testicles and got over himself.

'Put it on autopilot,' Stella said, pressing the beer into his hand. 'Come and sit with me.'

Yeh, that was just what he needed.

But he did it anyway.

'So, how's the book going?' he asked, nodding at the shut laptop as he took a man-sized swallow of beer to dilute the absolute unmanly curiosity over her current romance novel.

Stella nodded. 'Coming along very nicely. I'm just about finished with the first chapter. I've emailed Diana—she's ecstatic. I think Joy had threatened her with editing non-fic if I didn't deliver.' Stella grinned.

Rick smiled too. She seemed relaxed and willing to chat about the book. Maybe, instead of wondering whether Lady Mary was her, which was, quite frankly, driving him nuts, he could just come out and ask. Or at least start a conversation where he could work his way round to it.

'So, what's the book about?' he asked as he took a bite out of his bread roll.

Stella looked up at him from under the brim of her hat. 'You really want to know?'

Rick stopped chewing. 'Of course, why wouldn't I?'

Stella blinked. For as long as she'd known him Rick's tastes had run to non-fiction books on anything to do with the salvage industry and shipwrecks. And *Phantom* comics.

'It's not really your thing.'

Oh, if only she knew how suddenly it was exactly his thing. He looked at her. 'It's yours. I'm interested.'

Stella stared at him for a moment, taken aback by his sincerity. 'Good answer.' She smiled.

He smiled back. She looked so damn sweet, how could she have such a dirty mind? 'So?' He quirked an eyebrow.

She didn't know where to start. She wasn't used to sharing this sort of information with anyone. Only Diana had known about *Pleasure Hunt* and even then Stella had been reticent to share any of the details in the early stages of the book. Non-writers didn't understand how storylines and characters weren't always crystal clear and well defined.

'It's about a mermaid,' she said. 'Called Lucinda.'

And then for some strange reason, under his scrutiny, she blushed. She thought about all the times they'd played pirate and mermaid as kids, swimming through the tropical waters of wherever they happened to be at the time.

'You know I've always had a thing for mermaids,' she said defensively.

Rick's gaze locked with hers. 'I do.'

Stella shrugged. 'She came to me in a dream.'

He nodded, wishing he'd been privy to that dream. Hell, if her dream life was as rich as her on-page fantasy life he wished he were privy to all of them.

'And the hero?' he asked.

Something held Stella back. She straightened the hat on

her head, then whisked it off and let her hair tumble down, stalling for time as she looked towards the horizon. 'I don't know much about the hero this time,' she said with what she hoped seemed like artistic vagueness.

Rick followed the stream of her hair as the stiffening ocean breeze blew it behind her. His palm itched to tangle in it and he kept it firmly planted around his beer. 'Is that unusual?' he asked.

'I don't know. I'm new to this and it's just the way it's happened.'

Rick slid a sideways glance at her. 'Did that happen with your first hero?'

Stella's heart skipped a beat as she glanced at him. 'No,' she said casually. 'He came to me…fairly well developed.'

Rick bit back a smile. *Hell, yeah, honey, no prizes for guessing why.* 'Does he have a name at least, this new guy?'

Stella blushed again. 'Inigo.'

Rick smiled. 'Ah…good choice.'

Stella looked at him and returned his smile grudgingly. 'Thank you.' It was surprisingly hard to talk about the hero with Rick and his Vasco Ramirez eyes staring straight at her even from behind his midnight shades.

Rick knew he had a good opening but was surprised by the pound of his heart as he contemplated the question.

Did he really want to know the answer?

He forced himself to take up inspection of the horizon so the question would seem casual rather than targeted. 'Do you base any of your characters on people you know?' he asked casually.

Stella glanced at him sharply. Did he know? Had he read *Pleasure Hunt*? She'd sent a copy to the *Persephone* for her father, which Rick could have got his hands on, she supposed, but it had been in a box of things that had been cleared from his cabin and sent to her after his death still in pristine condition.

The spine hadn't been cracked and it had been obvious to her that it had been unread.

It was an innocent enough question on the surface—one she'd been asked a hundred times by fans and media alike—but her shoulders tensed as she inspected that inscrutable profile just in case.

He seemed his usual relaxed self, soaking up some rays and downing a beer with the unconscious grace of an Old Spice model.

Besides, she doubted there would be any way he would have read it and not realised immediately who Vasco was. And she knew Rick well enough to know that he wouldn't have been able to resist taunting her mercilessly about it.

'No,' she said faintly, hoping her voice sounded stronger than it felt.

Rick stifled a chuckle. *Liar.* For damn sure Vasco Ramirez was him.

'So they just come to you…like in a dream or something…?' he asked innocently.

'Something like that,' she said vaguely. 'Although if I'm to be honest,' she admitted, trying to divert his attention off the hero, 'I suppose that the heroine is me.'

Rick coughed noisily as he inhaled some of his beer into his windpipe, necessitating her to beat him on the back a few times. He gasped and wheezed and coughed while his airway cleared the irritant.

Vasco probably never did anything so undignified.

'So,' he clarified once he could speak again, 'the heroines are…you?'

Please say no. Please don't let me have to imagine that Lady Mary is really you.

Damn it. He should have left it alone.

Stella blushed as Lady Mary filled her vision. 'Well, to a degree, I suppose, yes. I'm a woman so I can write a female character from my own experiences. In that respect, in very generic terms, I guess they are.'

Rick breathed easier. She was talking in generalisations. Not specifics. 'So Lucinda isn't you?'

Stella shook her head. 'Well, she's more me than Lady Mary,' she admitted.

Rick felt the tension ooze away completely.

Hah! There. She wasn't Lady Mary.

Phew.

'Lady Mary's from the first book?' he asked innocently.

Stella nodded as her embarrassment slipped away. It was actually quite good thinking this sort of stuff out loud. Knowing the differences could only help with her writing process.

Maybe Rick was a good sounding board?

'Lucinda has a strength of character that Lady Mary didn't. She's not waiting around to be rescued—in fact, she's going to rescue the hero, who's being held in chains.'

Rick tried not to think about how that scene would pan out. 'And Lady Mary is weak?'

Because he'd thought, in her own way, Mary had a startling resilience.

Stella shook her head. 'No, she's not weak, she's just more passive. But that's really just a product of the times and her upper-class background.'

Rick thought of the scene where Mary had finally succumbed to Vasco's seduction. There had been nothing passive about her then. And nothing passive about the way she'd totally turned the emotional tables on him.

'Definitely not you, then,' he smiled, relieved.

Stella smiled back. *If only he knew.* Beneath Lady Mary's petticoats and pantaloons lay Stella's every secret desire. She drained her beer, then checked her watch. 'Right, enough time skiving off. Lucinda is whispering sweet nothings in my head.'

Rick frowned. 'They talk to you?'

'Oh, yes.' Stella nodded. 'Most insistently usually.'

He swallowed. 'The heroes as well as the heroines?'

'Yep.'

Rick's mind boggled. 'What do they say?'

Stella shrugged. 'Their thoughts, dreams, desires.'

Good God—had Lady Mary whispered those things to Stella? Had she told Stella she wanted to see Vasco naked in the bath, that she wanted him to suck her finger into his mouth and she wanted to be tied to his bed?

Or had it been Vasco telling Stella what *he* wanted to do to Mary? Describing it in all the erotic detail that it had appeared in the book?

Had Stella been hearing him in her head?

Rick had never been so happy to see terra firma in all his life when they spotted the Papua New Guinea mainland mid-afternoon. His attempt to dissipate the heat of his thoughts hadn't exactly gone to plan and he was pleased to be getting off the boat and distracting himself for a while.

They motored into Port Moresby harbour and docked at the Royal Papua Yacht Club. After seeing to all the official formalities they headed for the club.

'Remember,' Stella said as Rick smiled at a beautiful dark-skinned woman who openly ogled him as she passed by, 'you're on a dare.'

Rick almost groaned out loud. If he had to share quarters with a woman who wrote sexy literature for a living and dressed in next to nothing, then it was vital to put his flirt somewhere!

The fact that he was now bound to a ridiculous dare was just the really rotten icing on a really sucky cake. What was the world coming to when he couldn't negate some totally inappropriate sexual urges with some harmless flirting?

He smiled at her. 'Piece of cake.'

Stella grinned as she fell in beside him. She was so going to enjoy this!

He tried to ditch her first thing in the cool, modern surrounds of the yacht club, but there was no way she was letting him walk around unaccompanied, flirting with no redress. She stuck to him like glue as he organised refuelling and restocking of their fresh food supplies and some onwards paperwork for their visit to Micronesia.

They found a nearby craft market and she watched him get crankier as they moved through the stalls thronging with colour and spice and wall-to-wall gorgeous local women. She asked him his opinion about earrings, bikinis and having her hair plaited. None of which he had a strong opinion on other than exasperation.

She bought a sarong and an anklet that had a tiny shell and a little bell on a piece of rope. It was nautical and she was thrilled with her purchase.

He was plain annoyed.

By the time they'd returned to the boat after an evening meal at the club, he was withdrawn and every inch the brooding pirate.

Due to cloud cover and lack of interest there was no star gazing tonight. Just a strictly professional conversation about their onward leg and a discussion revolving around the weather, which wasn't looking good for the next couple of days, but the long-range forecast remained excellent considering they were in the monsoon season.

'You okay?' she asked innocently as she picked up their empty coffee mugs and padded barefoot towards the galley. 'You seem kind of tense?'

Honestly, the man didn't realise how much his very survival depended on his banter with women—he needed it as if it were oxygen.

'The no flirting getting to you?' she queried, suppressing the humour that bubbled in her chest.

Rick heard the laughter in her voice only on a peripheral level as the tinkle of her anklet obliterated all else.

Great.

As if he weren't conscious enough already of her every movement, he was going to *hear* her every movement as well.

He'd probably hear her at night rolling over in bed.

He plastered a smile to his face. 'I'm fine,' he said. It had only been forty-eight hours, for crying out loud—just how oversexed did she think he was? 'I'm going up on deck to plot the course into the sat nav.'

Stella smiled as he departed. She had this dare nailed.

CHAPTER SIX

ON DECK the humid night was quiet and still, clouds obscuring what would almost be a full moon. Not even a light breeze tinkled the halyards. Faint music drifted down from the yacht club but the moorings were otherwise peaceful. No boats had cabin lights on, no one walked about stopping to chat, no low muffled conversations could be heard.

No one around to witness Rick gently belting his head against the wheel.

When he'd embarked on this voyage everything had been clear cut. *The Mermaid* and Inigo's treasure lay out there somewhere and he and his good friend Stella, *whom he'd known for ever, who despite some disturbing dreams was like a sister to him*, were going to find it.

After all, it was what Nathan had wanted.

Now he had a whole other picture going on in his head and he was damn sure there was nothing brotherly about it.

And definitely *not* what Nathan had wanted.

Nathan hadn't told Rick to leave Stella alone that day he'd caught them almost kissing. But he *had* spoken about how special his daughter was and left Rick in no doubt that he'd wanted someone just as special for Stella. Certainly a bunch of transient deckhands and divers on a motley collection of salvage boats had not measured up to Nathan's expectations in any way, shape or form.

Nathan had wanted for his daughter the one thing he'd never been able to give his own wife—stability.

Someone who was going to be there for her always.

And Nathan had made sure every man in his employ had known that his daughter was off-limits.

Himself included.

But that was then. And this was now.

Nathan was dead. And Stella was all grown up.

She had breasts and hips and an imagination that would make a sailor blush.

How on earth was he supposed to ignore that? Particularly when she was downstairs right now—he could hear that bloody bell all the way up here—prancing around, enjoying herself, feeling all smug at his expense.

And it was only day two.

How nuts would he be by the end of it all?

Hell, how nuts would he be in a week?

Unless…

Rick pulled his head off the steering wheel as the cunning of a certain pirate came to his rescue. He sat ramrod straight.

What if he took control of the situation? Turned the tables on her a little?

What if he were to take some of those tantalising scenes from *Pleasure Hunt* and give them life? He'd already established that she wasn't included in their little dare. Maybe he could have some more fun…

Vasco Ramirez had been determined to make the voyage with Lady Mary a pleasure hunt—maybe he should too?

Of course he'd never step over the line, the bondage scene would have to go begging, but what fun it could be seeing if he could get Stella all het up. After all, those scenes were written by her about him. Maybe he could indulge those fantasies for her just a little, give her a taste of the real thing?

It would be fun to see how she reacted.

Would she guess what he was doing or would she be unaware? Would she reject his boundary pushing or would she embrace it with the abandon with which she'd scribed it?

His gaze fell on the shower at the stern of the boat and he smiled.

Stella was putting the supplies away in the galley when she heard a loud splash outside the porthole in front of her. She frowned as she peered out into the night.

Maybe Rick had thrown himself overboard, the dare just too much?

'Rick?' she called, a smile on her face. No answer. 'Rick?'

Still no answer.

Maybe it was one of Moresby's infamous rascals trying to steal from them and he'd knocked Rick unconscious and into the water.

Her smile died as her heart started hammering in her chest. She reached for the nearest weapon, a heavy-based fry pan, and decided to go up and investigate. She climbed the spiral staircase, one tread at a time, an itch up her spine.

She took a deep breath, then popped her head above the deck line, like a meerkat.

'Rick?' she whispered while her eyes took a second or two to adjust from the bright light below to the low cloud-affected moonlight outside.

Still nothing.

She caught a slight movement towards the helm of the boat as the sound of running water defined itself from the gentle slap of sea against hull and the trilling of insects. She squinted to make out the shape, her vision slowly adjusting to its night capabilities.

It was a person…

A man.

Taking a shower.

Taking a shower?

The moon chose that moment to come out from behind the

scudding clouds that had been hampering its brilliance all night and Stella was afforded a side view of the man standing beneath the shower spray as if someone had switched on a spotlight.

Rick.

A one hundred per cent, buck naked, Rick.

She stood there frozen to the spot for a long moment caught between two impulses. To get out now before he discovered she was staring at his naked body or just stop and take in every magnificent inch.

As the celestial spotlight continued to bathe him in milky brilliance the latter won out.

The shower head was behind him, his head tipped back, his face raised to the night as the spray bathed his shoulder-length locks into a sleek, silky sheath. His eyes were shut as if worshipping the moonbeams that painted him in alabaster.

He looked like a statue. A Michelangelo nude.

With all the beautiful symmetry of fluid muscles and the more subtle details of sinews, tendons and veins in living, breathing relief.

Water sluiced over his broad shoulders, his chest, his biceps. It ran down the planes of his back, following the curve of his spine, dipping into those two sexy dimples above the rise of his buttocks. It flowed down firm flanks and rippled like a waterfall across the defined ridges of his abdomen.

Rivulets of water ran down one powerful thigh pressed slightly forward, the knee bent, obscuring her view any lower, and Stella frowned.

Damn it, so close...

Vasco's bath scene had been written over two years ago, and while a lot of it had been scripted out of her imagination some of it hadn't. Having grown up with Rick wearing barely anything at all—boardies or a skin-tight diving suit being his everyday attire—she'd had plenty of inspiration for Vasco's body and had been able to portray it with startling accuracy.

There had been some parts, however, that she'd had to… embellish.

It would be nice to know the truth of it. Had her fevered imaginings accurately represented *all* of Vasco or had it been pure whimsy on her behalf?

And then, as if he'd read her mind, he shifted, twisting his body slightly in her direction, straightening his bent knee and transferring his weight to his other thigh, and she no longer had to wonder if she'd got it right because the evidence that she had was right there.

Riccardo Granville was most definitely Vasco Ramirez in the flesh.

Rick turned so his back was to Stella and smiled to himself as he tilted his neck from side to side, letting the lukewarm water run over muscle that was surprisingly tense. The concentration it had taken to appear unselfconscious and relaxed, as if he were alone and being unwatched, had been much harder to carry off than he'd thought. But to see Stella's head pop up and then feel her avid gaze on him as tangible as the water cascading from the shower head had made the exercise worthwhile.

He was back in control again and that was exactly the way he liked it. Even if he was playing games with someone he had no business playing games with.

But if she was going to secretly put him in a book and not expect him to have a bit of fun with that then she'd completely forgotten about his devilish sense of humour.

As long as he kept it light and remembered who she was—Nathan's daughter, not a single, fully grown woman who wrote dirty books—and where the line was, it would work out just fine.

They'd both have a laugh at the end of the voyage and get on with their lives.

It was win-win as far as he was concerned.

* * *

The second Stella strained to see that birthmark she'd been fascinated with since she'd been five years old she knew that happenstance had turned into voyeurism. She forced herself to cease and desist. With one long last lingering look at possibly the most beautiful rear end in the world, certainly in historical romance fiction, she slunk back down below deck, fry pan still in hand.

She should feel guilty; she knew that. If the positions had been reversed she'd have been mortified. But strangely she didn't. No harm had been committed. He didn't know that she'd been watching him or that he'd just fulfilled a particularly potent fantasy of hers—so potent she'd put it in a book!—and she certainly wasn't going to tell him!

But she would use it.

Late at night when a day of crafting sensual tension or a torrid love scene left her restless and achy and the dictates of her body would not be ignored, a naked Rick bathed in shower spray and moonbeams would come in handy.

Very handy indeed.

Vasco examined the milky white perfection of Lady Mary's hand. He cradled it in the palm of his much bigger, much darker one and admired the contrast for a moment. This was what they'd look like in his bed, their limbs entwined, their stomachs pressed together—coconut and coffee.

He stroked his thumb down the length of her index finger where the long slither of wood had embedded itself and let it drift across her palm. He heard the slight intake of her breath and felt her resistance to his hold.

He looked up into her emerald eyes. 'It's not as bad as it looks,' he murmured.

Mary swallowed. They were seated, her knees primly together beneath her skirts, his legs spread wide in that lord-of-all-he-surveyed way of his, bracketing hers. The fabric of his breeches pulled taut across his thighs as he leaned in over her hand, his head perilously close to her cleavage.

'It really just needs a pair of tweezers,' she said, trying to pull her hand back. He resisted and she resigned herself to the unsettling heat of his touch.

Vasco smiled at her, her pink mouth a tempting bow before him. 'I think I can do better than that.'

His voice was low and silky and Mary felt it in places that she'd only recently, thanks to him, become aware of. Her green gaze locked with the startling blue of his as he raised her finger to his mouth and sucked it inside.

Vasco watched surprise pucker her mouth into a cute little O shape as her pupils dilated. Her breathing was loud in the space between them as she lowered her gaze to where his mouth tasted her. He felt a half-hearted attempt to pull away again but countered it by laving her finger with long strokes of his tongue.

Her whimper went straight to his groin.

Mary felt the throb ease as Vasco ministered to her wound in this most unusual fashion. Her gaze returned to his, finding him watching her with something in those mesmerising eyes she couldn't fathom. She didn't know what it was but she did know she'd seen it there before.

And it was both dangerous and enticing.

Still holding her gaze, Vasco slowly withdrew his lips, his teeth seeking and finding the rough end of the splinter burrowed in at the tip. He nipped at it until he held it firmly, then slowly eased it out, her glistening finger slipping from his mouth altogether. For a moment he held the liberated splinter between his teeth, then turned his head and spat it on the floor.

He smiled as he turned back to face her. 'That's better,' he murmured.

Mary couldn't move. Her finger or anything else for

that matter. She just sat there, hand still in his, finger moist from his ministrations, staring at his mouth. A mouth that had turned her insides to jelly.

'Th-thank you,' she stammered, belatedly remembering her manners.

Vasco lowered his head to her finger again, and pressed a gentle lingering kiss to the exit wound.

He grinned. 'My pleasure.'

Mary felt a sudden urge to call for smelling salts.

After a restless sleep Stella wasn't in any hurry to look Rick in the eye for the first time since her voyeurism of last night. She'd gone straight to her quarters after her little peeping Tom episode, thus avoiding him altogether.

But she couldn't stay in her cabin for ever and it wasn't as if he knew that she'd spied on him. All she had to do was not blush and stammer when she greeted him and pretty soon the awkwardness would pass.

The memory would be emblazoned on her frontal lobe for ever but the awkwardness would pass!

'Hey,' she said to Rick as she wandered into the galley fifteen minutes later. He was sitting at the dining table poring over charts. Fully clothed. She looked away as he looked up at her.

Rick forced himself not to smile like a Cheshire cat, but just give a normal everyday *hey* kind of a smile. Which was kind of difficult when greeted with another pair of brief shorts and some kind of strapless shirt, leaving her shoulders bare and her cleavage…enhanced.

'Morning,' he said. You s*aucy little pervert in barely any clothes*. 'Sleep well?'

He assumed she'd had a pretty fitful sleep if that damn bell jingling was anything to go by.

Stella steeled herself to look at him again and gave a noncommittal shrug. 'Fine,' she murmured.

Rick stifled a smile as she looked away. *Liar.* Good, now they were even. Between the damn book, that silly little bell and an array of teeny tiny clothes, sleep had become a rare commodity.

'You were in bed early last night,' he mused, because he just couldn't resist teasing her a little as she had done over their flirting bet last night. 'Everything okay?'

Stella's breath hitched as she popped two pieces of bread in the toaster. 'Fine,' she replied, her gaze planted firmly on the job at hand.

Rick suppressed a chuckle at her monosyllabic replies. He'd have loved to tease her some more, hell he could have done it all day, but the weather wasn't the best out there and they should be getting under way.

He picked up his plate and glass and headed towards the galley, squeezing behind her to get to the sink. He felt her stiffen a little as he caught a whiff of browning toast and coconut. Her hair sat in a messy ponytail on top of her head, leaving her neck exposed, and he had the craziest urge to slip his arms around her waist and nuzzle into it.

He stepped away from the temptation—teasing her was one thing, acting as if they'd set up house was another. He placed his plate in the sink and downed the last of his orange juice in one gulp. 'It's going to be a bit choppy out there today so I'll get us under way,' he said.

'Fine,' Stella said again, keeping rigidly still until he'd safely disappeared up the stairs. When the toast popped thirty seconds later she realised she'd been staring out of the porthole thinking about him naked.

Oh, brother! Would she ever be able to act normally around him again?

As it turned out Rick was fully engaged in keeping control of the boat in the worsening swell so there was no time for conversation, awkward or otherwise. The sky was grey and the wind was brisk, keeping him on his toes. It was far from dangerous but it did require his attention.

She sat up front and worked on her laptop for a bit, but trying to type with the horizon undulating drunkenly played havoc with her equilibrium and wasn't very productive. Even reading through her previous day's work for editing purposes proved impossible to her constitution.

Stella had always possessed an excellent set of sea legs but they'd obviously become rusty from lack of use as nausea sat like a lead sinker in her stomach.

Which at least wiped away the images of Rick showering in the moonlight.

She gave up on the book, shutting her laptop lid.

'Do you want to go down and make sure everything's secured properly below deck?' Rick called out an hour later as she sat very still, keeping her gaze fixed on the horizon, and concentrated on deep breathing.

Stella stood. Good idea. Something to do to keep her mind off the unsettling up and down of the boat.

It started to rain lightly as she passed him and she shivered as the breeze cooled the water droplets on her skin. He'd taken his shirt off at some stage and his chest was speckled with sea spray.

It reminded her of the way water droplets had clung to his naked skin last night and she wondered if they were cool on his skin too. Whether they tasted of salt or of man.

Or some heady mix of both.

If she hadn't felt so rough, she might have been tempted to try. 'Do you want your spray jacket?' she asked, not quite meeting his eyes.

Rick nodded, examining her face. It had gone from pale to white as the sail billowing above their heads. 'Thanks. You okay?' he asked. 'The bureau says it'll only last for another couple of hours.'

Stella gripped the leather back of the high captain's chair

where his butt was parked. He looked totally in his element. Calm and confident. Relishing the inclement weather even, as if it were nothing more than a sun shower. Stella nodded. 'I'm fine.'

He grinned at her, his long hair blowing behind him in true pirate fashion. 'There are some sea sickness pills in the cupboard above the sink,' he offered.

'I'm fine,' she lied.

Rick laughed. 'There's a lot of that going on today.'

Stella was sure if her cheeks weren't so cool they'd be heating up nicely. 'I practically grew up on a boat.'

Rick shrugged. 'Just saying…'

She went below deck and checked every room, securing any items that were lying around. She grabbed her spray jacket and pulled Rick's off the hook on the back of his door and headed to the galley, finding a couple of cans of soup and emptying them into a saucepan. The boat rolled to the side as she placed it over the element and her stomach lurched.

Damn it.

She reached above the sink and threw back two of the little blue pills, praying they'd work in a hurry.

She stood over the soup as it heated, shifting her weight from leg to leg with the motion of the boat. When it was done she puréed it, poured it into thermal mugs, cut off thick chunks of bread from the loaf they'd bought yesterday and loaded it all onto a tray. She shrugged into her jacket and folded his over her arm.

By the time she rejoined him fifteen minutes after taking the anti-emetic she was actually feeling markedly better.

'Thanks,' Rick said, relieving her of the tray and quickly shrugging into the jacket.

She could see water droplets clinging to his eyelashes and spattering his bronzed chest. Just as the shower spray had done last night.

She dragged her eyes away. Must not *think about the shower.*

'Hmm, this is good,' Rick said, watching her face as two pink spots appeared on her pale cheeks. 'I think I'll keep you.'

Stella's gaze flicked to his, to the teasing light in his pirate eyes. Two could play at that game. 'I think I'll let you,' she murmured.

Rick cocked an eyebrow, surprised at her easy comeback, then chuckled. He warmed his hands around the mug, taking another sip of the rich, fragrant pea and ham soup. 'Weather's easing up.'

Stella looked out at the lurching ocean. 'It is?'

He chuckled some more. 'You've become such a landlubber. Can't you feel it beneath your soles?'

Stella felt the laugh reach right inside her and warm her from the inside out. She guessed she had. 'No, Captain Ahab, I can't.'

'Ah, Moby Dick, my favourite book,' he teased, because he knew how much Stella hated it.

She rolled her eyes at him. 'You've never read it.'

'I have,' he protested.

'When?'

'When you dared me to,' he said.

Stella frowned at him, thinking back through the mists of time to that long-ago summer dare. 'I was twelve.'

She'd been going through a classics phase and also trying to read anything nautical to connect with her father, to try and understand why he'd loved the sea more than her mother.

It hadn't helped.

'I never back down on a dare. Besides, I liked it.'

Not as much as the hot pirate sex in Pleasure Hunt...

They had a discussion about its merits while they finished off their lunch and even Stella felt the sea was calmer by the time she reloaded their tray. The wind had definitely dropped. The sprinkling rain had stopped and they shrugged out of their jackets. A bare bicep brushed against her shoulder as he threw his jacket over the back of his chair and she shut her eyes briefly as heat licked at the point of contact.

'I'll get rid of these,' she said briskly, pulling away from him.

Rick watched her go, her hips full and round and swinging enticingly as her gait compensated for the lurch of the boat. Hips that had appeared one summer along with the bra and, no matter how much he'd tried to ignore them in his day-to-day dealings with her, they'd been right there in his fevered teenage dreams.

A sudden gust of wind caused the boat to roll to the side and he watched as she shimmied to counteract the swell. He smiled, admiring the move until he realised she'd overbalanced and was going down.

'Stella!' he called as he sprang from his chair.

Too late. The boat had thrown her sideways and Stella hit the deck hard on her left upper arm, the tray flying as she extended her other hand to buffer the impact, skidding as she grabbed at the wood for purchase.

'Stella,' Rick called again as he threw himself down beside her inert crumpled body, his heart hammering. 'Stella? Are you okay?'

Stella groaned. She couldn't think for the pain in her left arm.

Rick touched her arm, trying to roll her over. 'Stella?'

She moaned and he stopped. 'I'm okay, I'm okay,' she panted. 'Just give me a second.'

'Where are you hurt?' he asked.

'Arm,' she said after a moment. 'Hand.' She looked up at him through her fringe. 'Dignity.'

Rick laughed, relieved that she couldn't be too badly hurt if her sense of humour was still intact. 'Do you think anything's broken?'

Stella zeroed in on the pain in her upper arm where she'd

fallen the hardest. It had initially been excruciating but the intensity had eased quickly. It only felt as if a brick had fallen on it now as opposed to a cement column.

'Let me help you up,' he offered.

Stella acquiesced with a brief nod of her head. With both arms hurting like blazes, she had no idea how she was even going to get up. Rick grabbed her around the waist and gently pulled her into a sitting position. His big warm body was behind hers and for a moment she was so relieved she wasn't destined to spend for ever spread on the deck like a stranded beetle she sagged against him and shut her eyes.

Rick rubbed his cheek against her hair, the scent of coconuts filling his nostrils. He picked up her right hand. The knuckles were grazed and the middle three finger pads were bleeding with splinters embedded in each one.

He tried really hard not to think about Lady Mary and her splinter, but with Stella all warm and pliant against him, smelling like a pina colada, it was hard not to go there.

'Nasty,' he murmured, anticipation already building in his gut, knowing that he was the one who would take them out. Kiss those fingers better just as Vasco had. 'How's your arm? Can you move it?'

Stella gingerly rotated her shoulder. 'Bloody sore,' she bitched.

He smiled into her hair. 'What about your dignity?'

Her arm throbbed and she couldn't even rub it with her opposite hand because it throbbed as well. And was bleeding to boot. 'Unrecoverable, I should imagine.'

He chuckled. 'Nah. You really fell very gracefully.'

'Oh, goody,' she said dryly. 'A critique.'

He laughed again. 'Come on. Let's get you down below and have a look at you.'

'I bet you say that to all the girls,' she muttered.

Stella blinked as the snappy rejoinder loaded with innuendo slipped from her mouth. What the?

He laughed some more. 'Just the ones who fall at my feet.'

Rick helped her up. The boat rolled again slightly and he grabbed her waist and her good arm to steady her as she wobbled against him. He sucked in a breath as, for a moment, every part of her from her soft breasts to her round hips was pressed against him.

He took a step back as his body leapt to life. 'You've got your sea legs?' he asked.

Stella nodded. 'Sorry 'bout that.'

'No worries.' He shrugged. 'Why don't you go on down? I'll fix a few things up here and then I'll join you.'

Stella, despite the throb in her arm and the sting in her fingers, was still stuck back in that moment.

She nodded her head dumbly.

No dignity anywhere in sight!

When Rick joined her half an hour later she'd recovered sufficiently to have taken some painkillers, located the first-aid kit, washed her hand in the sink and was sitting at the table valiantly trying to dig the splinters out. But trying to do it left-handed was a slow enough process without being hampered by a restricted range of movement from the soft tissue damage inflicted by the fall up higher, near her shoulder.

Rick shoved his hands on his hips. 'What are you doing?' he asked.

Stella, who had made more of a mess through pricking herself, was not in the best of moods. It really didn't help that he looked all hot and sexy in that shirtless way of his.

'What do you think?' she demanded. 'I'm trying to get the splinters out.'

Rick smiled down at the petulant set to her mouth. *Oh, goody, this was going to be fun.*

'Here,' he said, scooting her along the bench seat as he moved in beside her. 'Let me.' Rick held out his hand. When she didn't comply he gave her an impatient look. 'Stella?'

Stella was in a quandary as the scene she'd written for *Pleasure Hunt* looked as if it too was about to play out. Well, the G-rated version of it anyway.

She couldn't imagine Rick sucking her fingers into his mouth. Well…she could. And she had. She'd even written it down.

But that was Vasco.

Rick could almost read the thoughts in her very expressive eyes. She was torn between medical necessity and curiosity. 'You don't want them to fester, do you?' he asked innocently.

Stella swallowed as she offered him her palm, hoping that she was submitting purely on medical grounds but knowing there were other less sensible, less pure reasons.

She just prayed he never read her book.

Her palm was warm in his as Rick took an antiseptic swab and cleaned up the site so he had a clearer field of vision. This close, like Vasco, he could see Stella's mouth and the way her teeth dug into her bottom lip.

He raised an eyebrow. 'You ready for this?' he asked.

Stella doubted she'd ever be ready for Rick being this close, his sea-salt-and-ocean-spray aroma wrapping her in a hundred childhood memories that warred with the very adult visions of him naked beneath a shower.

'I promise I'll be gentle,' he murmured.

Stella rolled her eyes at the amused glitter in his tropical gaze. The only way she was going to survive being the sole focus of his stymied flirting reflex was to give as good as she got. 'Maybe I don't like it gentle.'

Rick's heart thunked hard in his chest as he pulled back a little in surprise. She had her eyebrow raised and a small smile playing on her lips.

She was flirting back.

He chuckled. It had been a long time since they'd traded banter like this. It made his plan that much more enticing.

As Vasco had, he ducked his head and leaned over her

hand. Given that his deck was much more polished than that of a pirate ship from the seventeen hundreds, the splinters were much smaller than the one Mary had embedded in her finger. Certainly they were not removable by his teeth and it took some time digging them out.

She didn't whimper or complain although Rick looked up at one stage and she had her eyes shut and face screwed up. Their legs brushed intermittently beneath the table, their upper bodies were almost touching, his head was level with her cleavage and he wondered what she'd do if he claimed that long-awaited kiss early.

Find out if her mouth tasted as sweet as it looked. If it really did taste like coconuts.

Stella opened her eyes and caught him looking at her. Her breath caught in her throat. 'What?' she asked.

Rick took a moment or two to answer. Then he shook his head and said, 'Nothing,' and returned to his ministration, his hand not quite as steady.

Another ten minutes saw the job done. 'There now,' he announced to her closed eyes. 'Isn't that better?'

Stella looked down at her hand, the splinters gone from the pads of her fingers, his thumb lightly brushing her palm—just as Vasco's had done. The instinct to shut her eyes and allow her body to feel the caress everywhere warred with her guilt about indulging another Vasco fantasy with an unsuspecting Rick.

It made her crazy.

And the pain made her bitchy.

'No,' she said testily. 'It bloody hurts, actually.'

Rick felt her trying to withdraw her hand from his but he resisted her attempt, knowing it was too good an opportunity to pass up. 'Fine,' he sighed, 'I'll just have to kiss them better.'

It took a moment for his intention to register and another moment for Stella to open her mouth and lodge a protest. But by then it was too late. He was lifting her fingers to his mouth, holding her gaze as he did so. Her protest stuttered to an inarticulate gurgle as his lips briefly brushed over first one fingertip, then the next. When he got to the third her eyes widened as she felt his tongue press against the pad, laving the wound gently before his lips met then slowly withdrew.

She made some noise at the back of her throat that sounded foreign in the charged atmosphere between them.

It might have been a whimper.

'There,' he said huskily, her dilated pupils not only doing funny things to his groin, but deep inside his chest too. 'Is that better?'

She wanted to shake her head, tell him no. That they burned. That he'd set them on fire. But she was only capable of a nod. A very weak nod.

'Good,' Rick said with difficulty as her mouth hovered so very close and that line became even hazier.

My pleasure.

CHAPTER SEVEN

Lady Mary sat awkwardly on the chair placed in the middle of the sun-drenched deck, conscious of the crew's barely concealed curiosity.

'You'll have to lean back,' Vasco said from behind her.

Mary turned slightly, catching him in her peripheral vision. 'Really, I don't think this is necessary,' she protested primly, her hands folded in her lap.

Vasco placed his hand on her shoulder, urging her back. 'The lady wishes to wash her hair. What the lady wants, the lady gets.'

Mary submitted to the pressure of his hand and turned to face the front again. 'I am perfectly capable of washing my own hair, Captain Ramirez.'

Vasco leaned down, his lips near her ear, inhaling the floral scent of her, so utterly female in this all-male environment. 'Ah, but where would the fun be in that, Mary?'

He smiled at her slight intake of breath at his familiarity. 'Undo your hair,' he ordered in a low whisper. 'Lie back.'

Mary felt her nipples pebble against the fabric of her chemise at the deep vein of risqué in the low command. Another protest rose to her lips but she stifled it. In her week on the ship she'd learned that the Spanish captain always got what he wanted.

And her hair really did need a wash.

Her fingers trembled as she pulled out the pins that secured her hair in an elaborate up do, one by one. She could hear her own breath loud in her ears as he towered above her. When it was all released she shook it out, then furrowed her fingers into the back of the curly mass to loosen any recalcitrant strands.

She became aware that the low chatter from the crew had stopped and she was the object of their blatant attention. 'Captain,' she said, feeling suddenly breathless, 'your men are staring.'

Vasco couldn't blame them. Her hair was like a Titan masterpiece, a flaming torch beneath the blazing sun burnishing the highlights into strands of golden thread.

He gently picked up a long spiral curl from her shoulder and pulled it out to its full length before letting it go, watching it recoil against the scarlet fabric of her frock.

'It's not often they see a woman of such beauty, madam.'

'I would prefer they did not,' she said, reaching for just the right amount of haughty as the low, almost reverent compliment unsettled her.

Vasco preferred they did not as well and he barked some orders at them, more than satisfied with the immediate response.

'Thank you,' Mary murmured as a dozen or so crew got back to their jobs.

'What the lady wants...'

He looked down at her crowning glory and imagined how it would look spread over the milky skin of her breasts. What would she want when he was looking at her like that?

For she would soon be his.

'Tip your head back.'

The command was betrayed by the roughness of his

voice and he expected her to object yet again. When she acquiesced without dissent, her hair falling over the back of the chair in a soft red wave, his anticipation built another notch. It had been many months since he'd last had a woman. And never in all his eight and twenty years had he ever had a creature so stunningly beautiful.

He picked up the bucket and poured the water slowly onto her hair, distributing it evenly, watching as the curls became drenched and the whole glorious mass darkened into a lustrous sheath of the finest satin. The excess pooled around his boots but didn't register as an errant droplet captured his gaze. It trickled onto her forehead and began a slow descent down her face, running over a closed eyelid, down one creamy cheek until it reached her mouth, where her tongue darted out, sipping it up.

Vasco almost threw the bucket down and lowered his mouth to claim those moist, upturned lips on the spot. The desire to kiss her, to ravage that tempting mouth, had been building for days. But even through the savage haze of lust that had set a raging inferno in his loins he knew that she wasn't ready. That the dance wasn't yet complete.

So he picked up the soap and rubbed it over the sodden silky layers. Then he dropped it into the bucket and let his hands take over.

Mary almost moaned as Vasco's hands furrowed into her hair, the pads of his fingers rubbing with sensual ease against her scalp. Her nipples and belly tightened. Goose flesh broke out everywhere. Quite why she had no idea, given she was hotter than she'd ever been.

The sun no doubt.

Nothing to do with his gaze, which she knew without having to open her eyes lay heavily on the pulse drumming a frantic tattoo at the base of her neck.

'How's that?' he murmured.

At some level, Mary knew she should be contained in her reply but the drugging magic of his touch, the aroma of lavender and chives and the warmth of the sun were addling her senses. 'Amazing,' she breathed and Vasco chuckled.

At home this would have been her maid's job, and it would never have felt this...decadent.

And Vasco certainly was nobody's servant.

Her aunt would have an attack of the vapours if she could see the pirate laying his hands on her niece in such a familiar fashion. But Mary, for one, was giving herself up to the experience as she angled her head down to allow him access to where hair met nape.

Vasco's soapy fingers massaged her hairline, dipping down to rub the back of her neck, and he swallowed as a sigh escaped her lips. He noticed how her hands clenched and unclenched the fabric at her lap, the agitated press of her cleavage against the prison of her neckline, and sensed she was feeling things she'd never before experienced.

He worked his way back up to her temples, slowly stroking her there, working his way down to the shell of her ear, drifting his thumb across its ridges, smiling as he heard the rough inward drag of her breath.

He leaned down, replacing his fingers with his lips. 'You are very beautiful, Mary.'

Mary opened her eyes as his words slithered like the serpent into every cell in her body. A dozen retorts came to mind. He should not be talking to her like this. But with his hands creating havoc and her body craving something she didn't understand only one thing came to her lips. She turned her head slightly, their mouths closer than was decent.

'So are you, Vasco, so are you.'

For he was, quite simply, the most beautiful man she'd ever seen.

AFTER two more days of similar weather they finally had a calm, sunny day and Stella was able to get out on deck, where she felt most inspired, to do some more writing.

Which was just as well because she was going totally stir crazy.

She'd spent a lot of time down below during the inclement weather, trying to type two-fingered in between doses of pain-killers as her arm swelled up and the bruising came out. Rick, worried that she'd broken her humerus, had wanted to turn back and get her some medical help but Stella had refused.

Yes, she'd fallen heavily and yes, the pain had increased since the swelling and bruising had come out, but she'd broken her radius a few years ago and her current pain was nothing like how excruciating that had been.

She was sure she hadn't broken it. She'd assured him all she needed was a few days for the swelling to go down and she'd be back to normal.

But in the meantime, even the most basic things had been difficult and she was cranky and out of sorts with her limited abilities. Rick, in true Vasco fashion, had gallantly offered to help her dress and bathe, which she declined not quite in the same spirit it was offered.

So she'd battled on by herself, making do with quick showers and dressing in sarongs that required minimal arm lift. More complicated things like shaving her legs and washing her hair seemed like distant luxuries.

It was most frustrating on the writing front. The words were flowing in her head but she just couldn't get them down quick enough and the grazed knuckles and sore finger pads of her right hand made typing slow and laborious. Every twenty minutes she'd had to stop and let her left hand take over, but it caused the throbbing to increase up higher and after about ten minutes she had to take a break.

So, it felt good indeed to have the sun on her face and the feel of a calm ocean beneath her feet again and for the first half hour they got under way she just sat in her low chair with her face turned to the sun, soaking it up.

But it was all downhill from the moment she opened her laptop. It didn't take long for her mood to evaporate as her useless fingers, despite the absolutely exhilarating day, made a hard slog of the writing process. And when her arm started to throb half an hour into the process she shut the lid of the laptop in disgust.

It had felt really good this morning too. The bruising was fading to a greeny-yellow and the swelling had reduced by about half. She could even lift her bent arm almost level with her shoulder before discomfort forced her to stop.

'You okay?'

She turned to see Rick coming up behind her, taking full advantage of the glorious weather by once again going shirtless. She winced as the sudden movement wrenched through her arm. 'Fine,' she said morosely as she blew her fringe out of her eyes on a huffed breath.

Even it was annoying her. It was strawy and scratchy from the rigors of sea salt and the tangling effect of ocean breezes. Conscious of needing to save water on a boat, she hadn't washed it since they'd left Cairns.

Rick chuckled as he sat beside her. 'You don't seem fine.' He laughed again at her responding scowl. 'Come on, what's up? Tell Uncle Rick.'

'The words are coming but my useless fingers can't type them fast enough.'

'I could type them,' he offered. 'You can dictate them to me.' He smiled at her. 'It'll be just like Barbara Cartland.'

Stella rolled her eyes. No way in the world was she ever going to let him anywhere near Lucinda and Inigo.

Rick grinned. 'I'll take that as a no, then. What else?'

'My arm hurts,' she said, aware that it could be interpreted as whining. 'And my head is as itchy as hell because it hasn't been washed in for ever and I can't even scratch it because my fingers are too sore.'

For a moment Rick couldn't believe his luck. He'd read the scene where Vasco washed Lady Mary's hair about a dozen times. He let his gaze run idly over her hair, chunks of it escaping a poorly placed plastic claw. 'Well, now, that *is* something I can help with,' he said, very matter-of-fact.

She glared at him. 'Offering to help me shower was not funny the first time,' Stella said grouchily.

'Oh, I don't know.' Rick shrugged. 'I kind of thought it was but,' he said, holding up his hand to still the protest about to come out of her mouth, 'I didn't mean that. I'll wash it up here, on deck.' He grinned at her. 'You'll be fully clothed, I promise.'

Stella stilled as the implications of his offer slowly sank in. Another Vasco and Mary moment. She searched his tropical blue gaze for a spark of recognition. Something that told her he knew what he was offering was far from innocent. He looked back at her with the same clear, blue-eyed brilliance as always.

She chewed on her lip as the idea teased at her conscience. 'What...you mean with a...bucket?' she asked.

Rick bit the inside of his cheek as he struggled to stay deadpan for her searching gaze. He returned her interest with his best I-have-no-idea-what-you're-talking-about look. 'No...' He pointed to the stern on the boat. 'With the shower.'

She turned gingerly this time to take in the metallic head under which she'd watched him shower the other night. Her cheeks heated as the illicit image revisited.

Rick decided to leap on her indecision and take charge, giving her no quarter. The boat was on autopilot and it was clear sailing today. 'You head on over, I'll get your shampoo. It's in your en suite, yes?'

Stella nodded dumbly, sitting in her chair unmoving, as Rick disappeared. Could she indulge herself for a third time? This voyage was turning into some kind of hedonistic exploration of her fantasies.

It was…immoral, surely?

Debauched, certainly.

Rick came back on deck and smiled to see her still sitting in the same spot, indecision on her face. 'Come on,' he called. 'I don't have all day.'

Stella turned to look at his naked back as he headed towards the stern. She stood automatically to his command, dragging her chair with her. He looked so much like Vasco when she reached him, her conscience piqued.

'I don't think this is a good idea.'

Rick doubted he'd ever heard a more feeble protest and knew he was going to have to hold her hand on this one.

'Are you crazy? It's a brilliant idea. The sun is out, there's a light breeze, it'll dry quickly. And as there's nothing I can do about your arm or help with your writing, you should let me do this.'

Plus, you want to.

He took the chair out of her unprotesting fingers and placed it under the shower head, busying himself with finding the right position. By the time he was done she seemed to have resigned herself to a little piece of *Pleasure Hunt*. She sat when he asked her and even snuggled down low in her chair so just her neck and shoulders were exposed above the canvas and her head could tilt back easily over the edge.

Of course that bent her sarong-clad body into a banana shape with her feet flat on the deck, her thighs bent before him like an offering from the gods. Thighs that her sarong fell away from, leaving them exposed to his view. Not skinny. Firm, rounded like her and smooth with the beginnings of a tan tinting the formerly milky skin.

He turned the water on and doused himself with it first before removing the hand-held head from its cradle, kneeling behind her and directing the spray at her hair. She startled slightly and he swallowed as he noticed her nipples pucker beneath the sarong. 'Too cold?'

Stella reined in her heartbeat as his hand sifted through her hair, wishing she could rein in her other bodily responses as easily. 'No. Just wasn't expecting it.'

'Sorry,' he said, his gaze fixed on the two round points tenting the fabric at her chest. 'Should have warned you.'

Should have warned myself.

He might have been doing this as a tease but he hadn't been immune to that hair-washing scene and already he could feel a tightening in his groin.

Stella shut her eyes tight as his hand sifted and lifted and caressed every strand of her hair to ensure it was waterlogged. His fingers occasionally brushed against her scalp and she squeezed her thighs together as the sensation seemed to travel straight to a point between her legs.

Like acupuncture. Or reflexology.

Whatever...he'd definitely found her sweet spot.

Rick flicked the taps off, determinedly dragging his gaze away from her thighs and nipples and fixing it on her hair, on the job at hand, determined not to get carried away by it.

She was supposed to be turned into a panting mess—not him.

'Shampoo now,' he said as he squirted a healthy dollop into his palm and a waft of coconut—of her—hit him square in the solar plexus. It was like liquid silk in his hands and he spread it over her sodden hair evenly before he started to rub it into a lather with the flat of his palms.

Stella almost sighed at his touch. His movements were brisk at first, but after a few moments they changed, became slower, more defined, the tips of his fingers dragging with languorous subtlety against her scalp. She felt the motion right down to her toes and all the hot spots in between.

Every cell went on high alert. Her back arched involuntarily as she bit back a whimper. The pain in her arm and the sting in her fingers floated away on a sexual high.

Shampoo foamed between Rick's fingers as he watched her shift restlessly in the chair. The image of him sliding his soapy hands onto her shoulders, over her chest, pushing the sarong down off her breasts and lathering them up, teasing the nipples into taut peaks until she orgasmed hit him out of the blue and the tightness became something more.

He was harder than the wood beneath his knees.

He needed to distract himself fast. 'You always had gorgeous hair,' he murmured as the thickness of it filled his palms. He remembered diving with her when they'd been kids and being mesmerised by the way her hair streamed behind her as she swam or floated around her like a crown when she stopped. He'd dreamt of it often during his teenage years. 'Just like that mermaid you always wanted to be.'

Good. That was good.

Reminding himself of why it would be a very bad idea to lean over as Vasco had also wanted to do and ravage her mouth.

Because they were friends. Long-term friends.

He was just having some fun.

Stella opened her eyes, thinking back to those days when she'd truly believed in the imaginary world they'd created. Instead of having to create this faux fantasy life to keep that connection alive.

'Everything was so simple back then,' she murmured.

Rick nodded. Back then he'd been plain Rick, she'd been Nathan's daughter and hadn't had breasts and hips. Now he was Vasco Ramirez, Nathan was dead and she had breasts, hips and a lot of other bits in between.

She bent her head forward, just as Lady Mary had done and he obliged, caressing her hairline, drifting his thumbs over her nape, going lower, kneading his fingers into the muscles of her neck and lower still to her shoulders.

'Mmm,' she groaned. 'That feels good.'

She couldn't help herself, it just tumbled out. Because it did feel good, it felt so damn good *everywhere* she wanted to turn around and French him as she almost had all those years ago, and decades of being buddies and business partners and all those other consequences be damned.

Rick swallowed. 'That's because you're so tense,' he said lightly, feeling pretty damn tense himself but working on the knots in her neck muscles until he had them all ironed out because she kept making these little gurgly noises at the back of her throat that he could really become addicted to.

By the time they were gone and he'd forced himself to turn on the spray he had an erection that could have been used on Vasco's pirate ship as the plank for prisoners to walk to their doom upon.

For his own sanity, he tried to make the conditioning process much faster but pretty much failed. She had her hands stuffed between her thighs and he spent the whole time wondering if she really was just holding her sarong in place or maybe easing a little ache down there.

His imaginings had gone from lathering her breasts to his head disappearing between those amazing thighs and he was fit to burst when he left her, hair brushed and drying off, in the sunshine.

'Thank you,' she called after his disappearing back.

Rick gave her a wave, not turning around because he looked perfectly indecent at the moment and probably would be for quite a while with her squirmy, back-archy thing imprinted on his retinas. 'My pleasure,' he murmured quietly to himself as he descended below deck as quickly as his legs would carry him.

* * *

At midnight Rick gave up trying to sleep and trudged up to the deck to lie under the stars for a while. They'd always had a calming effect and he needed that badly at the moment, when his body was raging with undiluted lust and no amount of diversion tactics seemed to be working.

The ocean was still and the night almost silent as he made his way to the middle of the deck. He could barely feel the bob of the boat beneath his back and his breath was loud in his head. The waning moon threw a narrow beam of light on the surface of the gently rippling water as it fought for space in the crowded sky.

He lay with his knees bent and took a deep steadying breath.

Now, *this* made sense.

Stella and what happened to him every time he looked at her didn't make sense at all.

But this—the ocean—did.

This was like coming home.

He remembered turning up at Dartmouth at the age of fifteen, a rucksack on his back and four pounds in his pocket. He'd hitched from London the previous day. Nathan had looked at him from the deck of the *Persephone* and said, 'Sophia's been on the phone to me.'

He'd looked at Nathan with mutiny in his eyes. He'd loved his grandmother, but she hadn't understood that the ocean ran in his veins. She'd wanted him to study hard and go to university and all he'd wanted was a sea breeze in his hair. He'd chafed against her bonds. Cut classes. Flunked out.

'I'm not going back. This is where I belong.'

Nathan had looked at him for long moments. 'It's not the glamorous life it seems on summer break or from your father's grandiose sea stories, Rick. You should be in school.'

He'd shaken his head. He'd always known from Nathan's quiet restraint that his father's embellishments were romantic sentimentality and that there wasn't a lot of romance or sentiment in salvaging. He'd learned early it was ninety-nine per cent grunt, one per cent glory. 'I should be here. The business is half mine.'

They'd both known that Rick didn't legally inherit until he was of age but Nathan hadn't called him on it.

'That it is. But are you man enough?'

Rick had nodded his head firmly. 'Yes, sir.'

Nathan had crossed his arms. 'You come on board, you answer to me.'

'Aye, aye, captain.'

'And you finish school.' Nathan had raised his hand at the objections that had been about to tumble from Rick's mouth. 'A man knows the importance of education, Rick.' He'd shoved a hand on his hip and said, 'Take it or leave it.'

Rick had bristled at the harshness of it when he'd reluctantly agreed and had done his lessons by correspondence with less than good grace, but he'd been grateful for the many years that Nathan had forced his hand.

It hadn't been until years later that he'd found out Nathan and Sophia had done a deal while he'd been hitching his way to Dartmouth. Nathan had promised to look after Rick and see that he finished school and Sophia had agreed to loosen the reins she'd held on her stubborn grandson.

Nathan had had the utmost respect for Rick's Spanish grandmother, who had selflessly taken care of him when her daughter, Carmela's, tempestuous love affair with Anthony Granville had finished and neither had known what to do with a toddler. Rick knew now that if Sophia had demanded that Nathan bring her grandson back then he would have been back in London faster than he'd been able to blink.

Nathan had always said to never get between a woman and her child but he had still gone into bat for Rick. Had been the father his own father had never been. Had been his family after Sophia had passed away the following year.

So, messing around with Nathan's daughter was not the way he repaid the man, even if it was just a bit of teasing.

That was getting out of hand.

Remembering what made sense—the pulse of the ocean, the business, Inigo's treasure—that was how he repaid him.

It was just a little difficult at the moment with so little to do on a boat that virtually sailed itself and a barely dressed first mate who didn't seem like so much of a mate any more. In a few days they'd be at their destination in Micronesia and then he'd have things to do other than look at Stella all day in hardly any clothes.

They'd both be occupied. Their days filled with diving and poring over charts and Nathan's research trying to pinpoint *The Mermaid.*

In the meantime he really needed to stop reading *Pleasure Hunt.*

Stella kicked at the sheets restlessly, straining to hear any more movement from above deck. She'd heard Rick's footsteps twenty minutes ago after hours of staring at the ceiling, trying not to think about how his hands had felt on her scalp. How if she just shut her eyes she could be Mary and he could be Vasco and how maybe they could skip a few chapters and she could be tied to his bed.

She shut her eyes and erased the image. She was taking shameful advantage of the situation. Indulging her fantasies when Rick was just being himself. The guy she'd always known. A friend. One who would do anything for her. From coming to tell her personally about her father's sudden death to washing her hair because it was scratchy and itchy and she was physically limited.

Still, there was a part of her, egged on by her hormones and a latent wicked streak, that couldn't help but speculate. Just what would he do? How far would he go? Would he cut up those ripe mangoes that they'd purchased in Moresby and that permeated the galley with sweet promise and feed them to her as Vasco had done with a juicy pear? Would he scratch that itch that drove her mad right in the centre of her back that she just couldn't reach with her current injuries?

And what about that other itch that seemed to build and build the longer she spent in his company? The one that tingled between her thighs, that made her breasts feel heavy, that caused an ache down deep and low somewhere behind her belly button?

Would he relieve that if she asked him?

Because she wasn't even capable of that at the moment and God knew she was fit to burst.

Not that helping herself was ever as good as the real thing. But it was better than death by deprivation.

Damn it!

She kicked the sheets off. This was insane. Lying here thinking about Rick like this was pure madness. Neither of them was ever going to do anything that ruined twenty-plus years of friendship so she just needed to get over herself.

She needed to go on deck and normalise their relationship. Lying in her bed, her body throbbing, put images in her head that didn't have any place in reality. Lying on deck, looking at the stars with him as she'd done a hundred times before, would help to put things into perspective.

And God knew, if her body couldn't have passion then it sure as hell needed perspective.

Rick heard the bell before she made it to the top of the stairs. He shut his eyes and prayed to Neptune for restraint.

'Hey,' he said as she tramped over, eyes staring doggedly at the sky.

'Hey,' Stella acknowledged as she drew level and looked down at him. 'Can't sleep?'

'Something like that,' he said as her face appeared in his line of vision. She was wearing some three-quarter-length grey pants, the fabric of which was quite thin, clingy around the thighs, loose around the calves. And what he could only describe as a boob tube.

'Neither can I. Want some company?'

'Sure.'

He was already burning in the fires of hell—what was one more lie?

Stella joined him on her back on the deck, making sure her injured left arm was on the outer and that she maintained some distance between them. Rick and her didn't really do distance so it seemed awkward.

'Any shooters tonight?'

He nodded. 'Saw one earlier.'

'Did you make a wish?' she asked, rolling her head towards him.

Not one that he could repeat in decent company. He turned his head too. 'I wished for—'

'Stop,' Stella said urgently, automatically silencing him with the press of a finger against his lips. A finger that still stung a little and protested the movement. 'You know you're not supposed to say.'

Rick stilled as her fingerprint seared into the DNA of his lips. There were a lot of things he wasn't supposed to say.

Or do.

And every single one of them begged to be ignored.

Stella's eyes widened as a glitter of something distinctly sexual enriched his blue gaze with something distinctly pirate.

Heat flared in her belly and breasts.

Between her legs.

And deep, deep inside.

So deep she doubted anyone had ever touched it.

Her gaze narrowed to his mouth as her finger moved of its own volition, tracing his lips, the sting instantly easing. She could feel the warmth of his breath against it, the roughness of every inhalation and exhalation.

Rick opened his mouth slightly, giving silent permission to that seeking finger. When it had circumnavigated every millimetre he grazed the tip gently with his teeth as he touched his tongue to where the splinter had been.

The way she stared at his mouth as if it were the most perfect creation went straight to his head. The sound of her indrawn breath travelled straight to his groin.

He swallowed as a jungle drum beat in his head and thudded through his chest. 'Stella.'

'Hmm?' she asked absently as she mapped his mouth with her gaze. Vasco's mouth.

Rick tried again. 'I don't think we should—'

This time she didn't cut him off with her finger. This time she used her mouth and Rick was totally unprepared. He'd always dreamt their mythical first kiss would be soft and gentle. Tentative. It was certainly the way he would have kissed her at sixteen. But there was nothing tentative about the way she opened up to him.

In seconds the kiss was wet and deep and hard, leaving no room for finesse or wishing on stars. There was just feeling, reacting. Letting all that suppressed desire bubble up on a wave of coconut and take him to a higher plane.

Stella moaned as fantasy fused into reality on a rush of high octane lust that blasted heat into every cell of her body.

And it was better than she'd ever imagined.

The dare faded as they both collected on the prize early.

Desire coursed through her bloodstream and she gasped against his mouth as Rick rolled up onto his elbow, his face looming over hers, his fingers furrowing into her hair.

She sucked in great slabs of air as the kiss robbed her of breath. They both did. Their breathing loud as they rode the dizzying heat and the high oxygen demand of the incendiary kiss. His lips were demanding against hers and she opened to him wider, revelling in the thrust and tangle of his tongue, her head lifting off the deck trying to match it.

Trying to lead. Trying to follow.

Trying to get closer.

She squeezed her thighs together as the heat there morphed into a tingling that became more unbearable with every second. Her pelvic floor muscles undulated with each swipe of his tongue and she pressed her hips firmly into the deck to soothe the pressure building deep and low.

Was it possible to orgasm from a kiss alone?

God knew she'd fantasised about his kiss often enough both as a teenager and as a writer crafting all those highly sensual, gloriously descriptive love scenes. Maybe it was?

His thumb stroked along her temple and her head spun from the rhythmic caress. Her hips rotated restlessly against the deck as she felt herself edge closer.

Maybe, after all this time, a kiss *was* going to be enough?

Rick had spent a good portion of his life *not* wondering what kissing Stella would be like and now he knew he *never* wanted to stop.

Suddenly it was the *only* thing that made sense. Not the stars or the ocean or Inigo's treasure.

None of it.

Just that little whimpering noise at the back of her throat that reverberated inside his head like a benediction—like his own private cheer squad.

And the sweet aroma of coconuts.

Lying by himself on deck before, Stella hadn't made sense.

Looming over her, pressing her into the deck, feeling the flesh and blood of her, the restless sexuality bubbling in her kiss, the harsh, desperate suck of her breath and the answering rhythm of his own body, she'd never made more sense.

He wanted more. He wanted all. He wanted everything.

His hand fell to her arm, to gather her closer, pull her nearer, imprint her along the length of him.

And then she stiffened against him, cried out, broke away…

CHAPTER EIGHT

RICK froze as he stared down at her, her right hand supporting her injured left arm, her teeth sunken into her bottom lip, plump and moist from his ravaging. He was dazed for a moment, trying to compute what had brought an abrupt end to the passion.

Trying to compute what the hell had happened in the first place.

'I'm fine,' Stella said, breathing hard through clenched teeth as the jarring settled. She could see his bewilderment and something else, a slow dawning that seemed to closely resemble horror.

No, no, no.

'Just give me a moment,' she scrambled to assure him as she watched his blue gaze lose its drugged lustre and slowly recoil from her. 'Now.' She smiled up at him, the pain in her left arm easing as she slipped her good hand onto his shoulder. 'Where were we?'

Rick shook his head to clear the remnants of a very powerful buzz. *What the hell?* He groaned as he collapsed back against the deck.

'Oh, my God,' he said to the sky, blind to the beauty of the celestial display.

'Rick,' she assured him again, brushing a finger against his hand, 'it's fine.'

'Oh, my God,' he repeated, moving his hand to his face,

covering his eyes and shaking his head from side to side. 'What have I done?'

'Rick—'

'No.' He vaulted upright, then sprang to his feet. 'No, Stella,' he said, looking down at her. 'This is…crazy.'

Stella blinked at his vehemence. It had been shocking and surprising and unexpected. Not to mention unbelievably good.

But crazy?

She sat up gingerly. Obviously this wasn't going any further and she couldn't have this conversation with him towering over her reclined body.

'Why?'

Rick stared at her as her calm response filled him with complicated angst. 'Because,' he spluttered, 'you're Stella and I'm Rick and *we*—' he pointed back and forth between the two of them '—don't do this.'

'We made a kiss a stake in your flirting dare,' she pointed out.

And as far as Stella was concerned it was the best first kiss ever. A kiss that had obliterated Dale's best for eternity. A kiss that would surely ruin her for all other kisses.

Rick shook his head vehemently. 'Not this kind of kiss.' He'd thought about how it might go down and it hadn't been anything like this. It had been slow, sweet, controlled.

And they'd both been vertical.

'Why not?' She wasn't sixteen any more. Did he think she'd be satisfied with something chaste?

He blanched at her simple query. 'How about twenty-plus years of friendship? Or a legal document with both our signatures on that states we own a company together? Your father, for crying out loud.'

Stella frowned. 'My father?'

'Yes,' Rick fumed.

'My father?'

Rick nodded. 'He warned me off.'

'My *father* warned you off?'

Rick hadn't been forthcoming about what Nathan had said to him that day and, with the slight impression that she too had somehow let her father down, she hadn't pursued it.

He glared at her incredulous expression. 'Well, not in so many words, no. But every crew member he employed knew you were off-limits, Stel. Nathan didn't want anyone messing with his little girl.'

It took her a moment to process that. Would Rick have made a move a long time ago had her father not been all Neanderthal about his daughter?

She'd known there was an undercurrent between them as teenagers but it had all ended abruptly that day and she'd figured it was for the best.

But maybe Rick had always pondered the what-ifs too?

Stella used her right hand to push up from the deck, wincing slightly. 'Well, I don't know if you've noticed, but I'm not a little girl any more, Rick. And my father is dead.'

Rick's gaze dropped involuntarily to her boob tube. 'Yeah.' He grimaced as he returned his gaze to her face. 'I noticed.'

Stella laughed at his forlorn reply. 'I got breasts, sorry.'

He looked at them again. 'Yes, you did. It was simpler when you didn't.'

She frowned. 'I've had them for a long time, Rick—what changed this time?'

He looked at her. That damn book. *Pleasure Hunt*. Thanks to Nathan and years of platonic childhood memories he'd managed to keep perspective in his dealings with Stella.

Until the book.

But his perspective was currently shot to hell.

'The moonlight?' he lied. He somehow didn't think she'd approve of him using her book for his own ends. 'I don't know.' He shrugged. 'I guess it's never been an issue before. We've never been alone before. Not like this.'

She thought about it. 'You're right, I don't think we have.'

They looked at each other for a long moment. 'I think we'd regret it, Stel. In the long run. We have all these great memories of growing up together. Summer holidays on the *Persephone*. Bringing up Spanish coins from the ocean floor. Playing mermaid and pirate.'

Although perhaps that wasn't the best memory to bring up now…

'And when I look at you, that's what I see—how you and your father embraced me as part of the family. They are such fond memories, Stel. They mean a lot to me. I don't want to ruin them by giving in to this…crazy thing. It wouldn't be the same between us any more no matter how hard we tried. And I like what we have.'

Stella knew he was making sense but, right now, she liked what they'd been having five minutes ago more. She could still feel the surge of blood tingle through her breasts and between her thighs. Just the bob of the boat was almost enough to push piano-wire-taut muscles into delicious rapture.

God, why was he so bloody gallant? She'd probably only needed another minute or so and she would have been well satisfied. *Embarrassed for sure.* But not going off to bed with her hormones still raging and bitching at her to boot.

Well, if she had to sit on her hands the next few weeks and pretend that he hadn't almost made her come with just a kiss, then she was damned if she was going to play fair.

'Fine,' she huffed, pushing past him, heading for her cabin. 'Glad I packed my vibrator after all.'

Rick blinked. 'You brought a vibrator?' Hell, she *owned* a vibrator?

She stopped and turned. 'I'm a grown woman, Rick. *I have needs.*' She turned and continued on her way.

Rick shut his eyes on a silent groan as a particularly graphic image entered his head. 'Not helping, Stel,' he called after her, his gaze transfixed by the swing of her hips.

She smiled over her shoulder at him. 'Sweet dreams.'

* * *

Rick did not have a good night.

Every time Stella's bell jingled he strained to hear. What, he wasn't sure. A sigh? A moan? Those soft whimpery noises she made at the back of her throat?

Oh, God, those soft whimpery noises were not conducive to sleep.

And what if he *had* heard them? Would it make it any easier lying alone on the moral high ground knowing she was getting off? Knowing that he could have been in there with her, helping out?

Kissing her more.

Touching her more.

No!

It was hard now but at the end of the voyage and for the rest of the years to come, they'd be glad they were sensible. Glad they hadn't gone past the point of no return.

Maybe one day they'd even laugh about it.

Maybe.

Rick got the boat under way by eight the next morning. Stella hadn't put in an appearance and sitting around thinking about all the reasons she might be sleeping late, including a bone-deep sexual satisfaction, was not improving his mood.

It was another glorious day and losing himself in the familiar routine of setting sail seemed like a better alternative than wondering what mischief Nathan's daughter had got up to between the sheets last night.

And it worked to a degree. Until Stella came on deck an hour later.

In a micro bikini.

He stared at her open-mouthed, pleased for the camouflage of his sunglasses. Two tiny triangles barely contained the swell of her breasts and the pants, high on her leg and low on her front, had two tempting little bows at the side keeping them from falling off altogether.

'Morning,' she said airily as she drew level with him, her laptop, some coconut sunscreen and a towel in hand. A smile on her face. 'What a magnificent day,' she murmured, inhaling the sea air deep into her lungs, feeling it resonate with her spirit.

Rick watched as her chest expanded, straining the fabric of her bikini top to indecent proportions. Lord*, was she trying to give him a heart attack?*

'Sleep well?' he asked, his neutral tone almost killing him.

Stella sighed as the air rushed out of her lungs. 'Like a baby,' she purred.

She hadn't, of course. How could she sleep with a fire ravaging every erogenous zone she owned and quite a few she hadn't even known existed?

She'd barely slept a wink.

Perhaps she should have helped herself as she'd led Rick to believe but, after their near miss, she'd wanted strong male arms and a warm solid chest, not just her and Mr Buzzy.

'How's your arm?' he asked politely.

'Good.' She nodded. It was the first morning it hadn't ached when she woke and the bruising was nearly all faded. She could even move it the full range, if a little gingerly. 'I reckon I can hit my word count today.'

'Better get started, then,' he prompted, desperate to get her coconut aroma and bare shoulder out of his direct line of vision.

Stella nodded, knowing it was best to get away from him yet strangely reluctant to do so. It was as if some tropical fever had her in its grip and he was both the cause and the antidote.

'I might catch some rays first, before the sun gets too hot.'

Of course. Why didn't she just roll around in some jelly while she was at it?

'Yell if you need a hand,' she murmured as she pushed past him, heading for the bow.

He watched her sexy sashay from behind his glasses. *Yell if you need a hand.*

* * *

Stella sun-baked for the first two hours. She wasn't entirely sure what she was playing at but it seemed to have something to do with goading a reaction out of Rick. After all, if he was really that into her, he surely wouldn't be able to ignore her best attempts at extreme flirting?

She shifted, she wiggled, she lay on her back, she rolled over, she sat up, she applied liberal amounts of sunscreen, she even retied the bows.

She got nothing.

Last night had obviously been some sort of anomaly for Rick. A mad moment when a balmy night and the moonshine had affected his judgement. This morning he seemed completely indifferent to her. Nothing like the man who had kissed her as if it were his last day on earth.

Nothing like the guy she'd known for ever either—quick to laugh and eager to share his joy of the ocean. He looked like a robot at the wheel, sunglasses on, scanning the horizon for who knew what. The meaning of life? They'd passed several islands in the distance and they'd slipped by without so much as a *land ahoy* and a finger point.

It was already weird between them and nothing had happened.

Well…nothing much anyway.

She gave up trying eventually and drifted off to sleep, exhausted after her long night of tossing and turning. But later she knew she was going to have to make amends. Get things back on track.

Because, one way or another, she needed him in her life. And if that meant going to her grave without carnal knowledge of one Riccardo Granville, then so be it.

After a day of watching Stella prance around in a bikini, it was a relief to finally drop anchor and go below deck. He had a shower. A very cold shower. And lectured himself on the same things he'd lectured himself about all last night.

This was *Stella*. Nathan's daughter. His old, old friend and business partner.

And no one had ever died from sexual frustration.

By the time he got out of the shower he'd almost convinced himself, then his gaze fell on *Pleasure Hunt* and he was lost again. He picked it up to where it was open. The scene where Vasco fed Lady Mary slices of ripe pear jumped out at him. The scene had been rich with visualisation and Rick had almost been able to smell the sweet pear juice that had trekked down Mary's chin and Vasco had lapped up with his kisses.

Rick shut it for his own sanity. He let his fingers linger over the raised gold lettering of her name. How could he reconcile the Stella Mills who'd written the sexy historical with the Stella Mills he'd known practically all of his life?

How could he ever think of her as sweet and innocent again when he'd been privy to her erotic prose?

When he'd been the subject of that erotic prose?

When the taste of her mouth was imprinted onto his?

He meant what he'd said last night. But he'd never thought it would be so hard. He'd never been obsessed by a woman before. Sure, he'd had his usual teenage infatuations and spent some exciting shore leave with some very generous women, but none had played on his mind like this. None had moved into his brain and taken over.

Stella was fast becoming an obsession.

The question was would the obsession end when they went their separate ways? Or was he destined to wonder for ever?

He shoved the book under his pillow.

Out of sight, out of mind.

Although if he had any sense he'd take it above deck and hurl it into the ocean. But it was Diana's so he couldn't.

At least that was what he told himself anyway.

Stella was throwing a line in over the side when Rick reappeared half an hour later. He looked sublimely sexy in his shirt, regulation boardies and bare feet. God knew why—it wasn't as if he were wearing Armani or Ralph Lauren. But there was something about the way he wore them that oozed a special mix of charisma and wonderful outdoorsy sexuality.

'Thought we'd have some fish tonight,' she said.

Rick nodded. She'd put a button-up throw on over her bikini a long time ago but it was as if he had X-ray vision suddenly and it was still *all* he could see. 'I'll set up the grill.'

An hour later the sky was just starting to blush a velvety pink as they sat on deck and ate their fish with the potatoes that Rick had also fried on the grill. A gentle breeze caressed Stella's neck, lifting the tendrils that had escaped her messily constructed bun. The ocean lapped gently at the hull.

'Did you get your word count done?' Rick asked after they'd been eating in silent contemplation for most of the meal.

Stella nodded, grateful for the conversation. She was excruciatingly aware that they'd been avoiding any mention of what happened last night, which seemed kind of ridiculous sitting together and sharing a meal. 'Just over three thousand words today.'

He took a deep swallow of his beer. 'Is that your usual quota?'

She nodded again. 'I try to do three k a day. Some days—' she grimaced '—that's easier to achieve than others.'

'Why's that?' he asked. 'Surely you just sit there until you reach your goal.'

Stella shook her head at him—such a boy. 'Well, it doesn't really work that way unfortunately.'

He gave her a blank look and she knew she was going to have to explain it to this goal-orientated male.

'It's like diving for lost treasure. Sometimes coins are just lying on the ocean floor ready to scoop up, other times they're locked in chests, which are trapped in impossible-to-reach pockets within an aged, treacherous, waterlogged wreck. They're there...you can see them...but they're tantalisingly out of reach. The muse is like that. Some days she comes out to play and the words flow and other days…' She shrugged. 'It feels like every word is locked away in a chest just out of my reach.'

Rick wondered how quickly some of the *Pleasure Hunt* scenes flowed before stopping himself. 'I don't know,' he joked to cover the errant thoughts. 'You arty types.'

Stella laughed. 'Sorry, I suppose that did sound a bit pretentious.'

From her it had sounded just right. 'Not at all,' he dismissed with a smile. 'Do some scenes flow better than others?' The question slipped out unfiltered and couldn't be recalled.

Stella looked away. The sex scenes in *Pleasure Hunt* had flowed like a gushing tap. Years of feverish fantasies let loose had informed the scenes to embarrassing accuracy. She looked away from the piercing intensity of his gaze.

'No, not really,' she lied, standing to clear the plates. 'They can all be as easy or as difficult as each other.' She balanced the plates a little awkwardly, mindful of her injury and thankful for the calm ocean.

'Here, let me take them,' Rick said as he stood.

She shook her head. 'No way, you cooked, plus you've been waiting on me for days. The arm's heaps better so just sit.' Rick sat and she smiled. 'You want another beer?'

He nodded. 'Sure, why not?' Maybe if he was a little cut he'd go straight to sleep.

Stella seemed to take a while. He could hear her banging around down below deck as the sun gradually set above, the evening sky slowly speckling with stars. It felt oddly domesticated and a deep spring of contentment welled inside him, bringing him to his feet.

He frowned as he prowled restlessly around the deck. The boards felt good beneath his bare feet.

His deck, his boat, his ocean.

These were the things that brought him contentment. Not some woman clattering around in his kitchen.

That never made him feel content.

In fact it usually made him want to get away fast. Ditch the chick at the nearest port and sail himself far away. Get back to his true mistress—the ocean.

Like Nathan. Like his father.

But here he was, nonetheless, on the ocean, sharing it with probably the only woman who truly understood the pull of such a demanding mistress.

The tinkle of her bell alerted him to her presence and he turned to see her walking towards him, holding the necks of two beers in one hand and a plate holding two mangoes, a knife and a cloth in the other.

'I'm having a mango,' she said. 'I wasn't sure if you wanted one or not.' She handed him his beer as she sat on the deck, facing the horizon lotus-style, balancing the plate on her crossed knees.

Rick nodded, taking one as he sat beside her. Not too close. 'Sure, thanks. I'll eat mine after the beer.'

Stella raised the large pungent fruit to her face. It was warm against her cheek and she inhaled deeply. It smelled sweet and wild like forbidden berries and exotic like balmy tropical islands.

'Mmm, that smells good,' she murmured. 'The whole galley smells of them suddenly.'

Rick nodded. He'd noticed earlier when he'd gone below but he didn't want to look at her getting all breathy and orgasmic over anything other than him, so he hung his head back and kept his eyes firmly trained on the sky.

Stella placed the mango on the plate, salivating at the thought of the sweet, warm fruit sliding against her palate. She cut into the soft flesh, a pearl of juice beaded around the incision as the strong aroma wafted out to envelop her in its heady fragrance.

She was conscious of Rick beside her not saying anything. Conscious of what happened between them last night when they'd been on this deck. Conscious that it had sat large between them all day, screwing with their usual effortless dynamic. Normally by now Rick would be talking about the stars or prattling on about Inigo and *The Mermaid*.

Instead they sat in silence as they had done for most of their meal.

Stella took a deep breath as she picked up one mango cheek and scored the flesh. They couldn't go on like this. 'About last night...'

Rick's breath seized in his lungs momentarily and he took a moment before looking at her, taking a swallow of beer to calm himself. 'What about last night?'

Stella didn't dare look at him. The weight of his gaze was intimidating enough. 'You were right,' she said, scoring the other cheek. 'We would regret crossing the line. I'm sorry I made it difficult for you.'

Rick swallowed as she picked up a scored mango cheek, inverted it and used her tongue and teeth to liberate a cube of the soft pungent flesh. 'Yes,' he said faintly, trying not to think of the pear scene in *Pleasure Hunt* he'd not long been skimming.

Stella would have sighed as the fruit zinged along her tastebuds if the topic of conversation weren't so damn serious. She turned to face him as she sucked another cube of mango into her mouth and savoured it. 'I mean, of course it would be awkward between us and would negate all the good memories we've ever made.'

She bit into another perfectly square piece of mango flesh.

Rick heard the soft squelch go right to his groin. He zeroed in on her mouth, which glistened with ripe juice. His fingers tightened around the beer bottle. 'Uh-huh,' he said, not really even listening, his reasoning dissolving into a red haze as her mouth and tongue slowly devoured the fruit.

Vasco had fed Lady Mary, taunting her with slithers of pear, inching them closer, stroking them against her moist lips, watching her as she sucked them inside her mouth, her gaze not leaving his face.

He itched to pick the mango up and re-enact the scene. Cut off thin slices and feed them to Stella one by one. Watch her pupils dilate and her breath become shallow just as Lady Mary's had.

Maybe even hear that whimper again at the back of her throat. The whimper that was all Stella.

Stella's breath hitched as Rick's eyes seemed to suddenly glitter like moonbeams on sapphires. She swallowed her mouthful of mango but juice escaped to her lips and she ran her tongue around them to capture the errant moisture.

Rick shut his eyes and groaned as all his noble intentions from last night faded to black with each revolution of her tongue. 'Stella,' he murmured, his eyelids fluttering open to find her staring at him.

Stella blinked at the ache in his voice. Had he edged closer? Or had she? She looked at his mouth, remembered how it had felt against hers. How it had been so much better than she'd ever fantasised. 'This *is* crazy,' she whispered, mango forgotten.

Rick nodded, his gaze fixed on her mouth, inching his own closer to hers, drawn to her as if she were a homing beacon, his heart rate pulsing to the beat of the sea. 'Certifiable.'

Stella felt his pull as a physical force, which seemed only fitting beneath a canopy of stars with the rhythm of the ocean lulling away the insanity of it all. 'What about the memories, Rick?'

Her voice was low and husky in the quiet of the night as she tried to hang onto the one thing that made sense between them, even though her pulse coursed like an ocean squall through every inch of her body.

Suddenly her mouth felt dry.

So dry.

As if she'd been drinking sea water for days and, not only was her thirst unquenchable, it was sending her slowly mad. She swallowed and licked her lips to ease the dry, parched feeling.

Rick's pupils dilated as her tongue darted out. 'Screw 'em,' he muttered as his final shard of resistance melted away. 'Let's make better ones.'

R-rated ones.

And he closed the distance between them, capturing her mouth. There was a moment, ever so brief, when she could have pulled away, could have protested and he would have been capable of letting it slide. But when she opened to him instantly on a deep-in-his-bones moan the moment passed in a blink of an eye and her mango and coconut essence wrapped him in a sticky web of desire that was impossible to break free of.

Even if he wanted to.

Which he didn't.

His heart crashed in his chest, his breath sawed in and out. Her hands crept around his neck and she made that noise at the back of her throat and somehow, some way, he had her on the deck, her breasts pressed against his chest, her hand shoved in his hair.

Where his beer or her mango had ended up he didn't know and he didn't care. All he knew was she smelled like paradise and felt like every erotic dream he'd ever had, and when she moaned into his mouth her desire tasted sweet like mango and he wanted to devour every drop.

He was hard and needy and something in his head insisted that he touch every inch of her, smell every inch of her, know every inch of her.

His hand drifted south to the wild flutter at the base of her throat and she moaned. It moved further to the top button of her wrap, where the swell of her breast was emphasised by the taut fabric of her bikini top, and she gasped.

It fanned down over her ribs and came to rest on the gentle rise of her belly and she arched her back and undulated her stomach and sighed, 'Yes, yes, yes.'

Rick pulled away, breathing hard. Her face was soft and full of wonder. If he were an egotist he might even have called it rapture.

'Let's go to my cabin,' he murmured, kissing her eyes and the tip of her nose and the corner of her mouth.

Stella opened her lashes, seeing nothing but Rick's face crowned by about a million stars—*when had they come out*?

'No.' She shook her head. 'I want it here, on the deck, beneath the stars.'

She'd wanted to write a similar scene with Vasco and Mary but she'd known that it wouldn't have been possible in the middle of the ocean with a boat full of pirates in the eighteenth century.

But now she got to live the fantasy for real and she wasn't going to have it any other way.

He nuzzled her temple, her ear, her neck. 'Kinky,' he murmured as his hand found its way beneath the hem of her throw to trace patterns on her bare abdomen. The same abdomen that had taunted him all day with its cute little perky belly button.

Stella almost moaned out loud as the buzzing of his lips seemed to stroke other places. Lower places. 'Not into kinky?' she asked, smiling against his mouth as his lips brushed hers.

Rick chuckled as his mouth inched down her throat. 'Kinky is my middle name,' he said as his hand crept inexorably north.

'Really?' Stella said as the possibilities swirled around her mind in a sexual kaleidoscope.

'Really,' he repeated as he pushed her shirt up, pulled aside one bikini bra cup, exposing her breast totally to his view. He smiled as she gasped and the nipple puckered beneath his scrutiny. He stared at it fascinated as his hand groped beside her until he found what he was looking for.

Stella was in a sexual haze so heady she doubted even an undersea earthquake could have shifted her. The way he looked at her nipple as if it were his own private property was utterly mesmerising.

This was Rick. Her Rick. Not a fantasy. Not Vasco Ramirez.

Riccardo Granville.

He raised his hand above her chest and it took a few seconds for her to focus on what he was doing, and even then it wasn't until the warm sticky mango juice dripped onto her nipple that his actions registered.

But by then he'd lowered his mouth to it and she'd gasped and arched her back and she knew she was totally lost.

Just as Lady Mary had been.

CHAPTER NINE

RICK had never tasted anything so sweet as his tongue lapped at the juice, removing every drop from the hard nub. Stella tasted exotic like forbidden fruit, smelled like an ocean breeze riffling through a stand of coconut palms, and the very unladylike expletive that had fallen from her mouth as he nuzzled her breast played like a symphony in his head.

He pulled away and watched as her wet, puckered nipple dried in the breeze. A little frown appeared between her brows just before she moaned a protest and opened her eyes. There was a feverish glitter to her gaze, which went straight to his groin.

He had put that crazy-drunk look there.

The air felt thick and heavy on her palate as Stella dragged in some much-needed breaths. His hand spanned her ribs beneath her breast exactly where her heart pounded like a gong and she wondered if he knew that he had done that to her. He was staring down at her, his gaze roving over her face and chest, lingering on her mouth and her impossibly taut nipple.

'I have another,' she murmured.

Rick smiled. He relieved her of her throw, then smoothed his hand to her other bikini cup and dragged it aside with his index finger, satisfied as her breast spilled free. 'So you do,' he agreed, watching with fascination as the nipple wrinkled then puckered before his eyes. He groped for the discarded mango cheek.

Her pupils dilated and he heard her breath roughen as he squeezed the cheek again and juice dripped onto her breast, coating her nipple and running in sweet rivulets down her chest. His mouth salivated as he inched his head closer to the gloriously sticky morsel. Her low whimper encouraged him to close the distance and he took it greedily instead of repeating the steady assault he'd used on the other side.

She gasped and he sucked harder, rolling the stiff peak around and around his mouth, grazing the tip with his teeth, pressing it hard between palate and tongue, satisfied only when she arched her back, silently begging for more. His hand found the other nipple, hard and ready. When he brushed it with his thumb she panted. And when he pinched it between his fingers she practically levitated off the deck and cried out so loudly he lifted his head and smothered the husky outcry with his mouth.

Stella, driven by a hunger so insatiable she was blind to everything else, lifted her head off the deck and claimed Rick's lips with indecent vigour. She pushed her tongue into his mouth and when he groaned deep and low and needy she swallowed the sound whole, lapping up his response, wanting to fuse their mouths together, to fuse their bodies together for eternity.

Her pulse pounded through her head, her nostrils flared with each laboured breath. His hand left her nipple and stroked down her belly and she shifted restlessly against the deck as muscles deep inside shivered and undulated. The boards were hard against her back but she didn't care. She wanted him on top of her, pressing down, sinking into her. She wanted to feel his skin on hers, wrap her legs around his waist, have the rock and the sway and the pound of them become one with the rhythm of the ocean.

His hand moved lower, whispering across her skin, skimming the edge of her bikini bottoms. Her hips shifted as heat licked from his fingers and bloomed in her pelvis. An ache took up residence between her legs and she moaned as his hand fumbled with a bow.

She felt the tug as he pulled at it and it came undone.

Then another tug as the other bow ceded to his questing fingers and she shivered as he stripped the tiny triangle of fabric away, leaving her bare to the ocean breeze and the stars and his touch.

'Those damn bows have been driving me nuts all day,' Rick said, lifting his head briefly before moving his lips to her jaw, her ear, her throat. And lower, trailing towards her nipple as his fingers slowly stroked her inner thigh.

Stella whimpered as more heat fanned downwards from his kisses and upwards from his hand, searing and ravaging everything in between with devastating ease.

Suddenly it wasn't enough to be just lying here. She wanted to touch his skin—all of it. Feel it smooth and warm and solid beneath her hands, dance fire across it as he was doing to her.

Wreak a little havoc.

Render him a little crazy.

She grabbed for the hem of his shirt, reefing it up and over his head at the exact time his lips met her nipple. She whimpered as he let go for the briefest second and moaned deep and low when his mouth returned immediately to her breast and his fingers found her thigh again. She sucked in a breath, dug her fingernails into the bare warm flesh of his shoulder as he tormented the sensitive peak.

His flesh shuddered beneath her palm and it vibrated all the way down her arm, stroking gossamer fingers over her neck and her chest and down her belly. Her hands kneaded his shoulders and the defined muscles of his back. Her palms smoothed into the dimples she'd seen all those days ago in the moonlight, slipping beneath his waistband to the firm rounded rise of his buttocks.

When he groaned against her mouth she squeezed them hard.

Rick reared back as his erection surged painfully, bucking

against its confines. 'Stella,' he muttered, seeing stars despite his back being to them.

He recaptured her mouth, plundering its soft sweet depths, getting lost in the taste and the smell and the touch of her. Wanting everything at once, impatient to know the noises she made when she came.

His fingers moved a little north and brushed lightly at the juncture. Her back arched and she cried out as he found her hot and wet and ready. 'God, Stel,' he whispered, his lips hovering above hers. 'You feel so damn good.'

Stella shook her head from side to side, her hips rotating restlessly as his fingers stroked and brushed and sighed against her.

It wasn't enough, she needed more. 'Please,' she whispered.

'Please what?' Rick murmured, licking along the plump softness of her mouth. 'What do you want, Stella?'

Stella arched her back as his finger pressed a little harder, slid through the slick heat of her. 'More,' she said urgently, rotating her hips as she gripped his buttocks convulsively.

Rick slid a finger inside and felt her clamp hard around him. Her gasp echoed around the empty ocean. 'Like this?' he asked, licking down her neck, trailing his tongue down her chest. 'Or this?' He claimed a nipple as he slid another finger home.

'Rick!' Stella clung to him as he stretched her, taunted her. His expert thumb zeroed in on the impossibly hard erogenous zone as if it were fitted with a homing beacon and the stars started to flash in the sky.

A pressure built from deep inside as his thumb fanned and stoked.

God, she was going to come. *Very, very soon.*

'Wait,' she said, removing a hand from his backside to grab his wrist and still his devastatingly rhythmic movements.

Rick lifted his head and frowned. 'What's wrong?' he asked, breathing hard.

If she'd changed her mind, got cold feet, he was toast. He might as well just jump into the ocean now and save himself the slow decline into insanity.

Stella licked her lips. 'It's been a long time,' she panted. 'I swear if you keep doing that it's going to be over very, very quickly.'

It took a moment for her meaning to sink into his lust-addled brain, then everything stopped as he smiled. 'Really? You mean this?' He rotated his fingers deep inside her and grinned at the whimper that rent the air.

'Rick,' she pleaded, squeezing his wrist hard.

'What, Stel?' he murmured. 'You don't like this?' He repeated the manoeuvre, applying pressure to the hard little nub beneath his thumb.

Stella gasped as she shut her eyes. 'Rick, please.'

'What about this?' he asked as he groped awkwardly one-handed for the discarded mango cheek.

Stella opened her eyes as she felt his heat move from her side. His eyes glittered down at her as he half knelt beside her, one hand stroking her intimately, the other paused above the juncture of her thighs.

'You like this, Stella?' he asked as he squeezed the almost spent cheek, wringing the last drops of juice from its now pulpy flesh.

Stella felt the warm sticky ooze mingle with her own slickness as a waft of soft ripe fruit and sex enveloped her. And when he bent over her, his tongue joining the delicious friction, it was too, too much. A sweet wild aroma filled her senses as he stroked and stoked and the pressure accelerated to warp speed.

Rick groaned against her as the salt and the sweet of her slid over his tongue. Her heady aroma surrounded him as he taunted the hard nub, flicking and sucking in equal measure. She bucked and writhed beneath him, begging him to stop, begging him not to stop, as she lifted her hips in silent supplication.

He pinned her down with his hand and his mouth, lapping at her sweetness, refusing to yield. Even when she shattered around him seconds later he gave more, wringing every last tantalising morsel from her as he had done with the mango.

Stella jackknifed up, crying out, 'Stop, stop, stop,' fearing that she might actually die from the intensity of the pleasure.

Rick was breathing hard as he withdrew, rocking back on his haunches, watching as Stella collapsed back against the deck, delightfully naked aside from two pushed-aside bra cups.

He quirked an eyebrow. 'You look like you needed that.'

Stella grunted, which was all she was capable of as strong post-coital aftershocks undulated deep inside her. The stars burst around her like fireworks. 'You have no idea,' she panted.

Diana would be proud.

He ran his eyes over her naked abandon one more time. She lay all loose limbed, her nipples still erect, her legs spread, and his erection twitched painfully in his boardies. 'I think I do.'

Stella saw a flash of carnal hunger glitter in his eyes, aware suddenly that she'd short-changed him. 'I'm sorry,' she said, her breath still laboured. 'I don't know what the equivalent of premature ejaculation is in females but I think I just had an acute attack.'

Rick chuckled. 'It was my pleasure.' He held out his hand to her and pulled her towards him as she took it, kissing her nose. 'Fancy a shower?'

Stella was pleased for the cover of night as an image of a naked Rick, water and moonlight caressing his magnificent body, sprang instantly to mind. Never, all those nights ago when she'd spied on him, had she thought she'd ever be joining him under the deck shower.

He didn't give her a chance to indulge the embarrassing memory or to say no, pulling her to her feet, dragging her towards the bow. He let go of her to flick on the taps and rip at the Velcro on his boardies. In a trice they were gone and he was standing before her, proud and erect, the jut of his sex a tantalising silhouette. An illicit reminder of her peep show with the full embellishment of her fantasy life included for good measure.

Rick felt a tug deep inside as she stared at his erection. Somewhere behind him the water sprayed unattended, his heart pounding just as erratically. The moisture in his mouth dried to dust. 'Your turn,' he murmured.

She frowned for a moment, confused by his comment, then she looked down at her half-on, half-off bikini top and understood. She pulled it off over her head, being careful not to jar her almost recovered arm. It dropped to the deck next to his boardies.

Rick devoured her curvy roundness in one long slow look. 'You're beautiful,' he breathed.

'So are you,' she murmured, her gaze roaming over the perfection of him. This was how she had imagined Vasco. But Rick was more. So much more. He was no figment of her imagination. He was solid flesh and hard muscle and warm blood and he wanted her—*Stella*—not Mary.

She hadn't even realised she'd been jealous of Mary until this moment.

But then Rick held out his hand again and she took it and everything else was forgotten. He stepped backwards into the shower and she followed, watching as the water soaked his hair and ran down his chest, before running free down his obliques.

She stepped closer, raising herself on tippy toe, gliding her hands up his pecs and onto his shoulders. His erection pushed against her belly, thick and rampant, and her hand reached for it as she lifted her mouth to his. She felt the jolt through his body as she palmed the length of him and swallowed his groan as their lips fused.

'Oh...dear...God,' Rick gasped against her mouth as she

increased the intensity of her intimate caress, using the water to her advantage.

Stella couldn't agree with his sentiments more. She could taste mango and sex on his mouth and the water flowing over their heated skin caressed like icicles and he felt good and right in her hand.

But she wanted him good and right elsewhere.

Inside her.

Deep, deep inside her.

'You need to be in me,' she panted, her pulse thrumming so loudly through her ears she was sure she was about to rupture her eardrums.

Rick didn't need a written invitation. He grabbed her around the waist, boosting her up. As she locked her ankles at his waist he turned around in one easy movement. He pushed her against the entirely inadequate pole the shower head was mounted upon and lowered his mouth to hers, plundering hers until nothing but their two frantic heartbeats registered.

Not even the push and pull of the vast, vast ocean.

And when that wasn't enough he dropped his head to her chest, devouring the delicious ripeness of her breasts, revelling in the arch of her back and the crazed keening coming from her throat.

'Now,' Stella begged, her head thrown back, her chest thrust out in pure debauched abandon.

Rick was hard and ready and done with denying himself. He lifted her slightly, aligning her, aligning himself, nudging her entrance, feeling the still slick heat of her.

'Rick!' she begged, lightly pummelling a fist against the muscles of his shoulder as she felt him thick and hard but still not where she wanted him.

Where she needed him.

Rick chuckled at her frustration. 'Easy, Stel, easy. Let's make it last this time, huh?'

Stella whacked him harder. '*Now*, damn it,' she ordered.

Rick grinned. 'Aye, aye captain,' he murmured, smothering the very unladylike bellow that came from her mouth as he pushed into her long and hard and deep.

Stella broke away, gasping for air as he slowly withdrew and steadily pushed his way back in again, hitting exactly the right spot every time. 'Oh, God, yes,' she panted. 'Just there. Don't stop. God, don't stop!'

She squirmed against him, her head lolling back, water flowing down her breasts, her lips parting in a blissful O.

Rick stroked his tongue down her throat, sipping at the rivulets of water as he kept up the slow easy pace. Her whimpers vibrated against his mouth and he pushed deeper as he slowed right down.

Stella moaned as the subtle friction drove her crazy.

In a good way.

In a never-ever-stop way.

The way she'd always imagined it.

Hard and slow and perfect.

But this was better. So much better. Because it was real.

Rick watched Stella's breasts rock as he slowly surged into her again. Water sluiced down her chest, traced the contours of her cleavage, clung in droplets at the ends of her nipples. Stars formed a crown above her head and with her blonde hair plastered in wet strips over her shoulders she looked like a water nymph.

'God,' Rick groaned, his forehead falling against her chest as the tightness in his groin started to tug at his resistance. 'You look great in a shower.'

Stella gasped as he pulled out further this time and thrust all the way in. *So did he.* 'I have a confession,' she murmured.

Rick felt his orgasm drawing nearer and beat it back. 'You do?' he panted.

She nodded as his pulsing became thrusting once again. 'When you had a shower the other night at the yacht club in

Moresby…' her teeth sank into her lower lip and she clenched his shoulder as he picked up the pace '…I was spying on you.'

Rick pulled out all the way this time, pushing back in until she gasped and arched her back. He was a perfect fit.

'I have a confession too,' he said as a more urgent rhythm took over, nudging the slow inexorable build into something much harder to control. He withdrew quickly and just as quickly plunged back in. 'I saw you.'

If she hadn't been about to come Stella might have been angry. *Embarrassed certainly.* But the fact that he'd known, that he'd turned so she could see all of him, was inexplicably arousing. That combined with the continual in-and-out thrust of him was a heady combination.

'Pervert,' she gasped as he hit the spot that made her shudder and quiver and cling.

Rick grunted as her fingernails dug in and everything started to unravel. 'Look who you're calling pervert, my lovely.'

Stella was going to say something else, but all that came out was a gurgly whimper as she let the hypocritical protest fly up and become stardust. 'Ah-h-h,' she cried out as time and space blurred and all that remained was him and her and the silent permission of the ocean.

Rick felt things heat and boil as his belly tensed to an unbearable rigidity. He pulled her into him and crooned, 'Yes, Stella, yes,' directly into her ear as she threw back her head and called out his name, clamping tight around him, falling apart in his arms.

It was all that he needed and he bellowed into her chest, thrusting with none of the finesse of earlier as he rode the savage dictates of his body to their final release.

After a long night of getting acquainted in a way they never had before, Stella woke late the next morning to find Rick propped up on his elbow looking down at her. His eyes seemed even bluer in the morning sunshine slanting through his undressed portholes, his eyelashes longer. His hair seemed shaggier as it hung around his face and brushed his broad bronzed shoulders. His lips fuller.

He should look girly but he didn't.

He looked utterly masculine with nothing but a white sheet riding low on his hips.

'Good morning,' she murmured, blushing as she remembered just what lay beneath that sheet and the things he'd done with it.

She'd done with it.

Rick smiled at the pinkness in her cheeks, surprised that someone who knew him so carnally was capable of such modesty. 'Good morning to you too,' he replied, dropping a kiss on a bare shoulder.

His smile slackened as a feeling he wasn't familiar with washed over him and took up residence in his gut like a lead sinker. Nothing like how he usually felt the morning after—loose and light with all his kinks ironed out. Stella wasn't some bar hook-up or one of his many port calls. He wasn't sure what came next.

Stella noted his pensive look. 'I hope that's not buyer's remorse,' she murmured.

Rick shook his head. If she slapped him in the face and swam back home to England right this moment and refused to see him again he would never regret last night. 'Never.'

He lowered his head again and kissed her on the mouth, a long, slow, lingering kiss that tasted of them and left him hard beneath the sheet and aching for more.

Stella sighed as he pulled back, brushing her fingers along the soft bristles of his perpetual three day growth. 'So what's up?' she murmured.

He turned his face, kissing the tips of her fingers. 'I guess,' he said, looking down into her sleepy olive gaze, 'I'm not sure what comes next…'

Stella smiled. 'Breakfast, I think. Unless you want to—' she dropped her hand to his chest, traced her index finger down his belly to the interesting bulge in the sheet '—fool around a bit more?'

Rick captured her hand before it hit her target and thinking wouldn't be possible. 'Stel,' he said. 'I'm serious. Normally I'd kiss you and tell you I had to be somewhere in a couple of hours but…this is you and…I don't have a well-rehearsed morning-after plan for this. Frankly I'm torn between freaking out and ringing Andy Willis to tell him I've seen your boobs.'

Stella laughed, letting her hand fall to the mattress. Andy Willis had been Rick's best friend when he'd been eleven and had spent a couple of weeks one summer on the *Persephone* with them. He'd also had a massive crush on Stella.

Rick frowned down at her. 'It's not funny, Stella.'

Stella sobered, finding his pout irresistible. She lifted her head to kiss it away. He resisted until she tugged on his bottom lip with her teeth and soothed it with her tongue. She smiled when he groaned and kissed her back.

She pulled away when they were both breathing hard, smoothing his brow with her thumb.

'You're not eleven any more, Rick. What's happened with us has taken us both by surprise so I don't have a plan for this either. But do we really need one?'

She remembered what Diana had said—*you're going to be on that boat with him for long periods of time where there'll be nothing to do.* She'd rejected it then as an impossibility but, after last night, maybe Diana had a point.

'You and I both know that we live two very different lives and also know through the bitter experience of two broken families that they're practically mutually exclusive. But for the next little while we're on this boat together—alone—and we're both single and of age and if last night is any yardstick, we're pretty damn good together. Can't that be our plan?'

Rick thought it sounded like possibly the best ever plan

he'd heard. But could things really be that simple between the two of them? If he shut his eyes he could hear Nathan telling him how special Stella was, what she deserved out of life. And what she didn't.

'I don't know, Stel, maybe your father was right—'

Stella shook her head vigorously, interrupting him, annoyed that her father had meddled to the extent he had. She'd always wondered why none of her father's crew had ever spent much time with her once she'd grown breasts and now she knew.

'No, he was wrong. About a *lot* of things but especially this. I understand, Rick. You're like him. I get it. The ocean runs in your veins and the sea is your mistress blah blah.'

She rolled her eyes.

'And I want marriage and one day babies and for the father of those babies to be around full time. I know all that. But that's not what this is. We're not talking marriage and happily-ever-afters here, Rick. We're talking a couple of weeks of hot, sweaty, sandy, frolicking-in-tropical-lagoons sex.'

Rick shut his eyes against the images she evoked as his hard-on voted yes. But…he looked down at her, her blonde hair spread out on the pillow around her, her lovely face so, so familiar…could a woman who immersed herself in happily-ever-afters ever settle for less?

'And then what? We just go back to being friends?'

Stella shrugged. 'Sure. It's not like we see each other much these days, Rick. What…two or three times a year? Probably even less now that Dad's not around. Hell, it'll probably be another year or so before I next see you.'

Rick had to admit she made a good point. 'That's true,' he murmured.

Stella smiled, her hand making its way back to where the sheet still bulged interestingly. 'The truth, the whole truth and nothing but the truth.'

Rick dropped his head to nuzzle along her collarbone. 'It certainly makes sense.'

Her hand dipped under the sheet and she hit pay dirt. Rick swore in Spanish, and she smiled, recognising the word he had taught her when she'd been twelve years old. She wrapped her palm around his girth and revelled in the silky hard length of him and the way he shuddered against her.

She stretched languorously, her free hand slipping under the pillow, grabbing a fistful of sheet as Rick claimed a nipple, sucking it into the heat of his mouth, lashing it with hot wet swipes of his tongue.

Her hand nudged something and it took her lust-drunk brain a moment to ascertain it was a book. Without thinking she pulled it out and looked at it.

The cover of *Pleasure Hunt* stared back at her.

She said a choice swear word of her own, snagging Rick's attention.

'Ah…' he said warily.

'You've read this?'

She frowned as he collapsed back on the mattress and nodded, her worst fears confirmed. She'd wondered when they'd first had that conversation about her writing process if he'd read it, but his comments had set her mind at ease.

His obviously misleading comments.

'This is Diana's copy,' she said as she thumbed through it. She'd have known it without the benefit of her autograph on the title page. She'd know this dog-eared copy anywhere—she'd seen Diana reading it often enough.

'Yes. She gave it to me just before we left your house that day.'

'Oh, did she, now?' Stella murmured, her ire rising as she formulated a rather stinging email rant in her head. But then another thought hit and she sat bolt upright. 'Oh, God,' she said as the most important thing of all occurred to her. She turned her head and looked down at him. 'So you know…'

She couldn't even finish the statement, it was so embarrassing.

Rick grinned at her mortified look as he crossed his ankles and clasped his hands behind his head. 'That I'm Vasco Ramirez?'

The pink she'd gone earlier was nothing to the deep red that currently suffused her cheeks. She opened her mouth to deny it but she couldn't. If he'd read it, he'd know. There was too much of *him* in it. Not just that tantalising birthmark but the essence of him. His mannerisms, his way with words, his sense of humour.

His sense of honour.

She looked away, her fingers absently stroking the raised lettering on the cover. 'Well, there's no need to get too big-headed about it,' she huffed. 'I needed a pirate of Spanish descent. It made sense to…model him on someone I knew.'

Whatever happened she couldn't let him know that she'd been fantasising about him for a long time before Vasco had come on the scene. That Vasco had walked into her head fully formed because of him. He was already freaked out enough about the development in their relationship.

'But any resemblance to person or persons alive or dead…'

Rick vaulted upright, fitting himself in behind her, his front to her back, covering her mouth with his hand, cutting off the lawyer speak as he kissed her shoulder. 'Shh, Stella,' he murmured. 'I love it that you *modelled* him on me.'

He brushed a string of kisses up higher as he dropped his hand to her shoulder. 'I'm not going to sue you, I'm…flattered. And impressed how…accurate…' he smiled against her skin '…your descriptions are. That bath scene…' He nuzzled her ear; his hands moved to cup her breasts, his thumbs brushing over the already erect nipples. 'It was like you'd painted a portrait of me.'

Stella arched her back and felt her eyes roll back in her head as his mouth and fingers turned her insides to mush.

Rick kissed up her jaw and when she turned her head towards him he feathered kisses along her lips. 'Like you'd actually seen me naked,' he whispered against her mouth as one hand left her breast bearing south.

His words triggered a thought and Stella opened her eyes. 'You knew,' she murmured. 'You'd already read the book when you spied me watching you have that shower.'

He chuckled unashamedly in her ear as both hands stroked her thighs. 'Guilty,' he whispered.

Her brow wrinkled as she remembered how cannily familiar some things on this trip had been. The shower incident. When he'd tended her wounds as Vasco had done. When he'd squeezed mango juice all over her body.

But he'd turned her whole body into an erogenous zone and when he urged her thighs apart she didn't object.

'Have you been deliberately enacting scenes from the book?' she murmured, raising both arms and linking them around his neck, arching her back as his finger slid between her legs.

'What did you expect me to do for fun when you took away all my recreational flirting? Anyway, do you care?' he whispered, his erection pressing into the cleft of her soft round buttocks.

'Yes,' she sighed. 'I'm mad as he…ll.' And she would have sounded much more convincing had he not driven a finger deep inside her.

He chuckled at her breathy whimper. 'Are you telling me you haven't been taking advantage too? That you didn't think about the book when you were spying on me in the shower? Or when I was tending to your wounds? That bringing those scenes to life didn't excite you?'

Stella knew he was right. Knew that it would be hard to take the moral high ground when she'd been using him to indulge a few of her own fantasies.

But she was damned if she was going to let him have it all his way. 'It's just a story,' she panted as he stroked between her legs. 'They're what excited Lady Mary.'

Rick remembered what she'd said about Lady Mary not being her in anything other than a generic female way. Her slickness coated his fingers and he picked up the pace. 'And you're not her, right?' he whispered.

Stella was so close to falling over the edge. So far gone she didn't know which way was up, but even she knew to answer that question truthfully would be madness.

'Right,' she gasped as she squirmed against him and he stroked harder.

She clutched convulsively at the back of his neck as a tiny pulse fluttered deep and low, fanning out in ever-increasing waves. Mary was forgotten, Vasco was forgotten as it pulsed and grew until nothing else mattered but the magic Rick could do with his hands.

'Oh, God,' she groaned, arching her back, tilting her pelvis. 'Don't stop,' she begged. 'Please don't stop.'

Rick felt the tension in his groin tighten to almost unbearable tautness. 'Yes, Stel, yes,' he panted, working her slickness, feeling her ripple around him. 'Come for me. Come.'

Stella bucked as the wave broke over her, undulating with a ferocity that tore the breath from her lungs and, for a moment or two, the beat from her heart.

It gripped her and shook her in endless waves and she knew there was no possible way she could be put back together right, once it ended.

CHAPTER TEN

Mary chafed against the four silken bonds that imprisoned her, legs akimbo, upon Vasco's bed. For no matter how many times she shared it with him she would never regard it as hers. She eyed the big brooding pirate as he prowled back and forth. He was wearing breeches and boots and nothing else save the sunlight slanting through the portholes.

He stopped and turned to face her from the foot of the bed, shoving his hands on his hips. 'I'm waiting, Mary.'

His low rumble set her heart aflutter and her nipples to attention. She watched as his glittering blue eyes took in their state of indecency. How could they not when she was barely covered? When he had stripped her to her undergarments not ten minutes ago this had not been the expected outcome.

Damned stubborn man.

'I insist that you untie me immediately, Captain Ramirez.'

Vasco chuckled, his gaze fanning over the hard peaks tenting her chemise. 'Methinks you like to be tied up, Lady Mary,' he murmured, planting a knee on the bed.

She glared at him both scandalised and titillated at the thought. 'Captain Ramirez.'

He ignored the warning in her voice, slowly advancing onto the bed. 'I do so prefer it when you call me Vasco. Like you did that day on the deck when I washed your hair.' He prowled closer on his hands and knees until he was sitting on his haunches between her spreadeagled legs. 'And when I first touched you here,' he murmured, stroking his finger down the open central seam of her linen drawers.

She sucked in a breath and he smiled triumphantly. 'Like you did last night and the night before that and the five nights before that.' He stroked again.

Mary squirmed against his hand. 'Vasco, please,' she moaned. 'It's the middle of the day. The crew...'

He shook his head and chuckled that she could still keep a sense of propriety while tied to his bed. 'Say it,' he insisted. 'If you want it, Mary, you're going to have to ask for it.'

Lady Mary Bingham had been a willing and eager bed partner but there was part of her he hadn't been able to reach, a part she kept aloof from him even when she was in the throes of her release. It made him feel like a common street urchin and she the lady who was condescending to allow him to use her body while she had nothing better to do.

He needed to know that this fever was burning in her blood too.

Mary shook her head. Gently bred ladies did not talk so.

She'd already taken a pirate as a lover. How much more did he want? 'I will not.'

Vasco smiled at her, watching as she bit down on her bottom lip and fought against closing her eyes. 'You know you want to, Mary, I can feel it right here...' He slipped a finger inside her where it was hot and slick and she gasped. 'I know you, Mary.'

Mary hated how he could addle her senses so quickly.

'You know nothing about me, sir,' she said vehemently as her hips moved against him restlessly.

Vasco grinned. 'I know you like this,' he said, pushing up her chemise with his other hand, exposing a creamy breast and rosy nipple that puckered quickly beneath the stroke of his fingers.

'I know you have this tiny strawberry birthmark just here,' he said, satisfied to hear her whimper as he withdrew his finger, shifting it slightly to the left to the crease where her inner thigh met the very centre of her. 'I know you like it when I lick you there,' he murmured, lowering his head and putting his tongue to where his finger had been, to the mark that had fascinated him right from the beginning.

'Vasco...' Mary cried, arching her back as his finger re-entered her and his tongue swiped in long, lazy, knowing strokes.

He smiled as he pulled away, sitting back on his haunches, his finger still stroking deep inside her. 'I know me tying you up excites you even though I know you're hearing your uncle's voice telling you you're going to hell.'

Mary also hated how he seemed to be able to read her mind. 'Well, I'll be seeing you there first, Captain Ramirez,' she said haughtily.

Vasco threw back his head and laughed. When he stopped his eyes glittered down at her and he started to stroke her in earnest. 'Ah, but what a way to go, Lady Mary,' he taunted as he relentlessly increased the pressure.

Mary especially hated how he could bring her to her peak so effortlessly. 'Vasco,' she whimpered and moved against him, desperate for the rush.

He quirked an eyebrow, easing back a little, refusing to give her what she craved. If she wanted to use him then she could damn well say the words. 'Yes, Mary, what do you want?'

Mary rocked her pelvis against his hand as the maddening friction plateaued, divinity frustratingly out of reach. 'Please, Vasco,' she gasped.

Vasco was harder than he'd ever been in his life, watching her lying before him half exposed, fully abandoned, head tossing from side to side, her body begging for that which she would not put into words.

He shook his head. 'Please what, Mary?' he demanded, quickening the pace for a few tantalising seconds, then backing off.

Mary bit into her lip hard, lifting her hips off the bed. 'Vasco!'

'Say it,' he growled.

She opened her eyes and glared at him. 'Damn it, Vasco.' But she knew in that second she'd have given him the world if he'd asked for it. 'I like it when you do this to me,' she said. 'I want you to do it to me. I just plain want you. Now please...please...' her wrists yanked at the bonds '...I beg of you...'

Vasco grinned. 'Of course, Lady Mary, why didn't you just say so?'

But the rebuke that came to Mary's lips was lost as Vasco drove her over the edge in ten seconds. When she was capable of opening her eyes a little while later it was to his smug triumphant smile.

'Okay, Vasco,' she said, her breathing still not quite normal. 'Untie me now.'

Vasco shook his head and the gleam in his eye was positively wicked as he unlaced his breeches.

'I'm just getting started.'

THE next week flew by. Between long nights—and sometimes long days—below deck they made it to Micronesia, sailing into Weno in Chuuk State where they restocked and sorted out the official paperwork.

Chuuk, home to a giant lagoon, the final resting place for over a hundred ships, planes and submarines that had perished during fierce World War Two battles, was a magnate for wreck divers worldwide. Time and warm tropical waters had seen the wrecks bloom into breathtaking coral gardens and artificial reefs sporting a kaleidoscope of colours.

But they headed beyond that to the lesser known outer reefs fringing the deeper waters of the Pacific where Nathan had been convinced Inigo's boat had gone down in bad weather. The islands of Micronesia had once been part of the Spanish East Indies and, Nathan believed, a rich hunting ground for a pirate who wasn't picky or patriotic when it came to loot.

The fact that a veritable maze of two thousand plus, mainly uninhabited islands lay at his disposal, providing the perfect cover to lay low in between raids, had no doubt also been a plus for Inigo Alvarez.

The weather stayed calm and visibility was excellent as, for the first six days, Rick and Stella island-hopped, diving the area Nathan had deduced from his lifetime of research was the most likely resting pace for *The Mermaid*. It was about a hundred nautical miles square so they divided it up into a grid and painstakingly explored each segment from sun up to sundown.

Had they been in the *Persephone* or one of the other boats in the salvage fleet, they would have had all kinds of equipment to help them in their quest. But this was just a basic exploratory—old-fashioned treasure hunting at its best. Like they were kids again, pretending to find Spanish galleons while their fathers undertook their latest salvage operation.

And neither of them would have had it any other way.

The deepest water was ten metres but it still took a couple of dives for Stella to gain her confidence. Ever since she could swim, Stella had dived, and she'd held her open water diving certification for many years, but she hadn't been in a wetsuit for some time now.

Rick, used to diving much, much deeper, enjoyed the slower pace and took time to admire the magnificent underwater scenery, including the curvy little water nymph in a wetsuit that left nothing to the imagination.

At night she wrote, more inspired than ever by being back in the water again, and he reviewed the data from their dives.

And then they burned up the sheets.

On the seventh day they rested. They anchored off one of the many sandy atolls, loaded up the dinghy and motored the short distance, beaching the little runabout high above the tide level. They lolled in the shallows, making love as the water lapped gently around their legs. They sunbathed nude and ate sandwiches and drank cold beer for lunch. They dozed under a stand of coconut palms.

Three other islands could be seen nearby, towering out of the glittering ocean, and in the distance another boat, probably a dive charter, slowly traversed the horizon. It was a reminder that they weren't the only two people in the world, which had been an easy assumption to make these last idyllic days.

'Maybe we could just move here?' Stella said sleepily.

Rick smiled as he rolled his head to look at her. 'Sounds good to me.' If he was going to be stuck on a deserted island with anyone, she would be his preference. 'What happens when the laptop runs out of battery?' he teased.

Stella smiled too. 'Don't be practical,' she murmured as she drifted off again.

When she woke the sun wasn't as high overhead and Rick was lying on his stomach propped up on his elbows beside her. A sea breeze ruffled the papers he was reading. She lay there for a few minutes listening to the swish of the waves against the beach and the rustle of the wind through the palm leaves.

I could get used to this.

She rolled up onto her elbow, dropping a kiss on his bare

shoulder. 'What if it's not here?' she asked. 'What if *The Mermaid* is like Atlantis or El Dorado?'

Rick turned his head and nuzzled her temple before returning his attention to the research material he'd printed off the web just prior to leaving the boat this morning. He'd pored over everything he could get his hands on since deciding to undertake this voyage and he'd come across some more potentially useful information last night.

'It might not be here but I think your father's research definitely supports its existence and his reasonings for *The Mermaid* being in these waters are very sound.'

Stella nodded. She hoped so. It would be good to know that something her father had committed so much of his time and energy to might be realised. They'd both been aware, subliminally, that this voyage had been a pilgrimage of sorts. A way to pay homage to Nathan and his dream.

Neither of them wanted to return empty-handed.

'I'm going for a snorkel,' she said. 'You want to join me?'

Rick shook his head. 'Maybe later.'

Stella kissed his shoulder again. 'Are you sure?' she asked. 'I'm going naked.'

Ah, now that got his attention.

He smiled at her before kissing her hard on the mouth. 'Temptress,' he muttered as he pulled away. 'Be off with you.'

Stella laughed. 'Okay, fine,' she said, standing and stripping off her bikini where she stood, throwing it down on the papers he was reading.

Rick chuckled as he picked it up and looked over his shoulder to find her naked, hips swaying seductively as she sashayed down to the shoreline, a mask and snorkel in one hand. Her skin was a light golden brown from all the sun she'd been getting and as she turned and gave him a wave he copped a magnificent side view of full breast and tiny waist before she waded into the ocean. He levered himself up, turning to sit, papers still in hand, watching as the warm tropical waters slowly swallowed her up.

He realised after looking up for the tenth time in ten minutes he was too distracted to read. The reef was close to the shore so she was only a couple of metres out and he could see the bobbing of her naked bottom as she lazily circled back and forth across the surface, occasionally duck diving and blowing water out of her snorkel when she reappeared.

When a coconut fell beside him, missing him by about an inch, he decided it was time to give up and just enjoy the view. He absently picked up the coconut and shook it, hearing the swish of milk inside. He grabbed his diver's knife out of his backpack and, being an old hand at husking coconuts, quickly did so.

By the time the outer shell was peeled away and he'd removed the stringy bark, revealing the hard smooth surface, Stella was emerging from the ocean like something from a James Bond film.

Except nude. Her blonde hair slicked back from her face, clinging to her naked back like a sheath of honey-gold silk.

Like a mermaid.

He brought the bald nut to his face and inhaled the sweet earthy aroma as he watched her walking towards him. The fragrance was pure Stella.

A fragrance he'd become quite addicted to.

Her bell tinkled as she drew closer, his erection increasing with her every footfall. When she threw the snorkel and mask down beside him his mouth was as dry as the powdery sand beneath him.

'Do women practise that little hip swing or is it just part of their DNA?' he asked, looking up into her face. Water droplets clung to her eyelashes and ran down her body.

Stella laughed as she deliberately reached behind her to wrap her hair around her hand and squeeze out the excess water. 'I don't know what you're talking about.' She grinned.

'Oh, yeah?' he growled as he threw the coconut down and gently tumbled her to the ground.

Stella went down laughing, clinging to his shoulders as she settled against the soft sand. He straddled her, looming above. The grains felt warm and powdery beneath the cool skin of her back, as did the sun on her face, their formerly shaded position now mostly in light as the day grew later.

'I'm going to have sand everywhere,' she grouched good-naturedly.

'That's the plan.' He grinned as he lowered his mouth to hers. Her lips and the curve of her waist were cool to touch. 'Water cold?' he asked as his tongue lapped at the water droplets still clinging and cooling her throat.

Stella shut her eyes and angled her neck to give him wider access. 'A little.'

Rick smiled against her neck. He sat and groped around beside him. 'Let's see if we can't warm you up.'

Stella opened her eyes just in time to see him holding a coconut and his diver's knife over her abdomen. As a teenager she'd often watched him husk a coconut, the muscles of his back and arms way more fascinating than they should have been.

She quirked an eyebrow. 'Been busy?'

He grinned as he struck the coconut with the handle of the knife right between the eyes. It capitulated easily, cracking in half, clear fluid running out over his hand and dripping onto her cool belly.

He eased it apart, gratified to hear her gasp as he poured most of the warm milk over her belly and breasts. Her nipples ruched before him and his erection surged. He groaned as the aroma of ocean and her wafted up to him and he bent his head to her.

'I want to taste you here,' he muttered. His hot tongue swiped over puckered nipples and she arched her back. He removed every trace of the warm juice before moving on.

'And here,' he said, going down, following the trail of liquid that had puddled in her belly button. He heard the suck of her breath as he lapped it up. She tasted sweet and salty. Like the ocean, tropical breezes and the soft sugary nirvana of coconuts.

He sat back on his haunches, watching her, waiting for her to open her eyes. When her eyelashes fluttered open he picked up the half-coconut that still had a little milk remaining.

'And here,' he murmured, trickling it between her legs, as he had done with the mango, supressing a groan as she licked her lips and panted, her thighs parting, the sunlight glistening there so he could see it coating all of her.

He tossed the shell aside, swooping his head down, his hands gliding up her body to cup her breasts, his thumbs brushing across the nipples.

It was then, as he used his elbows to push her open to him more, that he noticed it for the first time. The sun shone like a spotlight and it was suddenly obvious.

A tiny blemish. A pink birthmark.

Exactly where Lady Mary had hers.

He stared at it, as he tried to think past the pounding of his heart.

So...she was Lady Mary?

But the heady aroma of her drowned in coconut juice was rendering his thought processes useless. He wanted to ask her. Needed to know.

He should stop and demand that she tell him the truth.

But she was making those little noises at the back of her throat again and as another waft of coconut headed his way he actually salivated.

Stella rotated her pelvis as the anticipation built to breaking point. Rick liked to tease but this had gone on long enough. She knew the touch of his mouth was coming and every second he made her wait, she could feel herself get wetter.

'Rick!' she begged, unable to bear it any longer. 'Please,' she whimpered, lifting her hips involuntarily. 'Please.'

It was the whimper that did it—just as it always did. There would be time enough for questions later. So he shut his eyes and gave her what she was asking for, licking that cute strawberry mark just as Vasco had done, savouring the sweet coconut essence of her, pinning her to the sand with his tongue and not letting her up until her climax rent the air.

Stella woke the next morning to a tight feeling at her wrists and a strange sense of foreboding. It was immediately allayed when she saw Rick, one knee planted on the edge of the mattress, his face hovering over her, smiling.

'Morning,' he murmured, kissing her.

She kissed him back. It wasn't until she tried to move her arms to hug him that the foreboding returned. It only took a moment to figure out why. She looked behind her. Her wrists were tied with some kind of material to the posts of his bed. As were her feet.

She was naked and spreadeagled.

Her pulse leapt at the illicitness of it all. Was Rick going to enact the scene from *Pleasure Hunt* where Vasco had tied Mary to the bed?

She looked at him. 'You do know that, unlike Mary, I am perfectly willing to ask you for sex and, not only that, but to tell you how, when, where and the number of times I want you to do me, right?'

Rick chuckled as he sat on the edge of the bed. 'I've noticed. You're really not her, are you?' he asked innocently.

Stella nodded as she averted her eyes to her ankle ties. 'Is that one of my sarongs?' she asked.

Rick grinned. 'Sorry. I'm all out of eighteenth-century satin sashes and I thought it'd be gentler on your wrists and ankles than nautical rope.'

Stella pulled against the bonds to test them and had to

agree. Even if she wanted to get out of them, which she didn't, she knew it would be futile—sailors knew how to tie knots.

'How on earth did you manage not to wake me?' she asked.

He shrugged. 'Well, it took me a while and, thankfully, you're a heavy sleeper.'

Stella nodded. That was true. 'So, was there a purpose to this or are you just into bondage suddenly?'

Rick looked at her, naked and spread on his bed like a gift from Neptune himself. He was ragingly hard and pleased he'd decided to put on some boardies instead of being naked as he'd originally thought yesterday when he'd lain in post-coital glory on the beach beside her, formulating this plan to get a confession out of her.

He wasn't sure why knowing whether she was Lady Mary was increasingly important to him.

It just was.

He'd often wondered if she thought about him. Knowing that she might have fantasised about *them* while he'd been training himself not to was beyond tantalising. Maybe it was ego, maybe it was something else he didn't want to examine too closely, but he had to know.

And he'd known that there was only one way to find out.

He smiled down at her as he pushed off his bed. 'Oh, there's a purpose.'

Stella's nipples hardened beneath his incendiary blue gaze as she noticed she was the only one naked. 'You're dressed.' She pouted.

His smile broadened. 'For now.'

Stella's heart beat a little faster at the promise in those two incredible eyes the exact colour of the tropical waters surrounding them.

Rick prowled around the bed as Vasco had done, his gaze boldly running over every delectable inch of her. Blatantly lingering on her breasts and the strawberry mark he couldn't see from this distance but he knew the exact location of—low and to the left of her centre. Their gazes locked as he roamed, dragging out the moment.

He stopped at the foot of the bed, shoving his hands on his hips. 'I discovered something very interesting yesterday,' he murmured.

The timbre of his voice dragged silken fingers across her skin. 'Really?' She hoped she sounded nonchalant, that the vibration of her madly fluttering heart wasn't shaking the entire bed.

He nodded as he planted a knee on the mattress. 'It's intriguing to say the least,' he continued.

'Something to do with Inigo?' she asked as she watched Rick prowl towards her, the light of a fictional pirate in his eyes.

He shook his head. 'No. Something to do with you.'

'Oh?' Her voice sounded high and breathy as he came right in close, his knees brushing her spread inner thighs.

Rick reached out and brushed his fingertips down her exposed centre. Stella gasped and bucked. He smiled. 'You like that, don't you?'

Stella bit her lip and nodded her head as the brush became something more purposeful. 'Yes.'

The hammer of his heart was loud in his head as his finger followed the path of her heat and sank inside her. 'And this?'

Stella whimpered. 'Yes.'

'You want more?' he asked, sliding another finger home, using his thumb to rub the spot that was already tight and hard.

Stella was ready in an instant, balanced on a knife edge of anticipation. 'Yes.'

Rick smiled. 'Don't you want to know what I discovered?'

She arched her back as he picked up the pace. 'Yes, yes.'

Rick swallowed. She looked so bloody desirable at the mercy of his hand that he wanted to rip his boardies off and forget the damn birthmark but it was about more than the blemish.

Had she ever fantasised about them together? As he had despite Nathan's unspoken law? Had she felt something more than friendship for him?

As he had.

He had to know.

He withdrew his fingers from inside her. 'I found that you, too, have a birthmark.'

Stella felt her orgasm recede beyond her reach as her breath stuttered to a halt. She opened her eyes to find his blue ones glittering down at her.

'Strangely enough,' he continued, sliding his finger to the left, locating the blemish immediately, 'in exactly the same spot that Lady Mary has hers. Coincidence, Stel, or are *you* Lady Mary?'

She shook her head vigorously. *This was not what she'd expected.* 'No.'

What would he think if he knew? He'd already guessed too much about her fantasy life from *Pleasure Hunt*.

He quirked an eyebrow as he brushed his finger against the birthmark again. 'Really?'

Stella panted even as she fought not to. 'Really.'

He moved his hand from her completely. 'I think you're lying, Stella. Mary's so very, very familiar to me.'

It was something he'd only just realised, too caught up in the big things to recognise the subtleties of the character. The nuances. The jut of her chin, the turn of her head, the glimpse of her humanity beneath all her starched upper-class Britishness.

Stella glared at him, now torn between telling him to go to hell and lying to him so he'd finish what he'd started.

And she felt vulnerable.

A state that had nothing to do with her nudity.

He wanted her to look at things that she'd never questioned too deeply.

'What the hell does it matter?' she asked in exasperation, yanking against her bonds.

'Because...' He looked into her simmering olive gaze, knowing that if he was demanding the truth from her then the least he could do was return the favour. 'Because despite what your father decreed, I used to fantasise about you. Not consciously, *never consciously*. But in my dreams...that was different. And...'

This bit was the hard part. The bit he'd never admitted to before, not even to himself. 'I guess I'd always wondered... hoped, maybe...that you might have done the same.'

Stella's heart ticked away madly like a thousand halyards tinkling in a stiff breeze. There'd been a vibe between them as teenagers—not spoken about or acted upon. But if she'd known that he used to dream about her she might have ignored her father's silent censure.

He looked so serious kneeling between her legs. Torn, surprised even, as if his words had come as a revelation to him too.

How could she not reciprocate?

Her father was gone and, even if he hadn't been, she was an adult, no longer needy of his approval.

'Yes,' she murmured, their gazes locking. 'Lady Mary is me. Beneath all those layers of clothing she has my heart and soul. *And* my desires.'

The admission was amazingly cathartic. She licked her lips, her mouth suddenly as dry as the ties binding her to the bed.

'When Vasco stormed into my head, I knew he was you. Deep down anyway—it took me a little while to recognise it consciously. And when I knew that, I knew whoever his woman was going to be, she would be me.'

Rick smiled triumphantly as Vasco had done at Mary's capitulation.

Stella rolled her eyes. 'I fantasised constantly about you when I was a teenager. And when I was writing the book...'

She stopped and blushed at the memory. 'Let's just say that Mr Buzzy got quite the working out.'

Rick blinked, relief flooding through his veins. 'So, I wasn't alone?' he murmured.

She shook her head. 'You weren't alone.'

Rick laid both hands over his heart and mouthed, 'Thank you.' Then he leaned forward and brushed his mouth lightly over hers, murmuring, 'Thank you, thank you,' as he dropped a string of tiny kisses before sitting back on his haunches again.

She quirked an eyebrow at him, a smile on her face. 'You going to untie me now?'

Rick shook his head as he ripped at the Velcro fastener on his boardies, a wicked glint in his eyes. 'I'm just getting started.'

The next day Stella and Rick were at six metres and just about to head back to the boat for lunch when Stella spotted a large shape looming below them. Visibility was still excellent but the find was partially obscured by a cascading wall of coral. Rick's breathing and heart rate picked up and he made a conscious effort to control them as they headed down to explore further.

As they neared, the ghostly grey shape of a remarkably intact, large, old wooden ship appeared. It was wedged into some kind of rocky ravine, the outer ledge of which fell away into the deep blue abyss of Pacific Ocean.

They both hovered above it for a moment, their torches aimed at the broken waterlogged beauty, stunned to be finally staring at something they'd both wondered from time to time ever really existed.

Was it *The Mermaid*? They couldn't know for certain—yet. But Rick felt sure in his gut—either that or it was Nathan's presence. They glided slowly through the waters surrounding the ship, trying to find any outward identifying marks but, whatever the origins, Rick already knew from years of salvage experience they had found something truly amazing.

They circled it in awed silence, the coral encrusted ship spooky in its watery grave. Adrenaline buzzed through Rick's veins as he became more certain, the dimensions of the find putting it in *The Mermaid*'s league. They didn't attempt to go in—that would come later when a more detailed survey had been undertaken. Too many divers had got themselves trapped and died in wrecks to be foolhardy.

And, as Nathan had always drilled into him, a shipwreck was a sacred site. The final resting place of the poor souls that had perished along with it and as such was to be treated with respect.

They discovered a figurehead when the bow came into view but it was too decayed and encrusted with weedy growths and coral life to tell if it was the laughing mermaid that had famously spearheaded Inigo Alvarez's ship. The nameplate proclaiming the ship as *La Sirena* was nowhere in sight.

Of course. It was never that easy...

Rick and Stella made their way to where the ghostly shape had settled on rock. He shone his torch, inspecting the damage, trying to ascertain a point of impact. Stella shone hers too, the beam hitting rock, a flash of something reflecting back. Stella looked closer, her heart thumping loudly in the eerie underwater stillness, her hand reaching for the object. She scooped it up, lay it flat in the palm of her hand, shone her torch on it.

A gold coin.

Rick felt a tug on his leg. He turned to find Stella, who was grinning like a loon, holding up what appeared to be a round coin. His heartbeat climbed off the scale as she passed it over.

It was gold and in good nick. Gold coins of good purity usually survived in water unscathed, unlike bronze coins that were degraded by salinity.

It was also Spanish.

It still didn't confirm the ship was *The Mermaid*. Archaeologists were going to have to decide that. But it was another strong indicator.

He grinned back and hugged her tight.

A couple of hours later they were back on board and had finished notifying the necessary people. Rick had organised for the marine archaeology company they used to send a team and had started the application process for a permit to salvage.

Stella was on deck looking at the marker buoy in the distance when Rick came up behind her. She was in a vest top and sarong and he pressed the chilled bottle of champagne they'd brought way back in Cairns for just this occasion against one shoulder as he kissed the other.

Stella jumped at the shock of it, then turned in his arms, and hugged him. 'Thank you,' she whispered.

Rick held her close, the boat bobbing gently. Realising Nathan's dream had meant as much to her as it had to him.

'I've been thinking,' she said, pulling back slightly. 'When they confirm it's *The Mermaid*, I'd like to bring Dad's ashes out here and scatter them.'

Nathan had always wanted them scattered at sea, but until now Stella hadn't felt ready to let him go.

Rick nodded. 'Good idea.' He smiled. 'Let's drink to Nathan,' he said.

They eased apart and he handed her the flutes as he worked the cork. Its pop was lost in the vast ocean surrounds and he quickly filled the glasses, handing her one.

'To Dad,' she said, holding her glass aloft.

Rick nodded, clinking his flute against hers. 'To Nathan.'

He glanced at her as she sipped the frothy nectar and she grinned at him. The breeze caught her drying blonde hair and the sun sparkled on the sea behind her like the champagne bubbles. She looked like a mermaid, a *sirena*, and he felt deep, deep-down-in-his-bones happy.

'What?' Stella asked as the glitter in his gaze became speculative.

'I think I love you,' he murmured.

The words fell from his lips and he didn't even bother to recall them because he knew in that instant that they were the truth. He did love her.

He'd loved her for ever.

Stella blinked. 'Okay...no more champagne for you,' she joked.

He laughed, then sobered, his gaze roaming her lovely familiar face. 'I'm sorry, I know that's sudden but...it's not really. It's just been a long time coming.'

Stella realised he was serious. Her pulse tripped. 'But...I thought the ocean, this...' she threw her arm out, indicating the glory of the scenery around them '...is your great love.'

Rick shook his head. 'This is nothing without you.'

Stella's heart clanged like a gong. She didn't know what to say. The fact that she loved him too was a no-brainer. It was suddenly as clear as the tropical waters fringing the pristine Micronesian reefs. In fact, she couldn't remember a time she hadn't loved him. It had always been there, snuggled inside her. She just hadn't been free to admit it.

Until now.

But she'd already lived through one broken marriage because of the sea and, no matter how much she loved him, she couldn't be with a man who wouldn't put her first.

Stella shook her head sadly, not allowing her love to bloom. 'It's not enough, Rick. Love's not enough. My father loved my mother, after all. I need to know you want me more than the ocean. That you'll put me before it. Something my father and your father *never* did.'

Rick stood firm, understanding her reticence, knowing that what he did for a job was hard on relationships but refusing to be cowed by it. 'You want me to walk away, I'll walk away.'

Stella lifted her hand and stroked his whiskers. 'I can't

ask you to do that, Rick. I'm not going to forbid you from the ocean—I saw how much grief that caused my mother in the long run. That has to be your choice.'

Rick lifted his hand to cover hers with his. 'The sea is not an easy mistress, Stel. She's selfish and addictive. But I've seen what happened with Nathan and Linda, and lived with the consequences of my father's inability to choose between two loves. Believe me, I know the heartache of that just as well as you and I don't want that for you and me. Rest assured, Stel, I will never put the sea before you.' His hands slid to her shoulders. *'Never.'*

Stella wanted to believe him. His brilliant blue eyes glittered with openness and honesty and she wanted to fall into them for ever. But… 'So tell me how this works?'

He shrugged. 'Up until we decide to start a family—'

'Wait,' she interrupted, the boat suddenly rolling under her feet a little. 'We're starting a family?'

'Sure…one day. Absolutely.' He frowned. 'I thought you wanted kids?'

Stella felt a lump in her throat as she nodded. 'Absolutely. Not soon. But one day.'

'Well, until then,' he continued, gently rubbing his hands up and down her arms, 'we can divide our time between Cornwall and salvage jobs. You have a portable career, Stel, and you love the business as much as I do so…why not?'

Why not indeed? Stella thought. Just because her parents hadn't been able to compromise didn't mean that they couldn't. And he was right—as long as she had a laptop and access to the Internet, her office could be anywhere.

'And when kids come along I'll manage the business from land and get someone in to do the hands-on stuff.'

Stella frowned at him. 'You would do that?'

He nodded. 'For you, I'd do it happily. I guess I'd like to go and spend the odd few days here and there at sea, checking on things, and when the kids get older we can take them on the *Persephone* in the school holidays just like when we were young.'

Stella felt that lump thicken as he painted a picture she'd dreamt about all her life. One that she was supposed to have lived with her own parents, but her father hadn't ever been able to stay on land long enough.

'How do I know you're not just telling me stuff I want to hear?' she asked. 'How many times do you think Dad promised Mum things would be different next time he came home?'

Rick pulled her in close to him. 'I'm not Nathan.'

He held her fiercely for a moment before pulling back to look into her eyes.

'I loved your father, he was like a father to me, you know that, but I was a little jealous of you having Linda. I wished she could have been my mother too. I never got how Nathan had such a terrific woman like Linda and didn't appreciate her. I've seen two male role models in my life blow it with women who loved them with far-reaching consequences, so, trust me, I won't ever make that mistake.'

Stella nodded. She believed him when he said he didn't want to make the same mistakes. Hindsight had put them both on the same page and love would keep them there.

'I love you,' she murmured, freeing her heart, letting her love bloom.

Rick smiled a slow steady smile as she said the three words he'd been waiting to hear nearly all his life.

Better late than never.

'Is that a yes?' he asked.

Stella laughed. 'A yes to what?'

'Embarking on a lifelong pleasure hunt?' he teased.

She smiled and raised her glass. 'That's a *hell yes.*'

Rick lowered his head. 'Then let's get started,' he whispered.

* * * * *